Praise for *Frank's Shadow*

"Doug McIntyre does for alcoholics what Mickey Spillane did for detectives. A raucous, funny, sad, and ultimately moving tale of a self-deprecating addict stumbling toward redemption for both his dad and himself."

—Robert K. Wilcox, author, *Target Patton* and *Black Aces High*

"McIntyre's Danny McKenna channels Scorsese's Paul Hackett in *After Hours*, along with Alice McDermott's *Charming Billy*, while the Ol' Blue Eyes soundtrack makes the pages sing and swing."

—John Pizzarelli, GRAMMY® winner, author, *World on a String*

"A witty and heartfelt ride through twentieth-century American culture. As real as a memoir, *Frank's Shadow* is an expertly crafted story. The shoes keep dropping until its very meaningful end."

—Jim McGrath, author, *Pamplona*, Goodman Theatre, Chicago

"A sprawling study of one man's life as he plows through all the hurdles the twentieth century is able to throw at him. McIntyre does it with insight, detail, and depth."

—Merrill Markoe, author, *We Saw Scenery* and *What the Dogs Have Taught Me*

"Pour yourself a shot of Jack Daniels, tell Siri to play Sinatra ballads non-stop, and pore over *Frank's Shadow*. McIntyre is a superb writer. A stunning, utterly vivid novel."

—Lew Irwin, author, *Deadly Times* and *Sinatra: A Man Remembered*

"A moving, heartfelt novel with traces of Charles Jackson's *Lost Weekend* and Frederick Exley's *A Fan's Notes*. This is a hard-won, convincing valentine to family and the greatest generation."

—**David Evanier,** former senior fiction
editor, *The Paris Review*, author, *All the
Things You Are: The Life of Tony Bennett*

"With his wise, witty, and richly detailed prose, Doug McIntyre's probing, compassionate novel finds universality and even grandeur in the seemingly mundane; along the way he touches the heart again and again."

—**James Gavin,** author, *Deep in a Dream:
The Long Night of Chet Baker* and
George Michael: A Life

"*Frank's Shadow* is a chess game of suspense. Highly recommended!"

—**Douglas Brinkley,** *New York Times*
best-selling author, *Silent Spring Revolution*

"Masterfully done, brilliantly articulate, and emotionally moving."

—**Stacy Keach,** Golden Globe winner;
author, *All in All*

Frank's Shadow

Frank's Shadow

A Novel

Doug McIntyre

River Grove
BOOKS

Published by River Grove Books
Austin, TX
www.rivergrovebooks.com

Distributed by River Grove Books

Design and composition by Greenleaf Book Group
Cover design by Greenleaf Book Group

Publisher's Cataloging-in-Publication data is available.

Print ISBN: 978-1-966629-59-7

eBook ISBN: 979-8-886450-45-3

First Edition

To Robert and Jeffrey McIntyre, a father, a brother.
Geraldine DeFeo and Kathleen Herndon, a mother, a sister.
And Penny Peyser, everything else.

*"Fame is a fickle food served upon a
shifting plate . . . Men eat of it and die."*
—Emily Dickinson

*"Of all the people you are ever going to meet, you
will know your mother and father the least."*
—Allan Sherman

1

The Last Dance

I see his picture on the TV suspended from the drop ceiling at Logan Airport, Terminal A, Gate 15, the Delta Shuttle. The chyron graphic leaves no doubt: *Francis Albert Sinatra, 1915–1998*. This is the kind of story television hits out of the park.

Unable to hear the eulogistic blabber over the buzz of arriving and departing fliers, I cross closer to the television hoping to hear . . . what? The details of Frank's death? A soundbite of "My Way"? The CNN anchor weep?

This is a biggie. *Frank fuckin' Sinatra!* Last night the whole country was talking about the final episode of *Seinfeld*. Now we're all talking about this.

I'm not surprised Sinatra is dead. The warning signs were there—a collapse on stage in Virginia, forgetting lyrics to songs he'd sung for decades, glassy-eyed photos in the tabloids. I saw it with my own eyes at Radio City Music Hall, April 26, 1994, just a little over four years ago. I still have the stub in a drawer.

I had scored a great seat in the second row, so close I could actually smell the smoke wafting from Sinatra's Camel. I smoked vicariously through Frank the way two generations of men had imagined them-selves banging women who were hopelessly out of their league. Yes,

I was stag. The women I know aren't into Frank Sinatra. I'm a musical oddball. At forty, I'm supposed to be listening to The Who, Bowie, Zeppelin, or even the Beatles, right? Instead, I've always been drawn to the music of my father's generation, the songs written by immigrants or the sons of immigrants. Berlin and the Gershwins, Porter and Mercer—the great writers who spoke to the heart, or at least to my heart. Somehow music had turned angry or self-indulgently angst-ridden, and I had enough of that in my life without hearing it on a jukebox.

The Radio City audience guffawed at Don Rickles, a headliner opening for the ultimate headliner. I ducked and weaved in my seat, trying to remain invisible from "Mr. Warmth." While I crave attention, literally dreaming of fame, I would have died if Don Rickles singled me out. Luckily, he spotted an elderly Japanese man three seats over and did kamikaze jokes for five minutes. A brief intermission gave those of us who wanted a drink the chance. I *excuse-me, pardon-me'd* my way over a gauntlet of canes and ladies' handbags as I tried to get to my chair without spilling the eight-dollar whiskey and water I had smuggled in from the lobby bar. I hooked my foot on a plastic hose leading to a portable oxygen tank and apologized to the COPD sufferer.

I felt the tension in the room. These later-vintage Sinatra shows were minefields. Which Sinatra would show up? The listless, disoriented Frank we read about in the *Enquirer*, or the drunken Sinatra still grinding an ax at Lee Mortimer, Dorothy Kilgallen, and Kitty Kelley? Or maybe we'd get avuncular Frank, more grandpa than Rat Packer. And if we were truly lucky, we might even catch him on one of the increasingly rare nights when everything clicked, and, if you shut your eyes, you'd hear The Voice that made women moist and men hard with expectations. The Voice that killed the Big Band Era and opened the door for rock and roll and everything that's come in its wake.

Suddenly, with no timpani roll, no announcement of any kind, the man who needed no introduction received none. Sinatra stepped out of the wings into the light, and the crowd stood and cheered and clapped and shouted like fools. He was our god.

But Frank looked nervous, and nobody wants a nervous god. On this night, it was as if Sinatra himself wasn't sure why he was on stage rather than seated in the mezzanine with his brother Elks from the New Hyde Park lodge who rode in from Long Island on a charter. Still, he accepted our ovation like a birthright, casually, the way a trust fund baby doesn't sweat a dinner check. Can you imagine being so loved? Your jokes always land; doors are held for you. The hippest restaurants have a table when you want one; your bed is never empty. All of life's sharp edges are rounded off because fame is heaven on earth. When I was a little boy, I had this feeling: that I was destined for greatness, that my life was supposed to have some profound meaning—that I was meant to accomplish something really big.

I still dream.

At the precise moment our cheering reached its peak, Sinatra barked, "Go!" to Frank Junior, his son and conductor. The old warhorse plunged into his opening song, but something was wrong. Frank Sinatra wasn't singing. A croaking vibrato leaked from his famous throat. Worse still, he knew it. He knew it before we did, maybe when he'd gotten up that morning. Small wonder Frank was nervous.

He tried to compensate with motion, dragging one stiff leg behind him, movements that made him look even older than his hard-lived seventy-eight years. *Quasimodo in a tux*, I thought. Not the way I wanted to remember him. I gulped a mouthful of Dewar's, ignoring the judgmental looks of the rule followers who had left their drinks in the lobby. Sinatra went to the well, drawing on sixty years of showbiz tropes, hoping to distract us from the awful truth: He was singing on fumes. His once pitch-perfect pipes were shot. A supernova was imploding before our eyes. It hurt to look, but how could we not? Against our better judgment, we gawked the way we gawk at a flattened raccoon on the highway.

This was our fault. We were the ones still buying the tickets with unrealistic expectations. The ravages of all those late nights, all those tumblers of Jack Daniels, all the broads, smokes, and temper tantrums had collected their pound of flesh. Dean was dead. Sammy was dead. Count Basie was dead. JFK was dead. Ava was dead. Music was dead.

Fans are enablers, so we forgave him. No, that's not right. We loved him even more. We knew, and he knew, this was it, his last performance in the city that loved him like no other. If Frank Sinatra was only capable of a karaoke version of Frank Sinatra, so be it. His seventy-eight-year-old, flat, creaky voice was not simply forgiven; it was embraced.

Then disaster hit.

He lost the lyric to "Mack the Knife," and the giant teleprompters weren't bringing the words back. He tried to scat his way through. The crowd began to murmur. Six thousand murmurers make a mighty roar. He heard us. Concern became embarrassment. We felt sorry for Frank Sinatra. Even at a hundred bucks a ticket. So, one by one, the murmurs turned to cheers. We cheered Sinatra as he had never been cheered before. We cheered out of pity.

His eyes widened. He was moved by our affection. Or did the out-of-context ovation just add to his confusion? Whatever he was feeling, this is what I felt: neediness, of which I am something of an expert. We cheered Frank Sinatra because this night wasn't about singing; it was about love for the singer. Love for a man we had never met but felt as if we had known our whole lives. And in a way we had. He was a ruin, but so is the Acropolis, and people still marvel at it.

Then something clicked. The lyric returned, and he belted out the last eight bars with gusto and timbre and swagger, and the years fell off him. He stood straighter, taller, moving rhythmically and in perfect sync with the band, who swung even harder. It was the zenith of the evening, maybe of his entire career. I cried.

With the passage of time, I'll probably gild the lily and remember things differently; his pitch will have been perfect, the famous phrasing flawless. But Frank is freshly dead, and the splendor of his failure is still vivid.

My flight is called for the second time. I fight my way down the jetway with the rest of the salmon, plopping in the wrong row twice. I am distracted. My Cape Cod honeymoon has been cut short. My bride has been left to close up the house. Everything went sideways when the phone rang with the news.

My father is dead.

2

The House I Live In

Francis Xavier "Frank" McKenna's passing won't be on TV or the front page of anything. We'll have to pay to get him into the papers, in the back, buried among the racing results and mattress ads. I got the news the way most of us get it, with a phone call in the middle of the night. Nobody calls with good news after dark.

I collected myself and determined to get home as quickly as possible. I should have waited for Kimberly to pack so we could travel together. It's a mistake to leave her to fend for herself. I rented a car to get from Cape Cod to the airport, which means she'll have to drive my car to our place in Somerville, and she hates my car. But I want to go *now*, and Kimberly doesn't do *now*. To make flying as easy as possible, I gave her the number of a travel agent I use to get to conferences on the rare occasions I travel for work. She just has to call me with her flight info so I can pick her up in New York.

The rush is pointless, of course. Whether I get there today or twenty years from today won't change a goddamn thing, I just need to go. Kimberly was still sleeping when the cab picked me up for the ride to Avis in Barnstable.

It's a quick flight from Logan to LaGuardia and a toss-up whether it wouldn't be easier to drive the rental straight to New York. Hassle or not, I opted for flight, because that's what I always do when things get tough.

I stare blankly at the back of the salesman's head sitting directly in front of me. He is a big man, six-five, maybe taller. He chatters on a cellphone at a dollar a minute hoping to close a deal before they shut the cabin door. His hair is cheaply dyed, one of those over-the-counter shampoo-in jobs that fools no one except himself. I wonder what his story is, this huge man stuffed into a coach seat on his way . . . home? To see clients? What did he dream he'd be, back when that huge body was young and firm, and he had yet to make all the compromises life demands?

I have too many thoughts at once. I'll never hear my father's lilting Irish brogue again. I'll never smell his tobacco breath or hear his cartoonishly loud sneezes, which rattled the dishes in the cabinets. Crazy thoughts. Is Kimberly angry that I left her at the beach house? She said she was okay. And why, only a few weeks after marrying her, am I so happy to get away? I start to sweat. I unbutton my top button and loosen my seat belt. *Not now. Please!* I frisk myself. No pills. I cup my hands to my mouth and take deep breaths like Dr. Pincus said. It's been months since my last panic attack. *Not now! Where are my pills?*

I think about my friend Josh, the Hollywood writer. I don't know why, maybe just to redirect my brain. I've known Josh since childhood, before any mention of him carried the caboose "Hollywood writer." He was just a Jewish kid on my block, part of the Wiffle ball scene. He knew my father, and maybe that's why he popped into my head. Josh is smart and funny and makes ten times what I make writing his imbecilic sitcoms. I remember fighting with him over something terrible his name was on, thirty minutes of clichés and coincidences that murdered credulity. "You can't tell a story without coincidence," said Josh defensively. Maybe he's right. That's not my line of work.

Shallow breaths, Danny. Shallow breaths. I repeat over and over, a therapeutic mantra. A cigarette would help.

I teach history at a small college in New England. Professor Daniel McKenna, PhD, but everyone calls me Danny. I call myself Danny.

Not Dan, never Daniel. I spend my days trying to strip fiction from fact, and immodestly, I'm pretty good at it. But I am stuck with a big fat coincidence that not even Josh would have the balls to write: My father is dead; Frank Sinatra is dead—two Franks—both born on the same day, December 12, 1915, and now eighty-two years later, they have died on the exact same day, May 14, 1998.

You don't have to be a mathematician to calculate the odds of my father dying on the same day as Frank Sinatra; it's simple, one in 365. But in the same year, too? And to be born and die on the same day? Those are Mega Millions jackpot odds. Still, X number of people born in 1915 will undoubtedly die in 1998. Y percent will die in May. Even Sinatra couldn't expect to hog the fourteenth all to himself. It's a matter of probability, an accident of the actuarial tables. But I want it to be more than just the bounce of a ball. I want this coincidence to be profound, something grand, like Thomas Jefferson and John Adams croaking on the same Fourth of July, 1826, the fiftieth anniversary of the Declaration of Independence. That macabre coincidence made the country gasp in wonder. It was taken as a sign that America had been founded with God's blessing. How could it be anything else? Adams and Jefferson were the polestars of independence—friends, then enemies, and late in life, friends again. They deserved to be united in death as they often were in life. What connection could my father possibly have with Frank Sinatra?

Dad was in our driveway behind the wheel of his car when our forever neighbor, Ed Henning, spotted him. The Mets game was blasting on the radio. My father was deaf in one ear and practically so in the other. When he listened to a ball game, the whole neighborhood listened to a ball game. And he was always listening, a real nut about his Mets.

My father was born in the old country, and in the '60s he bonded with a team that employed pitchers with Irish names like McGraw, McAndrew, and Ryan. It didn't hurt that Rheingold was his favorite beer and the house pour at Shea Stadium. Of course, it had been years since Dad had actually been to a game. "Nothing but a bunch of spoiled millionaires," he'd grumble. Still, he followed the team with the fidelity of a yellow lab. The Mets are perpetual underdogs. So are the Irish. My father and the New York Mets were made for each other. Yankee fans have no idea how hard life really is.

I take more cupped breaths as the beads of sweat on my forehead merge and form rivulets trickling down my cheeks. The woman on the aisle knows something is wrong.

"Are you okay?" she asks, leaning across the empty middle seat.

"Migraine," I lie.

I close my eyes and keep breathing into my hands. My heart is racing; pain radiates through my jaw and down my left arm to my fingertips.

"It's nothing," I tell myself. But it's something. Suffocating. Embarrassing. It's terrible.

The shelf above the sink! I remember. *I left my pills on the shelf above the sink!*

I hear the jingling little bottles on the beverage cart as a male flight attendant pushes it up the aisle. The clinking bottles prompt a Pavlovian reflex, like the bells on the Good Humor truck when I was nine. The attendant sells a Chardonnay to my row mate. A drink would relax me like my forgotten Ativan. I consider it. I swore off the sauce two years ago, a couple of years after Sinatra's final bow at Radio City, but that was a terrestrial oath. Am I bound to honor a promise made on earth while soaring in the clouds? Drunks think like this.

"Diet Coke, please," I say. "With lots of ice."

My father liked sitting in his car in the driveway. He'd clutch the wheel and remember when he made long-ago drives to the Adirondacks, Montauk, and once all the way to Florida. He could smoke in the car, the house having been ruled out of bounds after ashes from his pipe set fire to the couch and a firefighter broke some of my mother's Hummel figurines, causing her to cry. After that, Dad would sit in the car in the driveway and puff away while waiting for the Mets to blow it. Around the fourth inning, my father saw his final inning. A stroke killed Dad while the San Diego Padres were killing the Mets, taking both ends of a doubleheader, 3-1, 6-2. My mother had warned him, "Someday that team is going to give you a heart attack!" A case can be made.

Ed rapped on the window to shoot the breeze, because that's what

Ed does, anything to avoid talking to Mrs. Henning. But Ed quickly recognized something was wrong. Ladder Company 164 was called, and soon Dad had paramedics pounding on his chest until they were satisfied he was dead. In Little Neck, Queens County, New York, there's always time for one last beating.

The woman in the aisle seat sips her cup of wine while reading *Pelvic Pain and Diagnosis* from a big heavy binder, the kind they hand out at seminars. Is she a doctor? Who else would be reading about pelvic pain? I like that she might be a doctor. If I'm having a heart attack, not a panic attack, she'll know what to do. Still, it's awfully early in the day for a doctor to be drinking. Maybe she's not a doctor. Maybe the pelvic pain she's reading about is her own. Cancer? Now I feel bad for her. I think about ordering a drink to absolve her of whatever guilt she feels for starting so early. But if I have one glass, I'll have every glass. I sip my Diet Coke instead, then go back to panting into my fingers as Narragansett Bay passes under the wing.

We circle for half an hour over eastern Long Island, flying above all those towns in Suffolk County I've never set foot in. A problem at our gate. We turn north toward Block Island, practically back to the Cape, before turning south again. We begin our descent, and there's turbulence. My anxiety rises and falls with each undulation. I make fish-mouth movements with my lips and jaw, hoping to take in enough oxygen to survive. I open the valve on the air vent all the way and aim it at my face, forcing oxygen into my nose and mouth. My row mate ignores my theatrical antics until she can't take it.

"We're landing," she says with relief rather than empathy, happy she'll soon be free from the twitching, gasping ninny one seat over.

Finally, we pass low over an empty Shea Stadium and touch down at LaGuardia. I am exhausted, soaked with sweat, but the crisis has passed. I'm the last one off the plane.

While waiting for my bag, I take in the splendor of the Marine Air Terminal, a neglected temple of aviation that once served as the North American hub for Pan Am's Clipper service to South America and beyond. Gleaming silver flying boats, multi-engined and phallic, rose and settled on the waters of Flushing Bay as well-heeled playboys, socialites, budding tycoons, and mobsters came and went to exotic ports of call—places with sultry names like São Paulo, Montevideo, Mar del Plata, Caracas, and Cartagena. It was a time when men wore suits and ties and snap-brim hats. Drinks were served in crystal, and your in-flight entertainment was the experience of flight itself. By contrast, I had just spent ninety minutes on a bus with wings.

Kimberly says I live in the past. She's right about that. Is it any wonder I teach history? Is it any wonder I listen to the music of someone else's youth? The present is an incomprehensible jumble, and the future is the future, and I'll worry about that when it gets here. The past is settled. We survived it. I like that. So why am I anxious about going home to my own past? My bag tumbles down the chute and onto the carousel.

The cab ride is uneventful. We make our way over the familiar auto-parts-strewn streets of my childhood. The bumps and muffler scrapes are almost musical, and I enjoy each violent thump and occasional Urdu expletive shouted by my Pakistani chauffeur, prefatory noise before the main event. When I walk through the door of my boyhood home, I'll be awash in sounds—weeping, consolation, commiseration, consternation, and, since it's family, aggravation.

Nothing brings an Irish family together like a good cry. As a race, we've had practice. Our Holocaust, our Trail of Tears, was the Potato Famine. Not a very threatening name for a catastrophe, is it? From 1845 to 1850, one out of every nine Irishmen died a slow, wretched death by starvation. When the potato crop failed, entire villages were left without a single living soul. Families were discovered in their sod huts, emaciated cadavers, often lying on the dirt floor where they had literally dropped dead. But when you say "potato famine," it's nearly impossible to take it seriously. No potatoes? Have the onion rings.

That silly-sounding Potato Famine killed a million men, women, and children while sending five generations into flight, including my father, a boy not yet fourteen, up a gangway in Cobh with his brother, Eamon, who had just turned sixteen. As they shoved off, the two lads stood shoulder to shoulder at the stern and watched their homeland recede, until Cork Harbor and then Ireland herself was swallowed by the fog and physics. The year was 1929, and the Potato Famine was still robbing my people of its sons and daughters. History wounds everyone.

We make the left off Northern Boulevard, and there it is: 23-10 Little Neck Parkway, on the corner of 44th Avenue, just across the street and downwind of the Scobee Grill, always open, holidays included.

I am home.

Set on a small rise, five steps above the sidewalk, the house is a faded green, a color that seemed weatherworn even when fresh out of the paint bucket. A big dormer faces the street, two windows for Mom and Dad's bedroom, one for the older McKenna boys, Al, and Kevin. A brick chimney runs up the south side, past the attic room my brother Sean still sleeps in. Our house remains unchanged and perhaps unchangeable. My old room is in the back, overlooking our small yard and the garage we share with the Hennings. The lawns and hedges and flower beds are, as always, perfectly manicured but without aesthetic consideration. My father spent twenty-five years as a mow-and-blow gardener for the New York City Department of Parks and Recreation. Our home was landscaped like a park, a New York City park, which means function trumped beauty. Who will trim the hedges and pull the weeds now?

"Danny!" shouts everyone.

"Danny's here!" hollers Aunt Bridget.

"Hey, Kate, your brainy son is home!" calls Big Aunt Mary to my mother.

I drop my bag and gather Mom in my arms, as my first tears fall. They come again a few minutes later when I pick up Dad's cold pipe from the bowl by the door, touch his reading glasses next to his recliner, and see his ratty slippers on the bathroom floor. These aren't just things; they are appendages. I cry, smelling those smells that are unique to our childhood homes and maybe only detectable to us. I am, by nature, prone to weeping, and now my Irish tears flow freely, willingly, cathartically. Yes, I am home, where I need to be.

The house is thick with visitors, a steady stream filing in every quarter hour. Aunts, uncles, cousins, nieces, nephews, neighbors, former neighbors, lodge members, and church people, including two nuns, old friends of my mother's, former teachers of all the McKenna boys back in our St. Anastasia days. The word had spread quickly, phone call by phone call, most hearing the news before I did. I am regaled with the heroic tale of who called whom to call whom to get the number at the Cape, and I suppose the point is to make me feel wanted.

Aloysius McKenna, my eldest brother and Al to everyone, wraps me in a tight bear hug. This surprises me because we are not the hugging kind. "We're orphans," says Al, who likes to make jokes, even if it's a stretch given our mother is still very much alive. Al is nearly ten years my senior. His wife, Beth, follows suit with a hug of her own, while their kids, Gail and Jay, opt for awkward handshakes after being prompted by their mother.

"Did they give you anything to eat on the plane?" asks Mom, because feeding people is her obsession.

"Starving," I tell her, and this makes her happy.

It's hard not to think of food. "The girls"—still called girls well into their seventies—have filled the house with covered platters and are rewarded with the obligatory flattery for their soda breads, au gratin potatoes, glazed hams, sugar cookies, or whatever it is they have mastered and bring to every gathering, joyous or tragic. These are familiar tastes and aromas, the same meals I ate as a kid, as a teenager, as a college boy home for the summer, and now as a recently married man of forty whose father has died. We gorge and drink, Hoffman's Black Cherry for me, the real stuff for everyone else, especially Kevin, the second oldest, who was born with bright red hair and has been angry about it ever since. He's three times the drunk I ever was and still drinks prolifically. Kevin sits close by the wobbly folding table that functions as the bar at all McKenna family shindigs, jumping up whenever anyone needs a drink. One for them, two for himself.

Sean, third in line to the throne, is only fifteen months older than me. Sean should have been my closest brother, but instead he's the mystery McKenna. From toddlerhood on, he's been a spectral presence in our house, like the pictures hanging in the upstairs hallway that have been there forever but none of us could describe if our lives depended on it. Sean is a slight draft blowing under a door; we know he's here, but that's all. I'm the baby in the family. The "surprise" child.

Fat Tommy Boyle walks in without knocking or ringing the bell, as he always does, practically filling the room by himself. Tommy is immaculately dressed in a coal black suit, white shirt, and tie, with shoes polished like bowling balls. His hair is perpetually swept back and slicked down and nearly as dark as the cloud over my mother's head. Tommy is blood, Mom's cousin, and has been called "Fat Tommy" his entire life, even to his face. I don't know how this makes him feel, and I'm embarrassed to admit I've never given it a second's thought until now. Tommy is one of those big men who is light on his feet, like Jackie Gleason or the delightful Oliver Hardy, a dancer almost. Fat Tommy is greeted warmly, but everyone knows this is more than a condolence call. He's the family undertaker, and this is his time to shine.

Fat Tommy Boyle worked in Great Neck as undertaker Ted Flood's right-hand man until they had a falling out over something no one has ever discussed. A woman? Hard to imagine. Money? Maybe. Some wounds are too deep for gossip. For the past dozen years Fat Tommy has been head man at the Doyle S. O'Connell Funeral Home, conveniently located in Little Neck, less than five hundred feet from our front door. But for how much longer?

Dad and Mom's crowd are the last bastion of Irish, a shrinking pocket of blarney holding down the fort in eastern Queens, surrounded by a tightening noose of Dominicans, Haitians, Puerto Ricans, and especially Koreans. It won't be long before O'Connell's is a Blockbuster or CVS or something else we don't need. Grieving Reeds, Ryans, Fitzpatricks, and Fitzgeralds are yielding to grieving Rodriguezes, Reyes, Dae-Chos, and Ch'ung-hons.

"Fuckin' pan faces," says Kevin, when someone mentions the Koreans. He's already four drinks into his morning. The names might be changing, but the tears are the same in every language. Word is O'Connell Jr. is going to retire, then what? This worries my mother greatly. Catherine Boyle McKenna thinks often of death. Fat Tommy Boyle was the first person she called, ringing him before she called Al at his place in Ossining and hours before she had Kevin call me.

Tommy holds court, recounting his every action from the second he grabbed the phone on the first ring. He was genuinely sorry to hear it was Dad. My father always called Fat Tommy, Tommy, even behind his back. Fat Tommy rolled out of bed and drove like a teenager, running all the yellows and at least one red.

When the cops and firefighters had finished their paperwork, Fat Tommy walked across the street to fetch the hearse. A small cluster of neighbors had gathered along with some of the late-night omelet eaters who had spilled out of the Scobee to see what was up. They watched as Tommy carefully zipped Dad into the body bag and drove him over to the O'Connell loading dock. The gawkers greatly irritated my mother. "No respect," she said. "No respect," she says again when Tommy gets to that part of his story. Having recapped his efforts at the granular level, Tommy turns to me and Al.

"Can you bring Kate over around 4:30?" he asks as he bites into a cruller. "There's stuff to go over. The casket. Flowers. You know."

"Sure," says Al.

"We'll be there," I add gratuitously.

"I gotta squirt," says Tommy, as he angles his girth through the doorway of the narrow downstairs toilet.

The phone in the kitchen rings and keeps ringing. I squeeze my way through a pod of aunts and grab it, expecting Kimberly with her flight information.

"Is Sean home?" asks a male voice.

"Sean!" I bellow over the mob. "For you!" And my brother takes the receiver.

My stomach gurgles. It's two o'clock. Why hasn't she called?

Some of the mourners have long drives and leave early. These are obscure relatives and vague friends of Mom and Dad's, names I have heard all my life but faces I wouldn't place if we met on the street. They have stayed just long enough so their departure does not cause tongues to wag.

With their exit, the McKennas, various in-laws, and familial satellites fall into our traditional roles. The girls convene in the kitchen, sorting out chafing dishes, gravy ladles, and Tupperware lids, eyeing one another as if they're shoplifters. Meanwhile, the older men sit on metal folding chairs borrowed from the neighbors, blowing pipe and cigar smoke out the window, where it mixes with the perpetual cloud of burned ground beef and potatoes wafting from the giant Scobee Grill exhaust fans. They lecture one another on exactly what roads they will take home to beat traffic, each with his own strategy, each convinced the others are assholes if they take the Long Island Expressway instead of the Northern State Parkway, or vice versa.

Technically, I'm still part of the younger crowd, but I can see the handwriting. One of Al's kids is already a teenager. It is both a comfort and unnerving to see how this collation of commiseration has subtly, inexorably morphed into every other family gathering, no different than a birthday party, Easter Sunday, Labor Day barbecue, or baby christening. Had I stayed here like my brothers, I would have eventually taken my place on a folding chair, pontificating on the merits of Greenpoint Avenue to Queens Boulevard as the only sane way to reach the Fifty-Ninth Street Bridge. Even Al, who lives upstate, falls into bitching about the Hutch and Sprain Brook Parkways. An unwatched television in the corner underscores our chewing and smoking and jawboning. The TV yakking fills a rare silence, and a snippet about Frank Sinatra's passing crisscrosses our reveries and requiems for Francis McKenna.

It is unanimously agreed that what happened to Sinatra is a terrible thing. This unanimity quickly dissolves as the old-timers bicker about their favorite Sinatra songs, confusing Perry Como and Nat King Cole hits with Frank's. I hold my tongue, because this isn't the time or place to be a know-it-all, even if I do know it all when it comes to Francis Albert Sinatra.

As the afternoon moves toward evening, Kevin continues to pour himself drinks until he's wobblier than the drinks table itself. When we run out of ice, he volunteers to get another bag, even though we know we won't see him till morning. He leaves to join other drinkers at the Little Neck Inn, the local gin mill that opened in 1909 and burned to the ground in 1981, only to reopen a year later smelling of stale beer and vomit. How do you build a brand-new dive?

Eventually the house clears until it's just us, the inner circle, the blood McKennas: Mom, Al, Sean, Beth, and the kids, Gail and Jay.

"We'll deal with the dishes later," says Al, as he tries to herd Mom to her appointment with Fat Tommy.

"I just want to put the salads in the refrigerator," she says, while unspooling two feet of plastic wrap. Fat Tommy will have to wait.

While my mother wraps and stows leftovers, and Beth wipes around the sink with a sponge, I dial Kimberly, first at home, then at the beach house.

No answer.

Why is she doing this? How hard is it to pick up the phone and let me know when she's getting in? I think this but don't say it. "Fuck!" I say out loud.

When the last of the spread is cellophaned and bladders have been emptied, we help Mom down the steps and walk past the barbershop with the pole that no longer spins. We pass a real estate office that used to be a shoe repair/key-grinding shop, but that was years ago. Places come and go so fast today. We cross Northern Boulevard at the corner and enter O'Connell's through the side door. Fat Tommy jumps up from behind his desk and gives my mother a hug and peck, then cuts to the chase.

"Did Frank leave any instructions?" asks Tommy, peering over his half-glasses.

"He has a will," says Mom.

"Anything about what kind of service he preferred?"

"I'm pretty sure he'd prefer he didn't have to have one!" jokes Al, earning a smile from me and a stone face from Fat Tommy, who is not in the joke business. Rather than lightening the mood, Al has embarrassed himself, and he knows it. "I'm Dad's executor," he continues with appropriate solemnity. "There's nothing in writing."

"But you talked with Frank, right, Kate?" asks Tommy.

"Something simple," answers my mother. "A funeral, Tommy. That's all we want." And with that my mother ends her participation in the business side of death.

"Would you like to say a prayer, Mom?" asks Sean.

She nods yes, and Sean escorts her to the small chapel down the hall. Sean is the master of our mother's moods. He watches from the back, as Catherine Boyle McKenna kneels before the tiny altar, blesses herself, and mumbles her prayers while clacking her rosary beads, which haven't been out of her hands since her husband passed.

Beth shushes the kids, who are running up and down the stairs because they're kids, while Fat Tommy pitches me and Al caskets, headstones, floral packages, and all the bells and whistles available from Doyle S. O'Connell, Inc. Al chooses the Trinity Oak model from the Batesville Casket catalog—satin finish, accent beading, and adjustable bed and mattress. We both prefer the Pembroke Cherry, but Tommy says he'd have to get it from the wholesaler in Harrisburg and that could take a week.

Dad will be interred in the family plot at Calvary, that much we know. Calvary is the final resting place for three million Catholic souls, including nearly all my mother's people. It's the gigantic cemetery everyone knows from *The Godfather*, the place where Michael learns Tessio is the rat who sold out the family to Barzini. Our plot is on the other side of the BQE, away from the Corleones, closer to the Expressway, in Section 2, not far from Steve Brodie, the famous bookmaker who, in 1886, claimed he survived a leap off the Brooklyn Bridge, giving birth to the now archaic cop jargon, "Taking a Brodie." Leap or no leap, Brodie did not survive diabetes in 1901.

Once we square everything with Fat Tommy, Al suggests going out for dinner, despite the fridge full of food at home. Twenty minutes later, we squeeze into a booth at Gabel's, an Italian joint in Bayside that serves you-name-it parmesan. Nobody is hungry, not even Al, but we have things to discuss, and when we talk, we eat.

You couldn't make up Gabel's with a government grant. It's been on the Boulevard for, I don't know, forty, fifty years? Gabel's never changes, not the menu, not the waiters, not the paper place mats decorated with colorful illustrations of cocktails that haven't been in vogue since the Gulf of Tonkin Resolution: Gin Rickeys, Rob Roys, Rusty Nails, Singapore Slings, Brandy Alexanders, Whiskey Sours, Grasshoppers, and Stingers. Gabel's is a hangover museum. The fashionable couples painting the town are long gone. Gone too are the mid-level mobsters who stopped in late for platters of spaghetti and *sugo da tavola*, and, as long as they were there, the cigarette machine money. Gabel's survives now on the survivors, the elderly who eat here out of habit and the occasional stray Korean salesman who tries to move fax paper over plates of clams casino.

Al raises his glass to Dad and in two big swallows drains the one beer a day he allows himself. Marriage and children have civilized Al. In his day, he could pound 'em with the best of us. Now he lives as one of those anomalies whose only addictions are an admirable love for his family and carbohydrates. The world needs more Als. I often wish I wasn't the youngest. By the time I recognized Al's virtues, he had been out on his own for a decade. My mother prays nightly that Kevin will find a woman of character like Al's Beth, hoping the right woman will work a similar miracle for Kevin. No Beth has materialized, because Kevin believes all women are cunts and whores, so that's exactly what he attracts.

A long time ago, when he was nineteen or twenty, Kev came home very drunk—no shock—but very upset, and that was surprising. He told Al he had met a girl at some big disco on the South Shore. She was drunker than Kevin and hanging all over him. When they gave last call, she waved off her friends and told Kev to take her home. In the car she kissed and licked him and pawed his crotch while he felt up her breasts and jammed his fingers between her legs. Bringing a girl back to our house was out of the question, so Kevin drove her to one of those cheap motels on Jericho Turnpike. Kevin told Al she giggled as they tumbled onto the bed. Afterward he drove her all the way out to Riverhead, where she lived. He scribbled our phone number on a matchbook as she fumbled with the door lock.

"Gimme a call," he said.

"I hate you, asshole!" she screamed before slamming the door.

Kevin thought he had gotten lucky. The girl knew she had been raped.

Over dinner Al tells a cluster of funny stories, every one of which we've heard before. Beth does her best to steer him to the matter at hand, but eventually she lets him have his say. A successful marriage requires enduring the endless retelling of stories. A waiter finally comes, and we order appetizers and get down to business; we have a funeral to produce, pallbearers to cast, hymns to select, a eulogy to write.

My mother perks up when we get to the hymns. She has surprisingly strong opinions and knows all the hymns Dad loved, which is news to the rest of us, because we don't remember Dad ever expressing a preference for any type of music—popular, liturgical, classical, and definitely not those corny Irish things they bellow in bars on St. Patrick's Day. As far as I know, Frank McKenna was agnostic when it came to music, maybe even one of the 3 percent of poor souls who suffer from musical anhedonia, a neurological condition that prevents people from enjoying music of any kind.

And he was deafened, a souvenir of the war. "War is loud," he explained.

I have to constantly remind myself how isolating his deafness must have been. He wore a big clunky hearing aid in his "good" ear that he bitched about constantly. How many of life's simple pleasures did he miss because he never heard them? So Mom selects all the hymns she'd like sung at her funeral, and in a convoluted way, they are the perfect songs for Dad, because every husband's life is easier when his wife is happy, even from the other side.

My mother also surprises us by emphatically rejecting any military component for Dad's service, even though as a Greatest Generation veteran, the army would provide a color guard and bugler to play taps at his interment. "No, no, no!" she snaps. "Your father wouldn't want any of that." And she's got a point.

He was not a flag waver. He never wore his uniform on Veteran's Day or Memorial Day. I'm not sure he even had his old uniform. He never joined the VFW or any veteran's group. "That was then; this is now," he'd say. Frank McKenna was a quintessential Greatest Generation combat veteran, a deflector of glory, unwilling to introduce the poison of war into his home.

When pushed to discuss the army, Dad talked about gathering food, as if World War II had been one big scavenger hunt. The joy of discovering a smoked ham hidden in a Belgian farmhouse chimney was his stock story. This was an oft-repeated tale and his default response, a crumb to shut up the nosy. When he finished his ham-in-the-chimney saga, the topic of war was closed. Frank McKenna retreated behind his own mental Maginot Line, an unbreachable barrier that forever quarantined his wife and children from his wartime experiences. Naturally, as a historian, I was interested even if the eighteenth century is my sweet spot. I pressed him, practically begging my father to tell me something. Anything. "I can't describe it until I forget a bit more," he said enigmatically.

After some nudging, Mom finally agrees to a flag on his casket, but that's as far as she'll go.

I am the obvious choice to write the eulogy, since I have had many articles published (almost exclusively in academic journals), and my biography of Bushrod Washington, George's able nephew and one of the first justices of the Supreme Court, sold close to five hundred copies. It could have cracked a thousand, but the *New York Times* reviewer called it "adequate," and the History Book Club passed, which is death for a book like mine. Still, I needed a book to secure tenure, and it served that purpose if no other.

As the Draft Danny movement sweeps the McKenna family convention, I take the floor to make a motion. "Why not let each of the sons say a few words?"

I say this in full knowledge it's a terrible idea. Sean will wilt in front of a microphone, and Kevin, being Kevin, will likely drop an f-bomb and make a scene. I pitched this idea mostly as a sop to Al, who likes public speaking and is good at it, having polished his chops at work with PowerPoint presentations and at Rotary Club luncheons that he emcees. But my motion is tabled without a vote, and it's agreed I will do the eulogy, Al will read the Epistle, while Jay, cousin Roger, and my brothers and I will be the pallbearers, even though Kevin is likely to be stiffer than Dad before we get to the cemetery. There's a role for everyone who needs to be included, and nobody has grounds for complaint except my niece Gail, who doesn't understand why her brother gets to carry the casket and a girl can't be a pallbearer.

I accept my assignment with genuine reservations. My attempt to duck Dad's eulogy isn't based on humility; I am the most qualified—that is, if it were a eulogy for anyone other than my father.

Here's what I can't tell them, what I'm ashamed to admit: I have no more idea what to say about Francis McKenna than I would if asked to give the eulogy for the Haitian busboy who is scraping breadcrumbs off our tablecloth with a plastic pocket comb.

Al drops us back at the house and wrangles the kids into the SUV, arms burdened with a CARE package from my mother. Beth carries away enough potato salad, cold cuts, and baked goods for a small city. They blow kisses and begin the long drive to Ossining. True to form, Sean retreats to his attic bedroom without saying a word. He'll spend the rest of the night watching a movie or doing whatever it is he does up there. With Kevin still at the Little Neck Inn, that leaves just Mom and me. We bus the last of the paper plates and plastic cups into the kitchen. We do this in silence, until she asks if I'm spending the night.

"Of course I'm staying," I say with feigned enthusiasm.

"You can sleep in your old room," she says. "I dressed the bed with the good linen."

I nod yes, unable to say no. I was hoping to stay at the Ramada, which is where I usually stay when I come home.

"You're exhausted, Mom. Go to bed. We've got a big day tomorrow," I tell her as I give her a kiss on the top of her head.

"I won't sleep," she says through a yawn.

"You'll sleep."

And with that my mother climbs the stairs to pull on her nightgown, brush her teeth, and scrub her face after completing her first full day of widowhood.

Alone at last, I dial the kitchen phone, carefully reading the beach house number off the slip of paper I had tucked in my wallet. No answer. I dial my place. Our place. No answer. My stomach grumbles. A swig of milk from the carton calms the storm, and I slowly hang up the phone, listening to it ring until the receiver hits the cradle and the connection clicks off.

It's deathly quiet now, literally. My father's passing has changed
the acoustics of the house. His absence is palpable, like an amputated
limb you keep reaching for. Everything is exactly where it should be,
yet there's a vacuum, a vacuum I can feel, which is oxymoronic, but I
don't know how else to describe it. I sit on the couch across from his
chair. I don't even consider sitting in the big recliner with its exhausted
cushions and shot springs. Nobody ever sat in my father's chair, not
even the dog, back when we had a dog. It was never explicitly pro-
hibited; he was not that kind of father. It was simply understood that
Dad's chair was Dad's chair. We respected this unwritten rule, even
Kevin, who respects nothing.

The couch is also past its expiration date, speckled with ancient
stains and fabric rubbed smooth from decades of derrieres in corduroy and denim. After today's collation, the coffee table needs Pledge
to remove the drink rings and pistachio shells and other schmutz. The
shade on the end-table lamp is yellowed with age and slightly cocked
to throw light on my mother's lap while she knits. All is as it should
be, as it's always been, yet it's completely different.

Upstairs, faintly, I can hear the tap running in the hall bathroom as
my mother washes off her makeup and brushes her teeth. Occasionally
Sean's footsteps reverberate all the way down from the attic. The carriage clock on the mantel ticks loudly, ten minutes slow by my watch.
Who will wind it now that Dad is gone?

I flip open the photo album that had made the rounds earlier in the
day and caused much pointing and laughing and reminiscing, which
morphed into arguing over muddled names, places, and dates. The
usual collection of snapshots tells our family's history, time traveling
from sepia to black-and-white to faded 1970s colors and even a few
Polaroids. The oldest pictures are from Mom's side of the family, the
Boyles: Pappy, Ma Boyle, my mom as a little girl, and, one by one, her
four sisters. A formal wedding portrait, the same picture that's been
on the mantel for years, and the group shot, a professional black-and-
white wedding-party photograph showing the maid of honor, Aunt
Mary; the best man, my Uncle Eamon; and four people I do not know.
All the men are in uniform, including my father and his brother. As the

youngest, I am the least represented in the album. By the time I arrived in '57, my parents had tired of milestones. The photos end abruptly with my high school graduation. The last dozen pages are empty. Is there anything sadder than a family photo album?

The mantel clock chimes midnight, which means it's ten after. I find a stray M&M on the rug and pop it in my mouth.

I grab my roller bag and start up the stairs, each footfall producing a different creak, some high-pitched, others nautical, like a wooden boat riding at anchor. Why am I winded? Parliament 100s, that's why. I used to take these stairs two at a time. Down the hall, on the right, is the door to my bedroom.

The posters and baseball cards are long gone, but the crucifix is still nailed above the door where it's always been. The globe shading the overhead light has a smudge of paint from when I helped Dad roll the ceiling. That was a long time ago. This was never a big house, not with six of us coming and going and growing. Tonight, it feels extra tiny.

As always, the twin beds are in the only place they fit, on opposite walls with the big cast-iron radiator separating them like a thousand-pound accordion. All the McKennas pronounce radiator "RAD-e-ator," except me. I corrected them once, pointing out it doesn't "RAD-e-ate heat, it RAY-dee-ates" heat, which prompted a pointed "fucking know-it-all" from Kevin, his favorite rejoinder to pretty much everything I ever say. When I was little, I shared this room with Sean, but puberty sent him to the attic, affording me the luxury of a room of my own, another source of resentment for Kevin, who had to bunk with Al. Sean's bed frame didn't fit through the narrow attic opening, so he sleeps on a box spring and mattress on the floor. His empty bed was my roommate. It's still here, waiting for Kimberly, as am I.

While I unpack, a welcome breeze flutters the shade covering the half-opened window, a window forever propped up with a hairbrush, an empty paper towel tube, whatever is handy. Currently, the handle from a broken ice scraper is jammed into the sill. The bedroom needs attention. My father had been a prolific tinkerer, a fixer, until age overtook him, and things started to slide. One Christmas—I had just gotten out of grad school—I mentioned that the living room rug looked shabby. Dad peered over the top of his *Daily News* and said in that soft voice of his, "'Tis a living room. There's been a lot of living in here." I never mentioned it again.

My old swaybacked desk with the orange drawers is a survivor from my high school years. This was a curbside find. Kevin helped me carry it home. After sanding it down, I painted the scratched-up drawers with a quart of orange enamel I found in the garage. The color is garish, but in the early '70s, what wasn't? There was nothing I could do about the big dip in the middle. Pens and pencils still roll to the center.

I plop down in front of it; my knees scrape the underside. Was it always this low? I open the top drawer and fish through the detritus of my youth: a Jon Matlack rookie card, a plastic comb with bent tines, two calcified Hershey's Kisses, five pennies, a Canadian dime, rubber bands, paper clips, and lots of cheap pens with chewed-up caps. I went through a biting phase. My teeth still fit in the depressions. In the bottom drawer, stacks of old school papers commingle with a tux rental receipt from my junior prom, a book report on *The Grapes of Wrath* lifted verbatim from *CliffsNotes*, and stacks of loose-leaf paper and scribbled-on spiral notebooks with lots of missing pages. I enjoy the archaeology of it all but sitting here makes me conscious of my urgent homework assignment, my father's eulogy. I grab an old notebook and scratch a dried-up pen back to life.

"Francis Xavier McKenna was born in Ireland," I write before crossing it out. "First, let me say on behalf of my entire family, thank you for being with us today." That's better. Welcoming. Graceful. Then for the second time I write, "Francis Xavier McKenna was born in Ireland" and promptly cross it out a second time. I go on in this vein until I surrender and go back to inventorying the desk drawers: some staples, an old pack of Kleenex, one of those tiny screwdrivers to tighten eyeglasses, a Uriah Heep cassette tape (not mine), a ticket stub from a Mets/Expos game in 1979, a business card from a Honda dealership, and a faded photograph of a girl I had a crush on in senior year. We never dated, and I have no idea how I got this picture.

I slide between the stiff linens of my childhood bed and try to read a few pages of John Niven's biography of Martin Van Buren that I brought with me to the Cape. I'm teaching a class this fall on the development of the two-party system, so it's time to bone up on Van Buren. But that overhead light is blinding, like an operating room. How did I ever read in this bed? My thoughts drift from President Van Buren to my father, to my mother softly weeping in her room across the hall, to Al, and Kevin, and even Sean, whom no one ever thinks about. I think about Frank Sinatra and all the events of the past twenty-four hours, of the last forty years. Then I think about my wife. Beautiful Kimberly. Why hasn't she called?

I sleep. Eventually.

3

Summer Wind

I'm awakened by the screech of seagulls gorging from the dumpster behind the Scobee Grill. I had forgotten how loud they are. Occasionally, a busboy brings out trash and swats at them, but the gulls come right back.

More visitors drop by the house, some welcome, others intrusive. The phone continues to ring like a PBS pledge drive. Finally, I get the call I have been waiting for.

"Where have you been?" I bark into the receiver.

"Good morning to you, too," Kimberly barks back.

"I'm sorry," I say, recognizing my mistake. "But I couldn't reach you, and I need your flight information . . ."

"You left me to do everything!" she says. "Maybe if I had a cell phone like everyone else . . ."

"Everyone doesn't have a cell phone. I don't have one. When are you coming?"

"The plane lands at four."

"That late? We'll have to go straight to the funeral home."

"That means I'll have to wear my dress on the plane."

"Get an earlier flight."

"Whatever."

After a slight pause, a prompt really, she says what I need her to say. "How are you?"

"Okay. Thank you," I say. Then, "Oh, can you bring my medicine?"

A few minutes past four, Kimberly walks hands free out of baggage claim with a college kid steps behind lugging her enormous suitcase. He is delighted to do so, because she's a stunner, no doubt.

At five feet five, Kimberly Clark, like the paper products company—although now, technically, Kimberly McKenna—always seems to tower above the women around her, an illusion she's mastered by wearing her hair up, employing extra-high heels, and some magic chick alchemy men will never understand. A natural blonde with better curves than Bert Blyleven, she quiets every room she enters, including, on this occasion, baggage claim at LaGuardia Airport. Once, in front of our place in Somerville, while Kimberly was bent over emptying groceries from the trunk of our car, a gawker drove onto the sidewalk and flattened a mailbox, a point of pride for both of us. She is impossible to ignore this afternoon, encased as she is in a little black dress with a plunging neckline, glaringly inappropriate for a wake or funeral or even a shuttle flight from Boston. Still, it is black, her only black dress, and I appreciate the effort, while the college boy, skycaps, town-car drivers, and random travelers appreciate everything else.

I yank her bag out of the young man's hand, crushing the frat-house fantasy letter to *Playboy* he had already half composed in his head. I kiss her. A little more kiss than necessary.

"Do you have my pills?" I ask.

"Here," she says, shoving a prescription bottle into my hand.

Kimberly and I met when I was in Florida for a seminar, "The Evolution of American Governmental Finance," a three-day inquiry into the metamorphosis of a loose confederation of thirteen stingy sovereign states into today's federal behemoth. I had been invited to present a paper, since my doctoral thesis had been a deep dive into the career of the Revolutionary War–era financial wizard Robert Morris, which, amazingly, was published as a trade biography to the general public and sold okay, thanks to an editor who hacked away all the academic gobbledygook. I was up late polishing my presentation when a friend—I'll call him "Eric"—a tenured professor from Tufts, buzzed my room and asked if I'd like to go for a beer. I passed on the beer but was happy to take a break from the eighteenth century. My employer, George C. Marshall College of Woburn, Massachusetts, hadn't authorized a rental car. Fortunately, the free spenders at Tufts had—a convertible, no less. With Eric behind the wheel, we took off in search of culture in Tampa Bay.

Exactly a century ago, in 1898, Tampa was the point of embarkation for the AEF, the American Expeditionary Force, liberators of Cuba from the yoke of Spanish oppression and seekers of righteous retribution for the sinking of the battleship *Maine*. Never mind that Spain had nothing to do with the *Maine*; a fire in the coal bunker was the likely cause. Yet Americans of every social order were gung ho for our first foreign war since we swiped the Southwest from the Mexicans fifty years earlier.

Chaos reigned in Tampa as troop transports and supply trains dumped horses, men, and a million tons of cargo on the single railroad siding leading in and out of the harbor, leaving individual soldiers to sort out the mess for themselves. Theodore Roosevelt's Rough Riders had a rough time in this malaria-riddled swampy morass, along with everyone else. Nobody knew what they were doing—well, nobody except the battalions of hookers who set up shacks of ill repute along the waterfront.

Eric and I had a good chuckle imagining Teddy, who was something of a prude, surrounded by whores in a nearly one-to-one ratio with his men. Then Eric pulled the car into Dante's Inferno, an enormous neon-signed strip joint with parking for a thousand cars.

"I'm from St. Pete," explained Eric, who has spent an unhealthy portion of his life in strip joints and fancies himself a connoisseur. "Strip clubs are the earthly realization of an egalitarian utopia," he told me while we were waiting for our drinks to arrive. "Race, gender, and class are irrelevant, and all men are not only created equal, we are, in fact, equal," he continued, reveling in his own acuity. "None of us are going home with one of these girls. That's equality!"

Eric is fustian, as we academics tend to be. At one point, he called the dancers "ecdysiasts," a highfalutin word for strippers. I had to look it up.

Eccentricities magnify as we mature, with some people becoming charmingly quirky, adorable even, while others become pompous and off-putting. Eric is leaning toward the latter, but I've known him since grad school, and at least he had enough self-respect not to spend the night at the cocktail reception kissing Arthur Schlesinger Jr.'s ass like everyone else.

A pudgy redhead in a micro bikini brought us one Sam Adams and one Diet Coke. "Cheers," Eric said, before excusing himself to stalk another redhead who sat in a corner booth.

I sipped my soda and observed, which is my station in life.

Dante's is the same as every other strip joint on earth, only bigger; the girls take their turns on stage, collect dollar bills from the amateur gynecologists who sit up front, then work the crowd, hustling lap dances at twenty bucks a pop. As a brunette harvested her tips, the deejay introduced the next dancer.

"Watch out for those claws, gentlemen! Kat is on the prooooowl!" And he said it like that, dragging out "prowl" like a Venezuelan soccer announcer shouting, "Goal!"

She was subdued by stripper standards, more fitness model than pole dancer. Beautiful in a wholesome way. Even if she hadn't been a stunner, Kat would have piqued my interest because, unlike all the other dancers, her music was my music. Kat had chosen to remove her clothes to "Summer Wind," the Sinatra version, the only version that matters. This was my stripper.

She finished her routine, which was, choreographically speaking, routine. Of course, nobody is ever going to confuse Dante's Inferno with the Bolshoi, and the patrons showered Kat with a thunderous ovation and a blizzard of bills, mostly singles, but fives, tens, and even a few twenties. She collected her tribute and smiled a Pepsodent-commercial grin. Her smile made me smile, and that's when our eyes met. Kat exited behind a curtain leading to the dressing room—literally a room where naked women get dressed—but I knew she'd find me after she checked her makeup, straightened her hair, and slipped on a robe.

I'm not one of those men women throw themselves at. I'm not hot. I don't have six-pack abs or that sullen, brooding loner look women for some reason find irresistible. I light up like a pinball machine around attractive women. I overtalk and underwhelm. I am over-solicitous and nervous and have trouble making eye contact. I look exactly like what I am: a forty-year-old history professor from a middling New England college. I don't have tattoos or *Miami Vice* stubble. I wear glasses. I own brown shoes. Still, nature provides every species the tools it needs to perpetuate the line. If I could get Kat alone, chat her up a bit, make her laugh, maybe then . . . After all, Irish blood courses through my veins. Are we not blessed with the gift of gab? I've been known to talk in my sleep. On occasion, I've talked my way out of trouble. I was about to talk myself into it.

"Would you like a dance?" Kat asked, her soft voice seasoned with a pinch of the South.

I looked up from my soda, and there she stood, modestly wrapped in a sarong, sipping lemon water through a straw to preserve her freshly applied white lipstick. Yes, white lipstick. I didn't know there was such a thing.

"Maybe later," I said feigning disinterest, so I didn't come off as a horndog. This offended her. I quickly reversed course.

"Please, sit with me for a bit," I said, tapping the back of Eric's empty chair.

Thus began the snowballing events that led a few months later to an impulsive wedding in Las Vegas and my current dilemma.

No surprise, Kat wasn't her real name. Kimberly Anne Clark was born and raised in Clearwater, Florida, a local girl with a hard-luck story, as if there's any other kind.

Sometimes I think I should have been a priest; how happy my mother would be! All my life people have confessed things to me, and I don't know why. Kimberly unburdened herself, reciting the full menu of stripper problems, starting with abusive parents, especially her mother, whom I've still never met but Kimberly says is as tough as a Claim Jumper steak. Things happen to strippers, and Kimberly has had her share of woes. She told me everything, which should have been a red flag. I was a total stranger, for Christ's sake. She said something about an uncle who touched her, a first boyfriend who date-raped her, a second boyfriend who hit her, like every boyfriend who followed. But she was so damn beautiful I didn't care how damaged she was.

I heard about pregnancies miscarried or aborted, days at the beach followed by long nights of rock and roll and drug-induced despair, a father whose only advice was, "Take care of that ass of yours. It's your ticket out of this shit-hole town." It was a lot to absorb and nearly impossible to follow over the thundering music and deejay shtick. I wanted her, which I honestly didn't think possible, but I let her talk and talk and because I listened, she practically begged me to take her to my hotel. She drove us.

Eric went home alone.

Early the next morning, I shaved, showered, and kissed Kimberly on the cheek as she pulled a pillow closer to her recently renovated breasts, a gift from an ex—although, let's face it, the boob job was really a gift for himself.

I was late for a breakfast reception. Joseph Ellis was scheduled to speak in the Palm Room downstairs, and I had been asked to introduce him. Jack Rakove was supposed to do the honors but was a last-minute no-show due to thunderstorms in Atlanta.

I slipped out of the room carefully, so as not to wake Kimberly, hanging the Do Not Disturb sign on the knob. She wouldn't be here when I returned. I had no reason to believe she even knew my name.

"You fucked her, didn't you?" asked Eric with a leering smirk while sawing into a stale croissant with a plastic knife.

My introduction for Ellis was a success, laughs followed by a hearty ovation as he took the podium. We had a break around eleven, and I dashed upstairs just in case, but the bed was empty. I took in the archaeology of last night's fling—the tangled blankets spilled on the floor, a small hair clip forgotten on the nightstand, the wrapper from a condom Kimberly had pulled from her bag. I was searching for something specific, and there it was. A handwritten note on the message pad next to the phone. Scribble marks, tight tornadolike circles that tore the paper slightly as Kimberly coaxed ink from the cheap hotel pen. A thank you for last night with lots of Xs across the paper and a lipstick kiss. Wow. Kimberly's number was hastily scrawled at the bottom—an afterthought, I thought. Were those nines or sevens? I kissed the note. I actually kissed it. I needed this little scrap of paper, even if it was only left as a courtesy. Her note was an affirmation that I had not been someone she regrets.

Later, my research paper was well received, with distinguished professors requesting copies and a promise of publication in an obscure journal nobody reads. I even got a thumbs-up and a wink from Gordon Wood as the Pulitzer-winner dashed past me on his way to the men's room. I had made the world a better place by offering cogent insights into the precarious and remarkable story of how Robert Morris, with smoke and mirrors and his own fortune, managed to fund the War of Independence and the early days of the Republic. Yet, all the professional attaboys, both sincere and feigned, left me feeling as empty as the bed in room 802. I could only think of her.

I skipped the banquet that night. Those things are a terrific bore, and without a couple of drinks, unbearable. I considered taking a cab back to Dante's. I wanted to see her again but was afraid she might not recognize me. I couldn't have stood that. And what if I walked in and found her spilling her life story to some fresh dope with a better per diem trying to hide his wedding ring? I fell on the bed fingering her note until sleep made the decision for me.

Home again, in Boston—actually Somerville, just above Boston—I went through the motions of my life. I had an easy schedule of classes, lecturing to disinterested students who believe their feelings trump facts. At first, I pushed back and challenged the brightest of them to aim higher. Slowly, unconsciously, I surrendered and now feed them whatever they want to hear so I'll get favorable evaluations. Students today are not scholars; they're customers.

I filled my days reading and napping and driving to New Hampshire on weekends. I spent my summer at Fenway Park watching the Red

Sox, a team I don't care for. This makes baseball much more enjoyable. I can't watch the Mets without two Ativans and a roll of Tums. I am my father's son.

When not teaching class and dreaming of the book or whatever that will propel me to fame and fortune, or at least fame, I killed time with the million prosaic details that consume our lives: dry cleaning, smog check, haircuts, laundry, calling old friends to talk about nothing. I was lonely. I unfolded Kimberly's wallet-worn note with the lipstick kiss. I dialed.

After a minute of real awkwardness, I jogged her memory and my name, Danny McKenna, was placed in context.

"Oh, great!" she said, genuinely happy to hear from me. "I thought you forgot about me."

"I'm sorry," I said. "I didn't want to seem like a stalker."

"Instead, you wanted to seem like an asshole?" she said with a smile in her voice.

We talked about this and that for a few minutes, and then I heard myself blurting out an invitation to come to Boston. She accepted so fast, I asked a second time, and she said yes again. I bought her a plane ticket before she could change her mind.

I took Kimberly to all the places I go, not to show her around, rather, to show her off. Maybe in Hollywood or South Beach they have girls who look like Kimberly Anne Clark, but I assure you, in the faculty lounge at Marshall College, she was without precedent. My colleagues debated her merits and flaws with the intensity of a tenure review. It was terribly superficial, misogynistic even, and Kimberly's very existence (or was it mine?) offended the faculty feminists as well as the eunuchs who hoped to get into their pants by echoing everything they said. The Fems, to their credit, never talked behind my back. They condemned my shallowness to my face. Screeching associate professors of lesbian-Sandinistan poetry and visiting professors of gyno-deism accused me of objectification at its basest level. I denied the charge, but of course I am guilty of all that and more. My real sin with these broads, though, had been a vote for Reagan in '84, something they'll hold against me until the Second Coming.

Soon, the novelty of crisp New England weather, a rocky coastline, and cheap lobster dinners began to fade. The geography placebo had worn off. Kimberly turned sullen. Accusatory. Oddly jealous. Of what I don't know. She blew her top over nothing. Well, that's not true. She was bored. I bored her, and that made her angry. She said cruel things, emasculating insults, attacking my looks, my profession, where we lived, my dick, everything, hoping I'd hit her and allow her to leave as a victim. I wouldn't give her that. I answered calmly, my hands always held behind my back, so I didn't reflexively smack her. This drove her crazy. My Gandhian nonviolence was a devilish new form of abuse she had never encountered.

Late at night, while she slept, I'd lie in bed staring at the ceiling and ask myself, "What are you going to talk to her about tomorrow?" The truth is she bored me as much as I bored her. Kimberly's tales of woe had been told and retold, with new horrible details, many of them improbable, which made me start to question everything. I bored her, and she exhausted me. Then she started waking at night in terrific pain, real pain, abdominal cramps followed by nausea that I prayed wasn't a pregnancy, because I crave fame, not children.

Kimberly's Florida tan faded to a sickly gray, and she stopped eating. Blood spotted the sheets and bathroom towels. Soon she was bedridden with a heating pad on her growling stomach I could sometimes hear in the hallway. I begged her to go to the doctor, but she was terrified and refused. Finally, she confessed something new.

A year earlier, she had similar symptoms, and a doctor suspected colon cancer. She freaked and never went back, instead wishing cancer away. Like that ever works. She spilled the whole story, as I struggled to suppress my own growing panic. She thought she was dying, and now I did, too. She wept, real tears, blurting out a litany of fears, including no health insurance. That I could fix.

We married.

Despite everything we had going against us, the wedding was a hoot—a fabulous distraction. We flew all the way to Las Vegas. Neither of us had ever been. We bypassed the quickie marriage mills closer to home, because somehow a Vegas wedding seemed more legitimate than getting hitched in Atlantic City or Maryland. We took a cab from McCarran directly to the license bureau, then across the street to a pawnshop for rings. We picked a chapel at random, debated and rejected the Elvis impersonator, and an hour later registered at a hotel off the strip as Mr. and Mrs. Danny McKenna of Somerville, Massachusetts. The next morning we flew home without hitting the tables. We had gambled enough.

The following Monday I took her to Mass General, where it took three shots of Demerol to put her under. As the doctor probed, pain jolted Kimberly out of unconsciousness, and the procedure had to be aborted. "Nobody gets four shots of Demerol," explained the anesthesiologist.

Ten days later, back we went. This time using liquid Valium. Kimberly went under and stayed under.

I turned all the pages in *Redbook* and half a dozen other magazines of no interest and watched the elderly Portuguese woman who sat across from me as she worked her rosary. I envied this woman. She had a believer's conviction. She knew God would intercede on her behalf. I was the agnostic in the waiting room, without faith or even an atheist's certitude of disbelief. I would have gladly made a deal with God, any god, if only I could make a commitment. I rolled snake eyes on Pascal's wager. Some cultures are tripping over deities. In West Africa, people pray to Ifejioku, the god of yams, while I have just one, good ol' Jesus. Where is the god of skeptics? That's the god I need. Instead, I prayed to Christ, as I'd been taught by my parents, the nuns at St. Anastasia, and even by Santa Claus who was somehow connected to the birth of Jesus and all that swag on Christmas morning.

I prayed selfish prayers in the waiting room, mentioning Kimberly but really asking the Lord to spare *me* pain. I felt guilty making these selfish appeals. Asking for God's help now felt like cutting the line at the DMV. So I prayed again, a never-mind prayer, this time asking God to help the Portuguese woman, since she had to be more deserving than me. Then I prayed a third time, asking Jesus for a fresh start with Kimberly. A real prayer. I forgave her everything. She was my wife, my lover, and if Jesus would make her whole, I would do whatever I could to deserve a second chance.

The waiting room filled and emptied and filled again with worried loved ones mumbling about biopsies, MRIs, prognoses, and the outrageous shysters who set the sky-high prices at the hospital's parking garage. Finally, the doctor shoved his way through the doors, rushing to his next patient, or lunch, or to check his portfolio. I literally grabbed his sleeve.

"So?"

"She's fine," he said, as if there could be any doubt. "I found hemorrhoidal tissue in the large intestines."

"No cancer?" I managed.

"She's fine." And he was gone.

Hemorrhoids. I got married because of hemorrhoids. Still, I was so damn happy I overlooked the doctor's hubris and my own foolishness.

She was groggy and pale, and I cried as I told her the good news. Kimberly trembled as a year of worry drained from her body. I said, "I love you," and told her how we could now have a happy life together, and I think I meant it. She nodded her head, just a slight nod. Ambivalence or the aftereffects of Valium? That night, at home, I proposed a honeymoon.

I've always loved Cape Cod but didn't force it on her. A guy I play softball with, Marc, owns a small cottage on the beach in West Yarmouth. I had been there a couple of times for cookouts and clambakes and thought it romantic. The house was pure Cape Cod—weathered and filled with the ghosts of Melville and Thoreau and the endless whoosh of the Atlantic just outside the door. "Your money's no good," said Marc.

Four rooms in all, furnished with Eisenhower-era sofas and armchairs upholstered in primary colors, with cheap sun-faded curtains fluttering from the perpetual sea breeze that leaked through the storm shutters and sand-scarred windowpanes. Like all Cape cottages, it had a name painted on a faded wooden sign above an arch over the front gate: Bliss. Cigarette burns formed a surprisingly attractive leopard pattern on the wide wooden arms of an easy chair I adopted as my own. I felt as if I belonged in that chair, as if I'd always sat in it.

I imagined quiet sunny days flipping through out-of-date magazines and long chilly nights with a single lamp over my shoulder as I plowed through the stack of Will and Ariel Durant, which I had promised myself someday I'd read. Instinctively, I flipped my cigarette ash into the pedestal ashtray by my side, as if it had always been by my side. We'd eat fish dinners cooked in someone else's pots, meals served on mismatched plates, the leave-behinds from forty years of summer rentals. It was a house filled with history, so naturally, I loved it; a cottage filled with fond memories of a life I hadn't led.

But my wife is a modern woman, and she considers history old news, mostly bad. To her, the house was dilapidated and depressing, which made me wonder what she must think of our house in Somerville. Kimberly had been raised on the beaches of West Florida, and the ocean's call had long since lost its charm. The sound of the surf lapping the shore brought back too many nights of insincere seduction by lawyers and other big talkers intoxicated by cocaine and ecstasy and their W-2s, too many nights of loveless sex in hot tubs overlooking the Gulf of Mexico. I should have taken her to the mountains.

Still, we went through the motions. We cooked together and talked without fighting, trying to connect in some sustainable way. Kimberly and I searched for common ground, but with each conversation, the gulf actually widened as our incompatibility became our honeymoon's third wheel. We overacted our parts, chewing up the scenery, each trying to top the other in insincere professions of love. In AA they tell you to "fake it 'till you make it." And that's what we tried to do. We pretended to be in love, tumbling in and out of bed in a desperate attempt to fuck ourselves to sustainability. On our last night on the Cape, a local disc jockey obliged by playing "Summer Wind," a good omen, I thought, as Sinatra's voice and Johnny Mercer's words brought back the memory of that silly night at Dante's Inferno. But it was too soon for nostalgia. As we recovered in each other's arms, I blurted out a question I had been afraid to ask.

"Why 'Summer Wind'?"

"Huh?"

"Why did you dance to that song?"

"High heels," she said.

The slow, swinging rhythm of "Summer Wind" was simply easier on her feet than Van Halen or Aerosmith or any traditional stripper fare. And safer. Eight-inch heels are a twisted ankle waiting to happen, a month's rent gone, and then the door would be open to crossing a line she had promised herself she'd never cross. Kimberly is nothing if not pragmatic; I'm the romantic.

We had nothing together, not "Summer Wind," not Frank Sinatra, certainly not love. Our only bond was mutual neediness, and now that she would live, even that had disappeared. That's when the phone rang, and I heard Kevin's booze-slurred voice telling me Dad was dead. Kevin had volunteered to make the call because he loves breaking bad news.

The next morning, I drove to Boston for my flight home, leaving Kimberly to close up the cottage and drop the key where Marc said he would pick it up.

The hugs and kisses at baggage claim are for public consumption, mostly to crush the horny college boy who thought he had a shot. In the privacy of a cab, Kimberly and I resume our Cold War. After a few obligatory remarks—"How's your mom doing?" from her, and "How was the flight?"—from me, we ride in silence toward the funeral home. Kimberly is anxious. She has never met my family. I am anxious because I have.

It's drizzling, and the heavy damp air amplifies the roar of the jet engines as travelers soar off to the hub cities of Chicago, Atlanta, and Dallas. These same planes come in low over my childhood home, rattling the windowpanes and filling the air with exhaust we natives no longer smell.

"It's stinks around here," says Kimberly, not trying to start something, simply stating a fact.

"You get used to it." Also a fact. You can get used to anything.

"Roll up your window."

"I just lit a cigarette."

"Please, Danny, the stink is making me sick."

So I toss my smoke out, and nothing else passes between us until the cab stops in front of O'Connell's. Kimberly makes a dash through the rain for the awning. As I lug her huge bag out of the trunk, the driver, a Ukrainian in a black T-shirt and skintight knockoff designer jeans, gets out to help. He asks in his version of English, "You go to funeral?" I give him a nod and stuff a fifty into his mitt. He pauses, wanting more details.

"My father died," I say flatly, pissed I have to explain anything to this guy. The cabbie's huge face drops.

"My father die, too," he says, shoving the fifty back into my hand. "In January. In my village, Kovel."

"I'm sorry," I say, pushing the fifty back at him, but he clenches his fist and won't take it.

"Someday I go back. It's no good here," he says, climbing into his car and leaving me at the curb, money in hand, lump in throat.

Inside, we hang our coats and are immediately assaulted by my cousin Roger, a big oaf who thinks about dinner while still eating lunch.

Roger is an angry ex-jock, a football guy, his formerly chiseled physique having softened with the years like neglected topiary. Roger is at the tipping point, one week of reckless eating away from a lifetime of obesity. It's not Roger's gluttony I find off-putting; rather, it's his meanness.

I had dinner once at his house, a meal during which he belittled his kids and berated his wife, who has gone gray in their eleven years together. Hardly anyone spoke during this meal. Instead, forks and knives scraping and clicking on plates and teeth stood in for conversation. Still, Roger lives for wakes and funerals, because death frees him to hug and even cry, a luxury he does not allow himself otherwise. If I liked him more, I would feel sorry for him. The first to arrive, the last to leave, Roger can be counted on to say nice things about the deceased—in this case, my father, a man he hadn't seen in three years.

Tonight Roger is particularly attentive because Kimberly demands it in her clingy black cocktail dress. As sleek as a panther, with her long blonde hair draped over one shoulder like a silky lightning bolt, she illuminates the room, a chandelier with legs. Roger continues chatting away with her, as his unhappy wife gives him the stink eye from a folding chair. They live in Farmingdale, and I take subversive pleasure knowing Roger will get an earful on the long ride home.

Al comes over and gives me another hug, two in two days, some kind of record. Nonetheless, I feel a tear run down my cheek, which is easy to do with Al because he's a nice man and also because I cry a lot, which makes me a pansy in Roger's eyes.

"Which one's your mother?" asks Kimberly.

We find Mom with Kevin and Sean in the main salon. Fat Tommy has given Dad the "Big Room" at no additional cost, a pointless extravagance considering most of Dad's friends are also dead, or in Florida, or had paid their respects at the house and won't be back until the funeral on Tuesday. The Big Room is reserved for the important dead—children or politicians or firefighters, the deceased that matter. Dad's open casket is lost in this huge, empty space, and I hate Fat Tommy for making my father seem smaller than he was.

I make the introductions starting with my mother.

"Kimberly Clark McKenna, this is my mother, Catherine Boyle McKenna."

"I hope you'll be comfortable enough to call me Mom," says Mom, her eyes squarely on Kimberly's face rather than her body, unlike everyone else, even Beth and Gail.

"I'm sorry for your loss, Mrs. McKenna," says Kimberly, declining my mother's invitation.

Kevin approaches and shakes Kimberly's hand as if he's running for Congress. Kevin is so unnerved by her, he glances twice from Kimberly to me and back to her, trying to square the sexual math: *How did this happen? How did my asshole brother land this amazing piece of ass?* He doesn't say this with words.

We mingle with the dozen or so mourners; I stumble a few times when I can't remember some of the names and whiff completely on Faye Massaro, my mother's oldest friend, whom I've known forever but haven't seen in years. I feel sorry for Kimberly and tell her so. This is a hell of a way to meet the in-laws. Yet I'm also grateful the circumstances spare us the pretense of acting the part of happy newlyweds.

To her credit, Kimberly has brought her A game. No temper

tantrums, no scenes. She remains charmingly demure around my mother, friendly with Al, Beth, the kids, Kevin, and Sean, and just flirty enough with Roger to keep things interesting. She revels in the attention, accepting it naturally as the birthright of the physically blessed. The mourners keep her busy, shaking hands and returning pecks on the cheek; Roger comes back for seconds and thirds. My wife is thoroughly enjoying the limelight, and because she's happy, I'm happy.

As Al launches into a funny story, my eyes drift to the ignored open casket on the far side of the room. I know I have to approach Dad's body, kneel and pray or something, but I stall. I had hoped to be stronger than this, but I feel my resolve dissolve. All my repressed feelings bubble up from some neurotic magma chamber and collect in my throat. The idea of kneeling before my father's corpse suddenly terrifies me, as if I'll choke on clumps of emotion the way drunks sometimes choke on their own vomit. Instead, I read the cards on the floral arrangements; half came from the people in this room. The centerpiece is a giant shamrock made from carnations dipped in green dye by the florist, sent with the condolences of the Ancient Order of Hibernians, who have a budget for things like this. I retreat to the lobby and scan the visitor's registry to kill thirty seconds. I begin to compose a list of all the old friends who should be here but aren't, taking on fresh resentments.

I spot a day-old *Daily News* abandoned on a folding chair and grab it. The *New York Daily News* was Dad's bible. I hope my reading it will be interpreted as an homage rather than an evasion.

When I was twelve or so, the *News* published a letter Dad had written to "The Voice of the People" column demanding the city install a stop sign on our corner after a child was struck and killed by a garbage truck. Dad was the talk of Little Neck Parkway and got pats on the back from everyone. The Hibernians even thumbtacked his letter to the corkboard above the urinals, a place of honor. That letter elevated the *New York Daily News* to near-Talmudic status in our house and possibly inspired Dad's youngest son to someday see his own name in print.

The paper is facedown, the back page crowing the news of yet another Yankees victory along with the painful recap of the Mets' doubleheader disaster in San Diego that ended too late for yesterday's edition. I flip it over. On the cover, a monster headline screams the redundant news of Sinatra's death, news the entire world already knows but still packs a wallop in those big black letters with a rare "Extra! Extra! Extra!" running above the masthead. This is the real deal, an authentic extra edition, with a special press run of a hundred thousand copies. There's never been a culture more obsessed with people we don't know and less interested in those we do.

I thumb through the abandoned paper, moving my eyes over the columns of type as if I am actually reading. There are tributes to Sinatra from celebrities both foreign and domestic. Remembrances of friends and hangers-on. A filmography. A discography. A lexicon of Frankisms with definitions to words like *Clyde*, *duke*, and *bird*. There's a lead editorial bemoaning Sinatra's passing, as if his heart attack had been a nitwit act of Congress the president should veto. The *News* promises a special twenty-page pullout in tomorrow's paper, anointing it a collector's edition before it even goes to press.

I raise my eyes toward Kimberly, who tells a story and gets a laugh even though funny is not one of her colors. A few chairs behind me, two elderly women, friends of my mother's, prattle on about Sinatra.

"It's a crying shame. Eighty-two's not so old today."

"He smoked, didn't he?"

"Who smoked?"

"Sinatra."

"I wouldn't know. I feel sorry for his daughter."

"Nancy."

"With the laughing face."

"What?"

"The song. 'Nancy with the Laughing Face.'"

"I love that one."

My eyes dart back to the paper, at Frank's picture on the cover, in a tux, as always, a tumbler of Jack Daniels held high. Then I look over at the box bearing my father's forgotten remains. Suddenly I hate

Frank Sinatra. I hate Kimberly. But mostly I hate myself. Somebody has to pay for this outrage, so I approach the casket and drop to my knees and look my father square in the face. I will pay.

He was never a large man. Of course, when we're kids, every father seems gigantic. Me being the youngest, my father appeared extra-large, but over time I learned he was just average. Francis McKenna was forty-two when his youngest son was born in 1957, the boomingest of the Baby Boom years. I never knew my father as a young dad. Al and Kevin roughhoused with him, Sean less so, me not at all. His youth was already behind him when I arrived. Francis McKenna was fully a man and steaming toward old age. I think he would have preferred a daughter.

He was barrel-chested, ruddy-cheeked with thick, curly, blindingly white hair like cotton, and the mounting birthdays heightened his Celtic ancestry, his features morphing into a cliché mick—a whiskey-sipping, pipe-smoking caricature missing only the green derby, shillelagh, and pot o' gold. He became a Barry Fitzgerald lookalike, and I suppose it's a reflection on my media-obsessed generation that I have to invoke a movie actor to describe my own father.

I inventory his features like a housewife eyeing fillets at the fish counter. Fat Tommy Boyle, who is forever nicking his own chin while shaving, nicked Dad's on his final shave. I examine Tommy's work like a tire kicker at a used car lot, tapping fenders for Bondo. My face is uncomfortably close to Dad's, and I feel I'm crowding him, which is a posthumous role reversal.

Makeup has been slapped on as if with a trowel; clown red rouge to simulate Dad's perpetual ruddiness. My father's red cheeks did not come from his years of working out of doors, which is how he always said it. The color was the canary in the coal mine, a harbinger of the chronic hypertension that ended his life. Rather than hide this defect, Fat Tommy has heightened it. Dad is not his best work.

I examine my father's Adam's apple, big enough to make a pie. I look at his enormous hands and am happy to see not even death can rob them of their strength. His lifeless fingers cradle a rosary, as I like to imagine they once cradled me when my mother first put me in his arms. Hair, cheeks, chin, chest, neck, nose, lips. I examine each of Dad's component parts, careful to avoid seeing him in full assembly, hoping his details will suffice and let me avoid the terrible truth: I am looking at a stranger, a man I hardly know.

The *Daily News* says Ava Gardner was the love of Frank Sinatra's life. Who was the love of Frank McKenna's life? My mother? On Tuesday, my father will be buried and take with him all the answers to all the questions I never asked. If only he could climb out of his shiny new Batesville Casket Company coffin and explain himself.

There isn't anything I don't know about Frank Sinatra. His favorite color was orange. What was Dad's favorite color? I know Sinatra was a forceps baby, that his father was a Sicilian named Martin, that Frank Sinatra never finished high school. I know little Frankie sang in saloons for nickels as a kid, that he was friendless, spoiled, lonely, and starved for love. I know the minutiae of Sinatra's life, while my own father's story is a collection of random facts passed along secondhand via relatives with faulty or conflicting memories.

Here's what I can tell you.

My father was born in a thatched cottage in a tiny village in western Ireland, a village frozen in time. While it sounds romantic, his childhood home was cold and tubercular, taking the lives of three siblings he never met. Then history catapulted Francis McKenna to a new world. The long tail of the Potato Famine sent him to a smoky, mechanized, cacophonous city of pavement and hurry, utterly alien to the pastoral life he had known.

He was a man of regular habits. My father walked in the house every night at 5:00 p.m. He was like a metronome, that reliable. At least until he retired. His shift at the park began at 7:00 a.m. and ended at four, with an hour break for lunch. In the summer he'd stop for a beer on the way home, usually at the Little Neck Inn, but sometimes at a place on Bell Boulevard. He downed his beer quickly, and by five the jingle of his keys dropping on the little side table by the kitchen door announced his return.

Without deviation, Dad walked directly to the sink, where he rinsed out his thermos and placed it upside down in the dish drain. If he crossed paths with my mother, she got a reflexive peck on the cheek. Then he'd climb the stairs and scrub himself in the shower, paying special attention to his fingernails. My father had worker's hands, knotted and calloused, but he kept his nails pristine, as if they belonged to a jeweler or surgeon. When he reemerged, he was invariably dressed in a pair of sharply pressed slacks and a white short-sleeved collared shirt. The dirty, sweaty man who had spent seven hours mowing lawns, fixing sprinklers, cleaning shit and piss from public toilets, and stabbing beer cans and used condoms with the "idiot stick" (a broom handle with a sharpened nail on the end used to spear trash), would come downstairs, pet the dog, then go outside to check on his tomato plants and nod at the neighbors as they shouted their hellos from the sidewalk. This would go on until Mom called him in for supper.

In colder weather Dad switched to whiskey and water on his way home, and flannel replaced the short sleeves. Instead of inspecting his tomatoes, he'd duck into the garage and tend to some minor repair project on his bench.

Most of the other dads in our neighborhood worked in the city and caught the 6:50 or 7:10 trains from Penn Station. They'd trudge past our house, coming up the hill from the station, a long parade of physically and mentally exhausted men—mostly men—in lumpy suits with ties askew, their briefcases weighing down their arms like farmers lugging buckets of water from a well. I saw more of my father than Josh or any of the other kids saw their dads, especially in the summer when we'd play stickball on 44th Avenue and he'd be in the yard shouting "atta boy!" when somebody got a hold of one. I got away with nothing, not with him lurking behind the hedges. I thought my friends were the lucky ones.

A tight-lipped man by nature, Dad let his eyes do his talking. He'd lock those peepers on us as a group, or, God forbid, as individuals. That's all it took to end whatever shenanigans we were up to. I still find it difficult to look people in the eye, and this makes people distrust me.

One summer, the Summer of Sam, 1977, my father pulled strings and got me hired as a seasonal fill-in with the Parks Department. That was an education.

He called me Danny at work, just like at home, but he never introduced me as his son. I called him Frank. He didn't ask me to. I just knew to call him Frank, and he never corrected me. At home he was Dad again.

At Alley Pond Park the younger guys on the crew called him "Prickenna," because Dad would bust their balls for clowning around. He wasn't their supervisor and had no authority. Occasionally, he'd screw something up, and his boss called him "shit-for-brains." One night he locked a kid in the ladies' room, and the fire department had to get her out. He couldn't hear her yelling, "I'm in here! I'm in here!" I watched in shock as the boss cursed him the next morning, and Dad stood there and took it. This other life of Francis McKenna's was a revelation. At home he was infallible, even when he wasn't.

I couldn't wait for that summer to be over. Every day I wished it was Labor Day, so I could go back to college and booze it up with my pals. Then one day, my father had heard enough and said the wisest thing he ever said to me: "You're wishing your life away, kid."

That's all I know of my father.

So I weep. Big, loud, embarrassing air-sucking sobs that kill Kimberly's humorous story in mid-guffaw and make me the center of unwanted attention. I weep for myself, since I don't know my father well enough to shed tears for him. I weep because I know as long as Francis Xavier McKenna remains a mystery, so will his son, Daniel Patrick McKenna.

Al throws an arm around my shoulder. Kimberly, God bless her, summons up actual sympathy and is a comfort, which doesn't sit well with cousin Roger or Kevin. My mother cries at the sound and sight of my tears, and Sean deftly yanks a fistful of Kleenex from his pocket and presses them into her hands. He has a genius for anticipating her needs.

"Come on, Mom. Let's get some air," says Sean and escorts her out of the room.

Kevin chooses this moment to slip out a side door and head down the street to Peck's, a hellhole two notches below the Little Neck Inn, which is saying something. It's times like this brothers need sisters.

While I am encircled in a family scrum, an old man enters unnoticed. Cue-stick thin with a fringe of gray hair above his enormous ears, this walking relic makes his way purposefully toward my father, his cane landing just ahead of his orthopedic shoes. I shoot Al a look, and he shrugs. The stranger stands over my father's body and reaches into his coat and pulls out a garrison hat, folded twice. He snaps it open and sets it on his head at a rakish angle, the same way he wore it in 1944 and on Memorial Days ever since. He's United States Army, an enlisted man, a grunt. He now has our full attention.

We wait for his salute, a moment of great poignancy, a tribute from one warrior to a fallen brother. We watch in silence as the old veteran clears his throat, then *ptui!* A clam-like oval of saliva splashes across my father's face.

"Jesus Christ!" shouts Al.

"What the fuck!" screams Roger, as he nearly knocks the old man to the floor.

I say nothing, immobilized with shock, my face frozen like one of those big heads on Easter Island.

"What's wrong with you?" demands Al, as angry as he's ever been. "Whatdidyoudothatfor?" we shout collectively.

"That's between me and him!" says the stranger, as he refolds his hat and stuffs it back into his coat.

"What's this!" yells Fat Tommy, as he rushes into the room from his office. "What's this noise about?"

Recovering, I grab the old man by one elbow, Al takes the other. Together we lift his feet off the carpet and sweep him out of the room, through the lobby, and onto the sidewalk.

"Don't come back!" orders Al.

Fat Tommy Boyle rushes from McKenna to McKenna apologizing. He tells Roger how sorry he is, as if he had been the one who had spat in my father's face. Beth and Kimberly get two apologies each. My mother and Sean enter from the hallway.

"What's wrong?" asks my mother. "I heard shouting all the way in the ladies' room."

Roger starts to tell her, but his wife tugs his sleeve.

"What's happened?" my mother asks again.

"A crazy man, Mom," says Al, locking down the lie. "He wandered in off the street."

"Who was he?" asks Tommy. Then everybody talks at once.

"Why don't you walk Mom home?" says Al to Sean.

"I don't understand what's going on," she says, as Sean escorts her to the coatrack and umbrella stand and then whisks her outside.

"I'll get your father cleaned up," says Fat Tommy. "You'll never know this happened." And he closes the lid on Dad's casket. But we will always know this happened.

"That was so fucked," says Kimberly on behalf of all of us.

"Tommy, do you have a security camera?" I ask.

"Only for the safe in the office," he says, wiping his prints off the shiny casket lid. "I never thought I'd need one in the parlors."

"Check the register," says Beth. "Maybe he signed the register?"

We gather around the register in the lobby, scanning the names.

"Compliments of Willie and Joe," I say, reading the old man's shaky handwriting.

"Who the fu . . . fudge is Willie and Joe?" asks my nephew, Jay.

"The comic strip?" asks Al.

"Yes!" I say excitedly. "Bill Mauldin. In *Stars and Stripes*."

"Totally fucked up," says Kimberly. And once again we all talk over each other.

Back at the house, we rack our brains trying to understand who and what could have prompted this desecration of our father. It's simply inexplicable. While pitching theories, we are careful to change the subject whenever Mom is in earshot. She knows we're keeping something from her, but we're always keeping things from her, so she doesn't probe too deeply. She's understandably exhausted. We all are.

"This mattress sucks," says Kimberly, as she settles into Sean's old twin bed.

More than the radiator separates us. The silence is broken by sighs, all mine. I exhale big pillows of air, like a breaching whale. These are needy sounds, prompts for a sympathetic . . . anything. Instead, my efforts produce a snippy "What?" from Kimberly, followed by an angry, pitiable "Nothing" from me. But I tell her anyway.

"I have no idea what to say about my father."

"You're smart. You'll think of something," she says, which sounds like a compliment but is her way of ending the conversation.

I turn out the light and fall onto my bed, rewinding the tapes of my father's life. A million memories of ordinary events, simple pleasures, and minor crises fight for space in my brain. There's no pattern to any of it, certainly not a eulogy, just a series of jump cuts always circling back to the veteran who spat in my dead father's face.

Kimberly falls asleep instantly, a talent I envy. I toss as always, struggling to find a sweet spot on the pillow. Finally, I give up and quietly get out of bed to sit again at the swayback desk with the orange drawers. I flip on the old desk lamp and shove the flexible gooseneck low to keep the light from waking her. The glare of the bulb bounces off a sheet of paper onto my face, as if I'm interrogating myself.

Frank McKenna was no Frank Sinatra who was loved and hated by millions. Yes, hated. My father was loved only by us, and until tonight, I hadn't thought it possible he was hated by anyone. What could Dad have done to provoke the shocking scene we had just witnessed? It's a puzzle, and I can't stand puzzles. I look over at Kimberly, carefully tilting the desk lamp in her direction, just enough to let some light illuminate her skin, her hair, her curvy silhouette. My wife is a puzzle. I gently slip into the narrow twin with her.

"No," she says, sleepily waving her hand. There will be no love made in this room tonight, even if we had love to make.

Wordlessly I return to my own bed.

4

Strangers in the Night

Up at sunrise, unusual for me. I have the kitchen to myself while my mother, Sean, and Kimberly sleep upstairs, and Kevin sleeps it off wherever he crashed last night. I find a can of Yuban in the cabinets, months past its use-by date, but this is a house of tea drinkers, so what did I expect? I drink the coffee anyway, fortifying myself until I can get the real deal at the deli by the train station. I have mapped out my day, a busy day, the day I will learn who Francis Xavier McKenna really was. I'll start where my father's American adventure began, at Ellis Island, in the middle of New York Harbor, looking up the hem of Lady Liberty's skirt.

Kimberly will spend her day with Mom and Sean. She'll hate this, but I've given her no choice. While she slept, I scribbled a brief note explaining my plans and left it on her makeup kit, where I know she'll find it. I gulp down one last blast of Yuban and dump the rest down the sink.

I pick up a paper along with a real coffee at the deli, then jump on the Long Island Railroad's 7:20 to Woodside. I take a window on the right-hand side so I can get a glimpse of Shea Stadium, even though the Mets are in San Francisco. It's always exciting to see a big-league ballpark, even an empty one. Even a shit hole like Shea. I spread out the papers, jettisoning the sections I never read. Comics gone. Business gone. I keep the main news, with the all-important sports section and the latest stories about Frank Sinatra's impending funeral services, and dump the rest on the empty seat in front of me. This isn't littering, rather a random act of kindness. Some paperless commuter will need something to read and will be grateful to the anonymous, slovenly Samaritan who left this for him. I get off at Woodside and join the stream of commuters on their way to wherever their life choices have led them. I board a local 7 train to Times Square.

It's a slow ride. I try to avoid body contact with the curvy Latina in Nikes who carries her work shoes in a plastic bag. At Court Square, a blonde in a sundress steps aboard, a rare sight on the 7 train. She's like an exotic bird that inexplicably appears outside your window. The sleepy riders perk up. They part to make room for her. A young Dominican jumps up from his seat, and she lands gently with just the slightest nod to chivalry's dying embers. She straightens the skirt of her pink and white dress, skillfully pops the lid on a plastic cup of pineapple chunks, and spears them one by one with a fork, oblivious to the smelly, ugly world that surrounds her. She's like a swan eating with the gulls at the Scobee dumpster.

My fellow passengers listen to their Walkmans, read their *Posts* and *El Diarios* and Asian papers with names I can't make out. I even spot an old man in tweed reading the *Irish Echo*, an echo himself. In English, Korean, Arabic, Hebrew, Greek, and Spanish, headlines and photos rehash Sinatra's passing.

I fold my paper, then fold it again. As the train lurches and sways, my eyes struggle to keep the words from bouncing off the page, a blur of names in tiny print, columns of sadness—the death notices—as if anyone will notice these people have died. I had deliberately avoided the obits while reading about the Mets and the teams they need to climb over and the latest foolishness in Washington. Now there are no other distractions left to read, and I see:

McKenna, Francis X. Age 82.
b. 12 December, 1915, County Sligo, Ireland.

d. 14 May, 1998, Little Neck, Queens, N.Y.
US Army 1944–1946. A.O. Hibernians, Division 9
Survived by wife, Catherine (nee Boyle)
Sons: Aloysius, Kevin, Sean, Daniel
Viewing: Doyle S. O'Connell Funeral Home,
Little Neck Parkway. Service: Tuesday 5/19 noon.
St. Anastasia, 45-14 245th St. Douglaston. In lieu
of flowers, donations to St. A's CYO.

I rip the little obituary from the paper and tuck it into my eyeglass case. These sixty-nine words, a total of 353 characters, eighteen agate lines by one column, cost my mother four hundred dollars. I toss the rest of the paper on an empty seat for someone else to enjoy. I fix my gaze on the middle distance, the commuter's gaze, a social convention that precludes eye contact and the possibility of an ugly incident. You never know what will make someone snap.

After nearly an hour we're at 42nd Street, where I change for the ride to South Ferry and the boat to Ellis Island. Once aboard the ferry I assume a professional demeanor, determined not to be mistaken for one of the frivolous tourists with their disposable cameras and fanny packs filled with protein bars Velcroed around their midsections. I am a historian embarked on important research; I can't bury my father until I know who he was. I will not be lumped in with the Kansas City Kiwanis Club tour group posing for snapshots at the rail as the ferry slips past the two enormous towers of the World Trade Center, where my brother Al has his office. I make an ostentatious display of my briefcase, taking my bag off my shoulder and digging through it as if I'm searching for something critical, anything to make it clear I am not one of them.

A helium-voiced girl runs around the deck joyfully shouting in Spanish, calling even more attention to herself than the yellow tube top and denim short shorts she squeezed into this morning. A father and mother with their three boys take in the view from the bow. The two oldest children scream with delight as they dangle their arms over the side, catching the occasional spray of seawater as it splashes up. The father struggles to hold on to his youngest, a pudgy carbon copy of himself, maybe five or six. I'm not good at children's ages. The father huffs while swapping the boy from one arm to the other; the child has outgrown his father's strength. After today, this kid will never be held by his dad again. While every parent remembers the first time they held their child, who remembers the last? Neither the boy nor his father realize they have just passed a milestone. I notice because I'm a professional noticer.

As the ferry plows through the chop, I try to imagine what it must have been like for Francis McKenna when he first glimpsed the Manhattan skyline. Why hadn't I ever asked him?

My father had it easier than the millions who had preceded him. Ships were bigger, faster, safer by 1929. He came after the *Titanic*, after World War I, without fear of icebergs, U-boats, or mines. He would have seen photographs of the world he was about to enter, perhaps a motion picture of New York, shown in the parish hall by a traveling showman who set up a screen and projector. His trip across the ocean lasted six days, not six weeks or even months as in earlier times when new arrivals would stumble down the gangway, shaking off their sea legs, their backs bent under the weight of all their worldly possessions as well as their dreams for the future. They were more than grateful to be in America; they were relieved they hadn't been swallowed by the ocean most had never seen before.

The ferry lands with a thud. I skip the Great Hall and the glass displays with their artifacts and insights. I go straight to the archives and show my Marshall College credentials to a uniformed attendant. The Ellis Archives won't open to the public for another couple of years, but professional researchers like me have the run of the place. I am directed to a computer terminal where a docent patiently explains how it works.

Soon I am scrolling through Boyles and Boyds, Burns with a u and Byrnes with a y. O's of every ilk. Coughlins and Colemans and Clarks, maybe Kimberly's people? Connollys and Donnellys, Finnegans and Flannagans, Feeneys and Finneys. Then come the Mc's; McArdles, McAteers, McAwards, McDermotts, McElligotts, McGarritys, and MacGarritys. The McKennas alone run to six pages. There are Cahir

McKennas, Liam McKennas, Cecil McKennas, Seamus McKennas, Padraig McKennas, Peadar McKennas, Fergal McKennas, Donal McKennas, Bartley McKennas, and Colleen McKennas. There are even sixteen Daniel McKennas. These are the irrelevant McKennas, as in the way today as they had been a hundred or more years ago. I am searching only for Francis McKennas, of which I find thirty-one.

I fall into a reverie of sorts, scrolling up and down the lists of immigrants, stopping occasionally at an unusual name or exotic nation of origin. Jomo Kibaki jumps out at me, his Black face staring at me from inside the computer screen, a twenty-year-old Kenyan traveling on a British passport, who landed at Ellis Island in 1909. A time traveler. Or am I the time traveler? How lonely he must have been.

Of the 17,672 Irish who passed through Ellis Island in 1929, fourteen were named McKenna; including Eamon McKenna, age sixteen, the uncle I never met, and lastly, thirteen-year-old Francis X. McKenna, who twenty-eight years later would become my father.

"Dad!" I say out loud.

My father and Uncle Eamon arrived in New York on the 11th of February, 1929, having sailed third-class aboard the S.S. *München*, the flagship of the German Norddeutscher Lloyd Line, under the command of Captain H. Gossling. Why am I only learning this now? What an embarrassment.

One of my many esoteric interests are steamships. I don't know why, because I'm definitely a landlubber. Frankly, I'm still a little woozy from the ferry ride over here. Still, while nautical history is not my area of expertise, I've got a pretty good working knowledge of the ships that conveyed the immigrant diaspora across the Atlantic. The *München* was large for her time at 14,600 tons and fast at sixteen knots. She had six decks to transport nearly eight hundred in comfort. Even the third-class passengers enjoyed luxuries they had never dreamed would be theirs: hot meals, plentiful and delicious; showers; and a clean bed all to themselves, with no brothers or sisters kicking them in the ribs while they tried to sleep. They moved their bowels on porcelain toilet bowls for the very first time. They pushed and pulled on the mysterious chrome handles until their discharge was washed away in a whirlpool. They were astonished to discover rolls of paper made specifically to clean their backsides. For the first time ever, they were treated like humans, not animals. It seemed too good to be true. For some it turned out to be.

As Dad and Uncle Eamon queued up at Ellis for the health and customs inspectors, they must have felt great anxiety, with uniforms and badges everywhere and the wail of the unfortunates pulled out of line for any number of transgressions adding to the tension. Some had criminal records. Back they went. Unaccompanied women were given the twice-over to stem the White slave trade. Back the girls went. Anarchists, atheists, rabble-rousers, and Bolsheviks need not apply. Back they went. As the American Labor movement flexed its political muscle, "contract laborers," immigrants brought here specifically to replace American workers, were *persona non grata*. Back they went. My father and Uncle Eamon had come for jobs, but they made it through.

But who brought them here and why?

He had a name, of course: James Wilson of Mamaroneck, Westchester County, New York. It's right here on the screen. His signature is flamboyant and bold with frills and flourishes John Hancock would envy. James Wilson had agreed to accept financial responsibility for sixteen-year-old Eamon McKenna and his thirteen-year-old brother, Francis. Why hadn't Dad ever mentioned this name?

As I waited for the boat back to Manhattan, I thought about February 11, 1929. I don't remember Dad celebrating it. There were no cakes or parties commemorating the day he landed. Maybe he didn't remember. He was only a kid, and what do kids ever remember? From the stern of the ferry, I watch the rotting docks of Hoboken recede on the Jersey side of the Hudson. That makes me think of little Francis Albert Sinatra, Hoboken's most famous son. He was also thirteen on the eleventh day of February, 1929.

Frank Sinatra was born at home, a breach birth. His mother's life hung in the balance. A doctor was called. Forceps ripped the huge baby from Dolly's womb, tearing the left side of the child's face, scarring him for life, perhaps in more ways than one. As the doctor worked to save the hemorrhaging mother, Dolly's mom picked up the abandoned baby. He wasn't breathing, his face a deep blue. The old woman carried her grandson to the sink and ran cold water over the infant's head. Finally, the boy coughed and then cried himself to life. Dolly Sinatra would have no more children. This one would be enough for anyone.

Frank Sinatra loved telling the story of his hardscrabble youth—a skinny Italian scamp raised on the mean streets of New Jersey, chased and beaten by gangs of tough, ignorant Irish kids who taunted him because of the vowels in his surname. This was mostly fiction, of course, a manufactured biography fed to the fan magazines for public consumption, although I admit Frank Sinatra's childhood was tougher than mine, because everything was tougher eighty-two years ago. Sinatra's embellished childhood poverty was worth its weight in gold records. He told of singing for nickels on bar stools while his old man busted skulls for bootleggers, and he repeated the story so many times he came to believe it himself. Who doesn't believe their own myths? I still cling to the dream of making my mark in the world. I can't tell you how, but I need it to be true.

As Hoboken washes away in the ferry's wake, I envision thirteen-year-old Frank Sinatra standing on those piers, eyeballing the New York skyline, as hopeful and itching to make the crossing as any immigrant from the other side of the Atlantic, a young dreamer imagining his Italian name in lights above the theater marquees and nightclubs he had yet to see.

What was my father's dream?

Francis McKenna has no fans weeping at his passing. If my father had sung songs for the public rather than mow lawns for the city, would he have been loved more? Would his memory survive the anonymity to which he has been consigned? The anonymity I fear for myself more than death? Had I told my father I loved him while we rolled paint on the ceiling of my bedroom, or any of a thousand other occasions, would I be spared the inexhaustible regret I now carry?

Half the day is shot, and I now have more questions than I started with. First up, who was James Wilson?

———

I don't know anyone in Mamaroneck, so I check the phone book at the main library branch at 42nd and Fifth. The list of a half-dozen Wilsons discourages me. What would they think of a cold call inquiring about a dead ancestor who might not even be an ancestor? A call like that would be crazy, more irritating than those calls during dinner asking if you want home delivery of the paper you already get. Instead, I turn to the papers of record for people who live in places like Mamaroneck, the *New York Times* and *Wall Street Journal*, the papers that matter.

The *Times* archive lists many dead Wilsons but only a handful of Jameses. I scroll through six boxes of microfiche before I find:

James Fox Wilson III, Founding Partner,
Brampton, Wilson & Hodge, Dead at 54.

This is a real obituary with a bold headline and photograph the Wilson family didn't have to pay to get into the paper. James Fox Wilson's death was news.

Mr. Wilson was of pure Anglo-Saxon stock, the exact kind of people who had subjugated Catholic Ireland and sent hundreds of thousands streaming across the Pond. As an investor, he was a percentage man and prospered, Bull market or Bear, until he thought himself infallible, which is a papal construct a WASP had no business appropriating. Wilson rolled his fortune on an inside tip, which today is a felony. When the market tanked in '29, James Wilson's world crashed with it.

On the afternoon of June 10, 1930, after lunching at the Century Club, Wilson sat at his mahogany desk and wrote a note to his wife on embossed stationary, sealed the note, then swallowed the barrel of his revolver, blowing his brains out the back of his skull and splattering the nineteenth-century portrait of his grandfather that hung directly behind him.

Scrolling backward through time, I find additional articles by or about Mr. Wilson. A lengthy piece under his byline (but likely ghosted) offers no personal information, just the typically rosy projections for that age of endless growth and gain, all of which came tumbling down within a month of publication. I scroll again, the microfiche blurring by like the numbers on a gas pump. Back I go to the good ol' days when James Fox Wilson was still a fully clothed emperor.

In the August 8, 1927, *Times* rotogravure, I hit the motherlode: a society page profile titled "The Wilsons of Mamaroneck." Black-and-white photographs immortalize the family's magnificent home; solidly brick, Georgian, it sits on a rise surrounded by rolling, tree-shaded lawns that stretch to the horizon. A formal pose captures James with Mrs. Wilson, who doesn't appear to have a given name. The look on her face barely conceals her contempt for the photographer and the invasion of privacy he represents. Or maybe she was just self-conscious because her hips looked enormous. Her husband, however, is ripped right out of Fitzgerald, the embodiment of the nouveau riche, a twentieth-century robber baron who engineered this puff piece believing the publicity would be good for business.

I look deep into the Wilsons' long-dead eyes. I spend time with this photograph because my father spent time in service to these people. I'm hoping this picture will offer some clues, but then I realize I'm looking at the wrong photo.

There's a second shot: Wilson in tennis togs, ready to serve on his grass court. In the background, incidental to Wilson, stands a stoop-shouldered old Irishman leaning on a rake, identified as the estate overseer. It makes perfect sense! The aging Irish caretaker requested a couple of young bucks to help hoe the gardens, muck the stalls, and manure the lawns. Master Wilson, as Lord of the Manor, arranged it, employing an immigration broker in the U.K. to snag a couple of Irish lads. I dashed for the door, euphoric and anxious to share my discovery with . . . who?

I wait impatiently at the only working pay phone in Manhattan for a Puerto Rican bike messenger to finish telling his life story. I know Kimberly won't care about James Wilson III, the S.S. *München*, or the subway riders reading about Frank Sinatra's death, but she might feign interest, and right now that's all I need. I jingle change in my pockets, but bike boy doesn't take the hint. As I wait, my mind drifts back to the monochromatic world my young father-to-be found himself in. Was he happy in Mamaroneck?

He had the proverbial green thumb and grew tomatoes in a garden on the side of our house below the ever-spinning electric meter. My mother distributed the surplus to the neighbors in paper sacks from Bohack or Waldbaum's. He remained the envy of the windowsill geranium set until arthritis ended his growing career, and Kevin took custody of the garden and grew pot plants with limited success. It's entirely possible my father learned the tomato arts from that ancient unnamed overseer on the Wilson estate.

The bike messenger finally hangs up, but not before giving me that go f-yourself look New Yorkers have perfected. I ignore him and shove a quarter into the slot.

"When are you coming home?" Kimberly asks with irritation.

I take a deep breath. A day with my grieving mother has exhausted her; that's understandable. They barely know each other. And she's bored. Kimberly is dangerous when bored. I start telling her about my day and what I've discovered. I tell it with enthusiasm, hoping I can sweep her along on the crest of my excitement, but she stops listening after I say "museum" and "library." That sounds mean, like she's an idiot, which she's not, but she's busting my balls for no reason, and now I'm pissed, too. I take another breath and start again.

"I don't want a fight," I say offering an olive branch.

"I'm losing my mind, Danny!" she whisper-yells. "I have nothing to say to her, and she just cries," says Kimberly, nearly in tears herself.

I take another breath.

"Why don't you go out with Sean?" I suggest.

"What am I going to do with that faggot?" she yell-yells into the handset.

A gut punch.

Kimberly has spoken the great unspoken. Of course my brother is gay. I've known it since we shared those twin beds when I was ten or eleven, before we called gays gay. Still, in the grand tradition of Irish families everywhere, our social compact is based on a strictly enforced "don't ask, don't tell" policy, and now Kimberly, the outsider, has violated a prime directive by saying the word we have studiously avoided.

"Tell Mom I'll be late."

"Fine, but I won't be here when you get back," Kimberly snaps, hanging up before her last syllable reaches my end of the line.

I drop the receiver and let it dangle from the metal cord, a silly discourtesy to the woman waiting behind me, but my feelings are hurt, and I want to pay my pain forward. I brush past her, bumping her shoulder, which sets her to hollering, but I just wave her off as I wander down the street with no destination in mind.

When I'm upset, my mouth dries out, and my tongue sticks to the roof of my mouth, and I want a drink, okay? Even if my mouth isn't dry, I want a big glass of something. But my mouth is dry. It really is. I know hundreds of saloons I can settle into for a good day's bender. Half a dozen Blarney Stones, all those joints along Irish Alley on the East Side. I think about the Ear Bar down in the Village. The name comes from a workman who spilled paint across the neon BAR sign, turning the B into an E. I think about one of the hotel lobby bars. Hotel bars are great places to drink, but pricey. I even consider The Sinatra Bar in the Village. That isn't its name; it doesn't have a name, but everyone calls it The Sinatra Bar because the jukebox only plays Frank.

I refuse to lie to myself with that old drunk's chestnut, "I'll just have one." I want every drink in New York City, then I want Connecticut to send all its drinks. I want to drink every drink I should have had these past two dry years but turned down to prove the nags wrong. "See? I don't have a problem!" Now I want to put a bullet through my head like James Fox Wilson III, whom I understand better than my own father.

Instead, I walk. I just walk and walk with my head down while thinking about the eulogy I am unprepared to give, about the man who hates my father, about my gay brother, Kimberly, and Frank Sinatra. Then I walk without thinking. When I finally look up, I'm surprised to see it's dark, and I am suddenly aware how hungry I am, having eaten nothing this entire day.

I wolf down a bacon and egg on a roll in a coffee shop, while the woman at the next table talks nonstop about her dog to an Asian woman who never says a word. The dog chatter is subsumed into the clatter of dishes in the kitchen, the fans over the grill, the flies buzzing and tapping themselves to death against the neon-splashed plate-glass windows, and cab horns honking at pedestrians outside. A hopelessly overmatched sound system adds "Stayin' Alive" to the cacophony. Shrill Bee Gees high notes cut through the din, and I find myself involuntarily chewing in sync to the backbeat. This nameless, characterless coffee shop, one of hundreds in the city, assaults my ears across the entire spectrum of audio frequencies.

I watch with interest as a young hipster couple nibble wraps, the male half a study in androgynous beauty. His River Phoenix–like looks supersede her prettiness, and she knows it. She chews nervously, as if she expects him to leave with the next woman or man who walks through the door. I drop a ten on the table and leave before he does.

I yawn and stretch, throwing my head back, which enables me to gawk at all 103 stories of the Empire State Building like a rube from Iowa. The very top is bathed in a soft blue light, Ol' Blue Eyes blue, lit in tribute to you-know-who. Now there was a man who knew how to drown his sorrow! Johnny Mercer, Matt Dennis, and a few others wrote their best songs just so Frank Sinatra could describe the therapeutic value of alcohol consumed in quantity to salve a broken heart.

I stand for a long time looking up at the famous skyscraper, like one of those lunatics who thinks he sees something in the sky and draws a crowd to look at nothing. Except I don't draw a crowd. I am completely alone on a busy street in one of the busiest cities on earth. The pedestrians veer around me, as if I am a pile of dog shit plopped in the middle of the sidewalk. I think again about that guy who made the papers when he threw himself off the observation deck on the eighty-sixth floor. The wind blew him back into the building at the eighty-fourth floor, where a startled janitor pulled him off a window ledge. Can you imagine? Even gravity failed him. I love this nameless incompetent jumper, because I feel like my entire life has been a leap to the death two floors at a time.

I can't stand here forever, so I duck into a discount men's store and buy a cheap blue suit for my father's funeral. Everybody looks better in blue. At least I'll dress the part.

It's midnight when I finally jiggle the key in the lock and let myself into the house. Mom is upstairs in her room, and Kimberly, true to her word, is gone. I throw my new suit on the back of the sofa and go into the kitchen for a glass of water, startling Sean, who drops the sandwich he's making. It lands facedown on the floor.

"I didn't hear you come in," says Sean, as he kneels to mop mayonnaise off the linoleum.

"Sorry. I thought everyone was in bed," I say as I cross to the sink, letting the water run so it will get colder.

As I gulp down two big glasses, Sean briefs me on everything I missed: Mom turned in early, Kevin hasn't been seen since yesterday, Father Considine is on vacation—yes, priests get vacations—so Dad is getting the Cuban priest nobody can understand. Then, and it must be hard for him, Sean asks:

"Danny, is everything okay with you and Kimberly?"

"Yeah, sure." A ridiculous lie.

"It's none of my business . . ." Sean starts to say, but I cut him off.

"Did she call?"

She has not. We can't think of anything else to say, so Sean leaves with the second draft of his sandwich. I listen until I hear the attic door clunk shut behind him. I light a cigarette, something nobody does in the house anymore, not even Kevin. It's quiet, so quiet I can hear the outer wrapper pop and crackle as the tobacco burns. In a few hours I'll be standing on the altar at St. Anastasia to put my father's life into words I don't have. Had I really believed I could dash into the city and reconstruct in a day a life it had taken Dad eighty-two years to live?

I finally acknowledge the truth: I didn't run to Ellis Island to find my father. I ran to escape my family, my wife, my life—seeking refuge in the archives, reels of microfilm, and library shelves that have been my sanctuary, hiding from the present in the past.

I dump the last mouthful of water down the sink and put the glass, unwashed, back in the cabinet. I considered rinsing it out, but it was only a glass of water, so what's the point?

What *is* the point?

I plop on the sofa and wait for the phone to ring. "She'll call," I tell myself. But not until I've suffered enough, and I am suffering. I flip on the TV and turn the sound down low, nearly to mute, leaving just enough volume so I don't feel totally alone. I surf through the channels not looking for anything specific, semi-hypnotized by the swirl of colors flashing by. Channel something shows clips from Frank Sinatra's movies, and I nearly go past, because movies bore me, even Frank Sinatra movies. But I leave it on the Sinatra channel, while I wait for the phone to ring.

I watch a skeletal-thin Sinatra in a sailor suit hop on a row of beds with Gene Kelly in the big scene from *Anchors Aweigh*. Frank is so skinny the MGM wardrobe people had to sew butt pads into the seat of his pants so his flat ass wouldn't disappoint his female fans. The purpose of this clip is to show Sinatra matching the great Gene Kelly step for step as they bed hop. Of course, Sinatra was a gold-medal bed hopper off camera, but nobody got that on film. *Anchors Aweigh* is ludicrous, and I laugh out loud while wondering where my wife could possibly be. Whatever channel this is keeps it up, running clip after clip, a montage of movies with Frank in various costumes and his tidal hairline waxing and waning until it surrenders to a full-blown toupee. There he is tying off a vein in *The Man with the Golden Arm*. Now he's doing Joe E. Lewis's drunk act in *The Joker Is Wild*. I see Sinatra singing in a Barbary Coast saloon in *Around the World in Eighty Days*.

I let the phone ring four times before I pick it up. It's Kimberly, in tears, calling from the St. Regis in Manhattan, a once fashionable hotel now drifting toward seedy. I don't ask if she's alone. It's not that I don't care. As a matter of self-preservation, I have to accept that what Kimberly does or doesn't do is none of my business. She quickly perceives my indifference and asks if I want her to come home.

"Hurry," I tell her, because what else can I say?

There is zero traffic at this hour, and the trip from Midtown to Little Neck should only take thirty minutes, but I know I'm in for a wait. There will be a snafu. There always is. The doorman won't be able to flag a cab. She'll have problems checking out of the hotel—that is, if she had ever checked in. She'll run into construction on the LIE. Something will drag this out and make a long day longer. I go outside and stand on the sidewalk, knowing she won't be here for at least an hour. I smoke and watch a cop car drive slowly up the block. The cop riding shotgun gives me the once over. Young lovers, kids really, tumble out of the Scobee, sated with carbohydrates, coffee, and each other.

When you grow up across from an all-night diner, you have a front row seat on the bigger world that awaits. Sometimes, after lights out, I'd sneak into Al's and Kevin's room and sit in the window watching people come and go from the Scobee—cops, couples (young and old), maybe kept women and straying husbands engaged in illicit affairs. I witnessed these scenes before I even knew what an affair was, but I sensed their behavior was forbidden and therefore found it compelling. At the peak of summer, when the temperature was up along with our bedroom windows, lovers' quarrels reverberated with perfect clarity.

"You fucked her! Don't lie to me, Vinny!"

"I didn't fuck her!"

"Sheila says you fucked her!"

"Sheila is a bitch liar!"

"She wouldn't lie about that, Vinny!"

And on it would go, until someone got slapped or the cops chased them off or they hugged it out and went home and settled it between the sheets.

The Scobee is brighter than when I was a kid. It's lit like a casino or a landlocked cruise ship, with tubes of buzzing neon washing across Little Neck Parkway, splashing red, blue, and amber on the front of our place. I don't know how Mom sleeps with all those lights shining in her window. Some of the regulars are also lit, stumbling to their cars, dropping their keys twice, and pissing up against the dumpster and occasionally in our hedges, which infuriated my father.

Through the Scobee windows, I see happy drunks laughing and sad drunks alone at the counter, struggling to count out coins to cover their tabs. At the big booth in the corner, three couples grab late-night cheeseburgers, all except the chubby girl who stabs at a salad. She wants a cheeseburger, too, but knows her *Vogue*-thin friends will dis her on the way home.

"Can you believe she ate that entire burger?"

"And all the fries, too!"

Later, she'll numb the pain with a pint of Häagen-Dazs, then cry herself to sleep.

Finally, a taxi comes around the corner, and Kimberly, exhausted, high, and weeping steps out, feet bare, her shoes dangling in her hand. She falls into my arms and kisses me, then kisses me again. I start to say, "I'm sorry," but for what I'm not sure. She clamps her hand over my mouth and says, "Don't."

We stand there for a minute, silently staring at the person we have married. She is so damaged, so hurt, it's everything I can do not to fall for her again. A cat screams a block away, the long guttural *meeeeeeow!* melding with the other street sounds echoing off the facade of my boyhood home.

"Danny, we have to divorce," Kimberly says, breaking the silence.

I nod, then speak. "I know," grateful she said it first.

"Thank you for marrying me when I was sick," she says.

"Thanks aren't necessary."

"I know, but anyway, thanks." And she squeezes my hand and moves in to kiss me one last time. One for the road?

"It's cold," I say, pulling away before our lips meet.

"Very." And she walks up the steps and into the house.

I stay on the sidewalk until I see the light in the upstairs hallway go out. I'm freezing, and I have to pee, so I go inside.

I stretch out on the couch and drift in and out of sleep with the flickering blue light of the TV dancing around the room. Frank Sinatra's face appears in the glass vase on the mantel over the fireplace. There he is again in the freshly Pledged sheen on the coffee table. His face is refracted everywhere; a prism Frank sings to me to from a boxing ring. It's *The Main Event* concert from '74 at Madison Square Garden. But I know differently. The main event has just taken place on the sidewalk outside.

5

Love and Marriage

It began with a gunshot.

Shortly after James Fox Wilson blew his brains out, the Wilson estate in Briarcliff Manor was auctioned by the bank that had repossessed it, his large insurance policy nullified by his self-destruction. The surviving Wilsons were forced to relocate two hundred miles north to Herkimer, an American Siberia. No more operas. No more art gallery openings or society balls. But there was money. Mrs. Wilson's sister, Kitty, had married into the Herkimer diamond fortune, enabling her to clothe, feed, and house her freshly indigent relatives without sacrificing anything. Her benevolence only deepened the humiliation. Meanwhile, the two young Irish groundskeepers were cut loose along with the maids and chauffeur, stable hands, and the old Irish caretaker, all as dispossessed by Wilson's suicide as his heirs, only minus the soft landing.

Frank McKenna, now fifteen, and Eamon McKenna, eighteen, found new lodging in the attic of a crowded house across from the Oneida Triangle in the Woodlawn section of the Bronx. They briefly enrolled at St. Barnabas, but as the Great Depression deepened, finding work became essential. The nuns pleaded with the boys to stay, especially Eamon, who was apparently a wiz at math. Instead, the

McKenna brothers left school. Eamon worked six days a week in a print shop, while Francis got a job on an ice wagon, hauling big blocks to the ritzy brownstones on the Grand Concourse and the speakeasies of Webster Avenue, where he was tipped in whiskey despite being underage. Francis also briefly jerked soda at Woolworths, where he stuffed himself with so much ice cream, he never touched it again. That was the only job he ever talked about.

But the job that forever changed Frank's life came when he and Eamon landed at the enormous Depression-proof Dugan's bakery. (On Jamaica Avenue in Queens, today it's the site of an MTA bus depot.) Thanks to massive wartime spending, the economy was finally pulling out of its decade-long tailspin. American workers were suddenly flush with cash after years of deprivation. Dugan's added a second shift and then a third to keep up with demand for crullers, cakes, and pies gobbled by the men and women building the tanks, Jeeps, bombers, and bullets we would soon be sending across two oceans. Francis and Eamon found a flat in Woodside, Queens, another Irish enclave— or ghetto, if you prefer to see the glass as half empty.

They started on the factory floor, Eamon wrapping cakes and pies for shipping, and Frank sweeping and scrubbing the big metal baking sheets still hot from the ovens. Eventually, Eamon's facility with numbers was discovered, and he got kicked upstairs to process time cards for payroll. Meanwhile, the younger McKenna jumped at the chance to drive one of Dugan's Divco delivery trucks and escape the sweltering bakery.

His route encompassed northeastern Queens, including the Bayside home of Daniel Boyle, universally known as "Pappy." His wife, "Ma Boyle," was baptized Delia Jennings, but few knew her actual name. She was Ma Boyle to everyone, even signing checks that way. Pappy worked as a motorman for the New York City subway system, and that had spared him the worst of the Depression. He was proud to raise his five daughters, Catherine, Margaret, Geraldine, Bridget, and Mary in Bayside, surrounded by grass and trees and the estuary of Little Neck Bay rather than the asphalt and alleys of the Lower East Side of Manhattan, where he had spent his first years in America.

Catherine Boyle, then twenty years old, worked at the Gertz department store's flagship in Jamaica. Her shift did not begin until ten, so she was at home the first time the new Dugan's man rang the doorbell.

Fresh from the shower, Catherine raced down the stairs as only young legs can. She wore a robe and slippers with a towel turbaned around her damp hair. "I got it!" she shouted, unaware her future stood on the other side of the door. When she saw the handsome twenty-four-year-old with his tray of breads, cakes, muffins, and more, she blushed and ducked away, running as quickly up the stairs as she had coming down, leaving a baffled Francis McKenna to transact business with Mary, the youngest of the Boyle girls. Mary selected a loaf of rye and a pound cake, which was her Achilles heel. She would hide the pound cake in a hatbox under her bed and sneak bites, because her weight had recently become an issue with her mother.

The next time the bakery truck pulled up, Catherine was ready, wearing a gray pleated skirt, white blouse, and heels with makeup and hair done fashionably, but not too fashionably, because Gertz was not Bonwit Teller. Now it was Francis McKenna's turn to be flustered.

The Boyle home soon became easy pickings for this particular Dugan's man. Over the next weeks, Catherine was always at the door when the bell rang, until one day Ma Boyle beat her to punch and told Frank to stop dillydallying and ask Catherine out already! The Dugan's tab was a strain on the family budget, and Mary had gained five pounds. Catherine nearly died of embarrassment but managed a "yes" when Francis asked if she'd like to go out the following Sunday.

Frank took the bus from Woodside and arrived at the door in his best slacks and shirt. Pappy Boyle met him at the door and finally got to see for himself the man who had been the talk of the dinner table ever since he first put his finger on the Boyles' bell.

"How long have you been in America?" asked Pappy, beginning the interrogation.

"Since '29," said Francis.

"How long have you been working for Dugan?"

"Almost four years."

"Do you have family here?"

"I have a brother, Eamon."

"Where do you live?"

"Thirty-ninth Avenue at 64th Street."

"Alone?"

"No, with my brother."

Where are your people from?

"Castlerea."

"Who's still back home?"

And on that topic Francis was nearly stumped.

His father, Patrick McKenna, had died in 1920 of the Spanish flu. His mother, Fiona, a widow at twenty-five, struggled to raise her three surviving children of the six she had birthed: Eamon, then three dead babies—two boys and a girl—then Francis, and finally Sioban. Fiona, illiterate, was dependent on her daughter to scribble a few words now and then to her sons in America. So Frank didn't have much he could tell Pappy Boyle, even if he was the talking kind. Still, Francis X. McKenna's brogue was real enough; he hadn't been to jail, came to the house sober, and had Dugan's in his corner, because Pappy Boyle was a sucker for Sunshine Cake.

It was no surprise Francis took Catherine to the World's Fair on their first date. Everyone went to the fair, forty-four million before it closed for good in 1940.

They rode the Long Island Rail Road the short hop to Flushing Meadows, two young people, attractive and attracted, taking the first steps in a courtship ritual that would culminate on the altar of St. Teresa's, followed by a World War, four sons, two grandchildren, and fifty-four years of marriage.

But this is about the beginning, not the end.

Catherine excitedly led Francis around the fair, since she had been many times and knew it like she knew the women's department at Gertz.

Francis and Catherine laughed as they watched penguins slide into water-filled sluices. They screamed as they plunged toward earth on the Parachute Jump, laughing again as the white canopy billowed open above their heads. Tea Cups whirled, the Cyclone coaster caused more screaming, and Francis got a peck from Catherine when he won a dollar on the winning cat at the Boxing Cats kiosk, where two kittens duked it out in a tiny ring, their paws stuffed into little leather gloves.

From the Meteor Speedway to dinner at the Famous Chicken Inn, Francis and Catherine talked and laughed and broke the ice with random details of their lives or funny commentary about their fellow fairgoers. At Shoot the Works, Francis tried but failed to win a stuffed bear for Catherine, missing the targets completely. He had never fired a gun in his life. Standing next to him, two soldiers, army privates, made insulting comments about Francis because he was a Harp and, worse, a civilian. "Let's go dancing," said Catherine, diplomatically pulling Francis by the hand.

At the Savoy Ballroom, featuring "The World's Best Colored Dancers," Catherine had to drag Francis onto the floor, where he stiffly followed her lead in the Lindy Hop and other steps of the day. The floor was crowded with bobby-soxers, who were just becoming a thing in the summer of '40. Teenagers, mostly girls, clad in blouse, skirt, and saddle shoes, danced with other girls; Black girls with Black girls, White girls with Whites, but all on the same floor, bumping into each other and laughing and having the time of their lives. The music was swing, the bands were name brand and hot, like the great Harry James, who a few months earlier had employed a skinny singer named Frank Sinatra who was now making a name with Tommy Dorsey.

It was getting late, and both Francis and Catherine had to work in the morning, Francis before sunup. Still, there was time for one last dance, a slow number, a house-band cover of the big hit of that year, Dorsey's "I'll Never Smile Again," featuring The Pied Pipers with the aforementioned Sinatra singing lead. With Europe already at war, "I'll Never Smile Again" was fraught with emotion.

It's a song of loss and heartache, incongruous with Catherine and Francis's mood. They were joyful as they danced in each other's arms, grins welded to their faces as the girl singer crooned on. Francis pulled Catherine closer and stole a kiss, once, then twice. He didn't have to steal the third.

In the weeks ahead, Francis and Catherine were seen together everywhere, their happiness as contagious as a cold. The new couple was met with universal approval with one notable exception, Ray Stankowski, the boy next door.

Ray Stankowski was the youngest son of the Boyles' longtime neighbors and had been in and out of the Boyle home a million times. In school, Stankowski inevitably became "Stanky" and worse, "Stinky," first by friends and soon by everybody. He hated that nickname and became compulsive about his personal hygiene. If anything, Ray erred in the opposite direction, nearly drowning in Vitalis.

It was well known that Ray had a thing for Catherine Boyle, from pulling her pigtails in grade school to, as a teenager, whistling Bing Crosby tunes at her bedroom window late at night. The mysterious whistler had terrified Catherine and caused no small embarrassment when the culprit was finally discovered. Francis got off on the wrong foot with Ray by whistling at him the first time they met. Everyone laughed but Stankowski.

Then came Pearl Harbor, and nobody was laughing.

Until then, Hawaii had meant grass skirts, pineapples, and Crosby's "Sweet Leilani." Neither the Boyles nor the McKenna brothers could find Hawaii on a map. Suddenly everyone was an expert. The Extra! Extra! Edition of the *Daily News* employed the largest possible font, screaming the news everyone had already heard on the radio: "JAPS BOMB HAWAII!" Two days later the headline said simply, "WAR!" as if war is ever simple.

The papers were filled with maps of island chains, including the Japanese mainland, and obscure places somewhere over there, where nobody Francis or Catherine knew had ever been—Borneo, Java, Sumatra, Bali, and Timor. The maps were overlaid with ominous hydra-headed arrows aimed at Japanese objectives either achieved or threatened. The Philippines, hit only nine hours after Pearl, were back in the news for the first time since the days of President McKinley. How could General MacArthur have been caught with his pants down? A thousand column inches briefed Americans on all things Hawaiian, from Captain Cook's fatal voyage in 1778 to sugar plantations, ukuleles, the hula dance, and the curious local custom known as surfing.

When the first photographs of capsized and smoldering battleships arrived on front porches to be consumed at breakfast with crullers from Dugan's, the magnitude of the catastrophe robbed even Sunshine Cakes of their sweetness. And yet, oddly, for millions, there was a discordant sense of relief. The boil had finally been lanced. Years of wondering, worrying, and lobbying were over. America was in it now: a two-ocean war, thanks to Hitler's impulsive December 11 declaration against the United States.

The pro-German Bund dissolved. So, too, the isolationist America First movement. When its star attraction, Charles Lindbergh, tried to enlist, FDR told yesterday's hero to fuck off. Millions of men lined up at their local recruiting stations. The Stankowski brothers, Connie and Ray, enlisted. The McKenna brothers did not. Neither did Frank Sinatra.

Eamon continued crunching numbers in the Dugan's payroll department, while Francis drove his route, bypassing the Boyle home except to flirt with Catherine. If the army wanted the brothers, it knew where to find them.

And it did. Two letters arriving at the Woodside apartment on the same day.

ORDER TO REPORT FOR INDUCTION
Greetings:
Having submitted yourself to a local board composed of your neighbors for the purpose of determining your availability for training and service in the armed forces of the Unites States, you are hereby notified that you have now been selected for training and service in the (Army, Navy, Marine Corps.) You will, therefore, report to the local board at Maspeth, Queens, New York at 7:55 AM on the 6th of January, 1944.

Catherine cried when Francis showed her the letter. Pappy Boyle did not.

Pappy Boyle loved a good fight. Or a bad one. He thought the best way to turn the other cheek was with a right jab. In his sixties, he decked some punk who cut the line at the bank. But the U.S. government had classified Pappy III-B, "deferred both by reason of dependency and occupation." They were right, of course. He had all those daughters to feed, and the New York City subway system was vital to the war effort. Somebody had to get Rosie the Riveter to her factory. And he was fifty-two.

Boyle would stay home and do what he could to win the war. He planted vegetables in neat rows, digging up the front yard to make a Victory Garden. He bought war bonds with enthusiasm. He considered it an honor to help his adopted country in her time of need, since America had helped him when he arrived with only twenty-five dollars to his name.

He had another reason to support the war; Ireland had declared her neutrality. In Pappy's eyes that was a humiliation, a black mark against his entire race. Kicking Axis ass was a fight that should not be ducked; there would be plenty of time to hate the British after Hitler was dead. Pappy never forgave Eamon de Valera for keeping Ireland on the sidelines, but he was proud there would be no stain on the Boyle name. The McKenna brothers would fight for all of them.

Francis began his army life at Camp Upton, in Suffolk County, Long Island, not far from home. Camp Upton was the birthplace of the GI's unofficial anthem, "Oh, How I Hate to Get Up in the Morning," written during World War I by Sergeant Irving Berlin, who also wrote "God Bless America" at Camp Upton but kept that one stashed in his trunk until a bigger war arrived. Here it was.

Upton was only a brief stop, a reception center where Frank's hair was shorn like the sheep on his family's farm back in Ireland. He put on fatigues for the first time and snapped his first salutes. One of his drill sergeants recognized him from the neighborhood—his family had been a Dugan's customer—so, naturally, the sergeant called the new recruit "Dugan," a nickname that followed him throughout the war. A few of the good ol' boys thought Dugan was an Irish slur and took to calling all micks "Dugans," thus making it one.

From Camp Upton, Francis was packed on a train with 1,500 other inductees and shipped to Camp Croft a few miles outside Spartanburg, South Carolina, a culture shock for a man who had never been farther south than Atlantic City.

For the next seventeen weeks, he learned the basics of army life—sweating, scratching, starving, bitching, smoking, killing time, playing cards, blowing on dice, masturbating, drinking, and even a few practical skills like riflery, grenade tossing, hand-to-hand combat, map reading, aircraft identification, and his name, rank, and serial number. "McKenna, Francis! Private! One! Two! One! Three! One! Two! Zero! Seven!"

Eventually, Frank was dispatched to the deepest of the Deep South, Camp Van Dorn, in Centerville, Mississippi, just a few clicks away from the Louisiana border. The heat, humidity, snakes, and mosquitos presented the private's first brush with death. For two weeks he burned up with fever, likely malaria. The only thing dry about Camp Van Dorn was its location in Clay County, where a man couldn't get a legal drink.

Come September, Private McKenna, aka Dugan, received his orders; he was shipping out, rumor had it, to the European Theater of Operations, as the newspapers called it. He got a two-week furlough to get his affairs in order. Catherine Boyle was his only affair. Francis asked Catherine to marry him. She choked out a "yes" and dissolved in joyful tears.

The night before the wedding, the bride-to-be tossed fitfully in her bed, her mind bombarded with practical thoughts: Will it rain? Is it safe to put Margaret at the same table as Bridget? Her sisters don't get along.

Catherine climbed out of her virgin's bed to brush her hair in the mirror over the chest of drawers. She remembered when she was too small to see herself over the tops of the perfume bottles and atomizers and had to stand on the hassock to see her reflection.

She harbored ethereal, loving thoughts, too, born of the heart and loins, not the head. They made her ache for his touch, even perhaps to touch herself, pretending her hand is his, although that part of her story is never told. "Soon," she says as she picks up her fiancé's framed photo from the table beside her bed. His face is the last thing she sees before she drifts off and the first thing she sees when she awakes. She's getting married in the morning. How could anyone expect her to sleep?

Catherine and Frank were wed at St. Teresa's. The bride's dress came from Gertz, thanks to a generous employee discount. The groom's wardrobe was courtesy of the American taxpayers. The wedding party was accompanied by the usual collection of relatives, friends, and neighbors, along with the old biddies who showed up uninvited to collect gossip. The gossips went home disappointed. Everyone behaved with propriety, even Ray Stankowski, who did not want to be there.

Ray still held a grudge against Francis for whistling at him when they first met. He also resented the McKenna brothers for not enlisting. He certainly did not want to be part of Catherine Boyle's wedding party and only agreed because it would have been awkward for his parents if he had refused.

Ray had one more reason to be miserable on this day, the same reason he had been miserable every day for the past two years: Connie Stankowski was dead, lost in the Pacific when his ship hit a mine one month after Pearl. Ray could never be happy in a world that did not include his brother.

After the "I do's," the wedding party and guests retired to the Boyle home, where Pappy threw the biggest bash his civil-servant's paycheck would allow. Catherine was the first of his daughters to wed, and war or no war, pennies would not be pinched. The reception began in the backyard under blue skies, but when clouds rolled in and the skies opened up, the party moved indoors with spirits undampened. After a decade of Depression, Dust Bowl, and now war, what was a little rain?

Ma Boyle cranked the handle on the Victrola, and the needle scratched across a record, "People Will Say We're in Love," one of the hits from *Oklahoma!*, the Broadway smash nobody in this house would ever see. The record was the a cappella version recorded during an endless musician's strike, with Frank Sinatra backed only by the Bobby Tucker Singers. Everyone assumed this song was the happy couple's "song." It was not. "I'll Never Smile Again" was their song, but it was too lachrymose for a wedding dance. Instead, Francis and Catherine danced to Sinatra, while their guests smiled and Ray Stankowski boiled.

"Why isn't that asshole in uniform?" shouted Ray, pointing his beer bottle accusingly at the Victrola, a proxy for the skinny crooner.

All heads snapped in his direction.

"Why isn't lover boy in uniform?" he yelled.

The girls shushed him. They were all Frankie fans and sick of Stinky's mouthing off every time they played his records or heard him on the radio. This made Ray angrier. "Mice make women scream, too," said Ray, voicing a complaint shared by millions of GIs who believed Sinatra's 4-F classification was a load of horseshit. A punctured eardrum? He looked plenty healthy to them. To Ray Stankowski, and all the other Private Stankowskis, Frankie Sinatra was yellow and a scab to boot. These were union men, and the orchestra-less record was proof of his malfeasance. In Ray's mind, every shirker, coward, and draft dodger had been as responsible for his brother's death as the Imperial Japanese Navy. Stanky snatched the platter off the turntable and smashed it to the floor.

"Rajmund!" shrieked his mother.

"That'll be enough out of you!" shouted Pappy Boyle as he pulled Ray away from the record player. "Eamon, be a good boy, and take this hothead outside till he cools down."

And Eamon did exactly that, practically dragging Private Stankowski into the yard, while Bridget went for a broom to sweep up the mess. Ma Boyle quickly set a Doris Day record on the turntable, and the party resumed. Nobody had a beef with Doris Day.

The cake was cut, the bouquet was tossed, and the newlyweds took the train into the city, a luxury since Pappy Boyle had a drawer full of subway tokens, and they could ride the IRT for free. The pair spent their first night as husband and wife at the Drake Hotel, where a nice room cost nine dollars even.

6

That's Life

As I lay on the sofa, waiting for sleep to blot out the failure of my marriage and my life, I can hear someone speaking from somewhere in the house. It's my mother, moving about in her bedroom, engaged in an animated conversation with my father. I can't make out what she's saying, but she's talking to him, no doubt. Occasionally, she breaks down, and her sobs add a disturbing contrapuntal beat to the Woody Herman Orchestra backing Frank on the television screen. I can do nothing to comfort her because I'm too busy licking my own wounds.

She chats away, half talking, half weeping. She has things to tell him because there's never enough time to say everything that needs to be said. My mother paces her room and uses the late-night hours to get it off her chest.

She remembers when Francis McKenna was Mr. Wonderful in a picture frame. She watched her lover age and slip and fail, as time chiseled away at him. She made the cakes that marked the passing years of his life, wondering each time he blew out the candles how many more candles there would be—sixty candles, seventy candles, eighty. Sometimes she'd wake in the middle of the night just to watch him breathe, relieved every time his chest heaved up and down, reveling in each snore, snort, nose whistle, and fart. Now there are no more plans to make; Fat Tommy and her boys have seen to everything.

She climbs in and out of a bed that once seemed crowded and now seems enormous. If I go upstairs to comfort her, I will be an intrusion, a distraction from the magnitude of her loss. The restless head on her pillow is overwhelmed with the trajectory of two lives: hers and his, lives that crossed at a specific time and place, all leading to this moment.

The church is booked, and the funeral is tomorrow, technically today, this being the wee small hours of the morning, May 19, 1998. My mother is burying her husband in the morning. How could anyone expect her to sleep?

———

Mom is at her post in the kitchen when I shuffle in after spending the night on the sofa. My mother suspects something.

"Did you sleep the whole night on the couch?" she asks.

"I dozed off watching a movie."

It's a lie, of course, but she doesn't have space in her head for more sad news and lets it slide. A soft lie is easier to swallow than a hard truth.

Over tea and toast, Mom expresses her worries du jour, mostly Kevin-related. My brother hasn't been seen since Dad's wake. Her worry isn't based on fear something untoward has happened to him. Bad things always happen to Kevin McKenna. Rather, she fears Kevin will miss Dad's funeral, which will be hard to explain to her friends and a major embarrassment, which is her ultimate fear.

"Find your brother," she says. It's close to a command.

"I'll try, Mom." But try isn't good enough. "I'll find him," I say more affirmatively, and that seems to offer a measure of relief.

Kimberly stumbles into the kitchen, hung over, her robe loosely tied. We avoid eye contact.

"Good morning," says Mom.

"'Morning," says Kimberly through a yawn.

"Did you sleep well?" asks Mom.

"Great," says my wife without conviction. "Is there coffee?"

"I'll make some," I say, happy to have an occupation.

Mom and Kimberly exchange banalities, both making an effort to find things to say but for different reasons. I begin struggling for breath while fiddling with a paper filter and scooping coffee into the machine. I steal glances at the two women facing each other across the kitchen table, my mother in her pilling terry-cloth robe, Kimberly with her tits nearly flopping out of the same translucent wrap she wore at Dante's the night we met. I pray she'll hold her tongue and not spill the beans about last night, at least until my father is in the ground. I cup my hands over my mouth and take long, measured breaths, but I can feel beads of sweat punctuating my scalp and upper lip. I clutch my jaw, then my arm. *Not now! Please, not now!*

What could I possibly have been thinking? I have brought a whore into my mother's house! I can't breathe! I run from the kitchen, bumping Sean into a floor lamp as he makes his way to breakfast.

"Danny!" shout my mother and Kimberly in unison.

I am surprised to find myself in the street. I stand with my hands on my knees, trying to pull in a deep breath, or as deep a breath as a pack-a-day smoker can. *God, please no!* I concentrate on each involuntary action, making every breath a conscious act. Inhale. Exhale. Inhale. Exhale. And on and on until I feel myself slowly recovering.

What must my poor mother be thinking? And Kimberly? Whore? Such an ugly slander. Unfair. I'm such an asshole and a coward, because I don't have the guts to go back inside and apologize. I take a quick inventory by patting myself down, pockets first. I have my pills, good. I take one, a rarity for this early in the day because they make me loopy. I check for my wallet and my lighter. Excellent. I have shoes on my feet. Okay, then. I duck around the corner, pressing myself against Ed Henning's hedges, hiding from my loved ones.

"Danny? Danny?" calls Kimberly from the front stoop, wrapped, undoubtedly at my mother's insistence, in one of Dad's winter coats. She calls my name as if I'm a lost dog. I *am* a lost dog.

I cut through the Hennings' yard, through the alley behind the barber shop like I did when I was eleven. I will make good my promise to my mother. I will find Kevin and deliver him to Dad's funeral. It's a short walk to the Little Neck Inn, a half mile. I've done it a thousand times. I'll find him there. Then I'll pray to the god of language that he'll bless me with words, good words, perfect words for my father's eulogy.

"I can fix this!" I shout to the sky.

I've mentioned it before, but it bears repeating: The Little Neck Inn has been in continuous operation since 1909, with the notable exception of ten months in 1981 when a fire gutted the joint. I hold the distinction of having the last beer before the blaze, even cautioning the bartender, Kenny Clay, that his place of employment was about to go up like the Hindenburg.

The lights had been flickering for a few days, and then they blinked twice and went out. I grabbed the flashlight from behind the bar and made my way into the basement. I have no idea why I volunteered; I know as much about electricity as I do particle physics. I was drunk, of course. Why else would I be in the Little Neck Inn at 2:00 a.m. on a weekday?

The fuse box was hidden behind cases of cheap vodka. This was the bottom-shelf swill in the plastic half-gallon jugs Kenny funneled into empty top-shelf bottles of Belvedere, Grey Goose, and Stolichnaya to cheat the drunks who can't tell the difference. I moved eight cases to get at the circuit breakers, only to discover there were no circuit breakers, only a clump of bare copper wires. Rats or age or both had eaten away the insulation, creating a 220-volt Rastafarian knot that even I recognized as a fire waiting to happen.

"Jesus Christ, Kenny!" I bellowed as I slammed the fuse box shut, smushing the wires together—and the lights came back on.

From above I heard Kenny holler, "Ya done it! Way to go, Danny boy!"

Back on my barstool, I regaled Kenny and two drinkers with my electrical wizardry, earning a couple of free longnecks. "You better get that looked at, Kenny," I cautioned, as if I were Thomas Edison.

"Fuck it," he said, popping the cap off a fresh bottle. "The fuse box is under the jewelry store." We laughed at his joke, Kenny the loudest.

Kenny Clay is one half of the Clay brothers, Larry being the smaller and younger of the two. They pump the pipes at the Little Neck Inn, and once you get past their surly, misanthropic, sexist, ignorant, abrasive personalities, the brothers are really just garden-variety assholes, of which the world has no shortage. Still, Kenny and Larry Clay are our assholes, and we like them plenty. Kenny is something of a legend in the neighborhood. At six foot three, with a walrus mustache and Bozo hair, he has a face that must weigh fifty pounds, framed as it is with thick rubbery jowls that swing left or right whenever he turns his head. Something had happened to Kenny as a kid, leaving him with a voice like a cheese grater—think Louis Armstrong with a bad cold and no sense of time. Strangers hearing Kenny speak for the first time offer him lozenges.

The free beers kept coming, and I kept drinking till four, closing time, after which I surfed home, collapsing in bed fully dressed, shoes included. My mother shook me awake a few hours later.

"You have a phone call."

"I'll call back."

"It's important."

"Says who?"

"Josh. He's at a pay phone."

I rolled out of bed, but the whirlies nearly sent me to the floor.

"Good Lord, Danny, it smells like a saloon in here," she said propping the window open with a paperback copy of *Siddhartha*. "The phone's waiting."

"The Inn's on fire!" Josh shouted over sirens and more shouting.

"No shit?" I said, while rubbing night goop from my eyes.

I flew out the door and around the corner just in time to see an engine company race toward the Inn. A huge mob had gathered across the street from the fully engulfed bar. We spilled onto Northern Boulevard blocking two lanes. The news spread, causing morning commuters at Penn Station to change platforms and backtrack to the eastbound trains, blowing off work to witness history. Men in suits and ties mingled with the rest of us in our work boots and tool belts or tank tops and shorts. One guy watched in his bathrobe and slippers, while I still wore the clothes I had slept in. Our world was burning.

"Is this my fault?" I wondered then and still wonder. Had I not slammed that metal door pinching those bare wires. . . . Look at the trouble we cause when we don't stay in our own lane.

While the fire raged, a big Buick arrived, and the crowd parted to make room for Cecil Cleary, owner of the Little Neck Inn.

Everyone knew Cleary's name, but few had ever seen him in the flesh. Cleary has half a dozen joints, including a couple places with kitchens and cloth napkins. He thinks of himself as a restaurateur, but the Inn is his cash cow, patronized by loyal customers with low expectations. A notorious tightwad, Cecil would let a man die of thirst before springing for a drink. Yet even his detractors acknowledge he has a flair for the dramatic. With all eyes on him, Cleary pushed his way through the mob of gawkers and shoved aside a NYFD sawhorse. It suddenly got very quiet, as if Cleary were the bishop or the cardinal himself come to administer extreme unction to his smoldering gin mill.

"We'll be back!" he shouted to the mob. "By God, we'll be back!"

We let out a roar even though we assumed this, like everything else that tumbled out of his mouth, was a crock. But, true to his word, ten months later, the Little Neck Inn reopened, an exact replica of its former shabby self, an 86-proof phoenix risen from its own ashes. My brother Kevin purchased the first beer at the new and not-at-all improved Little Neck Inn.

The inn is a drinker's Shangri-la, and I am confident I'll find my brother sipping an eye-opener—that is, if he ever bothered to close them.

I shove my way through the front door, grateful to be out of the sunlight and back into the darkness and refracted light of green and brown bottles in the room-length mirrors. I have not set foot in here for two years of spite-driven sobriety.

"Hey, Danny. Miller's?" asks Kenny Clay, as if he had seen me yesterday. He pops the cap off a bottle and sets the beer on a coaster, giving it a little nudge in my direction.

"Pass, Kenny. I'm looking for Kevin," I say, pushing the bottle just out of reach.

"The stupid fucker went for eggs," says Clay with irritation. "He'll be back. He's got one on the house." And he nods to an inverted shot glass, the bartender's buoy, a reminder of which rum pot has a buy-back coming.

"I haven't seen you around," croaks Clay.

"I've been busy," I say, not wanting to explain my abstinence or anything else.

"Staying out of trouble?"

"Something like that," I mumble. "How 'bout a coffee?"

He pours a glass of coffee since the Inn doesn't have mugs, only those silly Irish coffee glasses that are too hot to pick up. I blow on the liquid, take a tiny sip, and look around at the early shift. Old Man Imprevento sits where he always sits, sipping a scotch and water. He's had surgery—mouth cancer—and his face is puffed up from radiation and steroids. He can barely open his lips, just enough to insert a straw. A few stools down sit the Hayes twins, Jimmy and Steve. They're supposed to be at work but have ditched their carpet-cleaning van behind the McDonald's and are slamming shots of something brown with 7-Up chasers. A blubbery woman in drawstring pants and a Rangers jersey smokes and curses as she dry humps the pinball machine, trying to win at something.

I light a smoke and thumb through yesterday's *New York Post*, killing time until my brother returns from his eggs. Kenny Clay refills my coffee and slides the Miller bottle back within easy reach.

"This is on Cleary whenever you're ready." But, of course, it's on Kenny.

I nod thanks. He moves down the bar to freshen a young junkie's rum and Coke. The junkie is edgy. He paged his dealer and hasn't heard back. A few silhouettes sip or swill whatever it is they're drinking in the back room while clacking pool balls around, annotating their successes and failures with "Fuck!" or "Shit!" or "Yeesssss!" as if they are Marv Albert calling a Knicks game. I take it all in: Norman Rockwell's America, Queens County, New York, May 19, 1998.

"Well, if it isn't the perfessor!" says Kevin, as he walks through the door. He says it exactly like that, *per-fessor!* As if there were any way I could miss the contempt.

"Where've you been?" I ask.

"Your wife's pussy."

I swallow hard and let it pass, unwilling to take the bait, as Kevin belches up an echo of his breakfast, the first solid food he's had in days.

My brother takes his meals mostly at the Seven Seas Diner, having been eighty-sixed from the Scobee after shoving a waitress and puking in a booth. Kevin favors the "special," three eggs any style, bacon, hash browns, bagel, coffee, and juice. The third egg is what makes it special.

"Let's go. Mom's waiting."

"We got time," he says, looking at his watchless wrist. "What time is it?"

"Ten to eleven."

"We got time," he says again, as he hoists himself onto his barstool and flips the upside-down shot glass right side up. "Hook me up, Kenny."

Kevin McKenna works for an air-freight company in Springfield Gardens, across from JFK. This is the latest in a string of jobs that have ended for one reason or another, but mostly the same reason: "Those fucking pricks." He runs the pickup department and spends his days screaming at the Blacks and Hispanics who drive the vans collecting packages throughout the five boroughs. Kevin makes twenty-eight thousand a year, spends thirty, and believes himself superior to the couriers because he wears a collared shirt to work.

Kevin has his passions—alcohol, obviously, but also sports of any kind: baseball, football, hoops, or hockey. It doesn't matter, as long as there are two teams and a point spread. Not being a fan of anything, his interest is purely financial. My brother is really more Calvinist than Catholic, his worldview shaped by a jaundiced predestination that ordains all his misfortunes. He believes in luck. Talent and effort play no role in success. Athletes, actors, singers, doctors, inventors, CEOs, and anyone good at anything are lucky. He is unlucky.

He was an altar boy like the rest of us. One day, in the sacristy before Mass, Al dared Kevin to take a sip of altar wine. Kevin sipped and then chugged half the bottle and vomited in the sink. Then he drank the other half. He was a full-blown drunk from the start. It took me longer to get there. Being unlucky, of course, Kevin got caught by Father Byrnes, who was pastor back then. Kevin never got away with anything. However, Father Byrnes did. Having discovered my brother's soft spot, Father Byrnes leveraged Kevin's predilection to indulge his own. I can occasionally whip up sympathy for my brother, unable to fathom everything that has reduced funny, playful, hopeful little Kevin McKenna into the bitter wreck on the barstool to my left.

"So, are you coming?" I ask.

"I'm cuming! I'm cuming!" he shouts while pantomiming an orgasm. He does this without looking at me, talking instead to my reflection in the mirror behind the bar.

We settle into a comfortable lesser argument over our physical appearances, he calling out the rumpled clothes I slept in, while I point out his unshaven face, matted hair, and the booze breath I can smell three feet away.

"Who the fuck are you to talk?"

"I have a new suit waiting at the house."

"Whoop-de-fuckin'-do!"

And we go back and forth like this until Kenny Clay can't stand it.

"Put a cork in it! Christ almighty!" he growls. "The two of you sound like a couple of queers."

And that ends it, because at the Little Neck Inn, there's no place to go after the queers card has been played. Kenny then lightens the mood by expelling a long, wet fart.

"Jesus, Kenny, your ass sounds like an Evinrude!" shouts one of the Hayes brothers.

Everyone laughs. Kevin laughs. I laugh. I try a new approach.

"Let's go home, hit the showers, and do this right."

Kevin says nothing.

"For Mom," I say, playing my ace. Kevin sips his drink.

"Jesus, Kevin, what's the big deal?"

After another sip he slowly blesses himself.

"In the name of the Father, of the Son, and of the Holy Ghost.

Rub-a-dub-dub three men in a tub! E pluribus Unum! Yabba dabba do."

"Shit, Kevin."

"He was an old man who lived a long time, busted his ass with nothing to show for it, and now he's dead," says Kevin.

"That's some eulogy," I say with irritation.

"For you, Pop," says Kevin, raising his glass. Then, in one quick motion, he throws back his drink. It's a violent toast, the cubes smack against his teeth and spill down his chin, then skitter across the bar like dice.

I watch him carefully as he curses God and man, a molecular anger boiling over with long-festering resentments. Layer upon layer of hurt and disappointment pour out of him. It's etched on his face. It curves his posture, grays his hair, and sours any possibility of enjoyment in life.

Then I see something even more shocking, my own reflection in the mirror. My pasty complexion, red-rimmed eyes, and unshaven face peek from behind a picket fence of green, blue, and brown bottles topped with chrome pour spouts. They look like tiny conquistadors, their helmets refracting the neon swirl of the Michelob sign that hangs a few feet above. Who am I to condemn Kevin McKenna? Maybe he's right to hate the world; what has the world done for him? By thinking kindlier of my brother, I hope he will soften his stance toward me.

"Will you please go with me to the church?" I ask in my sincerest voice.

Kevin turns slowly, then smiles a Jack Nicholson in *The Shining* smile.

"You want *me* to do *you* a favor?" says Kevin punching the "me" and "you" to emphasize the outrageousness of my request. "Okay, I'll go to the funeral," he continues. "But first, you have to do me a favor."

"How much?" I ask reflexively.

"Asshole."

"Then what?"

"I'll go if you drink this beer," he says as he places the Miller bottle in my hand.

"Why are you doing this, Kev?"

"Drink it, and I'll go."

"What are you trying to prove?"

"I'm not proving shit," he says. "I just hate to see a good beer go to waste. Drink and I'll go."

I do it quickly, in four big gulps. The beer is room temperature and bitter after sitting untouched for an hour. I hold the bottle high over my mouth and let the last drop of foam dribble out of the neck and into my tar-and-nicotine-varnished throat. I slam the bottle on the bar and yell, "Happy?"

Kevin laughs, a big rolling laugh, the kind of laugh you hear from movie villains. It shocks me, this laugh. It's otherworldly in its meanness.

"What's so goddamn funny?" I snap.

"You," he says. "You're a fucking riot with your sanctimonious Diet Cokes, you fucking bum!

"Give this lush whatever he wants," says Kevin. "On me." And he flips a fiver on the bar.

A fresh bottle slides into my hands, ice cold, right out of the cooler. I polish it off as fast as the first. It's delicious and liberating and everything I ever loved about beer.

"I always knew you were full of shit, Danny. What's it been, three years?" asks Kevin.

"Two."

"Is your life better, Danny?" he asks, leaning inches from my face. "Are you happy?"

I feel his hot breath blowing into my eyes and nostrils. "Does that bitch you married fuck you, Danny?" he says, punching each "Danny" hard.

That's when I tell Kevin about Kimberly, how we met, why we married, and why we are through. He seems genuinely interested, but then he would be, because my failed marriage confirms one of his core beliefs.

"She's a cunt. They're all cunts," he says.

"Watch your mouth!" shouts Kenny. "There are ladies here."

"Here?" says Kevin, looking around with genuine surprise. Then,

"I gotta hand it to ya, brother," he continues. "Even if she is a bitch, quality pussy like that don't come along every day."

"Forget it," I say. "Forget I said anything."

Kevin pushes back from the bar, scraping his stool loudly.

"I'm gonna play something to cheer you up."

He crosses to the jukebox and sticks a crinkled dollar in the machine. The jukebox spits it back. He rubs the dollar on his thigh with his palm and tries again, twice more before it's swallowed for keeps. Kevin scans the song titles. He needs glasses. Finally, he jabs the buttons. "This is for you, brother!" And suddenly the Little Neck Inn fills with Mike Melvoin's booming, bluesy organ intro to "That's Life." Sinatra, of course.

> *That's life! That's what people say*
> *You're riding high in April*
> *shot down in May*
> *But I know I'm gonna change that tune*
> *when I'm back on top, back on top in June . . .*

This shocks me. Kevin knows! Somehow, it has registered that this song, "That's Life," is one of my all-timers. It's not high art. It's not Mozart or Bernstein or Gershwin. It's not Harold Arlen or Jerome Kern. But still, the way pop hits can work their way into our very souls, "That's Life" is an anthem for everyone who's ever been kicked in the balls, which is everyone. I am drunk. I want to be drunker.

"Kenny, you fat bastard!" I scream over Frank Sinatra. "Keep the beers coming!"

It's now booze o'clock. Like old times. Two brothers laughing and singing and remembering our father with fondness, gratitude, even love. We toast our father's memory, then toast him again. And we sing together, me, Kevin, Kenny Clay, the jittery junkie, the Hayes brothers, and the blubbery girl at the pinball machine, too.

> *I've been a puppet, a pauper, a pirate, a poet,*
> *a pawn and a king*

> *I've been up and down and over and out,*
> *and I know one thing*
> *Each time I find myself flat on my face*
> *I pick myself up and get back in the race!*

I stick in three more dollars and punch "That's Life" as many times as it will play.

Finally, after decades of estrangement, we are brothers again, picking ourselves up and getting back in the race. That's life! But then, as life often does, the song takes an unexpected turn. As the record plays for the fifth time, I hear the final chorus for the first time.

> *. . . But if nothing's shaking come this here July,*
> *I'm gonna roll myself up in a big ball and die!*

What does that mean? "If nothing's shaking come this here July"? If things aren't better by the end of June, kill yourself? What about all that "pick yourself up and get back in the race" stuff? I've heard this song ten thousand times, but this is the first time I absorbed its crazy bipolar message.

I check my watch. We have five minutes to get to St. Anastasia's.

> *My, myyyyy!*

7

Send In the Clowns

The Hayes twins volunteer to drive us to St. Anastasia. There are no seats in the back of the van. Kevin is on the floor; I'm on a five-gallon plastic bucket of rug shampoo wedged between a giant industrial vacuum and the spare tire. Our feet tangle in the hoses, brushes, and squeegees. We hold on for our lives as Jimmy Hayes races down the road.

"We look like bums," I say.

No shower. No brand-new blue suit. I brush the front of my shirt with both hands as if they are a pair of boney Maytags that will some-how wash, dry, and press my rumpled clothing.

"Fuck it," says Kevin, as he drains a beer he smuggled out of the bar. "Nobody's coming to see you."

"I gotta piss!" shouts Jimmy Hayes over the hollow metallic rattle of the van.

"Just drive!" I shout back.

We catch a break with the traffic lights but have to run every yel-low. Up ahead, my father's hearse has discharged his casket onto the church truck. After waiting for me and Kevin to appear, they can wait no longer. Fat Tommy Boyle leads the procession up the steps and through the church's polished wooden doors.

Jimmy stops the van at a rip in the chain-link fence that surrounds the school parking lot. This hole has been here forever, each generation pulling it open to create a shortcut to the netless basketball hoops. I jump out of the van and squeeze through the fence as I've done a thousand times before, as if this is the way everyone goes to their father's funeral.

"Hurry up!" I shout back at Kevin.

But Kevin isn't coming.

"Go!" yells Kev, as he climbs back into the van, wedging himself between the brothers.

I stand there as they drive off, the wind knocked out of me without a punch being thrown. The organist begins the "Ave Maria."

I am shocked at how drunk I am. I never should have taken that Ativan.

Fat Tommy leads the pallbearers down the center aisle; Al, Sean, cousin Roger, nephew Jay, and, pinch-hitting for me and Kevin, the limo driver from O'Connell's and my niece, Gail, who nearly skips with delight, thrilled she has shattered the glass ceiling of death. The priest mumbles a blessing as he clacks the thurible, prompting it to exhale burps of incense. The procession resumes, creeping down the aisle with Dad's casket rolling slowly along on the church truck, the Stars and Stripes draped over his earthly remains. About halfway down, one of the wheels locks like a Grand Union shopping cart, causing the coffin to pull to the left. Fat Tommy and the limo driver reflexively hip check the casket to keep my father from crashing into the pews.

Sean, Al, Beth, and the kids take their places next to my mother in the first row. Kimberly sits behind them with Aunt Mary, Uncle Ed, Roger, and his wife and kids. Scattered among the other pews are a handful of neighbors and friends, the same people who paid their respects at the house or at the wake. The crowd is padded a bit with a few surprise guests—two guys who worked with Dad at Alley Pond Park. Interspersed are the professional mourners you find in all parishes who attend every funeral whether they know the deceased or not. It's good they're here, because the church swallows up my father's loved ones.

The tiny Cuban priest nobody can understand mouths the words of the liturgy, his thick accent and monotone delivery rendered even less comprehensible by St. Anastasia's impossible acoustics. A cloud of spent incense wafts in two distinct layers over the congregation, causing Aunt Mary and the other asthmatics to cough. The priest disinterestedly mumbles my father's requiem, and his boredom spreads like a yawn. He's new to the parish, sent by the bishop to accommodate the Hispanic congregants who he wrongly believes represent the future of St. Anastasia. The bishop should have sent a Korean. All the old Irish fathers have been called home by their ultimate boss. Only Father Considine survives, but he's currently fishing on the Manasquan Reservoir and won't be back until the twenty-fifth.

I take all this in from the back of the church, woozy and nauseous from alcohol, Ativan, and shame. I step back outside. I should go. Run. But run where? The hearse driver gives me a suspicious look as he takes a drag on his cigarette. What I wouldn't give for a smoke! So I fire up a heater and think about hopping in the hearse and driving myself to a new life. Instead, I plunge through the church doors again and dip my hand in the holy water font. I splash my face, seeking a revival rather than a blessing. One more deep breath, and I charge directly up the main aisle, almost at a trot. My off-brand sneakers squeak on the marble floor. The faster I walk, the louder they squeak, until I sound like a hamster on a wheel. *Squeak! Squeak!* I shush them. "Quiet!" I say. "*Shhhhhh!*" And one by one the mourners turn to see who is late, who is making this racket.

I see their eyes. Fat Tommy's, Jay's, Gail's, Ed Henning's, the limo driver's, the little Cuban priest's. Sean's eyes, Al's eyes, and Kimberly's, with a look of utter disbelief on her face. Then—try as I might to not see them—my mother's sad and horrified eyes look directly at me and then through me. The room starts spinning, and I stumble and bump into an empty pew. I grab it to steady myself and labor to put one foot in front of the other. *Squeak! Squeak!* That's when I discover the physical force of silence, the wallop of a vacuum. The hush of judgment envelops me like smog shrouds LA. I am stinking drunk, and everyone knows it. Their disgust flies down the aisle like shock waves from an atomic blast. I stagger forward into the teeth of their silence, which quickly breaks into murmured condemnations, no louder than a whisper, but collectively like the roar of an angry sea.

The priest stops speaking in mid-platitude. He looks for someone to take charge, practically begging someone to intervene. Al shoots out of his seat, squeezing past my father's flag-draped casket.

"Sit down, Al!" I yell. "Sit back down!" My ferocity freezes Al in place. Beth tugs on his jacket and coaxes him back into his pew.

"Everything's okay!" I yell, as I finally make it to the first row, one hand on the post, the other on Dad's coffin, leaning on him one last time.

"My name is Daniel Patrick McKenna, and I am here to speak my father's eulogy!" I yell toward the priest.

"Danny, sit down!" Al and Sean both shout-whisper in unison.

I wave them off and speak directly to Father Mumbles, demanding he acknowledge me. "I said my name is Daniel Patrick McKenna . . . and I am here to speak my father's eulogy!" I say the whole thing again, word for word, even repeating the odd syntax to force the issue. I did not want to do this eulogy, but they insisted, so, goddammit, I'm going to tell them about Francis Xavier McKenna. The little priest looks to my mother. She nods her consent. Then the priest steps down from the altar and approaches. I puff myself up for a blow, but instead of a punch he offers his elbow. The priest gently escorts me up the steps toward the lectern.

"I can walk!" I bark.

"Be careful," he says. "Watch the steps."

I steady myself with the microphone stand, grabbing it like a subway stanchion.

"This is too low," I say, stooping over to speak. My voice booms over the PA system. "Father Tiny is so little," I say to lighten the mood. It doesn't. So I fiddle with the stand, raising it to my mouth and then high over my head. I let it sink back down below my chest. Al jumps out of his seat again, quickly making his way onto the altar.

"Come on, Danny," he says, concealing his fury. "Let's take a walk outside."

"I know what I'm doing!" I shout, as I yank my arm free from Al's grip.

And what can Al do? Not a damn thing, unless he's willing to bodily remove me from the house of God. I have called his bluff.

"It's my turn to say something," I say.

"Let him say his piece," the priest tells Al.

"Why won't this goddamn thing stay put?" I ask, still futzing with the microphone.

Like a Tim Conway routine, my head bobs slowly up and down following the trajectory of the falling and rising microphone. Al's kids find this hilarious, so too cousin Roger's twins, who are ten. I can see them pointing and fighting to stifle their laughter. Finally, in frustration, I grab the mic and hold it in place, embarrassed to find a lit cigarette between my fingers. I search for a place to ditch the smoke.

"You got an ashtray?" I ask the priest. This causes the altar boys to bite their lips. They will remember this funeral.

"Oh, God, Danny! Stop it!" shouts Kimberly.

I ignore her.

Al takes the cigarette out of my hand. It's deathly quiet again, so quiet I can hear the fizzle when Al sticks my smoke into one of the floral arrangements. The priest motions to the pudgy altar boy, who grabs the vase and disappears into the sacristy.

I begin my eulogy.

"Kevin will not be with us today," I say as an opener. "He sends his regrets." A nice touch, a good, solid, face-saving McKenna family lie. I am pleased with myself for thinking of it and for not sounding all slurry.

"My family has requested I say a few words about my father, Francis Xavier McKenna," I continue. But then I abruptly stop to make sure I have their full attention. It is hard to tell if they're listening or not. All their heads are down, and I only see hairdos, veils, and male-pattern baldness. They're fidgeting, looking at their shoes, and this makes me angry. My mother is the lone holdout; she looks directly at me, her face as expressionless as the face on a coin. My mother has anticipated this. If not specifically this, something like this. During last night's long vigil of sleepless worry, she had imagined some ugly scene that would bring embarrassment and disgrace. The only surprise is the perpetrator. The smart money was on Kevin. The only money really. "Get on with it!" shouts Al. So I plunge back into my father's eulogy.

"I have many things to tell you about Dad. Dad was a good man, a fair man, a good father, I guess. A good husband, right, Mom?" But I stop before she can answer.

My tongue is thick and my mouth dry. I am conscious of my tongue, and it's impossible to speak when you're thinking about it as a biological process.

"Can I get some water?" I ask no one in particular.

The priest looks again to the altar boys, and both run off to get water but mostly to laugh and high-five. I fumble with my eyeglass case as I wait for the kids to come back, but they take too long, and I have no choice but to continue.

"My father was from Ireland. My father didn't have a career; he had jobs. My father liked the New York Mets. My father grew the best tomatoes, or so I'm told. I hate tomatoes. My father smoked cigarettes, like I do. He also smoked a pipe. My father did not sing like Frank Sinatra. He did not sing at all. My father drank, but he wasn't a drunk like me or Kevin."

"Where are you going with this?" asks Al.

"To hell," I answer truthfully. "I am going to hell."

This is Kimberly's cue to leave. She shimmies out of her pew and clicks and clacks as she rushes out a side door. I watch her go but say nothing. What can I say?

The mourners mumble again. The church echoes with nervous coughing and whispered condemnations. I try to stare them into silence. Then I can't take it anymore.

"Does my father's life bore you?" I yell into the microphone, causing a shrill squeal of feedback. I yell it again, on purpose, so they have to cover their ears.

Belligerent. Furious. Insane. Kevin is here in spirit. I am Kevin. Rather, I am me, and now everyone knows how alike Kevin McKenna and Danny McKenna really are. Knowing that they know is more than I can stand. I turn savagely on my family.

"Maybe I should give Frank fuckin' Sinatra's eulogy!" I scream. "You'd like that, wouldn't you? Frank fuckin' Sinatra never bored you . . ." but that's as far as I get, because they're coming for me.

Fat Tommy Boyle is on his feet. Cousin Roger is already on the altar steps, taking them two at a time. Roger played linebacker at Cardozo and has me in his crosshairs. I scramble like Fran Tarkenton trying to evade a sack. I duck behind the altar, then quickly around the lectern. They're coming to get me, all of them! Fat Tommy, Roger, Ed Henning, even Sean, Jay, and Gail are on their feet. Then, out of nowhere, *WHAM!* My knees buckle, and I go down, slamming my head into the corner of the lectern before striking the hard marble floor. It's Al, my kindest brother, delivering a blindside tackle. Blood gushes from a gash above my eyes. Screams! Chaos! Keening! Wailing!

I throw off Al and kick away Fat Tommy, Ed Henning, and the little priest. I chomp on fingers and hands. I am rabidly mad with strength I have never possessed. I scare them all, even Roger, who is shocked to see a ferocious Danny McKenna, someone he has always considered a fairy because I was once in a high school play.

It hurts—my head, my ribs, my back where Al hit me. My glasses are gone, shattered, the frames and lenses crushed in the scrum. Flowers are overturned, the candles have been knocked off the altar, and the flag from my father's coffin falls to the floor and is trampled as more people rush up the steps to get a piece of me. My mother weeps uncontrollably, and Sean lets her. I did this. I caused this.

The little priest is livid. He has a cut under one eye; it will become a shiner, and I tell him I hope it was me who gave it to him. A police siren approaches. Are they coming for me too? Who dropped the dime? I blame the altar boys.

"Fuck you, 'ya little cassock-clad cocksuckers!" I scream, scaring the smirks off their pubescent faces.

Roger has me in a headlock and begins dragging me off the altar. He had put me in many headlocks as a kid, but this time it isn't horse-play. It was never horseplay. Roger hates me.

"McKenna, Francis X. Age eighty-two!" I shout, now decidedly off mic as I am manhandled down the altar steps. "Born, the twelfth of December! Nineteen hundred and fifteen! County Sligo, Ireland! . . . Died the fourteenth day of May! Nineteen hundred and ninety-eight! Little Neck! Queens County! New York! Survived by wife, Catherine, nee Boyle! . . . And sons, Aloysius, Kevin, Sean, and Daniel!"

And I would go on screaming, but I drop Dad's tiny *Daily News* obituary when the priest knees me in the balls. Without that slip of paper, I have nothing to say about my father, and I have no choice but to shut up.

Roger hoists me off the floor and onto his back. Al, Fat Tommy, and a cluster of men lift me bodily and carry me down the aisle like a rock star surfing the crowd. Only these are not fans, rather, an angry mob of my own blood, delivering kidney punches and elbows intended to punish rather than subdue. I have no fight left. Their blows hurt, and for that I am grateful. I deserve to suffer, and they are giving me the gift of pain. As I'm hauled toward the back of the church, I stare at the ceiling's peculiar paint job, like the bottom of a David Hockney swimming pool. "Whose idea was that?" I wonder. The church doors are thrown open, and a freight train of brilliant sunlight blinds me. I turn my head away from the glare, and there he stands, the ancient war veteran, cane in hand, hat cocked on his vein-mottled head, a satisfied smirk on his blue, cracked lips.

As I am carried out, he snaps a salute.

8

My Way

The '62 Mets lost 120 games out of 160 played, still the worst record in the history of baseball. Mets fans are proud of this record. Whenever a horrible team threatens to lose their way into the record books, we root for that team to win.

My eulogy has failed as spectacularly as the Mets. If you must fail, a crushing defeat is the best kind. It's definitive. There's no second-guessing when you're thoroughly trounced.

So I choose to believe my father would have appreciated the magnitude of my failure. Twenty years from now, maybe thirty or more, the legend of Frank McKenna's funeral will still be told. The Thrilla in Manila, the Rumble in the Jungle, and now the Slaughter on the Altar. My drunken tirade and the resultant spectacle have given my father a beachhead on immortality. Even when his name and mine are lost to the mists of time and the details embroidered to absurd dimensions—"He punched his mother!" "He shot the priest!"—at least we will have left our mark on the world. Infamy, if not fame, is ours. In our tabloid age, where Joey Buttafuoco begets Amy Fisher begets John Wayne Bobbitt begets Kato Kaelin, there is no longer a distinction between the notorious and the accomplished. There is only fame.

Of course, my family doesn't see it this way.

The spectacle on the altar has been shocking and horrible. Most have never seen me drunk, and my behavior is utterly inexplicable. The people closest to me ignored my drunkenness as we've ignored Sean's homosexuality and everything else that would require family introspection. Nothing keeps a secret like mutual guilt.

A word or two about booze. I like it. I like the way it tastes. I like the bottles it comes in. I like the names on the labels. I like the sound of ice cubes tinkling in a glass. I like what it does to my head. In every culture, in every corner of the world, in every epoch of history, men and women have turned to fermentation to find relief from life's burdens, to silence the voices of the childhood syllabuses and dogmas that programmed them to believe this life is not to be enjoyed.

The rich have options: therapists and vacations, cosmetic surgery, weekend seminars on "healing the inner child," or other jibber-jabber to go along with the fifty million self-help books that mostly help the people writing them. The rest of us have only the time-tested homeopathic remedies—beer, vodka, whiskey, gin, tequila, rum, and wine. A drink or two allows a shy, lonely man to get up his courage and ask the chubby chick in the pantsuit if she'd like to dance. A glass or two or three may empower that woman to experience the one great orgasm she'll have in this life, a few minutes of bliss she'll happily remember for the next fifty years.

Without alcohol, countless millions would spend their lives saddled with an oppressive virginity and life's worst curse, a case of the "what ifs?" One night of drunken passion is better than a lifetime of sober celibacy; booze is good for the world! It loosens us up so we can love and live and be loved and create. As Clarence Darrow said, "What kind of a poem do you think you'll find in a glass of water?" Would Frank Sinatra have been Frank Sinatra without his beloved Jack Daniels? The guy who sang "I'm a Fool to Want You" the way he sang "I'm a Fool to Want You" had to be a drinker. You don't get sounds like that from a smoothie.

Drinkers have all the fun. That's why it's called Happy Hour. Visit any bar in the world. Go early when everyone is quiet and taking their first sips. Stay for the magic, the stress-draining miracle of distilled spirits at work. It begins with strangers exchanging pleasantries. "Is anyone sitting here?" "No, make yourself at home." Soon these strangers are sharing their day, what happened at the office, how their kids are doing—"Would you like to see a picture?" The peanut dish is shuttled back and forth like a puck on ice. Hopes and dreams are batted around as well. Nobody judges what you say because nobody is actually listening. It's beautiful.

Ethanol is the secret sauce, a colorless liquid that puts color in our cheeks, in our language, in our lives. Soon, the chitchat intensifies, sixty decibels become eighty. Laughter enters. Real belly laughs. When was the last time you threw your head back in sheer hilarity? The room is now alive with animated conversations, heated debates over points of public policy, tales of heroic plays made between the foul lines, that orgasmic cheeseburger in San Diego, nostalgic reminiscence, dreams of future glory, thwarted and consummated seductions, the entire bibliography of the human condition is unfolding courtesy of our half-full glasses.

Yet I must caution, CH3-CH2-OH is flammable. Volatile. Ginger ale would not have compelled me to vandalize my father's service. If Happy Hour becomes Happy Hours, problems arise. Daddy comes home drunk. Or maybe not at all. Maybe your husband smells like Chanel but you wear Estee Lauder. As the drinks go down and the night speeds ahead, the magic can turn tragic. Voices get a little too loud. Points are made too emphatically. Arguments become personal. Courtesy dissolves in alcohol. So does character. Now you're in a fight. Falling down. Driving recklessly on the street where your own children play, struggling to remember which house is home. She's angry, and you might hit her. So you hit her. Then you hit her again. Rape. She stabs you with the scissors from the kitchen drawer. Be careful, my friends. Use the gift of liquor with discretion, otherwise you may end up a mush-mouthed ogre repellent to children and a source of worry and shame to your own mother. Now the cops are involved—rightly so—and your marriage is ruined, your kids traumatized, your job terminated, and you can't come up with a single reason to keep living. The booze bone is connected to the suicide bone.

Was my father an alcoholic? He was a drinker, but was he an alcoholic?

My mother did not like it when Dad came home drunk from a Hibernian meeting or a night of cards or simply late on a Tuesday. They would have words. One memorable night, he had a snootful, and they argued, one of the rare times my mother and father raised their voices with each other. Dad slammed the door behind him as he stomped out of the house. Hours later Mom found him in the backyard in the cheap folding lounger Sean used in the summer to sun himself. It had snowed, and my father was covered with a light dusting. None of my friends' fathers slept under a blanket of snow. Did yours?

When I was fresh out of college—this is years ago—on a very hot July Fourth weekend in beautiful Newport, Rhode Island, I found myself in handcuffs with a cop's knee on the small of my back outside the home of Lucy Webster. I didn't know Lucy Webster. I had no business being in her yard. It was close to three in the morning, give or take a few cocktails. I was busy chopping down Lucy's fence with an ax I had found in her shrubbery when Ms. Webster objected. Two enormously tolerant gendarmes responded to her call. Luckily for me, Newport being the summer party town it is, these cops were old hands at subduing drunken fools. In any other city in America, a man with an ax, even a man as White as I, would be quickly dispatched to the next world with more holes in his body than he was born with.

At the time, I was unfamiliar with the term "suicide by cop." I have since learned it's a common phenomenon, and I can't rule out that somewhere in my booze-marinated mind the idea hadn't pinged in my brain to bait Newport's Finest into putting me out of my misery.

A week later, though, I stood before Judge Martin Grohman in the Newport Municipal Court. It was Houston-hot, swampy, ninety-plus degrees. The courtroom itself was more Dixie than Yankee, with slowly rotating ceiling fans shoving clumps of humidity from one side of the room to the other, like something out of *Scopes v. Tennessee*, only I was the monkey on trial.

I hired an attorney out of the phone book. My very first attorney.

I told the lawyer my story of stupid drinking with college chums in every gin mill on Thames Street. The lawyer knew every bar, which made me question his habits.

I recounted what I could—the heavy rain, rain that killed all our outdoor plans and lit the drinking lamp early. I told him how we laughed and tried to get laid and, in the process, how we scattered all over a city we barely knew, chasing skirts we would not catch. I explained how I got lost in the warren of narrow colonial-era roads that make up the oldest part of Newport, cobblestone cart paths going back to the 1680s. The lawyer glanced at his watch. I saw him do it, so I sped up my story to keep from spilling into to a second billable hour.

"What do you think? I asked.

"When the judge asks how you plead, tell him *nolo contendere*."

"Like Spiro Agnew?"

"Like Agnew."

"That's it?"

"You're asking for pity, Mr. McKenna," he said, as he stood up. "That's your only play."

We shook hands, and I gave his girl at the front desk my Mastercard and never saw the lawyer again.

When it was finally my turn in the docket, I answered, as instructed, "No contest, Your Honor," and a benevolent Judge Grohman let me off with $250 dollars restitution to Ms. Webster and a mandatory alcohol treatment program because he believed I had a problem. That's what sent me briefly to AA. I took my tap on the wrist like a man. An angry bailiff pulled me by the sleeve into a hallway behind the bench. "You're a lucky son-of-a-bitch!" he stage-whispered.

Was I? Am I?

For years the people who know me best have worried about my drinking. Josh, the night before he moved to California, begged me to give AA a shot. I made some dumb joke about a "shot" of whiskey or something and blew him off, never telling him or anyone I had already been to AA, courtesy of a Rhode Island judge. Then there was a pointedly uncomfortable annual Marshall College evaluation by my department chairman and friend, Louis d'Arnaud. After recounting several embarrassing incidents, including a slurry speech at a faculty meeting, he took off his glasses, looked me straight in the eye, and said, "Get your shit together." That took guts. I stopped drinking that day to prove him wrong. To prove them all wrong. But I was wrong, and Kevin McKenna was right. I am a bum.

Now I have ruined my father's funeral. I have humiliated my mother. My wife has left me. I'm professionally nowhere, and my only prospect is more of the same. We really only have one absolute obligation, and that is to die. Everything else is a choice. I definitely will kill myself, but first I have to shake Roger, who drives me back to Mom's with instructions to sit on me while the rest of the family does their best to restore order to Dad's funeral.

I'm not a total asshole. I am contrite and filled with genuine remorse—*regrets, I've had a few*—but Roger makes it difficult to stay sorry. The big lummox drinks three of Kevin's Budweisers while chewing me out for being a drunken bum. Thoughts of suicide become visions of homicide, but I have to be careful, knowing Roger will jump at the chance to pummel me again. I bookmark my rage and wait for an opportunity to escape.

I don't have to wait long. Outsmarting Roger is a low bar. When he excuses himself from the kitchen to "drain the dragon," I give him my word I won't do anything stupid. At the sound of his zipper uncoupling, I flee the house for the second time today. Staying would be stupid, so I'm not really breaking my word.

I'm in too big a hurry to wait for the train, so I flag a cab. "The City," I say. I'll be safe in Manhattan, hidden among the millions.

The cabbie gives me the once-over in the rearview mirror. I watch his big eyes calculate how much trouble I might be. My bruised face and blood-matted hair scream danger. I expect him to say, "Get out." Instead, he turns and smiles a genuine smile without a trace of condescension. A Jamaican? He has Rasta hair and pot-shot eyes and that lovely lilting island accent as he loudly sings, "The beat-up man from Little Neck wants to go to the biiiiiig town!" And with that, we take off. The driver chatters away, occasionally singing nonmelodic lines of a complex story, his life story, picked up exactly where he left off when his previous fare got out. It makes no difference to him who hears it, as long as he has someone to tell it to. I pretend to listen, throwing in an occasional, "Is that so?" or "You're kidding?" when he comes up for air. I have plans to make.

I'll find a room. Someplace nice. Someplace extravagant. Why not? The Waldorf? Too stuffy. The Plaza? I love the bar—the Oak Room. And the high ceilings over the beds make you feel important, because only important people can afford to air-condition a room with twenty-foot ceilings. I think about how I'll order a steak and an ice bucket filled with Beck's. No Millers for me. Not tonight. Tonight, I am going top shelf all the way. I'll get the best imported beer, the best USDA beef. I'll flip through the Yellow Pages and order an escort service to send their finest girl. Fuck it, their finest *girls*. My wallet is fat with cash, honeymoon money, all that dough I took from the bank before we left for the Cape. And I have credit cards, of course. What American doesn't? I am ready to blow it all on one fantastic night of hedonistic debauchery, if you'll pardon the redundancy. I am Caligula in a cab!

This is the grandest ride of my life, so wonderful I don't even mind my driver's interminable life story that occasionally prompts him to lit-erally sing out random sentences. "I miss my chilllllllldren! They're all grown nowwwwww!" Tuneless but joyful singing even when what he sings about is tragic; his happy sadness contributes to my own eupho-ria after a two-year sabbatical from booze. I command the cabbie to stop at a delicatessen on Utopia Parkway. "The Liiiiiittle Neck man wants to stop at a deli!"

I purchase a tall boy to lubricate the remainder of the ride. Tightly wrapped in a brown sack, I flip the top and suck the foam and drain it dry, crushing the can in my hands, squishing it into an aluminum disk, impressed by my own manliness as the driver sings about the time he was shot by a drug lord.

I throw the can out the window as we merge onto the LIE. It skit-ters on the pavement and vanishes under a box truck.

"Litter, litter, what a shitter!" sings the driver.

Then I wad up the bag and toss that, too. The bag unravels and is swept upward in the vortex of whooshing cars. It floats over the guardrail, landing among the trail of trash and detritus trapped in the high weeds and grass of the embankment. I hate litterers. Now I'm a litterer. I am unshackled from common decency. I will make the most of it. As we creep toward the Midtown Tunnel, I make a decision.

"The Plaza!"

"Oh, the Plaaaaaza!"

I am no longer drunk but soon will be again. I look drunk, dressed in the clothes I wore yesterday. Unshaven, hair matted with blood, a bruised face, and an oozing wound on my forehead. They'll give me the thrice-over at the Plaza, but what can I do? We enter the circle off Fifty-Ninth and pull to a stop at the main entrance on Central Park South. The uniformed doorman opens the cab door and watches as I climb out. His face turns to stone.

"Can I help you?" he asks.

"No," I say.

Now the ball is in his court. Does he let me into the lobby or shoo me away to the Milford Plaza or some pit where bums like me belong? I put myself in his shoes and try to imagine what I'd do if I were him. It's a coin toss. Everyone is so litigious now; what if he turns me away and I lawyer up and sue? Who can tell who has class today? I decide not to give him a hard time. He must have a family to feed; why else would a grown man dress in that asinine Vatican Guard costume and spend his life obsequiously opening doors for perfectly healthy, fully ambulatory adults and even children? He is my senior by ten years. I pity this doorman, and that makes me feel better about myself because I'm not him, and it proves I still have ego if not empathy. I slip him a twenty. That brings back his unctuous smile.

"Welcome to the Plaza Hotel, sir."

He got his taste. I have cleared the first hurdle.

Inside the hotel's gilded Beaux-Arts lobby, I know I will be confronted by a desk clerk who will pose a bigger challenge. I duck into the men's room to clean up as best I can. The soap and water feel great on my face, and I watch as my dried blood returns to a liquid state before circling the drain. I rub my face with a fresh hand towel from the neat stack thoughtfully provided by the housekeeping staff. I use more towels than necessary because, why not? A jar of blue sanitizer stuffed with floating black combs sits on the vanity next to a tray of sundries, Q-Tips, floss, nail files, and a dispenser of mouthwash with a stack of tiny paper cups like they use to distribute meds in a mental ward. I take liberal advantage of this, swishing and spitting again and again until my mouth is decontaminated. I love lobby bathrooms. Marble everywhere, dark wood paneling, and the latest editions of the *New York Times, Wall Street Journal,* and even *Le Monde* carefully draped over beveled wooden dowels near the stalls, anything to take our minds off shitting. I help myself to a handful of shrink-wrapped mints, popping one in my mouth and pocketing the rest for later. In the lobby shop, these things go for three bucks a roll.

I give myself one last look in the mirror. Better, but will anyone else think so? It will be difficult to fool the desk people. They've seen everything. I wipe the bottoms of my sneakers with a towel so as not to track anything on the Breccia-marble lobby floors. With each step I take my sneakers punctuate my movements with a high-pitched squeak, a repeat of my long, wobbly walk up the aisle of St. Anastasia's. I sound like a calliope.

"Good afternoon," I say cheerfully to the polished African American desk clerk. "I would like a room."

"Do you have a reservation?" she asks.

"I do not," I say, as if not having a reservation is a virtue.

"I'm sorry, sir, but without a reservation, there's nothing we can do," she says, employing the royal we.

"You've got rooms," I say firmly as I slide my Massachusetts driver's license toward her, none too subtly wrapped in a one-hundred-dollar bill. This offends her, and she slides my license and C-note back without comment. She repeats, "Without a reservation, I'm afraid I can't help you, sir." But this time "sir" has an edge.

This leaves me no choice but to ask for her superior. After a brief interlude, I am greeted by an attractive Middle Easterner named Ashaki.

"Ashaki?" I say, just to say it. "What does that mean?"

"One who is beautiful," she says shyly, dipping her eyes slightly, indicating a genuine humility even though the name fits.

"Your parents knew what they were doing," I say, laying it on thick.

"What does Daniel mean?" she asks, reading from my driver's license.

"God is my judge," I answer. "It's from the Hebrew."

"Are you Jewish?"

"No. Are you?"

And she smiles, bringing an end to this volley of competitive charm. Now it's down to business.

"How can I help you, Mr. McKenna?"

"I would like a room for tonight. Just tonight. But your under-ling . . ." and I shoot a glance at the desk clerk, "tells me there are no rooms."

With that, Ashaki pecks away on a keyboard, her eyes scanning a screen.

"Aha!" she says. "We do have a room, but I'm afraid it's one of our Ambassador Class suites."

She says this, confident I'll blanch at the price and lodge elsewhere.

"Perfect!" I say with a bright smile. "By all means, give me an Ambassador Class suite!" I say this with so much pretentiousness she doesn't take me seriously. I take it up a notch.

"And, Ashaki, make it a real ambassador's suite, like the Court of St. James or Russia, not one of those petty ambassadors like Honduras or Luxembourg."

She doesn't chuckle or smile at my joke. She may not even recog-nize it as a joke. Ashaki is tired of me.

"That will be $965 for the one night," she says, emphasizing the "one night."

Wow. Crazy expensive! But I don't say anything and do my best not to show it. Instead I pull out my wallet and withdraw the wad of new hundred-dollar bills I got from the Plymouth Savings Bank near home. I count them out, even though I know I only have four hundred dollars and will have to use a credit card to cover the tab. Still, flash-ing the cash takes the wind out of Ashaki's sails, and that's the point.

I light up a smoke, a violation of lobby etiquette, but I'm nervous despite my resolve.

"Tell you what," I say, pulling out the American Express card I use only in emergencies. "Put it on Amex." And I flip the card across the counter like I'm a blackjack dealer. After running the card, Ashaki hits a button, and the printer spits out an invoice I have to sign in two places.

"Shit, that's a lot of money," I say out loud without meaning to.

"I assume you'd prefer a smoking room?" she says, fanning away the plume I deliberately exhaled her way.

"I'd like a smoking *suite*," I say, correcting her.

Finally, the supervisor slides the heavy metal room key in my direction. I smile as she taps the brass bell summoning a hop. The kid, a young Black man from the islands, jumps up from a bench.

"I'm luggage-less."

"You don't have any baggage?" asks Ashaki.

"We all have baggage," I answer, because I can't resist the setup.

I make three lefts and a right and find myself in the Oak Room, with one foot on the brass rail and my elbow on the dark-grained wood bar. The bartender comes over.

"You okay?" he asks, looking at my bruised face and torn shirt.

"Get me a Beck's."

"I don't know if that's a good idea."

"I don't care about your ideas." And I show him my key.

He folds, and I get the beer. After a few sips, I consider my options.

How should I kill myself? I have to come up with something guaranteed to work, but also something not too painful. I don't want to fail like that poor sap who jumped off the Empire State Building and survived. Kevin will say, "He couldn't even get that right!" So I rule out grand gestures like hurling myself off landmark buildings. I consider again buying a gun, but with all these goddamn New York gun laws, the Brady Bill, cooling-off periods, background checks, and me with an out-of-state license, it'll take weeks, and I need a gun now. Maybe the bellhop who was so eager to take my bags can hook me up? Then I chastise myself for assuming the Black kid could get me a gun. Still, the idea of some cheap peashooter misfiring or worse, leaving me a crippled, half-brained, tube-fed, idiot vegetable unable to do anything but blink my eyes and piss myself. . . . Well, no to that.

A shotgun would work. Hemingway used one. Kurt Cobain, too. I could prop myself up in my big Plaza Ambassador Suite bed and spray my brains all over the hand-carved headboard and freshly papered walls. You don't have to aim a shotgun, and even if I flinch, I'm sure to hit something critical. This appeals to me. But how do you fire a shotgun with the barrel in your mouth and the trigger way down there? I'd need arms like Phil Jackson.

I pantomime putting a shotgun in my mouth, which earns a few quizzical looks from the bartender and specifically one table of diners, a father and mother with two young girls, in town to see *The Lion King*. The father looks right at me and then whispers something to the wife who chuckles. I order another beer. My thoughts drift to the unfortunate housekeeper who will have to clean my room. She'll find my head-mess all over the wall and will have to scrub everything. How much could the Plaza possibly pay a housekeeper? A shotgun is out.

I consider staging an accident, throwing myself in front of a bus so Kimberly can sue the MTA and have a pile to keep her off the pole. Then again, people get mowed down by buses every day, and most survive. The paramedics and trauma teams are so good now.

Maybe poison. But what kind of poison? Where would I get poison? What must that feel like? Drano will kill me. I can get that anywhere. But Drano is lye, and that would hurt like hell. A horrible death. Pass on poison.

Pills of some kind. Maybe Ativan? I have some with me but not enough for an overdose. Sleeping pills? That sounds peaceful, like people say drowning is supposed to be. But every time I see someone drowning on TV or in a *Titanic* movie they're screaming and splashing and terrified. Where can I get sleeping pills? Maybe the slow-as-molasses bartender who hasn't come back with my second beer?

"One more!" I shout, tapping my empty Beck's bottle.

If I do get pills and swallow enough to die, will my Ambassador Suite become notorious? Will my death make the news, *Daily* or otherwise? Will it become a kinky thing to ask specifically for the room where the guy killed himself? I try to imagine the next couple who will sleep on my hotel bed. Will they get off knowing what had happened on that mattress? In French, "orgasm" is *la petite mort*, the little death. I don't speak French. Someone who does told me this.

When I was ten, Sean found a dog behind the Scobee, so he brought her home. He named her Snoopy, not the most original name, but *It's the Great Pumpkin, Charlie Brown* had just aired, and Sean was Snoopy crazed. That little dog quickly became the center of attention, not just in our house but in our lives.

Snoopy had power in our family. She was loved beyond reason, except there *was* a reason. It was safe for us to love this silly little dog. We could hug her, kiss her on the nose, talk baby talk to her, and spoil her rotten. In other words, all the affection we dared not show each other we showered on Snoopy. The dog became the conduit for our love; she was the intermediary that allowed us to express tenderness without embarrassment or, worse, rejection. When Snoopy died, we grieved terribly, even Dad, who, on his own, took a spade and Snoopy's favorite toy, a little chewed-up stuffed penguin, and buried the two of them together in the backyard. There were no more family pets after Snoopy. The McKennas hardened.

Some things stay with you. When Pappy Boyle died, Mom and Dad hugged by the telephone, the receiver still in my mother's hand—a forever memory, the only time I remember seeing my parents embrace. I don't write poetry. I don't read it. I'm too literal for poetry. I don't even like poetry unless it's sung by Frank Sinatra, but one night while drinking alone, I wrote this:

> *The phone rang early today, and my mother cried.*
> *The news is bad, her father has died.*
> *As a child I watched as her world crumbled.*
> *Mom's tears didn't flow, they literally tumbled*
> *onto my father's shoulder as he held her*
> *and hugged her and said, "It's alright."*
> *For me, just a child, a terrifying sight.*
> *It took death to bring them together.*
> *It took death to draw them close.*

Would I have to die as well, since I love them both?
Pappy is dead, and mother is sad. I am confused

and, truthfully, mad.

Why is love easy when you are dead?
Why is love then so easily said?

Before I can invent any of a thousand additional suicide scenarios, the maître d' taps me on the shoulder and requests I leave the Oak Room because I am sans jacket. "It's our policy," he says. I show him my room key as if it were a police badge.

"Beck's, please," I say to the bartender.

"Why don't you take your key and go to your room?" says the maître d'.

"Why don't you go fuck yourself?" I reply.

"Okay, out!" he says, pointing to the exit door to the street.

All heads swivel in my direction. *The Lion King* dad looks right at me. We lock eyes, and now he is the center of my fury, because he's violated one of life's prime directives: Never make eye contact with the crazy person.

"What are you looking at?" I yell, as club sandwiches freeze in midair like in one of those old E.F. Hutton TV commercials. The Oak Room is suddenly populated with mannequins. Chicken Caesars dangle from forks as I rush to the gawker's table, sticking my face inches from his. He flinches, recoiling into his chair.

"Didn't your mother teach you it's rude to stare?"

"I wasn't looking," he says, terrified.

I love that I scare him. Weakling! Jellyfish! I have humiliated him in front of his wife, and, better yet, in front of his daughters. No child wants to remember their father as a coward. I will ruin this man who dares judge me.

I can't stop myself. The crazy tumbles out of me like boulders in an avalanche, propelled by Newton's First Law and a millennium of inertia suddenly unsprung. What have I become? Or is this who I've always been?

"Sir, please, be quiet!" shouts the maître d'.

"Apologize!" I yell, pounding the table for effect, which bounces a peppermill to the floor. The bartender picks up a house phone.

"Todd, apologize," says Todd's wife. The two little girls burst into tears and hide behind napkins, which is fantastic!

"Apologize, Todd!" I shout, now armed with his name, which makes my attack even more personal. Like a great ham actor, I throw my voice across the room. "Ladies and gentleman of the Oak Room, Todd has something he'd like to say to you!" But before Todd can speak, a security guard approaches.

"Is there a problem, sir?"

"There was a problem, but Todd's gonna make it right. Aren't you, Todd?"

"Sir, let's talk about this outside," says a second guard, joining the scrum.

"I prefer to talk about it *inside*."

But they have heard enough. The square badges each take an elbow and shove me through the revolving door, spitting me onto the sidewalk where the goons are less polite.

We exchange a volley of expletives, and I make the obligatory, feckless threat of reporting them to their superiors. They aren't impressed by my room key, and one suggests where I can stick it, while the other one goes to get a real cop. That's my cue to back down. There's no point fighting a battle I'm guaranteed to lose, especially with a stocked minibar waiting for me upstairs. I apologize for causing trouble and explain I just buried my father, further degrading myself by using Dad's death as an alibi for asshole behavior. But it works. He softens a bit, and I promise if I am let back in, I'll go directly to my room and bed down for the night. We strike a compromise: I can go to my suite, with an escort, but I am banned from the Oak Room for the duration of my stay.

Inside, the maître d' is busy apologizing to Todd, his wife, and daughters. Their meals will be comped. I nod to Todd as I'm led by. He doesn't thank me for the free meal or the story he'll tell for the rest of his life, recasting himself in a heroic light.

It's time to see what $965 gets you at the Plaza.

Each of the hotel's gilded elevators is topped with a clock set to a different foreign capital: London, Paris, Tokyo, etc. I wait for a car with a cluster of guests returning from their day on the town. My security escort waits with me. We do not speak. A middle-aged woman loaded down with shopping bags stands with a businessman in a designer suit and wristwatch that cost more than my car. A bellhop joins us, the same island bellhop I had rebuffed earlier. He shoves the shiny brass-plated luggage cart into the Tokyo elevator. I let the other guests go ahead of me. What I lack in hygiene, I make up for in manners. The security goon gives me a little tap to get in, then follows. It is uncomfortably crowded. I stand with my back to the door, looking directly at the other guests. My appearance confuses them. I look too much like the panhandlers who had been hassling them a few minutes ago in Central Park. A father and mother, both tanned, beautiful, fit, and under forty, stand in color-coordinated outfits as one of their two young boys starts pushing the elevator buttons.

"Don't do that, Trevor," says the mom.

These boys are also beautiful. That's the only word for them, *beautiful*. This is not an adjective I'm in the habit of applying to children. As a rule, children are invisible to me. But these two, dressed in matching Lakers pullovers, are blissfully, prepubescently unaware of exactly how stunning they are and all the opportunities genetics and their father's W-2 will afford them. The elevator stops four times, and people get off, including the beautiful Californians. By the time we reach the eleventh floor, it's just me and the guard. He leads me through a labyrinth of hallways to suite 1100, right where it should be for this kind of money, on the corner, with a panoramic view of the park.

I offer the goon a dollar tip. I mean it to be an insult, but a dollar is a dollar. He pockets it. I close the door and throw the bolt and watch through the peephole as he retreats down the hallway, reporting to someone on his radio.

Magnificent! The sitting room is luxurious with a fully stocked wet bar I will do my best to unstock. The bathroom is bigger than the kitchen at my place in Somerville, and the bedroom looks like the bedroom in Thomas Rowlandson's pornographic engraving *The Larking Cull*, which I once saw in an illustrated edition of *Fanny Hill*. Flowing green drapery cascades from the ceiling to the thickly carpeted floor. Throws and cozies of every shape and size are placed on settees and armchairs and loungers. I wish I could show off these rooms to someone. I think about all my old friends from high school and college and those early jobs before I fled to Somerville. Maybe I can call Dougherty or Finnigan; they still live in the city. I want to brag to my pals like a kid on Christmas morning who can't wait to rub his fabulous new toy in his friends' faces. But I haven't seen Dougherty or Finnigan in years. They're married and fathers, and why would they care? Josh is still single, but he's out in LA. I consider calling him anyway, the way people used to call from airplanes to tell their kids they're calling from airplanes. I don't call anyone. Tomorrow some other fool with 965 bucks to blow will be standing where I now stand. There is no glory in spending.

I pop the cap off a four-dollar bottle of Heineken and strip down for a shower. It's a little stuffy, suite or no suite, so I throw open a window. Surprisingly, the Plaza's windows open wide enough to go out, an amenity for those inclined to take a leap, which I am. This is a good jumping window. I can't believe the hotel's insurance carrier allows this. These thoughts run through my head while I stand naked in front of the window. The warm spring air washes over my body. It feels nearly as good as a shower, and for a second, I consider not taking one.

From my perch above Central Park, I see tourists waiting for their hansom rides with their children laughing every time a horse craps out a load. They snap photos of each other with the famous Plaza as a backdrop, unaware of the tiny penis they'll find in their prints when they get back to Boise or Oslo or wherever they live. Let them see my dick, I say, giving it a little shake, hoping to fluff it up enough so it will be clearly visible in their vacation photos. We enter the world naked; it seems right to leave it that way. But I don't jump.

I stand at the window a long time, waiting for someone to notice my nakedness but give up when there is a knock at the door. I put on a robe and accept a fruit basket, compliments of the hotel management. Is this sarcasm? Or is Ashaki trying to make amends? Then it dawns on me, the fruit baskets are sent pro forma to anyone crazy enough to book one of these ridiculously expensive suites. This ruins the gesture. I climb into the bathtub and turn on the shower full blast. I scrub myself red, removing the stink of booze and smokes and blood from my skin and hair.

I dry myself with all the towels, intentionally tossing them on the bathroom floor, where they pile up like drifts of snow. I powder myself with talc, spray myself with deodorant, then brush my teeth with a hotel toothbrush for five full minutes, using some generic brand of paste that tastes like gum. I celebrate each of these mundane tasks because this is the last time I will perform them, and the last of anything is special.

My clothes are a problem. I have nothing clean to wear. I jettison my stinky socks and underwear, going commando. I am truly sorry I hadn't grabbed that cheap blue suit I bought for Dad's funeral. They'll bury me in it now. It'll never fit Al, and what would Kevin do with a suit? Sean, maybe.

I pop open another Heinie as I comb my hair, a minor obsession, and step back to examine myself in one of the many mirrors pinging my reflection all over the bathroom. Versailles with a toilet. I look good. Not good, but better. The gash on my forehead has stopped bleeding. My eyes are still a little glassy, and my shirt and pants are trashed, but the shower has worked the miracle that showers always perform. I am now delightfully sloshed, like William Powell in *The Thin Man* movies. The shower and mirrors and towels and alcohol have made me believe I'm both witty and charming. I have regained my confidence. I am ready for a girl.

The telephone directory lists hundreds of escort services with names like Malibu Blondes Plus, Private Joy, Abby's Live Playmates, and Sophisticated Lady. Their suggestive ads offer "dinner companions," "theater dates," and multilingual "tour guides," preposterous euphemisms for hookers. I choose only the ads that are accompanied by photos. I know these are stock pictures, still, no picture, no call from me. Platinum Entertainment features a trio of vixens, a blonde, a brunette, and an Asian. I dial.

Vic, the hooker dispatcher, promises he can have a raven-haired goddess named Tiffany at my door in fifteen minutes. I pass because there are no goddesses named Tiffany, and tonight I require a goddess. I call half a dozen agencies and pass on them as well. I find a new reason to reject each one, yet every call causes a rush, the potential of someone fantastic to spend my last night on earth with. I'm hard. I'm ready. But finally, I have to acknowledge I don't want to spend this night with a rented lover.

I need air. I grab my smokes and my lighter. I don't bother closing the door as I retrace my steps to the elevators. In the lobby, I check to see if the coast is clear and make a quick exit.

9

New York, New York

Out on the street, I think about taking yet another cab but don't have a destination in mind, so I walk until I can think of one. You never know what might happen when you walk. I make my way to Seventh Avenue and then, out of habit, south toward Times Square.

I worked briefly, but memorably, in Times Square. This was right after I finished my master's and needed dough while filling out applications for doctoral programs. Through a friend of a friend, I got a freelance job at an ad agency writing copy for a glue company, "Beno-Beta for Better Bonds." This was at a tiny agency, a father-son partnership, and they were crazy. Really crazy.

In the early 1980s, Times Square was still a filthy, lurid cacophony of peep shows, live sex acts, and triple-X theaters with remarkably graphic posters in the windows and single-entendre titles on the marquees. *Young Nympho* on a double bill with *Intrasexum*. Across the street they were playing *Sweet Cakes*, *Naked Are the Cheaters*, and *The Senator's Daughter* with Leslie Bovee. *Taboo II* was the big draw, starring Kay Parker and Dorothy LeMay. The House of Paradise offered a hot-rock sauna, steam room, "five lovely hostesses," and, as an added inducement, air-conditioning, which, I imagine, was a nice amenity after half an hour in a sauna with a skank.

One joint on the top floor of an ancient brownstone went by the name The Sensitive Meeting Place and offered "real sizzlers." In the basement of a hotel on Madison—not really the Theater District but not far away—A Quiet Little Table in the Corner provided just that, dinner in a darkened alcove screened by beaded curtains. It was a popular place for waitresses, because their customer's hands were already occupied. Times Square still had a live burlesque show, *The Follies Burlesk*, directly above another relic, the Howard Johnson's that opened in 1955 just as *Guys and Dolls* was closing. Walking through Times Square was like going on a sin safari. It was a fabulous place, especially at night, when a stroll down Broadway was like being inside Kafka's brain, if Kafka happened to be reading Damon Runyon at the time.

Times Square is going through its own metamorphosis, with corporate America moving in. Storefront by storefront, the peep shows and gray-market electronics shops are being squeezed out. National brands have replaced the XXX titles; Gap, Jordache, Swatch, Burger King, Arby's, and United Colors of Benetton have taken over—a different sort of public indecency. Times Square is cleaner, safer, family friendly, Disneyfied, a *Stepford Wife* version of what I grew up with. Yes, Father Duffy and George M. Cohan still have pigeons sitting and shitting on their heads, and if you look carefully, you can still find the occasional pimp and working girl or boy, but you really have to want to find them. Giuliani and the moneymen have shoved the hookers west, all the way to 11th Avenue, where the tourists are warned not to go. I don't like it.

I keep walking west, to 10th Avenue, past the Port Authority Bus Terminal and the last bastion of old Times Square squalor, a few straggling peep parlors and jack shacks, the Alamo of porn. They hold no interest, and I pass them as if they're already gone. On this night of all nights, I crave a real experience, one of those meetings that occasionally happen in our lives, mostly when we're young and beautiful and the odds are in our favor.

I remember once walking on the East Side and meeting a girl, although "meeting" hardly describes what happened.

It was late, 2:00 or 3:00 a.m., and she was wearing leopard-print tights, on her way home from who knows what. As I passed her, she reached out and took my hand. She just grabbed my hand. Who does that? I went where she led me, to her place, and spent an hour loving her on a bare floor, worried more about splinters than birth control or STDs or AIDS, which hadn't become a thing yet. We barely spoke, and I left immediately at her request. A sex miracle!

Tonight I need a similar miracle. I need to feel another human's beating heart like I did that night long ago. I want to feel the touch of another person's skin, to feel her hands rub on my neck and shoulders and tear into my chest reflexively. She must need me as much as I need her. Where can I find that woman?

In the movies, here's where they'd put the montage—a series of quick scenes set to a pop tune: me wandering the streets, a lonely man in the loneliest place on earth, a crowd that doesn't care. You'd see me go aimlessly down into the subway, then back up onto the street. Me eating a pushcart hotdog, settling for Sabretts when I promised myself New York prime. I watch a vendor as he thumps rock-hard pretzels on the side of his cart. These are end-of-shift pretzels. The vendor dips his fingers into the gutter and spritzes his stale pretzels like a priest splashing holy water, hoping to soften them up. I buy one anyway and nearly chip a tooth.

As the montage continues, you'd see me walk three full blocks just to watch the cheeks of a young woman's perfectly shaped ass undulate with every step she takes. A tall redhead, incandescent in her sensuality, she walks like a ballad. I follow her at a distance, so she won't be frightened or whistle for the cops with one of those steel whistles women keep on their key rings, or pepper spray me, or hit me with the business-end of her heel. I can't let any of this happen, so I follow her carefully, hoping she is as lonely as I am. I wait for her to turn and catch my eye and invite me upstairs to her expensive, elegantly furnished love nest subsidized by a contemptible sugar daddy who has no idea how much she hates him. But Red turns instead into a corner market and buys a bag of plums from a Chinese fruit vendor, then sweeps past her doorman. She will never know how much she means to me.

A posse of young Black men bop toward me. Instinctively, I switch to the other side of the street. They ignore the slight, numbed by generations of worse slights. There are five of them, walking in sync with a pounding percussive beat roaring from a shoulder-borne boom box. Clad in color-coordinated tracksuits and obligatory bling, their heads undulate forward and back like giant pigeons, their bodies rhythmically fluid in a way a man as terminally Caucasian as I can only dream of. It's a full-blown cardio workout. Being young and Black must be exhausting.

This montage needs trimming, yet it continues.

I walk more, turning corners until I see P.J. Clarke's across Third Avenue. This surprises me because I hadn't realized I was so far east, but that's where I am. Clarke's is a legendary watering hole dating back to 1884. Billy Wilder shot *Lost Weekend* here. It's an excellent place to rest my feet and mull things over, even if mulling is maudlin, but what montage isn't? I jog across Third, dodging a FedEx truck barreling ahead to beat the light. Kimberly might get that insurance yet.

I order a black and tan and play with the foam while listening to "All or Nothing at All" on the jukebox. Frank Sinatra drank here with Jimmy Cannon and Pete Hamill, a washed-up prizefighter, Jan Murray, and a couple of broads. The name Clarke might be Irish, the bartenders might be Irish, but the music is Italian. Sinatra, Bennett, Martin, Martino, Como, Darin, Vale, and Damone . . . *bel canto* is in their blood.

I throw back the pint and leave an unmerited tip, since the bartenders at Clarke's are notoriously sullen, having transplanted feuds from the Old World to the New. The big bushy-browed mick and his beet-faced nemesis pour their drafts and shake their cocktails in stony silence, squeezing past each other as if they'll catch poison oak should they touch. Theirs is an endless stubborn pantomime, now in its second decade. I won't find her here. Not at P.J. Clarke's.

The search continues at the other P.J.'s: P.J. Carney's on Third and 38th and, as long as I'm in the neighborhood, Cleary's on 39th, but the girl I'm looking for isn't in either place; only a few old men drinking alone and a married couple silently eating fish and chips, the husband's eyes on a soccer game playing simultaneously on four TVs. I drop down to 23rd Street and have a pop at the Glocca Morra Pub, then up to Donahue's on Second and 48th. I stop in to Eamonn Doran's, which is only a few blocks away, mostly because of Uncle Eamon, despite the superfluous second "n."

I zigzag my way back to the westside, stopping at Tommy Markem's on Park Avenue and then Rusty Staub's on Fifth because everybody loves Mets legend Rusty Staub, even Yankees fans. It's a sports crowd, and women are in short supply. Still, I linger because sometimes the least likely place is where you'll strike gold.

Laughter bellows from a corner table, three young men burning the candle after work, like I did, like we all did when we were twenty-four and had our whole lives in front of us. They have yet to sprout the bellies they will carry into the future, when it's their turn to run the world, until another generation comes along and kicks them to the curb. I ask the bartender for an ice water. He gives me a look. I flip him a five, and he pours me a glass. The water goes down easy after all those beers. I tap my glass for a refill.

"Another pitcher?" shouts one of the young men.

"Fuck yeah!" shout the others.

And they laugh raucously as only the young can. She isn't at Rusty Staub's. Neither is Rusty.

She isn't at McAnn's in the bowels of Penn Station, and I would have been shocked if she had been. McAnn's is a commuter bar with drinkers packed three deep at rush hour, but at this hour the place is deserted. I have a shot and a beer out of habit and move on to Quinn's, Flanagan's, and Murphy's. I take on fresh liquor at each stop to keep the machine running. It's getting late. Where is she? Below 34th Street the bars thin out, so I buy a can of beer at a deli and continue south toward Greenwich Village, where they hand out liquor licenses like parking tickets. I drink as I walk and throw coins at a brace of bums pissing in the doorway of a shuttered custom-shutter shop. Watching them piss reminds me how badly I have to piss, so I join them.

I pass through Mulberry Street, which seems to be perpetually preparing for, or recovering from, the San Gennaro Festival. An elegant silver-haired gentleman walks in my direction. His leather loafers click on the sidewalk like tap shoes; his white linen shirt is open to the fifth button framing his silver chest hair. It's a little chilly for that, but he's Italian and can't help himself. Then I notice Signore is wearing a pale blue lace bra. He smiles as we pass.

I ask for a draft beer at McSorley's, where you can only get draft beer. McSorley's is way downtown, Seventh Street on the Lower East Side, off my beaten path. I have been here before, because sooner or later every mick ends up at McSorley's Old Ale House.

"We were here before you were born," says the sign. Established in 1854, McSorley's has been immortalized on canvas, song, and in words by Joseph Mitchell who described the place as well as language can. I've come to McSorley's because I had a good time here once, and maybe lightning will strike again. Of course, addicts are always chasing the one good time. Sadly, and that is the exact word, it's more depressing than I remembered. I would leave after I finish my beer if it weren't for the woman sitting alone at the table near the door. She's kicked her shoes off, and her bare feet rest on an empty chair. She is lost in thought. I sip and stare at her, trying to interpret her mood.

It's unusual to find a woman at McSorley's. This is a man's bar, literally until 1969, when an activist/attorney, Faith Seidenberg, walked through the door with her friend Karen DeCrow. Bells were rung, and the all-male clientele clapped and stomped their feet while the waiters and barkeeps whooped and whistled. But the fun stopped as soon as Seidenberg and DeCrow asked to be served. They were quickly escorted off the premises and promptly filed a lawsuit, which had been their objective from the start. In *Seidenberg v. McSorley's Old Ale House*, the courts ruled in the gals' favor, and women have been drinking with the men at McSorley's ever since.

In tiny numbers.

The first ladies' restroom wasn't installed until 1986. Old habits die hard. This is what makes the barefoot woman with the sad face sitting alone by the door noteworthy. And there's something else about her.

She is Black. African American. A woman of color. A Black woman here is about as welcome as a Black man everywhere else. In some ways, it's still 1854 at McSorley's. *It's her*, I tell myself. This is the woman I've been looking for. I wait patiently to see if she invites me to join her. She doesn't. Instead, she smokes and stares into the middle distance. I go to her. I ask her name, and she tells me, angrily, as if she has already told me eighty times. "Jane." Just plain old Jane with no fancy-assed Black spelling. "J. A. N. E.," she says, sounding out each letter as if she were talking to an imbecile. I sit down without being invited, which isn't uncommon at McSorley's because seats are at a premium. However, at this hour, on this night, there are plenty of empty chairs, and Jane has every right to feel her space invaded. "What do you want?" she snaps.

The shock of her hostility sends me back onto my feet, and I mumble an apology. As I move away, she calls me back and tells me to buy her a beer. I buy two beers and she doesn't object when I sit the second time.

"What happened to you?" she asks.

"It's a long story," I say, touching the wound on my forehead.

"Don't tell me. I don't care."

Jane is neither pretty nor ugly. Striking. The more I look at her, the more adjectives I audition, finally settling on "Olympian," muscular, as if she'd been chiseled from obsidian. Jane is more powerful than I am. I feel it. She's exotic and dangerous, with high cheekbones and manly features. For a second, I worry she is a man, but when she turns her head back into the light, her face softens, and she's fantastic. I talk my head off trying to make an impression.

I tell her about the famous McSorley's wishbone wire stretched over the bar festooned with old turkey bones lined shoulder to shoulder and crowned with two inches of dust. I explain how they were put there by soldiers on their way to fight in World War I. They were talismans to be reclaimed when they returned home. "Every wishbone represents a soldier or sailor who didn't make it back."

Who talks like this? Am I trying to get laid or tenure?

But I talk away, until she tells me to buy her another beer. I get her one and another for myself. After a few silent sips she asks my name.

"Danny."

"Do you want to fuck me, Danny?"

"Yes," I say, relieved I can finally shut up.

Jane is offended when I ask, "How much?" But she doesn't tell me to leave or leave herself, and she doesn't name a price. Now I'm positive she's the woman I've been looking for.

She sticks another cigarette in her mouth. I light it for her, but she doesn't notice and tries to light it a second time with a match. Without saying a word, she gets up and exits the bar, leaving her shoes under the table. She doesn't say "good night" or "goodbye" or "fuck off," so, unbidden, I grab her shoes and follow. I offer her the shoes, but she continues barefoot. We go to an old brick building jammed between all the other old brick buildings. I stop twice for air as we make the climb up the steep, crooked stairs that are more like a ladder. I make a crack about putting in a chairlift, but Jane has never been on skis, and my joke is taken as a complaint. "Leave if you don't like it," she says.

Hers is a poor person's flat, a small apartment, a quarter of what was once a large apartment. It needs paint and plaster and roach traps, and the bathroom door doesn't close properly, even if Jane had made the effort, which she has not. I put her shoes on the floor.

Jane pulls off her shirt and drops her pants. She sits naked on the toilet, releasing a jet of pee while I stand dumbly watching. Is this meant to be seduction? Is Jane an exhibitionist? Is it some sort of power play? Lyndon Johnson famously made senators and generals meet with him while he grunted away on the toilet. If she means to rattle me, she has succeeded. Still, she pees for so long with so little inhibition I finally turn away and check the fridge for something else to drink. I find a single bottle of Grolsch, that ridiculous Dutch beer with the ceramic stopper. I sit on the couch and sip while she flushes.

She seems even bigger in this small space. She has small firm breasts that barely move when she moves. These are natural breasts, unevenly shaped, unlike my wife's, which are factory symmetrical. Her left nipple is pierced with a sterling silver hoop the size of a quarter. Jane's buttocks are also solid, high riding and hard. Her waist, tapered and defined, ripples above a neatly shaved diamond patch of pubic hair over her privates, which are now public. The apartment window is curtainless and wide open. I can see into the apartments in the next building as clearly as they can see Jane push me back on the couch and move between my legs and kick my knees apart before dropping to her knees.

"Fuck me," she says, and I quickly undo my belt.

"Call me bitch! Call me cumster! Street squish, cuntwhore!" she says, not begging, demanding. Ordering. And I do. Then she asks for a word that's hard for me. It's distasteful. But she wants it. It's her thing. I oblige with that one and every foul word I've ever heard on a playground, at a Mets game, at the Little Neck Inn, or from my brother Kevin's mouth. I unleashed a volley of vile invective that would make David Mamet blush. I call her every filthy name at my command, and with each insult she moans louder and thrusts harder until I exhaust my lexicon of degradation.

I am spent, and Jane wants me to leave, although she is suddenly too polite to say so, the first hint of weakness she has shown. I wash my face in the kitchen sink and pull on my pants, gingerly zipping up as Jane sits naked in the window, blowing smoke from her Salem toward the neighbors who have collected in their windows to watch the show. As I button the last button on my shirt, Jane tells me to take a bag of trash on my way out. She doesn't turn to speak; she simply points to a plastic sack hanging from the doorknob as she continues gazing into space, her eyes aimed above the rooftops of the adjoining buildings.

I stall, hoping I can find something appropriate to say. "Thanks? You were great?" What I want to say is, "Now I can die," but that's not her business. Instead, I unhook the trash bag and leave without saying anything.

I'm on the street before I realize I've forgotten to toss Jane's garbage down the chute. I consider dumping it in the gutter with all the other trash, but there's a can on the corner and that's the direction I'm headed. The can is overflowing with KFC boxes and copies of the *Post, Daily News,* and some communist rag they give away. The headlines still feature Sinatra stories; even the Reds have a piece about

Frank's upcoming funeral. The world wants to know who's going and who's been snubbed. I swing the trash bag and let it fly toward the garbage can like a smelly hammer toss, but the bag rips apart in flight, spraying rubbish everywhere. Coffee grinds, orange peels, broken hair clips, and a condom wrapper splat on the sidewalk.

"Pick that shit up, asshole! screams a tiny Asian woman as she shakes her broom at me from the stoop of her building.

"Goddamn city that never sleeps!" I mutter as I kneel on the sidewalk and scoop up the mess I've made.

I pull the top of an Adidas box out of the garbage can and use it as a shovel, raking Jane's crap back into the bag. I see something shiny and fish with my fingers through the coffee grinds, searching for the glint of gold: a locket, plated, not solid, on a short choker chain. Jane's locket? I fumble with the latch; I can never open these things and nearly smash it on the ground in frustration before it pops open in my fingers. There's a tiny black-and-white photograph, maybe taken in one of those booths they have at Coney Island, a smiling Jane, her face not at all manly, with a little boy sitting on her lap. Her little boy? Yes. That's a mother's smile.

Jane will go crazy looking for this. She'll tear her place apart never knowing her precious locket went out with her one-night stand and the coffee grinds and used rubbers—not ours, either, because we hadn't bothered with condoms. I start back up the Matterhorn of stairs as the angry Asian woman returns to her obsessive late-night sweeping.

Jane won't be happy to see me at her door. I collect my breath on the second-floor landing. Too many smokes. A mouse skitters up a pipe. Maybe when I give her the locket, Jane will say something kind. Maybe she'll thank me. That will make dying so much easier. Up the last of the stairs I go.

I tap on the door and then tap louder. Is she asleep? She only had a few beers. She didn't seem drunk enough to pass out. Maybe she's afraid, like any sensible woman would be. Jesus, it's nearly three. I'm gonna wake the building.

I jiggle the knob, and the door swings open. Hadn't it locked behind me? "Jane?" I say softly, as I poke my head in. I call her name again, and that's when I see her on the kitchen floor, a long knife, ridiculously long, a serrated knife, the kind you use to cut a loaf of garlic bread, sticks straight out of her abdomen.

"Oh, my God!" I scream.

I turn away, unable to look. I think about running down the stairs and away from this horrible place, but I can't move, as if my sneakers have been nailed to the floor. I have no idea what to do.

"Where's the fucking phone?" I say, searching helter-skelter. There is no phone. "You don't have a phone?" I yell angrily at Jane as she continues to bleed out on the floor. I run to her.

Her eyes are glassy, dead eyes, like the eyes on a statue or a *Little Orphan Annie* comic. And there are other wounds—in her side, her thighs, and in both breasts, a horrible mutilation, the knife worked around her extremities until she made the final thrust through her own belly.

I puke up Beck's and Heineken and Grolsch and all those watery draft beers from Third Avenue and McAnn's and McSorley's and everyplace else I've been tonight, all the way back to the first warm bottle of Miller's I drank at the Little Neck Inn. Up comes the Plaza Hotel mint, the pushcart hot dog, and the granite street pretzel softened by gutter water. Vomit splashes on the floor next to Jane, onto Jane even, then trickles down my chin and all over the shirt I have so carefully buttoned after fucking this poor girl.

"Oh, my God!" I scream. "Oh, my God!"

I do all the things I've seen on TV shows. I feel her wrist without knowing what I'm feeling for. A pulse? What's a strong pulse? I can't feel her heartbeat because mine is jumping out of my chest. I call to her, speak her name but hear only gurgles in reply. Horrible, dripping, bubbling noises come from her open mouth and also from the wound in her stomach, which pumps fresh blood onto the cracked linoleum with convulsive spasms. She is alive, barely, and I hold her hand as I yell for help. Jane Last-Name-Unknown's life is leaking away onto the floor in an ever-expanding crimson pool. I will not let her die alone. "I'm here, Jane. I'm here."

A barefoot neighbor still tying her bathrobe pokes her head in the door, just far enough to see. She screams a horror-movie scream that carries down the hall and wakes everyone on Earth. I scream back at her.

"Call 911!"

But she just runs off yelling to no purpose other than to attract more neighbors, who add their screams to the mix. Jane's lips quiver. I bring my head down close to hers, tilting my ear up against her mouth. "What?" I ask. "What, Jane?" Her tongue moistens her lips.

"What have you done to me, and why?"

"What?"

"What have you done to me, and why?" she repeats.

Is she hallucinating from blood loss? Am I hallucinating? Is Jane accusing me? With her cloudy, dying eyes, does Jane even know who she's speaking to? What if one of those screaming neighbors comes in and she says it again? They'll think I did this. So I begin to pray for Jane to die.

"In the name of the Father, and of the Son, and of the Holy Spirit. Please, God, take her this instant!"

That's when a large bare-chested African American man barges through the bevy of keening neighbor women. He sees me on my knees leaning over Jane's body, her blood staining my puke-covered shirt. I look up at him and watch the wheels spinning behind his eyes. He grabs me by the collar with both hands and slams me sideways into the kitchen counter, hard enough to pop open a cabinet door. He hoists me by the back of my belt and shoves me into the open cabinet under the sink, smacking my head again and again against the U-shaped elbow pipe as I bowl over green cylinders of Comet and crusty sponges and Brillo pads and a toilet-bowl brush. Plaza Hotel mints fly out of my pockets and roll across the kitchen floor. I check to make sure they're not my teeth.

"I'm gonna kill you, you mothafucker!" he yells with a slight lisp, as he kicks me deeper into the cabinet.

"Stop!" I shout.

He's going to beat me to death. This is how I'm going to die. Murdered was not how I thought I'd go. None of this is how I want things to be. I pull up my knees to deflect his blows, screaming my innocence and begging some Good Samaritan to call an ambulance because I know it will sound good in court and because I will soon need one myself. Then, suddenly, my luck improves. One of the women from the hallway screws up her courage and enters the apartment. "The po-lice is coming," she says. The shirtless man backs off and turns his attention to Jane.

He kneels next to her and listens for the sound of her breath. Jane obliges with one long exhale, her very last. *Thank you, God!* I think but don't dare say. Now I am the sole custodian of her final words, and they will die with me. From under the kitchen sink I peek out and watch as Jane's bowels relax and her fluids spill onto the floor mixing with her blood and my tears. I am repulsed by what I see next, my semen, dripping from her dead vagina. *La petite mort.* The giant sees it too.

He grabs my ankles and rips me out from under the sink, fully intent on bludgeoning me. Then, we both hear cops coming up the stairs, clumping step by step with their equipment belts jingling and radios squawking.

"You're fuckin' lucky," says the giant.

I think fast, constructing the story I know I'll have to tell again and again. The shirtless giant believes I have murdered Jane; so do the screaming women in the hall. The cops will think I raped and killed her. The angry Asian woman will ID me and say how she saw me come out of Jane's building and then go back in. She'll tell them she saw me litter. The neighbors in the next building will say they watched me fuck her, but they'll claim it was by accident and not with their dicks in their hands. Everyone believes I killed her. Who would believe anything else? Could someone else have come in and stabbed her during the brief time it took me to go downstairs and come back with her locket?

The locket! It's still in my pocket.
My fingerprints are all over it.
But they're not on the knife! Or are they? Did I ever touch it?
I don't think so.
Remember, Danny! Remember!
Did I brush up against the knife? Think!
No, no I did not. I never touched the knife.

Each of these thoughts comes one by one, like bullet points. I construct my alibi working backward from the accusations I know will be leveled against me: opportunity, motive, DNA, timeline, all the *NYPD Blue* clichés and legal mumbo jumbo I have picked up watching a lifetime of television and every second of the O.J. trial. I play lawyer in my head, arguing my own case, telling the jury about the locket in the bag of trash, the unlocked door, and the mystery man who slipped in after I had left Jane smoking in the window, very much alive. Then I get a crazy idea. Why not tell them the truth? Jane is the killer. Jane murdered herself.

I know she took her own life because I saw her sitting naked in the window blowing smoke up to the stars. I know because I saw the lost look on her face as she sat alone at McSorley's. It was that look that drew me to her. I know Jane killed herself because I watched her orgasm on the sofa and again on the floor, joyless sex scored by a shower of verbal abuse. Joyless for both of us, a mutual degradation. I know Jane killed herself, because when I looked into her eyes, they mirrored my own. She had planned to die tonight, too, only she actually did, proving she was the stronger one after all. It's terrible!

Jane's death has changed me. All my indulgent years of self-pity and flirtation with theoretical suicide have been vaporized by the gruesome, repulsive reality of her self-destruction. I am ashamed. How could I ever have considered death as an alternative to life? I must do penance for all my selfish years. Jane's death is an epiphany, and those are rare. I cannot waste this.

I will live now. I must live as long as I can, as long as my father. As long as Frank Sinatra. Longer. Jane Doe's spectacular self-immolation has saved me. She died for my sins. Jane is my Christ.

I decide I will tell the truth. Tell them everything: the end of my marriage, my bender after two years of white-knuckle sobriety, the fistfight on the altar at St. Anastasia, the old spitting veteran, the long night of walking and drinking, looking for a woman who turned out to be Jane.

The cops handcuff me. They do it roughly, shoving me around and clamping on the shackles so tight they break the skin. This pleases the women in the hallway and the shirtless giant who is still busy convicting me until a detective finally tells him to wait his turn. A team of sweat-soaked paramedics enter after humping a gurney up five flights. They hate these old elevator-less buildings almost as much as they hate me.

I walk the cops through the sequence of events that led to this tragedy. I emphasize "tragedy," not crime, not rape, certainly not murder. I do it coherently, without a trace of drunkenness. My composure is impressive. Maybe too impressive. Should I break down? No, I'm not an actor. Clear-headedness is what this calls for. And sincerity, which I do not have to fake. The senior detective turns his attention to the shirtless man and begins taking his statement as a young cop and a junior detective lead me out of the apartment. The neighbors yell expletives as we descend the stairs. Their rage follows as an echo.

A small crowd has gathered on the street despite the predawn hour. They cheer and boo as the cops stuff me into the backseat of an unmarked car, a Crown Victoria, just like the cab that had brought me to the Plaza. But this car has no ticking meter or friendly celebrity voice telling me to "buckle up for safety," and no singing Rasta driver.

A photographer from the *Daily News* hops out of a van. His police scanner has tipped him off, but he's too late for the money shot—me in handcuffs, running the gauntlet of furious faces outside the crime scene. He pounds his fist on the trunk of the cop car. I turn my head reflexively, and the camera flash goes off.

In a few hours, my face will make page one of "New York's Picture Newspaper." That paper will land in my mother's driveway. It will be sold at newsstands and coffee shops and be seen on trains and subways and buses everywhere. At last, fame!

I slump deep into the backseat as we speed away, partly from the centrifugal force of the lurching car but mostly from the force of my collapsing world. The photographer continues to fire off shots, worthless snaps capturing only the back of my head. Later, he will talk his way into the crime scene and shoot two rolls of gruesome unpublishable photos of Jane's naked, mutilated body that he will print and add to his personal collection. I just know he will.

10

Nice Work if You Can Get It

Two days after Francis and Catherine were married, Eamon McKenna caught a southbound train to Fort Dix before his long rail ride cross-country to his post in California. Meanwhile, on the Jersey side of the Hudson, Catherine, Pappy, Ma Boyle, and all the Boyle sisters waved farewell to Francis from the pier as he lugged his duffel bag up the gangway of the U.S.S. *Florence Nightingale*. At least they waved to someone they thought was Francis. With all those men in uniforms, it was hard to tell. The sisters bickered until they finally settled on the Francis that Catherine had chosen. "She knows best," said Ma Boyle, which caused Catherine to blush and her sisters to giggle, because Catherine had picked her Francis based on the shape of his ass.

The *Florence Nightingale* was one of the rare warships named for a woman, the only thing feminine about her. She began life as the *Mormacsun*, which sounds like a tribal casino, but was a mash-up of Moore-McCormack, the Bay Area–based cargo company that built her in 1941. At 492 feet, she was far from the biggest ship hauling troops across the ocean, but the need was urgent, and the Navy was quick to draft her into service. On October 8, 1944, she shoved off from Bayonne, New Jersey, passing the Statue of Liberty and Ellis Island, where only fifteen years earlier Francis X. McKenna had disembarked from the German liner *München*. Now, he was one of 2,017 soldiers sailing off to kill Germans.

At the exact moment Catherine's Frank shipped out, Frank Sinatra was rehearsing for his much-anticipated return to the Paramount Theater in New York City, his first time as the headliner.

A young publicist named George Evans paid a handful of girls to faint when Sinatra came on stage. Like tiny pebbles triggering a full-blown avalanche, Evans's shills were soon subsumed in a spontaneous explosion of wartime loneliness and estrogen-induced hysteria the world would not see again until a beautiful White boy from Tupelo, Mississippi, swiveled his hips on TV. "Swoonatra" was born, a mania that swept the country introducing teenagers as a distinct demographic group with their own tastes and economic clout and turning Frankie Sinatra into a cultural phenomenon.

Thirty-five hundred bobby-soxers poured through the turnstiles, utterly ignoring the feature film, *Our Hearts Were Young and Gay*. Instead, they stood on their seats, waving copies of fan magazines plastered with Sinatra's kisser, rhythmically clapping and chanting, "We want Frankie! We want Frankie!" until the film finally ended, and they got Frankie.

When the curtain dropped on the first show, the audience refused to leave. And they wouldn't budge after the second show either. Or the third. The manager took to the stage and begged the girls to go home. They booed and heckled and threw saddle shoes and nail files until he fled to the wings. The fourth show came and went, then the fifth. Rivulets of urine trickled down the theater's aisles as bobby-soxers answered nature's call where they sat, and thousands of furious ticket holders continued to pound on the doors demanding to be let in.

The next day was Columbus Day, a holiday, and the crowds were even wilder. Sinatra was spotted on the sidewalk heading for the stage door. The girls mobbed him. One fan got him by the bow tie and would have snapped his neck if a big Irish flatfoot hadn't broken her grip. Fists and feet flew as cops with batons and shields moved in to break up the crowd. Store windows were smashed. Cars overturned. The newspapers had a field day; editorials warned that the end of civilization was nigh. Stick a fork in America if *this* represents the future! J. Edgar Hoover opened a file on Sinatra for corrupting the morals of America's youth. It was a dream come true for the skinny kid from Hoboken who required more love than normal men.

Was Francis Albert Sinatra a draft dodger?

Why wasn't he on the *Florence Nightingale* with Francis McKenna? Was he a coward like Ray Stankowski believed? That's what the sailors who threw eggs at his giant puss on the Paramount marquee thought. Sinatra's 4-F status followed him for the rest of his life. He was Velcro. Everything stuck to Frank Sinatra, both good and bad.

Early in the morning on the fifteenth day of October 1944, Frank McKenna stretched his legs on deck and watched the sun rise. Instead, he saw something more spectacular: Eagle Island and the mouth of Blacksod Bay, Belmullet, County Mayo, Ireland, a puny eighty-five miles from his mother and sister and the home fields of Castlerea. Yes, Ireland! Francis was gobsmacked. Secrecy had kept him in the dark.

As the convoy forged ahead, rumors picked up. England? Scotland? France itself? Or would Francis McKenna actually find himself back in Eire? When they turned east, splitting the waters between Rathlin and the Mull of Kintyre on the southern tip of Scotland, all doubt vanished. Ireland it was. The *Florence Nightingale* entered Belfast Lough, steaming past the Harland & Wolff shipyards where the *Titanic* was built, and finally landing at the quay nearest the River Lagan. He was home. Sort of. Is a Catholic ever at home in Ulster?

Francis McKenna's unexpected return to Ireland made his someday dream a sudden reality. He dashed off a letter to his mother as soon as he stepped ashore. When his sister, Sioban, read it aloud to Fiona McKenna, the older woman fell to her knees right there in the pigpen and thanked Jesus for bringing her son home to her, although it was actually Adolf Hitler who made their reunion possible.

Leave was out of the question for Francis, so Fiona and Sioban would have to go to him. They arranged for the sheep and pigs to be fed and the cow to be milked while they were away. Fiona baked a loaf of soda bread, her sons' favorite when they were boys. She wrapped the bread in a sweater and put it carefully into her bundle before heading off.

The women walked the forty miles to Enniskillen, passing through the villages of Manorhamilton and Belcoo. They spent a night in each place, lodging with relatives or relatives of neighbors who gave them letters of introduction, guaranteeing hospitality everywhere they went. In Enniskillen, they discovered that fuel rationing had cut the Belfast bus to only three days a week, adding an extra day to their journey. As Fiona and Sioban entered Belfast, a train carrying Francis McKenna left for Cobh on the southernmost tip of Ireland. War giveth and war taketh. Mother and son never saw each other again.

In Cobh, Francis was quickly herded aboard the U.S.S. *T.H. Biss* for the short but dangerous trip to the recently liberated French port of La Havre. Twenty-two hours later, he was on another train, this one covered in aircraft camouflage, with all the windows painted black. The train traveled east, gathering speed and rumors with every click and clack of the tracks. Nobody knew anything. Everyone had an opinion. Eventually even the know-it-alls quieted down, as the swaying cars rocked them to sleep, but for how long nobody remembered.

A sergeant entered the car where Francis slept. "Longuyon! *Viva la France!*" he shouted. "On your feet, jabronis!"

The soldiers stretched and smoked and scratched their balls, then fumbled their way forward through the gates of a barely there compound consisting of a headquarters, mess hall, hospital, officers' club, and shower tent. The rest of the camp was nothing but a sea of green canvas, shelter halves stretched over straw. Private McKenna stowed his gear before making his way to the mess hall with everyone else. He slept well that night. They all did, even the worriers.

Reveille sounded at 6:00 a.m. sharp; thirty minutes later Dugan was back in line for pancakes, powdered eggs, and boiling coffee too hot to hold without gloves. At 7:30 a.m. he was directed toward a long line of deuce-and-a-half trucks. More orders were barked up and down the line: "Twenty-four men per vehicle! Go! Go! Go!"

They formed into columns of two and tramped forward, duffel bags bobbing and swaying from shoulder to shoulder as the heavy packs dug into their backs. Francis McKenna climbed into the first available truck, ducking his head under the canvas canopy before landing on one of the two facing benches.

"Shove over, Dugan," said the GI next to him. Butt cheek by butt cheek, he crabbed deeper into the deuce until he was thigh to thigh with the men on either side of him. Gear clinked and rattled as the men muttered apologies for encroaching upon their neighbors or crushing their toes. Some nearly came to blows. The optimists were grateful for the proximity, their collective body heat tempering the cutting winds from the north. These were no summer soldiers. After what seemed an eternity, the truck engines fired up in unison, and they jerked ahead, slowly, then even slower as forty drivers worked to establish the spatial relationship that enables a convoy to move as one.

They traveled over rutted, ruined roads through tiny, nameless villages and a dozen stand-alone farms before crossing the border into Belgium. Private McKenna lifted his feet for the tenth time to unstick them from the dark goo on the truck bed. Long sinewy strands stretched from the floor to the soles of his boots. It was congealed blood—the blood of the men who liberated the road they traveled on, the men they were on their way to replace. The living went east; the dead went west.

After six hours of nearly continuous bumping and swaying, the men literally fell out of the trucks when they arrived in Schönberg, a Belgian village ten miles north of St. Vith, just across the border from Germany.

Dugan stomped the circulation back into his feet; they all did, as if a thousand men had suddenly been given a hotfoot. Four sergeants barked commands, and once again they formed columns of two and marched into the replacement depot, "repple depple" in GI slang. That night would be the last for many months that Private McKenna would sleep with a roof over his head.

The next morning, he ate more pancakes and powdered eggs before rushing to fall in on the giant parade ground that would never see a parade.

A lieutenant with clipboard and whistle bellowed names, as soldiers sprinted to the left or right as directed. A skinny kid from Georgia, Travis Lugo, went left when he was told to go right, earning an abuse bath from the lieutenant.

"McKenna, Francis X! B Company!" shouted the same lieutenant, and Francis joined Lugo and a dozen others as a redheaded officer so young he still had his milk teeth—a captain no less—led them to a field behind the latrines. The captain was also a replacement, fresh out of OCS. This was his first command.

"Gather your gear. We ship out at zero eight hundred," said Captain Warton.

And with those words, Francis McKenna was officially welcomed to B Company, 23rd Infantry Regiment, 2nd Division of the 1st Army of the United States of America.

Before enlisting, Captain Walter Warton was stationed at his child-hood home, serving under the command of his mother and father in Pine Bluff, Arkansas, where he slept in a bed with his kid brother, the same bed he had always slept in. Warton was an educated man, having finished high school, and he hoped to advance within the ranks of the *Arkansas Gazette*, where he worked as the Pine Bluff bureau chief. This would have been an impressive title had there been a second employee. Warton diligently corrected the grammar, punctuation, and frequently the facts of stringers to whom he was authorized to pay three dollars a story if their stuff made the paper. Phantom car wrecks and barn fires nobody remembered were frequently called in by reporters who were three bucks shy on their bar tabs. Warton became an expert at sniffing out bullshit, a skill that would serve him well in the army. The new commanding officer of Baker Company was twenty-three years old, five years younger than Dugan.

B Company had fought through Saint-Laurent-sur-Mer, attacked across the Aure River, helped liberate Trévières, and then secured infamous Hill 192, the key German stronghold on the road to Saint-Lô. All this in their first five days after landing at Normandy on D-Day, plus one.

In late July they moved across the Vire with the rest of the 2nd Division to help capture Tinchebray before driving further east into Brittany for the Battle of Brest, a thirty-nine-day bloodbath made bloodier by Hitler's order to fight to the last man. Of the 150 members of B Company who came ashore on June 7, only fifty were left to witness the surrender of Brest on the eighteenth of September. Their C.O. was not among them.

On the final day, Captain Ira Goldschmidt lost both legs and a hand. He had gotten his men onto Omaha Beach intact, then led them out of the hedgerows and through the worst of Brest before a German mortar ended his war. Young Captain Warton had enormous shoes to fill.

At St. Vith, B Company's replacements met up with B Company's veterans. Warton shook hands with his executive officer, First Lieutenant Bryan Suits of Port Angeles, Washington, who got him up to speed on their situation. Francis McKenna fell in with the 1st Platoon, saluting his platoon leader, Second Lieutenant Wade Chase of Vidor, Texas, a good ol' boy who had never heard an Irish brogue and thought a snafu had sent them a British soldier by mistake. It was pulling teeth to get a nod or a name from the other grunts, and Francis soon stopped trying. He went about smoking, rubbing the barrel of his M-1, and lying low until he could figure out what was what.

Captain Warton and the platoon leaders met to go over their maps and then vanished through a forest of fir trees to reconnoiter the position B Company would occupy that night. The field kitchens would not arrive for hours, so the men of the 1st Platoon did what soldiers always do when not in combat: Some slept, a few wrote letters home, while others moved their bowels. Francis wrote a brief note to his mother and sister, apologizing for missing them in Belfast, and then he wrote a letter to Catherine, using the pet names they had for each other.

Bunny,

I'm well. Hope you're the same. Nobody speaks English here, especially the Sgt!!! Haven't seen any Germans. Food is something. The cooks were all morticians before the war. They embalm everything. I sleep like a log. Speaking of logs . . . Wink, Wink.

Jack Rabbit

A few hours later, Captain Warton formally introduced himself to his men and briefed them on what lay ahead. At 2100—which is 9:00 p.m. civilian time—B Company would move across the border into Germany and relieve I Company, which had been manning a series of captured pillboxes, the outer works of the notorious Siegfried Line, the 390-mile German answer to France's Maginot Line. The chain of eighteen thousand bunkers surrounded by mile after mile of razor wire and concrete dragon's teeth had been built to stop Sherman and Comet tanks. For two weeks, these bunkers had gone back and forth between the Germans and Americans. Tonight it would be Francis McKenna's job to keep the Nazis from retaking them.

As the hour approached, the men of B Company gathered their gear and fell in. By 2200 hours, they had crossed the main road out of St. Vith and into the Schnee-Eifel Forest.

"You are now entering Germany, an enemy country. Be on alert!" read a big wooden sign. And they were on alert, the green troops and their new commanding officer jumping at the sound of every snapping twig while the veterans shook their heads and spat.

B Company entered Grofkampkenberg, a tiny farming village that hadn't seen electricity since 1942. You smelled Grofkampkenberg before you saw it, thanks to large piles of manure heaped beside each dwelling. They were crazily close to the houses, thought Francis, who knew a bit about manure from his Irish boyhood. "Why would they pile shit under their own eaves?" he wondered in a letter to Catherine. For the first time, Dugan considered the possibility that Krauts were different from normal people.

Dugan's new home was a giant shell crater, reinforced with scrap lumber and dug even deeper by men experienced at turning small holes into big ones. A camouflaged canvas canopy offered some protection from rain but none from lead, while wooden pallets stacked two deep kept mud from sucking the boots off their feet. His first frontline post was a lucky one; the 3rd Platoon had drawn the right flank, an exposed hilltop with nearly solid granite only inches below the topsoil, making it impossible to dig in and suicidal to stand up during daylight hours. Snipers made quick work of the careless.

That first night was cold, with not-quite-rain soaking everything, including Dugan McKenna, who pulled his two-hour watch from 0100 to 0300 before being relieved by another greenhorn, Private Anthony Insalaco of Steubenville, Ohio. Insalaco shared his birthplace with Deano Paul Crocetti, the future Dean Martin, a big-nosed croupier and local band singer nobody had heard of in 1944 and who was currently defending Akron, Ohio. Everyone groused and wondered why they couldn't bunk in one of the empty concrete pillboxes instead of sleeping in a hole in the rain.

Captain Warton was not being a prick. He had been warned that three nights earlier, just a few miles south, a flamethrower tank swooshed a tongue of napalm through a pillbox gun slit, sucking out the oxygen and incinerating an entire platoon of sleeping men. B Company slept outdoors because some deaths are more horrible than others.

Small-arms fire and the occasional burst of heavy machine guns kept the new men awake, while the veterans of Normandy, Brittany, and Brest slept like bears. At sunup, Francis got his first real look at war—cows, dead, inverted, and bloated with limbs and utters pointing stiffly skyward. And there, not twenty yards from the lip of his foxhole, Francis saw his first casualty: a German, also dead and bloated. This was no Aryan superman, but rather a short, dark-haired man of thirty-something, possibly a Lithuanian or Estonian, one of the millions of hapless men shanghaied into the German Army after their homelands had been occupied by the Reich. Wherever he was from, this is where his life ended, in a cow pasture with heaps of manure stinking up a town he had never heard of.

Dugan studied this dead man the way all soldiers fixate on their first glimpse of death, the freeze-frame of rigor mortis preserving the exact moment of his passing. He lay there with one outstretched arm, the fingers of his hands clawlike, his skin stretched tight to the point of rupture. He'd been there a couple of days. A third of this poor man's face was missing, pushed inside his skull by a light machine gun fired from the very foxhole Dugan now stood in. Francis McKenna's first sunrise was a microcosm of what was to come. For every famous battle history remembers, millions, literally millions, died or were maimed in nameless, forgotten skirmishes that neither gained nor lost ground, only lives. Darwinism squared.

As his platoon mates stretched, yawned, and farted themselves awake, Private McKenna's eyes remained locked on the dead Nazi. He could see into this man, literally, right into his frontal lobe, speckled as it was with white flecks of skull bone and dura mater mashed all the way back into his parietal lobe. It was both sickening and riveting. By Friday he wouldn't think twice about a horror like that, not even when feral hogs ate through the distended bellies of the fallen. Still, this dead Kraut was his first dead Kraut, and he'd never forget him, like he'd never forget his first girl, whoever she was. The spell was finally broken when word spread that the kitchens had arrived, and a hot breakfast would soon be served.

Francis's first full day on the front line was uneventful by rifle company standards. The periodic tattoo of trigger-happy Germans and the inevitable return fire from the GIs quickly became part of the ecosystem in which he lived. The call and response of incoming and outgoing fire was more annoyance than threat, the way car alarms, leaf blowers, and loud cellphone talkers have been folded into the ambient sound of our world. It was only when the sharp report of a single sniper rifle was heard that everyone took notice.

The cry "Medic!" went up and down the line, and the corpsman scrambled forward, duckwalking from hole to hole until he finally reached the fallen. Of course, he was dead. He was dead the second he carelessly stood up to stretch.

Veterans and greenhorns alike looked to Captain Warton to see how he would respond. He grabbed the 536 and asked Battalion for an artillery strike. Looking at his map, Warton called in the coordinates. "Concentration number two, two, one," said Warton into the field phone. Ninety seconds later, the 15th Field Artillery unleashed three rounds from the big 155mm guns in the rear. They roared overhead and exploded just short of a small copse of fir trees half a mile away. Warton radioed an adjustment. "Plus two hundred yards."

Seconds later another volley fired, this time tearing into the trees, sending limbs both wooden and human flying. The sniper rifles were quiet the rest of that day, and only the occasional chatter of good-guy machine guns responding to the bad-guy burp guns broke the monotony of sitting in a hole waiting for your next meal or bowel movement, as if there was a difference. Warton had passed his first test.

The infantryman's life is hard, always hard, scrolling backward through time to the Meuse-Argonne, Gettysburg, Valley Forge, Waterloo, Alesia, and Thermopylae. We remember the leaders—Blackjack Pershing, Lee and Pickett and Meade, Washington and Cornwallis, Napoleon and Wellington and Blücher. Caesar is an immortal. So, too, Xerxes and Leonidas. But what of the three hundred? What of the archers and foot soldiers slogging across the Rubicon through mud and blood and death for the glory of Rome? What glory rebounds upon the grunt in a muddy hole cowering under an artillery barrage so concussive and membrane-rupturing that blood drips from his eyes and ears while urine and feces soil his pants? Sixteen million Americans put on a uniform during World War II. Only 14 percent got it dirty. The infantry was a helluva way to earn seventy-one dollars a month.

A man in a rifle company can only dream of the luxuries enjoyed by the other branches. They find their comforts where they can, often while plundering the homes of the terrified civilians who have the misfortune of having a war knock on their doors. Then the infantryman will feast on fresh eggs with a thick slab of smoked ham liberated from inside a chimney, the best meal Francis McKenna ever ate. Or he'll find a vintage bottle in a nook deep in a cellar. Some will even lie with a comely Fräulein whose own father shouts at her, "*Schlafen mit der soldat!*" while she quietly whispers, "*Bitte nein,*" into the uncomprehending ear of a rutting twenty-year-old who believes every day may be his last.

Over time the fragile start to crack. "I'm gonna die! I know it!" Or "Captain hates me. He's trying to get me killed!" Accidents start to happen on purpose. Toes happily fly away. The fatty part of a thigh is pierced. Men vanish before coming back with an alibi and the clap. This is the war Studs Terkel called *The Good War*, the war without moral ambiguity, the war history thanks the victors for winning. And it was still shit.

Francis spent his second freezing night in a foxhole, another night of standing watch, two hours on, two hours off. Another cold K-ration supper, another long night of exhausting sleep and rumors and false reports of the enemy's approach.

Then the enemy approached.

A corporal in a forward foxhole on the right flank saw something. A glint of steel? He fired a burst from his rifle just to be safe. But the men were nervous and unleashed a terrific volley of contagious fire up and down the line. Unfocused and wasteful, the men shot at a phantom enemy. Worse still, each blast from their muzzles revealed their exact positions, giving the German artillery something to aim at. Captain Warton screamed into the field phone.

"Hold your fire! Hold your fire!"

Order was restored as "Hold your fire" rippled from lieutenant to sergeant to corporal to private. All was quiet again, until a distinctive *plock* announced the launch of a flare arcing high above the field ahead of the forward positions. And there they were—forty Germans, bayonets deployed, crawling elbow by elbow toward Baker Company. A suicide squad sent to take the American line with cold steel.

This was war at its most elemental. Hand-to-hand combat, fists and blades and rifle butts, even more personal than the sniper's aim. Instantly, the silence was ruptured by the roar of heavy machine guns sweeping the field to keep the Germans down, while grenade pins tinkled on the pallet boards. Instinctively, every man in every platoon hurled a pineapple at the cowering enemy.

The grenades arrived simultaneously, raising a terrific roar with flashes of light and flames and screams. Dirt and rocks and legs were launched fifty feet into the night sky.

"The Germans are beat," Francis McKenna had heard back in Longuyon. "The war is practically over," said the heroes in the rear with the gear who never saw action. The Reich was contracting everywhere. The German juggernaut was now a backward blitzkrieg, with the Panzers and storm troopers retracing their goose steps in double time. The much-feared Luftwaffe's wings had been clipped, leaving the skies open for Bomber Harris and Curtis LeMay to incinerate one German city after another. Hitler had lost France. Hitler had lost Holland. Hitler had lost Belgium. Hitler had lost his mind.

The men in the foxholes had different intelligence. A private in a rifle company only trusts what he sees with his own eyes. B Company had just seen forty Germans crawl on their bellies and try to run them through with bayonets. Those Krauts still had plenty of fight in them. What the big brains in London, Paris, and the War Department failed to note was an ancient phenomenon impossible to quantify. Once the Huns felt their jackboots back on the soil of the Fatherland, the spirit of Fredrick the Great, Bismarck, Goethe, and Wagner with his Valkyries and Götterdämmerung compelled them to fanatically defend their Führer to the very last. The Germans even had a word for it, *Fahneneid*, the ancient oath of the Teutonic Knights who were sworn to obey the emperor. Even if that emperor was a hateful, drug-addled, flatulent madman with a tenuous hold on reality and an apocalyptic denouement planned for his thousand-year Reich that would not see its thirteenth year.

Morning was particularly welcomed by the men of B Company. Yet, in war, even sunrise on a cloudless autumn day brings its own horrors. Private McKenna got an up-close look at the men who had been sent to kill him the night before. Some lay on their backs, in peaceful repose, as if napping in a park after lunch. Others were frozen by the retreating night air in unnatural contortions, legs twisted at odd angles, feet pointing the wrong way and arms raised to shield their eyes from whatever it was that killed them. Many were dismembered, some beheaded, all were covered with an eerie patina of frost, like macabre powdered doughnuts. The frost melted quickly with the rising sun, giving each cadaver a sweaty sheen, as if they had just gone for a run.

Nobody on either side lifted a finger to collect the dead Germans. They remained where they fell for the next three days and nights, first turning a light shade of green, then darkening like weathered copper.

Private McKenna fired his weapon every night, sometimes at the enemy, sometimes at a sow in heat, at an owl swooping for a field mouse, or simply at the wind. Sometimes Dugan squeezed the trigger just to reassure himself he was not defenseless. There was comfort in knowing your rifle was a killer, even if you were not.

On November 7, 1944—while Americans were going to the polls to reelect FDR to an unprecedented fourth term—the tanks appeared, first in sound, then in silhouette, backlit by a burning farmhouse just over the crest of a distant hill. The field phones chirped with excited chatter until Captain Warton cleared the line. He called Battalion for the 155s, "Concentration Queen one-six-three." And the big guns boomed. "Minus sixty yards." And again they roared to life. A Panzer erupted in a giant fireball. The men cheered. But it was a mine that had taken out the tank, not directed fire.

Captain Warton shouted again, "Minus sixty yards. Six, Zero." And this time a pair of tanks were torn to shreds, with flaming crewmen scrambling to get out, only to be gunned down. The men trapped inside the burning tank were reduced to liquid, literally grease dripping out of the undercarriage vents. At that moment, every man in Baker Company was happy he wasn't in armor.

Volley after volley of 155s pockmarked the ground directly in front of B Company, with the three flaming tanks lighting up a field of fire. The soldiers approaching from behind were picked off one by one. The sky was heavy and cold, and the low clouds trapped the smoke and dust. The stench of cordite enveloped friend and foe alike. A battle with no name and no objective other than death—an epic struggle for every man who was there, yet overlooked by history except as recorded in the yellowing pages of a report written by a young captain, who had the good fortune to survive and write it all down.

And the Battle of the Bulge was yet to come.

11

Dream

I'm only in the police car a few minutes before we pull up to the Seventh Precinct.

"Out of the car," barks a cop.

"Watch his head," says another as they hoist me from the backseat.

In one of those little cubicles like they have at car dealerships—an empty desk with no pictures or pens or even a stray paper clip, just a bare metal desk and chairs—I try to answer all their questions without betraying my terror or anger or just bawling like a schoolgirl home alone on prom night. I almost lose it a couple of times when their questions become transparent attempts at self-incrimination. A chipmunk-voiced female detective tries, none too subtly, to get me to pick up Jane's knife. I refuse to touch it, knowing damn well my prints aren't on it. I understand that cops have a job to do, but Jesus Christ!

As the questioning drags on, I become lightheaded from exhaustion, stress, and a monster hangover. I start making demands: a lawyer, which I don't have, then, amazingly, stupidly even, I try to bully my way out.

"Charge me or let me go."

I don't know what made me make this foolish bluff. I'm a notoriously bad gambler, a Mets fan, for God's sake. Still, I know I didn't kill Jane, and being a White male of Irish descent, I believe in the fundamental goodness of cops, because cops are in our blood. But not these cops. They take my pills, my watch, my wallet, my belt, and my shoelaces. Funny, I never considered shoelaces. Now that I'm committed to living, I've lost the means of dying.

I ask to make a phone call. I am told to shut up. They put me in a holding tank with a transvestite, a bleeding Haitian who had beaten his father-in-law and taken a couple of blows in return, and two male prostitutes who rolled a drunken john and stabbed him. All of us are innocent, especially me, and I quickly tire of talking about how innocent we are, so I curl up on the cement floor to sleep.

I am in heaven, or what I imagine heaven to be, since it's a white place and sublime. I'm a physical being—by that I mean I have a body and mass, and I'm not a spirit or an angel with halo and harp. I feel clean, healthy, rested, and very much alive, more alive than I've ever felt. I have no business being in heaven, of course. I'm a gate-crasher and expect to be found out.

I walk toward a light, which is an enormous cliché, but there is a light, and I walk toward it. I don't see any people. There is wind, a powerful, howling wind, but it's filtered, as if I'm protected by a bubble. It's a safe feeling and adds to my sense of well-being. As I get closer to the light, I have to squint. The light intensifies, blinding me, but I press on until all shapes and colors vanish in a swirling ball of brightness. If it's possible for light to have physical mass, this light does. I feel it on my skin, not as heat, the way you would sitting too near a campfire, rather as pressure, as if the light is pressing against my flesh. I pass through the light at its zenith, crossing a doorless threshold. On the other side, the light is softer, and my eyes slowly dilate. That's when I see him. My father. Francis X. McKenna.

Dad reaches out and takes my hand. We walk together wordlessly until we arrive at a little stream running gently to infinity. I finally speak, asking Dad if he is okay. He says he is. Then he points to the ground, or whatever it is we're standing on, and we sit together with our suddenly bare feet dangling in the stream.

A second chance! I have been given a second chance to ask him in death everything I never asked in life. Dad smiles, as we sit dipping our toes in and out of the water. We begin our talk.

"How was your day today, Dan?"

"Difficult."

"How come, Dan?"

"That's two Dans. What happened to Danny?" I ask.

"Danny's a boy's name. You're a man, aren't you?"

"It's good to see you, Dad."

"The car's dripping oil," he says. "I saw stains in the driveway. Tell your brothers to park it in the street."

"I'll tell them, Dad."

"How's your mother?"

"She misses you."

"Baaaah!" He waves off the notion. "She's strong as steel, that one is. She'll git along fine."

"Did you love her, Dad?"

"Who?"

"Mom. Your wife."

"Now, what kind of question is that?" he asks, his voice rising an octave before hitting the punctuation mark. A characteristic nonanswer answer.

"Did you enjoy your life, Dad?"

"Are you enjoying yours, Dan?"

"Honestly, no."

"That's a shame," he says. "You're still a young man. Have fun while you can."

"I'll try."

"You have to learn to enjoy your own company."

"I'll try."

"Why have you come?" he asks.

"I have questions."

"You always were big with the questions. Always asking."

"But you never answered."

"Here I am." He spreads his arms with his palms up. "Ask away."

"Did you love us?"

"Do you think I didn't?"

"Not always," I reply.

"Maybe you weren't always lovable."

"That's not an answer."

"Don't be silly. Of course I loved you. Even when you didn't deserve it."

"Like when?" I ask.

"Like now."

"Did you know I loved you?"

"You're my son." He sighs.

"Not every son loves his father."

"Kevin," he says.

"Yes, Kevin."

"Kevin doesn't love himself."

"Does that make you sad?"

"Children always make their parents sad."

"Are you still sad?"

"There's no sad here. No deafness, either. I hear everything." And he taps his right ear. Then, after a long pause. "Is there anything else?"

"Are you in a rush?" I ask sarcastically. "Who is the man who spat on you? Why would he do something like that?"

He says nothing.

"Did something happen during the war?"

"No!" he snaps and closes his eyes.

"A man came. An old man. He hates you."

"I said no!"

And with that my father sheds his clothes. They fall off him like rain running down a pane of glass. His clothes simply melt away, and with them his skin peels off, revealing not muscle and bone but scales. His arms and legs and torso ripple with shiny, silver scales flecked with blues and grays. And then he slides gracefully into the stream, a sleek, eel-like fish. I run along the riverbank shouting for him to come back, but he swims away.

Suddenly, I feel a sharp pain, a boot in the small of my back. My eyes pop open, my dream aborted by my reality.

"Where am I?" I ask the cop who had kicked me awake.

"Disney-fucking-land. Up, McKenna. On your feet."

This is a new cop, a shift-change cop, but he's heard about me. I crawl off the floor, feet swollen and blistered, my body stiff from yesterday's maniacal liquor-fueled walkabout, my double beatings, and the concrete mattress I've slept on for how long I don't know. I want to kill this son-of-a-bitch cop. I want to grab him by his throat and feel his larynx crack between my fingers. I want to pull his thick, unthinking head off his body and kick his skull like a soccer ball. Just a few more minutes with my father! But instead of murdering the cop, I meekly put my hands behind my back and accept his cuffs with the passivity of an old hound acquiescing to his master's leash.

As I shuffle down the hallway, I make a list in my head of all the questions my father had evaded or didn't answer in my dream. Did he love my mother? Evasion. Did he enjoy his life? No answer. What happened in the war that made that living fossil hate him enough to spit in his dead overly made-up face? He refused to answer and swam away from the question.

Then there are all the questions I never got to ask.

"What made you proud?"

"What do you regret, Dad?"

"What do you cherish?"

"Was I the son you had hoped for?"

"What would you do differently?"

"Is there anything I should know that only you can tell me?"

"Why could we never speak to each other, even now?"

"Why do I know Frank Sinatra was a forceps baby and yet know so little about you?"

"Who are you, Francis X. McKenna?"

A minute later, I face two detectives: Horton from Jane's apartment and a Black cop, Lieutenant Mills, who drops a copy of the *New York Daily News* on the table directly in front of me. My face looks back from inside the police car. The headline screams: "He's History!"

The subhead says: "Cops Nab Prof Who Stabs."

A sub-subhead reads: "Suspect collared in LES murder." LES being tabloid speak for Lower East Side. I'm a three-headline story! I've bumped Frank Sinatra off page one. Christ almighty.

My face and name and shame will get picked up in a day by the *Post*, the Metro section of the *Times*, *Newsday*, *Amsterdam News*, *Staten Island Advance*, *Bergen Record*, *Newark Star-Ledger*, and maybe even the *Connecticut Post*. When word reaches Massachusetts and they discover I am a resident of Somerville, the *Herald*, the *Patriot Ledger*, and the *Globe* will carry the story. My students and colleagues at Marshall College will read about my horrific crime while they wait in the drive-through for their Egg McMuffins. I am ruined.

But I am alive and Jane is not.

I take some small comfort knowing Sean will hide this from my mother. He will get the paper from the driveway. He won't let her see it. Kevin is a different story. He'll buy extra copies and wave them around as if the headline reads, "Men Walk on Moon."

"I want a lawyer," I say, pushing the paper away.

"Calm down, Danny. You don't need a lawyer," says Horton, using my first name for the first time.

"I am calm."

"You want something? Coffee?" asks Mills.

I say nothing.

"Get him coffee," Mills tells a female cop, as if she is a waitress.

The tone has shifted. My guard goes up. When the coffee arrives, I won't touch it. I want coffee badly, but I refuse to take anything from these bastards.

"We have a few more questions, if you don't mind," says Horton.

"Ask," I say, wiggling my chair back from the table.

"Where did you meet her?" begins Horton.

"I told you."

"Had you met before?" asks Mills.

"I told you."

"How well did you know Ms. Freeman?" asks Mills.

"Ms. Freeman?" I ask.

"Jane Freeman," says Horton, reading her name off a document.

"Help us clear this up, Mr. McKenna," says Mills with formality.

"How long did you know the victim?" asks Horton, using the v-word, which angers me.

"I've known her forever," I say, causing Mills to arch his eyebrows and put down his pen.

"Did you know her or not know her?" snaps Horton.

"You can know someone ten minutes and know them forever," I say. "Others, you can know a lifetime, and they're still strangers."

"We got a philosopher," Mills says to Horton.

"Answer the damn questions," Horton demands.

I explain how my father died a stranger, but Jane, whom I knew only long enough to fuck in front of an open window, I felt I'd known forever. Her sadness was my sadness. The cops look at each other like I'm some kind of nut, and maybe I am, but I stick to my story because it's the most honest thing I've ever said. Mills hands me Jane's locket.

"Who's the kid?"

"That's Jane's son, and something terrible happened to him."

"What happened?" asks Horton, perking up.

"I don't know. But that's why she killed herself."

"You don't know?" says Mills.

"I don't know," I reply.

"Where is he?"

"I don't know."

"What's the boy's name?"

"I don't know."

"But you know something happened to him?" Horton squints at me.

"She failed him in some awful, unforgivable way." I say this without taking my eyes off the tiny photo of Jane and her boy.

"Did she say anything before she expired?" asks Horton casually.

The question! He went there. I try not to flinch. He slipped it in, offhand, to trip me up. *Do they know, or are they fishing?*

"Like what?" I ask. A stall. *Do they notice?*

"Did she say why she did it?" asks Horton.

"Did she say if someone else did it?" asks Mills.

I hear Jane's voice, "What have you done to me, and why?"

"Did she?" asks Mills, leaning forward aggressively.

"Only one word."

"What word, Mr. McKenna?"

"Rosebud," I say and look past them to a better time, a better place.

"Asshole," says Mills, as he pushes back from the table. He snatches his papers and walks out of the interview room, throwing the door open so violently it bangs back and forth twice before coming to a stop.

I'm put back in the holding tank, and I sit for a long time, I don't know how long, because they have my watch. I complain loudly. I am told to shut up. They offer a wrapped sandwich from a vending machine. I refuse it on principle. I squawk again about my one phone call, and they bring me to a cubicle. I dial the house in Little Neck. Sean picks up.

"Danny?"

"I'll explain later," I say preempting his many questions. "Is Al there?"

"He went to the bakery for rolls. Where are you? When we got back from the funeral, Roger said you vanished. We were up all night. Al filed a missing-persons report!"

"Tell him to come get me."

"Where?"

"The Seventh Precinct."

"Where?"

"Seventh Precinct."

"Where is that?"

"What's the address?" I shout to a desk cop.

"19½ Pitt Street."

"19½ Pitt Street," I say to Sean.

"What happened, Danny? Are you okay?"

"Don't let Mom see today's paper."

"What?"

"19½ Pitt Street!" I slam down the phone, not knowing why I have been abrupt with Sean. I regret not asking how Mom is doing.

Around 5:00 p.m., Al shows up with a lawyer friend of his. I hear them but can't see them from the cell. They arrive a few minutes after the preliminary report from the medical examiner comes over the fax machine. The cops huddle in private for what seems like hours, while my brother and his lawyer buddy cool their heels out front. Finally, Detective Horton speaks with "my" attorney, a man I have never met. The M.E.'s report says the angle of Jane's puncture wounds "are consistent with self-inflicted injuries." The only prints on the knife are Jane's.

They put me in a small room with Al and the attorney. Al says nothing. He won't look at me even. The lawyer does all the talking. Al stands against the wall with his arms folded tightly across his chest.

"The cops have been busy," says the lawyer. They talked to Jane's neighbors—the women who screamed in the hallway, as well as the broom lady who described me in great detail. He says they also talked again to the shirtless giant; he'll go to his grave believing I'm a murderer. They talked to the bartender at McSorley's, who doesn't remember me because all drinkers are the same to him but remembers Jane because she was Black. The Plaza confirmed I was a registered guest and gave them an earful about me. They tracked down Jane's sometimes boss at a nail salon she occasionally worked in, discovering she had twice before tried to off herself, even landing in Presbyterian Hospital on a 51-50. And she had a record: drugs, shoplifting, check kiting, and on and on, but not a word about the boy in the locket. All told, the M.E.'s report backs my version, and they don't have my prints on the knife. Their case is crumbling. My lawyer insists they have no grounds to hold me. This guy is good.

Another half hour passes before I'm escorted from the holding tank. Horton asks for all my information again, even though I've already given them everything: my address and phone number in Somerville, my office phone at Marshall College, even my mother's number in Little Neck. He has the female cop Xerox my driver's license, and then he takes my fingerprints, although I'm pretty sure I could have refused that. But I don't object. Horton says the investigation is still open, and I can be called back in.

"Can I go?" I ask.

"Go," says Horton.

I retrieve my Ativan, watch, belt, and shoelaces from the desk sergeant and find Al waiting in the lobby. The lawyer has split. I've made him late for the Yankees game.

As we exit the station house, I squint to bring the world into focus. I can't believe I got around last night without my shattered glasses. One of many things I can't believe about last night. As we walk to Al's car, people stare at me. I am a sight. My clothes are disgusting, ripped and stained with blood and vomit, my face swollen from yesterday's double beatings. I limp along on my throbbing sockless feet. Passersby flinch. I look like a deadbeat. No, worse. I look like the guy on the cover of the *New York Daily News*—the pervert murderer who butchered a girl. The law says I'm free to go, but I will never be free from Jane Freeman.

"Get in!" says Al, practically the first words he's spoken to me.

I crawl into the passenger seat.

"Please don't yell at me," I say pathetically.

"I'm beyond yelling," he says.

"I'm sorry."

"Save it for someone else."

As we speed away, I turn my head from the window to hide from my own reflection. I lean against the glass and think about my epiphany. How does one turn an epiphany into action? I think about my eel-father and the man who hates him. I think about the fruit basket I left in suite 1100. I wish I could give it to Beth when we get to the house. I think about my mother and what I've done to her. I think about Jane Freeman and her little boy. I think about Frank Sinatra, whose funeral is tomorrow and whose fame I have temporarily eclipsed.

I don't think about Kimberly.

12

The Best Is Yet to Come

I wake up in Ardsley when Al stops at a Dunkin' Donuts to take a dump. He is in there forever, so I flip on the sports station to catch the end of the Mets-Reds game, but they're in a rain delay.

I hold my breath during the top-of-the-hour newscast when a staff announcer reports on Jane's death. Amazingly, he doesn't mention either my name or Jane's, saying only, "A body was found yesterday in a Lower East Side apartment," and that a "person of interest was questioned and released." He then moves on to an apartment fire in the Bronx and a jackknifed big rig blocking lanes on the Williamsburg Bridge. When the Kars4Kids jingle plays, I exhale.

Al returns with a container of chocolate milk for himself and a coffee and two doughnuts for me. "Here," he says, handing me the Thin Blue Line Special. I mumble a thank-you between ravenous bites and slurps.

Aloysius McKenna is ten years my senior and works diligently to support Beth and the kids in a comfortable fashion, even if he had to move to Ossining to do so. Al has been with Marsh & McLennan for nineteen years, coming over after a short stay at RMJ Securities. To be honest, I don't really know what he does. Some kind of support work for the big insurance brokers and consultants who make all the money. He does well for himself but nothing like the brokers who take home piles of cash.

One of the perks of his job is his office, literally a window on the world, the ninety-sixth floor, one floor below the famous restaurant atop New York's tallest building. From Al's desk, he can look down on jets landing or taking off at JFK, Newark, and Teterboro. He has a spectacular view of the harbor, of Ellis Island and the Statue of Liberty, and across New Jersey. On a clear day he can even see Pennsylvania, visible as a fuzzy, purple smudge where the earth ducks out of view.

Al's desk also gave him an excellent view of the cute girl in Human Resources. He married Bethany Anne Wittenwyler two years to the day after they met. As newlyweds, Al and Beth were Upper East Siders, pinching pennies to save for the home in which they would eventually raise their children. His life is organized, disciplined, and admirable in every way mine is not. He is a problem solver, and I am a problem factory. I marvel how he has taken me on as just one more thing to do.

Al's anger has dissipated enough for him to ask how I'm doing. I don't know what to say, so I tell him the truth.

"I'm horrible," I say. We drive the rest of the way to Ossining in silence.

I'll be safe at Al and Beth's, because they don't keep liquor in the house, not since Jay got caught with booze on his breath after a night at Rye Playland. It's late when we pull into the driveway. I give Beth a kiss while apologizing for my appearance. Jay and Gail say hello, but tepidly, from the stairs, just in case I'm still the raving madman they saw at their grandfather's funeral. It was funny then. Now I'm in their nest.

The house is roomy and tastefully decorated in a colonial, yard-sale kind of way. Beth has sandwiches waiting in the kitchen, which I gobble down like the starving dog I am. I eat them so fast I don't even know what they are. Al hit the lottery when he married Beth. My mother is right about that.

"Let's talk upstairs," says Al.

"Upstairs" means the little room he carved off for himself, filled with books and records and all kinds of hats, mostly baseball caps, but nutty ones too, like a plastic Viking helmet with horns and a Green

Bay Packers cheese head. I knew this was coming and don't try to worm out of it.

I light a cigarette, and Al produces an ashtray from a bottom drawer without me asking. He quit years ago.

"Should I go first, or do you want to start?" he says.

I let him start because, frankly, I don't know if my version begins with yesterday's madness or the day I was born.

"Did you have anything to do with that girl's death?" he asks, getting right to the point.

"Of course not," I tell him, looking at my shoelaces. And he believes me, as I knew he would.

"Danny, what the fuck?"

"Exactly," I say. "What the fuck?"

I give him the *Reader's Digest* version: the breakup with Kimberly, the deal I made with Kevin at the Inn, the catastrophe at the church, the decision to kill myself, the horror with Jane, the cops, the *Daily News* photographer, and along the way lots of digressions into sidebar issues that seem pertinent to me but are irrelevant to him. Al listens to all of it without interrupting. I speak for more than an hour. His face is sympathetic sometimes, angry, and occasionally disgusted. He'd make a terrible poker player. Still, I know he feels bad for me. Worse than bad. He pities me. I don't resent his pity. I need it. I am beyond vulnerable; I am lost. Al takes a drag from my cigarette; that explains the ashtray in his drawer. Finally, he speaks.

"Do you still want to kill yourself?" he asks, exhaling a plume.

You don't just flip a switch, so I give him an honest yes. But I also tell him about my epiphany, about my commitment to live no matter what. He makes me promise I will call him anytime, day or night, before doing anything stupid. I give him my word. He passes back my cigarette like it's a joint in a dorm room.

I turn to other topics of a pressing nature.

"He was there."

"Who?"

"That old bastard who spat on Dad."

"Where?"

"At the funeral."

"Where?"

"In the back."

"No shit?"

"He saluted me, Al. The motherfucker smirked and saluted me! I'm going to find him."

"You're not doing anything until you get your head out of your ass."

"I'm going to find him."

"And do what?"

"Find out why. Why he did what he did. Don't you want to know?"

"Right now, I want to know what you're planning to do to fix yourself," Al says, as he pulls a sheet of paper from his printer. "Beth made some calls. There's like fifty places around here that can help you."

"I'm not going to rehab!" I blurt.

"You're going," he says, literally pointing a finger at me.

"I don't have a month to piss away in some booze camp listening to a bunch of drunks and druggies . . ."

"Stop!" Al says. "It's May 20. You've got nothing on your calendar until classes start after Labor Day."

"I have a wife!"

"Had a wife," says Al, but without rancor. "You pick the place, or I pick it, but you're going."

I sit in silence, looking directly at him. My brother is trembling, the paper shakes in his hand. He's twitching, his face flushed with anger and heartache.

"Gimme the list." I snatch it from him.

The conversation continues throughout the night. It moves to other rooms. Beth joins in. So do Jay and Gail before they go to bed, which I don't think is fair but Beth says is fair because my insanity has been like a pebble in a pond. Worse, a boulder in a puddle, impacting other people's lives, including my niece and nephew about whom I know almost nothing. You can't argue with a mother who plays the kid card.

But I'm stubborn. I fight for the best possible deal. I dig my heels in and get Al's most onerous demands off the table; I will not be checking in to one of those ridiculously expensive recovery resorts like Smithers, Hazelden, or Betty Ford, the places the Mets were always sending Doc Gooden and Darryl Strawberry. Finally, I offer a thirty-day commitment to AA—one meeting a day, every day, for the next month. Al accepts, but only if I spend the month here, in Ossining, in their guest room, because he does not trust me. I say that's insulting. He says tough shit. Still, I'm out of wiggle room, so we shake on it. I celebrate with a Diet Coke. Al has a regular Coke, which I remind him is bad for his blood sugars but mostly to knock him down a peg. He's not perfect.

I call the house in Somerville. There is no answer. Is she there and not picking up, or did she return to her life in Florida or somewhere else? My head hurts. I crawl into bed to contemplate my new reality. I make a schedule, because I'm a teacher and teachers love schedules. Monday, Thursday, and Friday, AA meetings in the morning, afternoons at the library or at Al's desk, as I begin the tedious job of tracking down my father's military records, hoping they'll lead to that ancient spitting asshole. Tuesday, Wednesday, Saturday, and Sunday, I'll do evening meetings and write letters of apology during the day. It's a lot to take on at once.

———

The next morning, I borrow some of Al's clothes, his skinny stuff from ten years ago. At six o'clock I drive Beth's car to Scarborough Presbyterian Church in Briarcliff Manor.

Built with Vanderbilt money by a nephew of Stanford White, the congregation at Scarborough Presbyterian at one time included some of the wealthiest people on earth. This is robber-baron country, where the Rockefellers, Goulds, and Livingstons lived on estates with names like Kykuit, Lyndhurst, Van Cortlandt Manor, Washington Irving's Sunnyside, FDR's Hyde Park, and Martin Van Buren's Lindenwald. Today's corporate titans continue the tradition; Jamie Dimon, Steve Rattner, and other Masters of the Universe hang their hats in the Hudson Valley. The church is magnificent, but an AA meeting is still an AA meeting.

I find a door with the AA logo—a pyramid inside a circle—in the church annex, a generic function room with folding tables and chairs and fluorescent lighting. I help myself to a tiny Styrofoam cup of coffee so hot I'm still blowing on it five minutes later. I don't see any robber barons here, only drunkards.

The 6:30 meeting had been added to the schedule for the Wall Streeters who wanted a meeting before taking the early trains to Grand Central. However, the drug of choice for this generation's nouveau riche is blow, and the cokeheads gravitate to the Narcotics Anonymous meetings in Tarrytown or even Yonkers, where there's less chance they'll run into someone they know. This meeting is mostly populated by the local peasantry, which suits me just fine. My fellow sots are the handymen or domestic help working the surrounding estates, just as my father and Uncle Eamon did for James Fox Wilson III a lifetime ago. Plus, this is a smoker's meeting, and there's no way I can quit drinking and cigarettes at the same time.

Collectively, we fog up the room with so much secondhand smoke the guy running the meeting is more hologram than human, a pixilated person speaking from behind a shifting curtain of smoldering Marlboros, Merits, and Winstons. A backbeat of coughing, wheezing, and throat clearing nearly drowns out the hazy speaker. "Better to die of cancer at sixty than cirrhosis at thirty," goes conventional AA wisdom.

As the new face in the room, I am asked to identify myself in accordance with AA protocol.

"My name is Daniel M., and I am an alcoholic."

"Hi, Danny," they say in unison, despite my specific decision to use my full first name.

"Daniel," I correct them, and the meeting chairman has them say it properly.

"Hi, Daniel."

Some of them say "Daniel" begrudgingly, as if I'm being a prima donna, but by using my full name, a grown-up's name, not a boy's name like my father said in my holding-tank dream, I've taken a tiny step forward.

An elegant older woman dressed like Joan Crawford lights a Davidoff with a monogrammed lighter. She looks at me as she blows a tight jet of smoke in my direction, a carbon-monoxide dart putting me on notice not to stir the pot. I let it slide. Instead, I spend a minute wondering if she had been a martini abuser or an all-day champagne swiller like Winston Churchill or Dudley Moore's character in *10*. She reeks of Chanel and alimony. Her name is Phyllis P., the socioeconomic outlier of this group.

For those of you unfamiliar with the mechanics of AA, the 6:30 is billed as a Step Work Meeting, focusing on the famous Twelve Steps that are the foundation upon which AA recovery is built. "Blah, blah, blah, God, blah, blah, higher power, blah, blah, blah," is what I hear. Then a skinny Black man in a New York Giants windbreaker says something that makes me sit up.

"The first step is really two steps," he says.

He then reads from *Alcoholics Anonymous*, the AA bible, universally known as the "Big Book": "We admitted we were powerless over alcohol—that our lives had become unmanageable."

And he's right. That em dash makes it Step 1 and Step 1A. I *am* powerless over alcohol. The last forty-eight hours have removed any doubt. What stumps me is accepting my life as unmanageable. Who should run it, these people? Al? God? The meeting ends, and I leave as quickly as possible to avoid engaging.

Back at the house, I call Kimberly again, but again she does not answer. I sit in front of Al's typewriter, ignoring his word processor because I can't turn it on and wouldn't know how to use it if I could. I roll a sheet of paper into the carriage.

Dear Mom,

I cannot tell you how deeply sorry I am for my actions at Dad's service. I can't explian it other than to say I was out of my mind. I beg your forgivenesss but will understand if you don't want me in your life.

Love, Danny

I pull the paper out of the machine and circle two spelling errors, typos really, because I haven't used any difficult words, and I cross out the last maudlin, oleaginous sentence and change "Danny" to "Daniel." I have chosen to write to my mother rather than call because we're less inclined to say something stupid when we have to check our spelling.

"I've got some errands to run. Do you need anything?" Beth shouts from downstairs.

"Wait up!" I shout back as I quickly retype my apologia. "Can you drop me at the library?" I ask as I come down the stairs.

"Sure," says Beth, as she fixes her eyeliner in the hallway mirror.

"Sorry to be a pest. Do you have an envelope and a stamp?"

"You're not a pest," she says. But I am a pest, and we both know it.

I scratch my mother's address on the envelope as we drive the short distance to the library. I could walk, and I tell Beth that's how I'll get back.

"When will you be home?"

"Later," I tell her with a teenager's vagary. I drop the envelope in a mailbox just outside the library door.

I quickly find the reference books I need and copy the address for the National Personnel Records Center in St. Louis, the repository for military records. I write it on a paper towel with a borrowed pen. On the walk home I buy a *New York Post*. Fuck the *Daily News*. I go directly upstairs to Al's office and write to the personnel people, requesting an SF-180 form, the first step in retrieving my father's military file and hopefully some connection that will lead me to the man who hates my father. It's a first step in a day of first steps. It's only 9:30. I have the rest of the day to do . . . what?

Ruminate? Speculate? Castigate? Procrastinate? Obfuscate? Exaggerate? Celebrate? Commiserate? Regurgitate? Meditate? Ameliorate? Emancipate? Emasculate? Dissipate? Repudiate? Hesitate? Alienate? Excavate? Urinate? Defecate? Mutate? Fixate? Hate? So I ate—two peanut-butter sandwiches and a chicken leg, then some potato salad, and everything else I can fit in my mouth. I eat as if I have never been fed.

And then I cry for no reason, or maybe for every reason. I weep with cathartic tears, foamy beer tears, shed in sobriety. I cry until I am empty and so exhausted that I can't even read about Frank Sinatra's final words, which the *Post* teases on the front cover, "Family Reveals Frank's Last Words." Nor do I care about the lottery frenzy sending New Yorkers by the thousands to Connecticut hoping to cut off a slice of a $175 million jackpot. I don't even read about the Mets taking both ends of a doubleheader against Cincinnati.

Instead, I distract myself with a cable channel and watch a recap of yesterday's funeral Mass for Francis Albert Sinatra.

The service began promptly at noon Pacific Daylight Time at the Church of the Good Shepherd, which lists a Roxbury Drive address in Beverly Hills but actually faces Santa Monica Boulevard.

The curious and celebrity-besotted jostled for position, angling for the best possible view. As you would expect, the civilians were quarantined behind an unbroken line of BHPD sawhorses and K-rails, the line of demarcation between the applauded and the applauders. In front of the barriers stood a wall of flesh, a battalion of cops every bit as starstruck as the aged bobby-soxers and other spectators they had been sent to keep in their place. The latecomers had to settle for narrow gaps between the news vans and satellite trucks.

With the arrival of each Mercedes and stretch limo, a kick line of red-jacketed valet parking attendants sprinted across the street like synchronized swimmers diving into a pool. Doors flew open, depositing one notable personage after another, each famous name called out by the mob of paparazzi angling for a salable shot. The photographers' shouts turned the media jackals into de facto emcees, identifying each celebrity as they made their entrances.

"Liza! Over here!"

"Give us a wave, Liza!"

"Liza, a big smile!"

Delighted to see Ms. Minnelli, or the back of her head anyway, the throng whooped it up as the cameras went *click, click, click.*

Then the lenses whipped to the right as a sultry Sophia Loren slithered up the walkway in a red-tinged, formfitting metallic dress. A school bus, halted on command from a white-gloved traffic officer, blocked the spectators and paparazzi. The crowd booed, and photographers banged their fists on the bus, frightening the children.

"Jack Lemmon!" shouted someone. "What's with the eye patch? Like Sammy after his car wreck." *Click, click, click.* "Lee Iaccoca!" yelled someone good at faces. "Remember when Frank did those Chrysler commercials?" Only a few clicks for Lee. "Is that former First Lady Nancy Reagan?" Yes, it is! "She's so skinny." *Click, click, click.*

Janel Dreeka, a twenty-eight-year-old advertising saleswoman, dressed head to toe in black, including the Jackie Kennedy veil, tried to pass as family by presenting a driver's license borrowed from a friend named Lisa Ann Sinatra, no relation. But the veil was too much even for Hollywood, and Dreeka was promptly turned away. No camera clicks for Janel.

"There's Jack Nicholson!" yelled everyone, then "Bruuuuuuce!" announced the arrival of The Boss. Springsteen and Sinatra, a couple of Jersey Boys, the Garden State's favorite sons. *Click, click, click, click!*

The crowd parted for Paul Anka, the man who wrote "My Way." *Click, click.* Wayne Newton was there, as large as Anka is small, and Jerry Vale, Vic Damone, Diahann Carroll, and Carol Bayer Sager. Dionne Warwick and the great Rosemary Clooney arrive. *Click, click, click.* "That's Rosemary Clooney? She's so fat!" murmured a dozen women just as fat, if not fatter.

The line stalled as a brace of *alter cockers* shuffled from their cars toward the church steps: Milton Berle, *click*; Kirk Douglas, *click*; Anthony Quinn, *click*; and Red Buttons, the roast master general of the Friars Club, the club for which Mr. Sinatra reigned as abbot emeritus. Not many *clicks* for the old-timers. Stardom has a shelf life.

Rat Packer Joey Bishop arrived to respectful applause from those old enough to remember, and so did honorary Rat Packer Angie Dickenson, who still looks sensational. *Clicks* for Joey and Angie. Tony Bennett was greeted like the great big star he is, heir to Sinatra's throne. *Click, click, click.* He saluted the fans with a little wave before vanishing inside the church. No cameras allowed in there.

Away from the press and their adoring fans, the seven hundred chosen ones had the luxury of assuming their human incarnations, coughing, fidgeting, and suppressing farts, as they fanned themselves with their programs like regular people. The non-Catholics thumbed through the missals as if hunting for coupons in the Sunday paper. Fourteen hundred nostrils were assaulted by thirty thousand gardenias, chrysanthemums, and white roses, battling it out for olfactory supremacy with the gallons of Chanel No. 5 and Armani Acqua di Gio worn by the mourners.

Mia Farrow, the third Mrs. Frank Sinatra, was a late arrival but managed to find a seat in a pew near the altar, as did the first Mrs. S., Nancy Sr., the mother of Frank Sinatra's children. Of course, the kids were there: Nancy Jr., Frank Jr., and Tina, all seated in the pew of honor next to the fourth and final woman to hold the title—Barbara Ann Blakeley Oliver Marx Sinatra. Only plane fare and death kept Ava Gardner away. Let the haters say what they will; Frank's people loved him.

The funeral Mass lasted a full two hours with the usual rituals of incense, holy water sprinkling, kneeling, standing, genuflecting, mumbling of prayers, and shifting from glute to glute on the hard, polished wooden pews. During lulls, the flagless coffin up front allowed the veterans in the church to remember where Frank was during those long four years of war—or more correctly, to remember where he wasn't. Ed McMahon was a Marine pilot and flew eighty-five combat missions. Tony Bennett helped liberate death camps. Kirk Douglas left the Pacific with a Purple Heart. Tony Curtis was a submariner, and Don Rickles hurled hand grenades instead of insults in the Philippines.

The Cardinal gave the homily, not a word of which made the papers. Kirk Douglas, Gregory Peck, Bob Wagner, and Frank Jr. added their personal touches, with Junior earning a nice hand for remembering his father as "a reckless rogue, a sentimental fella." Tony Bennett sang a magnificent "Ave Maria," topped only by a recording of the man himself singing his own closing theme, "Put Your Dreams Away." That brought out a cloud of Kleenex, and then it was over, because who could ever follow Frank Sinatra?

When the church doors swung open, the crowd roared to life,

sending the paparazzi scrambling to refocus their cameras. Once the family and special guests were back in their limos, the motorcade picked up a police escort and began the drive over the hill to Van Nuys Airport.

As the Sinatra family boarded the charter, a crew of Mexican and Guatemalan laborers in the Coachella Valley erected a canopy over a freshly dug grave, plot B-8, #151, at Desert Memorial Park in Cathedral City, near Palm Springs. The cemetery was closed, giving a measure of privacy to the final moments of a very public life.

Soon after landing, Frank's casket was transferred to a waiting hearse as a small fleet of limousines took the burial party on the short drive to Desert Memorial. The route was lined with spectators—a mix of divorcees, sunbaked swingers, gays, and desert rats who snapped pictures and waved, some with homemade signs, "I ♥ You Frank!" At the cemetery, Father Jack Barker of St. Francis of Assisi in La Quinta sprinkled holy water on the casket. It was so hot you could hear it sizzle when it hit the lid.

In a few days a stonemason will install a small gray marker inscribed:

THE BEST IS YET TO COME
Francis Albert Sinatra
1915 – 1998
Beloved Husband & Father

The epigraph is the title of a Cy Coleman/Carolyn Leigh song made famous by Sinatra in the '60s, a little postmortem hyperbole from the widow, because not even heaven could top the life Frank Sinatra had led.

At dinner I tell everyone about Sinatra's funeral, and then Al tells me about my father's burial, which I had missed due to circumstances entirely within my control.

After calm had been restored at the church, Dad was taken to Calvary for interment. Forty minutes later, the funeral party gathered for a post-service collation at Patrick's Pub, a lace-curtain Irish joint we only go to on special occasions, including my father's eightieth birthday. My breakdown, or whatever it was, fueled whispered conversations, until Roger showed up with news of my escape, and then I was discussed openly. I ask Al to stop there because I'm not strong enough to hear the rest.

13

Soliloquy

I sleep late the next morning. When I stumble downstairs looking for coffee, Al is already at work, having caught the 7:19, his regular train. Beth is out as well; she dropped Al at the station before heading to Ossining High School for a parent-teacher conference, which, for some reason, is scheduled during the day, meaning the kids don't start school until ten. The always-thoughtful Beth set up a fresh pot of coffee before she left. All I have to do is push the button.

As I sit at the yellow Formica table slurping coffee, Jay and Gail drift in looking for things. Kids are always hunting for something; this time it's scissors and Scotch tape for her and food for him. I try making small talk but fail. Talking to Jay and Gail makes me feel like a first-semester French student suddenly dropped into the Assemblée Nationale and asked to make a speech.

I admit it: Children scare me. They get to you. When Gail was little, she had a wandering eye and had to wear a patch to school. The bullies piled on the pirate jokes and other taunts. She came home weeping from her one unpatched eye. I happened to be visiting. I couldn't stand seeing her upset so I drew a funny red eyeball on a fresh patch. I don't know what made me do this. I just wanted to make it better so I wouldn't feel her pain. The next day all her friends wanted a funny red eyeball, and she came home happy. This is the only time I can remember helping a child, and even then I was really helping myself.

Jay and Gail chatter as if I'm not in the room. Jay opens cabinets and drawers as if he didn't live here until he finds a sandwich plate and milk glass and a box of Pop-Tarts. Gail busies herself digging through the junk drawer, grabbing clumps of worn-out doodads, the kind of stuff they sell near the cash register in grocery stores—dried up tubes of Krazy Glue and opened packs of birthday candles, long expired AAA batteries, toothpicks and twine, matchbooks and two wire Easter Egg dippers—and depositing it all on the kitchen counter.

Jay's tarts pop, and he plucks them from the toaster with his fingers, burning himself. He swallows the f-word, a courtesy to me. His restraint is endearing, given what he heard come out of my mouth during his grandfather's funeral. Jay blows on his fingers while his sister finally finds the scissors and tape. She sweeps the junk back into the drawer and gives it a shove, but it won't close. She gives it a couple more shoves, but no matter how hard she pushes, it will not budge. I start to tell her she needs to reach in and smooth everything out, that she probably pushed something out the back of the drawer and she'll have to get a flashlight and a coat hanger. But I say nothing. Why be the know-it-all adult? Teens hate that, and I'm already an intrusion in their lives.

Jay and Gail mumble goodbyes and split, leaving the junk drawer three-quarters open and the empty Pop-Tart box on the counter, along with Jay's milk glass, sandwich plate, and crumbs. I am now alone.

And this is where time stops.

———

For the next thirty days I live under my brother's roof, treading as lightly as possible around my sister-in-law and niece and nephew, not because they don't make me feel welcome, but rather because they do. My life during this hiatus consists of recovery meetings, smoking—mostly in the backyard—waiting to get my father's military records, and calling the house, hoping Kimberly will answer. I would call my neighbors and ask them to check on her, but I don't know my neighbors, not even the people who have lived next to me for years. I consider calling Lou d'Arnaud and asking him to stop by the house, but how embarrassing would that be? Yes, he's a friend, but he's also my department chairman, my boss. It's all so exhausting.

I am tired at the molecular level. Still, I drag myself to meeting after meeting and listen to the other drunks recount their rock bottoms and their personal relationships with their higher power, as they understand them, while smoking pack after pack of Parliament 100s and washing it all down with lava-hot coffee in tiny Styrofoam cups.

I grow to resent everything about AA: the coffee for being too hot; the way everybody scrapes their chairs on the floor; the fluorescent lighting, which buzzes like an angry hive; the AA aphorisms like "Keep Coming Back" and "One Day at a Time." The little silver cardboard ashtrays scattered on the tables bug me, as do the tables themselves, the undersides of which are spackled with petrified wads of Hubba-Bubba, Bazooka, and Trident. I resent the insights I hear, the wisdom and practical advice offered by those with years of sober living under their belts. I hate the old-timers' boastful humility with their twenty, twenty-five, and forty-year sobriety birthday cakes. I loathe their serenity. Then, one day, I slip, not with alcohol, but with negativity, which is the opening act for a bender. I tell them AA is full of shit, and that's when the skinny Black man in the Giants windbreaker calls me outside. I follow him because I don't know what else to do.

"Go home," he says. "This isn't for you."

"I'm going!" I shout and walk away.

"But come back when you're ready."

That stops me. I turn back. "I'm never going to be ready for this."

"That's up to you. There's plenty of drunks in the world," he says without rancor. "We'll fill your chair."

I return the next day. I sit in the same seat, drink the same coffee, and smoke the same number of cigarettes. I raise my hand and ask if I can speak.

"I'm sorry about yesterday," I say. And then I fall silent because I have said everything I have come to say.

"Welcome back," says a voice from the other side of the room. It is the skinny Giants fan. I keep *comingbackonedayatatime*. Every day. Some days twice a day. I learn his name is Gordon. Gordy H. I ask him to be my sponsor.

I now do as I am told by people healthier than me—by Gordy, by Al, Beth, Jay, and Gail. I listen to anyone and everyone healthier than myself. My management got me into this mess. I let wiser hands steer.

Then something changes. The meeting room does not fill with a transcendent light as it did for Bill W. in his hospital room at the dawn of AA. Rather I feel slowly enveloped in an absence of sensation, not a vacuum, but rather a soothing muting of sounds as if someone is slowly turning down the planet's volume. I feel weightless yet still answer to gravity—but without gravity's oppressive pressure.

What is this feeling? Absolution? Yes, absolution! And I am catapulted into what Bill W. called "the fourth dimension of existence . . . happiness, peace, and usefulness." I can feel the purgation of my addiction and with it the relentless compulsion to self-destruct. I am now liberated from the madness of clock watching, ass covering, breathmint sucking, and micromanaging the minutia of the drunkard's life of lies. I close my eyes to soak in every second of this amazing moment and do not open them until the last words of the Serenity Prayer are said, and we collectively shout, "Keep coming back!"

I eat meals now at regular hours with my brother and his family, appreciating for the first time that his family is also my family. I go to bed at a normal hour the way normal people do. I sleep. Real sleep. Good sleep. Recuperative, restorative, rejuvenating sleep. And slowly I begin to dream again but not about my father and certainly not about fame. I toss away the last of my Ativan. I feel better, first physically, then, dare I say . . . no, not yet.

Beth takes me to her optometrist, a Persian man who talks a lot but about what I don't remember. He fits me for new glasses to replace the pair smashed in the altar brawl. I make do with an old pair of Al's until mine are ready. Al's are the wrong prescription and give me a headache, but they're better than nothing. As Gordy says, we seek progress, not perfection.

The district attorney's office calls. They want me in for another interview. This rattles me, of course, but my lawyer thinks it's pro forma and sends a junior partner to accompany me. And it turns out to be nothing. A political box needed to be checked, because I'm White and Jane was Black, and a street-corner activist raised a stink. Two African American city councilmen squawked, so the D.A. called me in. Of course, had Jane been White and I been Black, well, we know how that would have played out.

Legally, this is the end of it.

On day thirty of my exile in Ossining, Gordy H. presents me with my one-month chip. I accept it like a Grammy and thank everyone profusely, because this is a different sobriety from my previous court-ordered, unmoored, white-knuckle, wobbly attempts. I have kept my word to my brother. Thirty meetings in thirty days. It's time to go home, but home to what?

The following morning, I say goodbye to Jay, Gail, and Beth. Beth tells me to take care of myself and to not isolate.

"I'm thinking of getting a dog," I tell her.

"You're not ready for a dog," says Beth. "Get a cat."

I ride the train with Al into Grand Central. I give him one last thank-you and a big hug—yes, a hug—before hopping the shuttle to Times Square and the 3 train to Penn Station. I buy another coffee and two papers before plopping into a window seat on the 8:25 to Boston. I sleep most of the way, despite the loud talker behind me who doesn't stop until he gets off in Bridgeport. At North Station, I get a taxi to my place in Somerville.

I had picked Somerville by accident, meaning I did not seek it out specifically as a place to live. Somerville checked all the boxes: cheap, close to campus, easy access to Boston, with enough history to make me feel I'm part of something. Of course, every town has a story, except those cookie-cutter places in Arizona I could never live in.

After a cursory search, I had found the larger half of a two-family house on Flint Street, in East Somerville. I signed a lease in '88 shortly after landing at Marshall College, an appropriately thrifty and noncommittal address for an assistant professor fresh out of graduate school and just climbing aboard the seven-year tenure train.

My neighborhood is to the right of Winter Hill, home of Whitey Bulger and his notorious gang of hooligans, and a short walk to Assembly Square and the Mystic River. It's an old wood-frame house on a stone foundation, and after ninety winter freezes and spring thaws, it's off plumb, and there isn't a straight line in the place. My half is really two-thirds of the house, because I have three bedrooms and the other side has only one. The rent is practically nothing, especially compared to New York prices. The kitchen is warm in the winter if I leave the oven on, which is more than I can say for the bedrooms, one of which I converted to a home office.

To be blunt, my house is ugly, with a tiny patch of weeds and dirt and a preposterous chain-link fence to keep out . . . what? A gaggle of wires droop from the weight of snow and age and whip around in the wind that blows off the river. It's a miracle this house hasn't burned down like the Little Neck Inn.

On move-in day, I dropped a mattress on the floor in the biggest bedroom, where it stayed for two years until I bought a real bed off a friend. This guy was a notorious skirt hound, and I hoped that by sleeping in his bed, his pheromones would rub off.

Then, one year became two, two became five, and on and on. I filled the house with yard-sale bargains, curbside cast-offs, or easy-to-assemble laminated particleboard shelving. My home is not furnished much differently than the dorm rooms of the students I teach. I figure I'll get nice things when I deserve them.

Kimberly did bring a woman's touch. While I was at work, she was at Walmart or Target and occasionally Filene's Basement, picking up whatever caught her eye. I'd come home to an obstacle course of shopping bags stuffed with throw pillows, candlesticks, place mats with birds or seashells or flowers, and enough flatware for the House of Windsor. Small pots of plants appeared in windows, and crystals dangling from filament were hung to bring us positive energy. She bought a large vase filled with puffy paper flowers and a "Made in

Indonesia" sticker on each stem. Scented candles burned day and night. The expense of it all worried me, but I worried even more when she stopped shopping, knowing it wasn't the house she had lost interest in.

Over the years, the other half of the house has been occupied by, in order, a male flight attendant, a line cook at some fancy place in Cambridge, a lesbian couple with a dog that never stopped barking. (Yes, I reported them. You would have, too.) And finally, my current neighbor, an old man I never see, ever. His age is a supposition, because I hear him through the common walls, coughing and clearing his throat like an old man, so I assume he is one. I checked his mailbox to learn his name, but everything was addressed to occupant. I call him "Mr. Occupant" but not to his face, because, as I said, I've never met him.

I no longer think about moving because this is simply where I live. I pay the cabbie and open the squeaky gate while digging my keys out of my jacket pocket.

My mailbox is jammed, mostly with junk, but also bills. One of them is an invoice for seven thousand dollars and change for Kimberly's surgery, her claim rejected as a preexisting condition. Jesus.

I had put a hold on the *Globe* for our honeymoon, but delivery resumed while I was rehabbing at Al and Beth's. Stacks of papers have been tossed to my side of the porch, either by Mr. Occupant, the mailman as he came and went, or maybe even my wife when she returned from Dad's funeral. I boot today's paper aside and put the key in the door.

"Hello?" I shout, not expecting an answer but hopeful nonetheless.

The television plays loudly from upstairs, which is not unusual, because Kimberly habitually leaves the TV on when she goes out. Most of the lights are on as well. When I enter the kitchen, the faucet is running, meaning my water bill is going to choke a horse. I look for a note, anything from her—a goodbye, thanks, fuck you. I find nothing. The ultimate fuck you.

It's eerily similar to the emptiness I felt at Mom's house after Dad died. And why not? Isn't the end of a marriage, even a stupid marriage like ours, a kind of death? I walk from room to room and find evidence of her hasty departure—stray bobby pins on the floor, a broken lipstick in a bathroom vanity drawer. Her dresser is empty except for two mismatched socks, a pair of torn stockings, and the robe she wore at Dante's the night we met. That she left on purpose. I know it. The scent of her hair spray and perfume still hangs in the air, but I'll soon smoke that out. Kimberly hadn't been here long, just long enough to be missed. Or maybe I just miss the idea of her?

After a month in my brother's home, I feel the absence of love in this house. I land in a chair—a chair I fall into by happenstance, lucky it's under me when my knees buckle. I'm on the pity pot, a dangerous place for a recovering addict to be.

But I will not surrender!

I jump up and push the play button on the stereo, and music changes everything. The house fills with the joyful sound of Frank Sinatra belting out "Here's to the Losers," a so-so song saved by a terrific Marty Paich arrangement that makes it sound better than it is. I turn the volume way up, almost to the point of distortion.

Frank was in great voice the day he recorded "Losers"—July 31, 1963. His pal the president was still four months away from Dallas, the Beatles seven months from Ed Sullivan. Frank Jr. had yet to be kidnapped by a pair of imbeciles. *The Feminine Mystique* had just hit bookstores but not hard enough to take chauvinism down a peg. Drinking, smoking, and philandering were still considered male virtues. *Vietneverheardofit* wasn't a thing yet, at least not a thing anyone cared about, and Dr. King's dream was still a dream. Of course, a case can be made it's still a dream.

In 1963 Frank Sinatra was living his dream, his voice rich with joie de vivre and testosterone, overflowing with love, even for losers. He was bigger than ever, huge in the movies and with network television specials, headlining casino showrooms and nightclubs, and heard on jukeboxes, car radios, and every hi-fi where lovers gathered to spoon. Pitch perfect, emotionally engaged, masculine yet vulnerable, sexy, timelessly tasteful, Frank Sinatra sang in the tempo of the beating human heart.

Before my epiphany, tonight's reverie would have been scored with a darker soundtrack. I would have seized on my empty house as carte blanche to wallow in melancholy songs backed by strings, muted trombones, and oboes, the saddest-sounding instrument of all. This would be a night of Frank noir, and nobody has ever plumbed deeper or darker into heartache. These are the recordings that gave men permission to cry: "I'm a Fool to Want You," "Willow Weep for Me," "Blues in the Night." I'd put on *Only the Lonely* and play the whole album twice. I'd play it on vinyl, on my old college turntable, so I could hear every scratch and bump as the needle completed each orbit. I'd brace myself for "One for My Baby (and One More for the Road)" with my eyes instantly tearing up with the first tinkling notes of Bill Miller's piano.

Bill Miller was Frank's accompanist for nearly fifty years. They met when both were at professional and personal low tides. Together they would soar. Miller's minimalist piano on "One for My Baby" is instantly recognizable, a play within the larger play of any concert or whatever Sinatra album it lands on. Written as an up-tempo dance number for a Fred Astaire picture, Frank and Bill slowed it to a crawl and turned it into a three-minute masterpiece. During a brief falling out, a rupture neither man would discuss, Sinatra pulled the piece from the band book. It's one thing to cheat on a wife, but Frank Sinatra would never cheat on a song.

I play only happy Frank, all the brassy, finger-snapping Billy May/Basie-beat discs, starting with *Songs for Swinging Lovers, Come Swing with Me!, Come Fly with Me*, and of course, *Come Dance with Me!*, since you can't hear one without the others. I play *Ring-a-Ding-Ding!* and wish Sinatra had done more with Johnny Mandel. I play great stuff by Billy Byers and Ernie Freeman and a young Quincy Jones. I play *Sinatra at the Sands* and even listen to Frank's cringe-inducing comedy monologue, counting the seconds until he gets back to singing.

I pull out obscure Sinatra nobody listens to anymore: stuff from the Columbia years when he was still the "Bony Baritone" wearing floppy bow ties the first Mrs. S sewed for him, back when my mother and father were freshly in love. *Songs by Sinatra, Sing and Dance with Frank Sinatra, Hello Young Lovers*. I keep grabbing and shoving

CDs into the new, giant one-hundred-disc player I bought on a whim the morning after Kimberly said she would live with me. I exhaust the Columbia catalogue and switch back to the Reprise years. I open the fridge for a Diet Coke. Good God, what a stink! I slam the door shut and choke back an upchuck, then get a warm can out of the pantry.

While celebrating my epiphanous new life, I toast Francis X. McKenna and Jane Freeman. Then I toast all living things, including Kimberly Clark and Kimberly Clark McKenna, two names for one person, both strangers. I toast Kevin McKenna and the Hayes Brothers, the angry Chinese woman sweeping the sidewalk in the dead of night. I even toast that fucking *Daily News* photographer who nearly ruined me.

I raise my warm Diet Coke high above my head, a carbonated aspartame tribute to Pelawatta Gayan, the cabbie who drove me from North Station to Flint Street earlier today. I toast Beth and Al and Jay and Gail and the Mets bullpen. I salute Sean and Mom, but not the New York Yankees and not that cadaverous old prick who hates my father. I only think a couple of times about the neighborhood package store where they know me and would give me whatever I want, even if I leave my wallet at home. Instead, I kneel like an altar boy and pump CD after CD into the machine until my legs cramp. I am high on syncopation, drunk on rhythm and rhyme.

My head spins, and I have to sit down. I crawl back to my chair and shut off the table lamp. I sit in the dark, enjoying the soft cerulean glow of the CD player's LEDs. I light a cigarette, even though I still have one burning in the ashtray. I click "random" on the remote, and the discs spin and the lights blink. I kick off my shoes as the gears and whirligigs of the shuffler do their thing.

> *The summer wind came blowing in*
> *from across the sea . . .*

No!

Click.

I'm not ready for "Summer Wind." I don't know when I will be. The silence is ghastly. I can hear my thoughts. I turn on the TV to drown myself out. I land on the Red Sox/Rays game. I don't make it far. I sleep where I sit the entire night through.

———

I drink my first coffee of the day black, because the half-and-half in the fridge is a solid block of curds, spoiled like everything else after sitting a month. I light a breakfast smoke and think.

I need a routine.

The car won't start. I ask my neighbor across the street to give me a jump. I'm embarrassed because I don't know his name. I try faking it with "Thanks, pal. Appreciate the help, buddy." But he knows my name and uses it liberally.

"I'm sorry, but I can't remember your name," I finally confess.

"Dan," he says. "Same as yours."

The car turns over, and I make the short drive to Marshall College.

The campus is deserted, and I park in the Dean of Students' space, a huge no-no during the school year. I think better of it and move my car to my regular spot. This is probably more integrity than my epiphany requires, but I need to get in the habit of doing the right thing. I wave to one of the guys from Buildings & Grounds, as he drives by on a big lawn tractor. He gives me a puzzled look because I never wave to the Buildings & Grounds guys.

The windowless hallway on faculty row is dark. I flip a switch, and the fluorescents flicker to life. I see something taped to my office door.

"Oh, fuck!" My face on the cover of the *Daily News*! I quickly rip it down and ball it up.

My hands are shaking, and I drop my office key. I have to push hard to open the door, plowing away a month's worth of mail shoved under my door. Someone's been in here though; a sealed envelope leans against the telephone, marked CONFIDENTIAL typed in all caps.

To Professor Daniel McKenna, PhD:

In light of the negative publicity surrounding the death of Ms. Jane Freeman on 19 May 1998, and our inability to contact you in the intervening weeks, it is the unanimous decision of the Board of Trustees, President Campbell, Dean Sullivan, Human Resources, as well as myself as your Department Chairperson, to suspend your scheduled classes for the fall semester. You are hereby placed on mandatory sabbatical, at full pay, per your employment agreement, unless or until additional information comes to light that may necessitate further action by the Trustees.

Sincerely,
Louis d'Arnaud, PhD
Chairman, Department of History,
Marshall College

Then, in his own handwriting, a postscript: "Danny, WTF? Call me. Lou."

I call. Something I should have done as soon as I got to Al's and Beth's. Lou's office phone rings and rings. I run down the hall and knock on his door. Not here. I call him at home. His wife answers. She's frosty. Not her usual chatty self. Lou is curt. He tells me where to meet him. I wait in a booth for half an hour at a Wendy's near campus. Finally he shows.

"How was the Cape?" he asks sarcastically.

And I tell him the whole sordid story. I also tell him I am one month sober.

"Why didn't you call?"

"I wasn't thinking, Lou."

"No, shit!" he snaps. "Campbell is pushing hard for termination. So is Development. If you didn't have tenure, you'd be out."

"Thank you for defending me."

"Who says I defended you?"

"You defended me."

"I simply told them because you're an alcoholic, the college might be vulnerable in an ADA lawsuit."

I smile hearing this. Lou knows how the game is played.

"We're still getting calls from parents," he says as he puts a third sugar in his coffee.

"I didn't kill her, Lou."

"You know there's the internet now?" he says.

"I know."

"You don't know, Luddite! This will never go away. A hundred years from now that picture will still be out there."

"I can't change history."

"Bullshit. We change history all the time." He says this while shimmying out of the booth. Then, "Enjoy your time off."

I sit a while watching cars go by. There's a close call when horns honk and a box truck swerves around a cat dashing across the street.

I've had my own close call. Instead of twenty-to-life in Elmira or professional ruin, I've landed on a silk pillow, while Jane landed . . . where?

I stop at a market and fill the cart with foods I never eat but know to be good for me. I enjoy shopping in the aisles I never visit: the fish counter, the produce section, where I stuff vegetables into plastic bags that are difficult to open. I grab a box of Raisin Bran and a bottle of vitamins. Just buying this stuff makes me feel healthier. I try to imagine actually eating it.

At home, a letter is waiting from the National Personnel Records Center. My father's military records!

I tear it open like it's a birthday card with money inside. Instead, a form letter explains a fire in '73 gutted the giant warehouse in St. Louis, wiping out fifty years of military history. My father's were among the eighteen million files lost. This is a setback. Now I'll have to find some other way to track down the man who spat in my father's face.

But first I tackle the rancid refrigerator.

I prep by opening every window in the house and turn on the wobbly ceiling fan. I light some of Kimberly's scented candles and wiggle my fingers into rubber gloves. I tilt my head away as I open the fridge and quickly remove a pack of rotten chopped meat from the bottom shelf. I drop it in a plastic trash bag and then toss in three liquified tomatoes, fermenting plums, and moldy cottage cheese. This was Kimberly's food. The stuff I eat never expires.

Out go leftover containers filled with God-knows-what. I double wrap it all in a leaf-and-lawn bag and dump it in the garbage outside, pulling the can away from the house. I scrub the refrigerator walls and racks and bins with soap, water, Windex, and a splash of Clorox. A purification. Only then do I put my groceries away. I do all of this without complaint—frankly, with gratitude—because this is what healthy people do.

After dinner, Al calls to check on me. I tell him how the *Daily News* cover followed me here and will likely follow me forever. I recap how close I came to losing my job. I tell him about the fire that destroyed our father's military records and how much harder it will be to track down the man who spat in Dad's face. But I also tell Al truthfully that I'm okay. Or I will be.

Over the next few days, I audition local AA meetings until I find a few I'm comfortable with. I call Gordy and go over the pluses and minuses of each meeting before I pick a home group. This was high on my to-do list. Next, I knock on the other Dan's door and give him an Entenmann's crumb cake for jump-starting my car. I join a gym and actually go. The StairMaster reminds me again that I have to quit smoking.

Undoing my marriage is not difficult, but finding Kimberly is. She's in Florida, that I know from my Mastercard statement. She bought a plane ticket the day after Dad's funeral. But where in Florida? I hire a P.I. to track her down to some guy's condo near St. Pete. I had hoped we could get an annulment, a matrimonial mulligan, but there's some kind of legal mumbo jumbo that makes this impractical, so divorce it is. A paralegal sends paperwork that asks why our marriage failed. I check the box next to "irretrievable breakdown of affection," because there is no box for stupidity.

When the process server hands her the papers, she immediately calls me, furious. I have no idea why. My house is rented. We have no matrimonial assets to divide. Finally, she calms down, and we say goodbye civilly. In six months, it will be all over.

A few days later, I come home from the gym to find my street blocked by emergency vehicles. Neighbors and dog walkers gather on the sidewalk as paramedics wheel Mr. Occupant out of the house, strapped to a gurney. I ask a cop what happened, and he tells me to buzz off until I say I live in the other half of the house.

"Stroke," says the cop. "Fire thinks he was on the floor for two days. Shit and urine . . . feces everywhere," he says, correcting himself.

"That's terrible."

"You didn't hear anything?"

"No."

"We got a call for a welfare check from his daughter."

"I didn't know he had a daughter." But the cop has moved on, stopping a furniture truck so the ambulance can pull out from the curb.

I think about my nameless, unmet elderly neighbor dead for two days on the other side of my bedroom wall. If only I had heard him groan or thump to the floor or something. Then I think of Jane. Did anyone come to her funeral? Did she have a funeral? I wonder where she's buried. I wonder *if* she's buried.

I stare at the bedroom ceiling, punching my pillows and jamming them under my neck and flipping them over to the cool side. The pillows aren't the problem. I get out of bed and open a notebook and start making a list of all the people I have harmed. This is Step Nine of Alcoholics Anonymous. Direct amends. The expensive step. The one where you have to make good on all the money you borrowed or stole and undo the damage you caused, as long as doing so won't cause more harm.

My list is long, spilling onto a second page. I put the obvious people first: my mother, my brothers, Kimberly, every woman I have ever slept with, including Jane. I keep going backward in time to childhood, to things nobody on earth remembers except me, like when I was six and Aunt Bridget gave me a tin windup horse for Christmas, and I wouldn't thank her because I didn't like horses. What a brat! Aunt Bridget's name goes on my list.

The depth of my guilt is inexhaustible. When I brush my teeth, I feel guilty watching the water swirl down the drain. I think of foreign legionnaires dying of thirst as they crawl across the desert, like this actually happens. I shut off the faucet, hoping that will somehow fill the canteens of the lost battalions. I'm not just my father's son. I have a mother, too. I call her.

"Danny?" she says with surprise. "What's wrong?"

"Nothing's wrong, Mom."
"What time is it?"
"Late." Then I ask if I can come see her.
"Of course," she says.
I ask if she got my letter.
"I did," she says.
"And?"
"And it was very nice of you to write."
Step Nine is going to be a bitch.

14

It Had to Be You

Two days later, I throw an overnight bag in the trunk and back out of the driveway, which should be easy, but today is trash day, and cans line the street, making it a slalom in reverse.

I drive an '89 Chevy Cavalier, silver, although like all silver cars, it's starting to flake. I bought it two years ago from a kid around the corner. This is not a car that's going to get anyone laid. Honestly, I'm not sure what the Chevrolet people were thinking when they named it Cavalier, unless they were trolling the car-buying public or meant it ironically. Historically speaking, the Cavaliers were backers of Charles I during the English Civil War, hardly a selling point for a midsize family sedan. *Cavalier* is also a synonym for insouciant, dismissive, take it or leave it, and indifferent. Would anybody drive a Chevy Indifferent? Cavalier is a dumb name for a generic automobile, but I only paid nine hundred for it, so I can't complain.

I unconsciously light a cigarette because the driving bone is connected to the smoking bone. I smoke with the windows up, steering from inside a cloud, occasionally flicking ashes in the direction of the tiny ashtray by the gearshift. The ashtray is jammed with filters. They poke up, growing like carcinogenic stalagmites. I empty the ashtray at a Dunkin's, and, as long as I'm here, I grab a doughnut and coffee before squeezing onto I-93 South. It feels great to be behind the wheel. There are possibilities when you travel, even to familiar places. I fall into my own private reverie, humming along to a Dinah Washington cassette that's been stuck in the deck for months. I hit rewind and play it again and again.

The morning sun promises a hotter afternoon. I keep one eye on the road and one eye on the idiot lights, looking for any sign of trouble. Last summer, I boiled over outside of Woonsocket, and I can't get that out of my head even though I replaced the thermostat and radiator hose, and everything's working fine. I enter and leave Rhode Island.

In Milford, Connecticut, I stop at McDonald's because I'm on a road trip and I'm an American. I pick up an abandoned *National Enquirer*, so I have something to look at while gobbling my Quarter Pounder with Cheese. After months of sugarcoating Sinatra's biography, the first wave of Blue Eyes blowback has arrived. Kitty Kelley is quotable again.

The columnists and Billingsgate hacks have been let off the leash to look again under the rocks of the icon's life: his Sicilian temper, his coldhearted abandonment of poor, sweet, loyal Nancy Barbato for that boozy temptress, Ava Gardner. All the lurid stories going back decades are regurgitated: Frank with notorious mobsters named Giancana, Cohen, Costello, and Gambino; stories of pimping for JFK—there's Judith Exner's picture—slugging Lee Mortimer, skipping World War II, browbeating that poor blackjack dealer in Atlantic City; getting trapped in Australia after shooting off his mouth about a female reporter; singing for Ronald Reagan; and smoking in public. It's open season on Frank Sinatra because he rose too high and must be taken down a peg, unlike Frank McKenna, whose anonymity ensures his secrets will be kept. And to think I once thought obscurity was a curse. Living to be remembered is no way to live.

I leave Connecticut.

It's purgatory, waiting to pay the toll at the Whitestone Bridge— $3.50! It's like New York has a cover charge.

The Cavalier sweeps across the bridge high above Long Island Sound. I steal a glance to my right at the remarkable skyline. It never gets old, no matter how many times I see it. From up here, the sky-scrapers look like Atlas rockets ready for launch. I risk a second glance, swerving a bit out of my lane, but it's worth the angry horns and raised middle fingers, because I can see the Chrysler building, more beautiful than any car Walter P. ever built. A fellow doctoral candidate dismissed the Chrysler Building as "a stupid person's idea of architecture." When I objected, she destroyed me with "Of course you like it. It's a giant shiny cock." She now teaches at Mills College in Oakland and moonlights as a dominatrix, which I don't know for a fact but choose to believe.

Even with the toll-plaza jam, I've made excellent time and decide on a whim to work Step Nine for Jane before going to see Mom. I exit west, heading across Queens and toward Manhattan, rather than east toward Little Neck.

The city morgue is on East 26th Street. It's part of the Bellevue Hospital complex, which must be unnerving to patients hoping to recover. My mood brightens when I find a legal parking spot only four blocks from Bellevue, sparing me the pound of flesh at the garage.

I stand in the lobby like an immigrant stepping off the boat at Ellis Island, dumbstruck by the mysteries of a foreign land. A bored, morbidly obese security guard points me to a less obese but equally bored security guard hunched over a desk by a bank of elevators. She sends me up to the fourth floor, where I meet more bored security people, which begs the question, why do the dead need so much protection? I approach the counter and wait for a clerk to acknowledge my existence.

"Yes?"

"I'm the one who called about Jane Freeman."

"Freeman?"

"Yes. I spoke to someone yesterday. I'm here to claim her remains," I say, using the term *remains* because that's what Fat Tommy calls them.

"When was she brought in?" he asks, as he types on a keyboard without looking up.

"The eighteenth. No, nineteenth."

"Nineteenth of what?"

"May."

With that, he looks at me with arched eyebrows.

"She's probably at Hart Island."

"The woman I spoke to yesterday said she was here."

"I'm checking."

"What's Hart Island?" I ask while he types.

"Potter's field," he says. "In the Bronx." Then, with surprise, "Hey, you're in luck. She *is* here. What mortuary are you with?"

"No mortuary. I'm just me."

His face becomes a fleshy question mark.

I rapidly and stridently explain what I've been told over the phone: how I have every right as a friend of Jane's to claim her unclaimed body so she can have a proper burial. I sound like a guy ready for a fight, but he stops me by raising his hand.

"How do you plan on moving her?"

"She's been cremated. No?"

"No."

"After all this time?" I ask.

"Mister, we have bodies here for months, sometimes longer. Some go to the medical schools; most wind up at Hart Island. In another week that's where Ms. Freeman would be." He says this matter-of-factly, then hands me a clipboard and pen. "Sign here," he says pointing. "Call us back with the name of the funeral home once you've made your arrangements."

Gordy warned me Step Nine would be difficult, but I didn't expect this. Do I call Fat Tommy? I debate what to do as the elevator brings me back to the lobby. No, Tommy will blab it. This is between me and Jane. I go to a row of pay phones, to the Yellow Pages, and find a funeral home on 14th Street. They take my credit card. Her ashes will be ready Friday. An hour later, I park the Cavalier cavalierly on the street in front of Mom's house.

"Is that you, Sean?" she shouts at the sound of my key in the lock.

"It's me."

"Danny?"

"Yes, Mom. It's me."

I give her a peck, and she kisses me back.

"Are you hungry?"

"Starved," I say, even though I am stuffed with road junk.

We sit at the kitchen table and talk about nothing in particular. I make a few attempts to bring up the catastrophe I had authored the day of Dad's funeral, but she skillfully deflects each attempt like a goalie kicking away slap shots.

"Do you want cheese on your sandwich?"

"Is whole wheat okay? That's all Sean will eat."

"Yellow mustard or brown?"

Food, food, food. I answer her questions, until Sean comes home from work and the window closes on my apology. Sean is surprised to see me.

"How long are you staying?" he asks.

"A couple of days."

Satisfied, he fills a glass with water and exits.

"How's Kevin?" I ask.

"Kevin is Kevin," she says, and that says it all.

I finish my sandwich and wash the plate and milk glass, which my mother insists on drying. The crumbs are swept up, and all evidence of this unnecessary meal are erased.

"Can you run your father's things to St. Vincent de Paul's for me?"

"Sure," I say, happy she asked. "What things?"

I follow Mom upstairs to her bedroom and help her empty Dad's clothes from his dresser. This is the nitty-gritty of death—tossing out socks and underwear and Dad's toothbrush and razor and old rolled-up tubes of Preparation H.

It's odd being in this room. Mom and Dad's bedroom was off-limits, not by decree, rather by practice. Once we were past Tooth Fairy age, we simply did not cross this threshold. Being in here is like sneaking under the museum ropes.

We throw everything on the bed, spring and summer clothes to the right, winter and fall to the left. My mother pulls slacks and polo shirts out of the bottom drawer, tenderly folding each as if she still worked at Gertz. Tiny beads of perspiration crown her forehead just below her hairline. I suggest we turn on a fan or at least open a window.

"There's not much left to do," she says, as if that will cool the room.

"Mom, there's no rush. It's not like you need the closet space."

"Someone can use them," she says hopefully.

But nobody will wear this stuff, not even to a costume party.

I grab an armful of hopelessly out-of-date blazers and plop them on the bed. Polyester checks and plaids, the kind of coats you only see at a racetrack.

A well-worn corduroy jacket with more roy than cord slips off the bed onto the floor. Mom carefully brushes it as if it had fallen in the road rather than on her spotless bedroom floor. She gently places it back on the bed, as if Dad were still inside it. The corduroy is the only coat I remember him wearing. My father looked his most Irish in it. With a pipe in his mouth, books of matches stuffed in his pockets, a tweed Scally cap on his head, there was no mistaking his ancestry. Mom volunteers no stories about the time Dad wore this or that. I ask about a few items, and she says, "That old thing!" or "He never even tried that on."

I unzip a garment bag to discover a Johnny Carson–brand suit that hasn't seen the light of day since 1976. It's hard to believe some of this stuff was his. That's the downside of living a long life; nobody remembers that you were once young.

My mother has begun the process of scrubbing my father's history, expunging his garish sports jackets, the waxy Q-tips that fell behind the toilet, the eighth of a bottle of whiskey in the liquor cabinet, along with all his lighters, pipes, and that corny novelty clock in the kitchen he thought was so funny—the one that says, "No Drinking Before Five!" with twelve fives on the face. All of this must go to make room for the authorized version of Francis X. McKenna, the cornerstone of which is already in place, the eight-by-ten Sears studio portrait in a silver frame on the end table next to the sofa, where everyone can see him. This edition of Dad will not swear, will not get drunk, will not smoke or sneeze loudly or yell at the Mets; he will not lose his hearing aid for the tenth time or fart in church. Nobody will challenge this version of Francis McKenna, because nobody cares except us and one malignant old man whom I haven't forgotten about.

We will respect the curated Francis McKenna out of consideration for my mother's feelings until she, too, is gone. And when the last of his children's children have passed, Francis McKenna will disappear entirely.

I blurt it out.

"Mom, did you see that *Daily News* picture? The one with me . . ."

"I saw it," she says without looking at me.

"Can we talk about it?"

"We just did." And she exits to the hall, closing the bathroom door behind her. She turns on the hot and cold faucets to drown out her sobs.

I carry everything downstairs and put it into Dad's car, which has a bigger trunk than mine. My father's car has barely moved since May. Kevin and Sean take it out once in a while, but mostly it sits here, baking away in the summer sun. When I open the door, a fist of heat punches me in the face, followed by the stench of stale tobacco. I slide in and put my hands on the wheel in the ten-two position. I grab it tight, squeezing it as my father likely did in his last moments of life. I turn the key, and the radio comes on, WPLJ, the rock station. Undoubtedly Kevin drove it last. The Mets will never be heard in this car again. I back out of the driveway onto 44th Avenue, scraping the muffler where the driveway meets the road. Half an hour later the car is back home.

"I got a receipt from the St. Vincent's people."

"A receipt for what?"

"For Dad's clothes." But this doesn't click. "For your taxes."

"Oh," Mom says, realizing for the first time she now has to do the taxes and register the car and do all the things her husband had done for the past fifty years. This makes her uncomfortable, and she sticks her head deep into the fridge. "I know there's a Fresca in here somewhere."

"I don't want a Fresca," I tell her.

"Found it!" she says, handing me the soda. "Maybe you could help your brothers in the basement?"

"What's in the basement?"

"I asked Kevin and Sean to throw away those old boxes by the oil tank."

"Dad's boxes?" I ask with surprise, because those boxes were strictly off-limits, so much so, I had forgotten they were still down there.

Kevin is awake. I hear him belching upstairs in his room. I put the Fresca back in the refrigerator and leave Mom at the sink, peeling a bowl of potatoes.

Kevin is thrilled to see me, almost giddy because I have one-upped him as the family embarrassment. He's been waiting to rub it in my face.

"So, Perfessor . . . did you kill that coon?" asks Kevin, with a smile uglier than his words. It takes an uncommon act of willpower to keep from smacking him.

"Her name was Jane, asshole."

"Jane Asshole?" he says, thinking he's being clever. "Is that the Harlem Assholes or the Bed-Stuy Assholes?"

"Stop it, Kevin," I say with existential exhaustion.

"Do you have any money?" he asks, whipsawing the conversation without a trace of self-consciousness. "I'm good for it."

"You're good for nothing," I tell him. "Who do you owe this time? Your drug dealer or your bookie?"

"Your wife! She said she'd blow me for a twenty!"

He's on his feet, and there's no place to go from here but fists. I swallow hard. He wants to fight me. I want to fight him. A deep breath.

"Kevin, please. We can't do this anymore. We're too old." I let that soak in. "How much do you need?"

"Two hundred."

"I'll give you sixty. That'll leave me only twenty." And I show him my wallet—four twenties.

I drop three at his feet, and one bill floats under his bed. He gives me a look but says nothing. The immediate crisis recedes. I don't like Kevin McKenna. It's hard even to love him.

He grunts as he reaches under the bed. I look down on the crown of his head. "You're going bald," I say with surprise. I watch him closely as he grimaces, trying to grab the twenty. It's physically challenging for him. My brother is an old man at forty-six; he has bags under his runny eyes, a greenish-gray pallor, a distended belly, and sticklike legs, a textbook late-stage alcoholic's physique. What's he got, five years? Ten max. I lose all my anger toward him.

"Kev, you need to take better care of yourself."

"I'll outlive Bob friggin' Hope."

"Bob Hope is ninety-five. You're supposed to outlive him."

"Got it!" And he grins as he waves my stray twenty as if he's won a prize.

"Mom wants Dad's boxes out of the basement. Gimme a hand."

Surprisingly, he's game. He steps quickly into his bedroom slippers and walks out of the room as if moving the boxes had been his idea.

"Sean! Basement!" I shout up the attic stairs.

We played in the basement as kids. We played hide-and-seek, although, as a joke, when Sean would hide, nobody sought him, not even me, the baby in the family. In my defense, I took my cues from Al and Kevin. They thought it was funny, so I thought it was funny. Sean sat patiently waiting to be discovered. I'm sure it was only ten minutes, but ten minutes of hiding is an eternity in kid time. Sean is still waiting to be discovered.

We learned about sex in this basement. We showed each other our little bald pee-pees, and there wasn't anything homo about it, but maybe for Sean there was.

I saw my first tits down here. Not real tits, pictures of tits. For about a year, my friends and I would pinch the new *Playboy* from the local candy store and stash it behind a loose cinder block in the wall above the slop sink. It was a secret compartment that only we knew about. My smut vault was my special place, and I bet if I yank at that block right now, I'll find a moldy Miss January 1970.

Of all the games we played as children, our all-time favorite— and most imaginative—was Submarine. Our basement is unfinished, with no drywall or drop ceiling or flooring. The cellar is a cold, hard, damp concrete space with bare lightbulbs and pull chords instead of switches. The ceiling is ribbed with the beams and joists of the kitchen, dining room, and living room above. Pipes with valves run from the giant oil tank to the hot-water heater and furnace. In winter the heater hisses and the furnace bangs, as it comes on and off. In our kid brains, it looked and sounded like every submarine we'd ever seen on TV or in movies, like *Run Silent, Run Deep*; *We Dive at Dawn*; and *Operation Petticoat*. We spent countless hours down here firing pretend torpedoes at imaginary Jap destroyers, while bracing for the inevitable depth charges meant to send us to the bottom. I had a carrier in the crosshairs of my cardboard periscope the day Dad clomped down the stairs to tell me Snoopy had died. Now Kevin, Sean, and I are back in the conning tower, preparing to jettison our father's boxes from our submarine.

There is a lot of heave-hoing and "one, two, three, lift!" with Kevin barking the orders and me and Sean obeying like the veteran submariners we once were. Kevin is good at boxes. He's a professional after years in and out of the shipping biz. He sees this as an opportunity to demonstrate his practical, real-world skills as a rebuke to my ivy-covered, theoretical, bullshit academic world. I submit to Kevin's authority until curiosity gets the better of me.

"What's in this one?" I ask, unfolding the flaps of a box.

"Don't start opening shit," orders Kevin.

"We should look at this stuff before we dump it," I explain.

"Jesus Christ!" says Kevin, literally throwing up his hands. "We'll be here all day." But now his curiosity is piqued.

Kevin begins opening boxes, examining things that catch his eye.

"How much do you think this is worth?" he asks, showing us an old wristwatch. Sean names a price. Kevin argues for a higher price.

"What do you think this lighter is worth?"

"Twenty grand, Kev. That's why Dad kept it in a wine box in the basement next to the washing machine."

Kevin rips opens a small box.

"This one's shit," he says. "A bunch of old checks."

"Checks?" I say with excitement. "Let me see."

There must be five hundred in here, some going back to the 1950s. A box of canceled checks is like finding Eldorado. I live for things like canceled checks. When I was working on my doctoral dissertation on Robert Morris, I slaved over ancient ledgers, trying to untangle the thicket of confusing accounts, debits, and credits surrounding Morris's fiscal schemes. Without his ledgers, it would have been impossible to understand Morris's enormous contribution to America's founding. I don't know what I'll discover with my father's old checks, maybe nothing. I'm not even sure what I'm looking for, but I have to have them.

"Gimme," I say, literally snatching the box out of Kevin's hand.

Kevin looks at me as if I'm crazy and stomps up the stairs and out the kitchen door, still in his bedroom slippers. He has my sixty dollars to drink or snort.

"Help me put this stuff in my car," I tell Sean, as if he works for me.

"All of it?"

"Yes."

I pull my car into the driveway behind Dad's. Together, Sean and I pile boxes into the Cavalier, filling it to the headliner.

At dinner Mom serves chicken and mashed potatoes. It's just the three of us; Kevin has not come home. As we eat, Mom keeps jumping up to tend to one minor detail after another.

"Does it need salt?" she asks.

"No, Mom," says Sean.

She gets up anyway and grabs the saltshaker from the windowsill, which doubles as her spice rack. She sits again and eats a lump of chicken. "Did I leave the oven on?" And up she pops before we can answer. She turns a knob and sits again.

"Does anyone need a knife?" she asks, stabbing a carrot.

"No, Mom," says Sean.

But up she goes to get two knives, one for Sean, one for me. She sits.

"You didn't get one for yourself?"

"Oh! I guess not," she says, getting up again. "I'd forget my head if it wasn't attached."

It's like this throughout the meal, bite, chew, *boing*. Bite, chew, *boing*. It's like eating with a kangaroo.

I ask Sean how his job is going, and he tells me he hates it and he's going to quit as soon as he finds something better. He's been saying this for five years.

Sean works at a shower-door company in Astoria. They make custom doors for upscale bathrooms. He's the quality-control supervisor, meaning he walks the factory floor correcting mistakes, which makes him extremely unpopular. It pays reasonably well, enough for him to get his own place, but, apparently, he prefers his room in the attic.

After dinner I sit with Mom in front of the television, while she sips a cup of tea. The volume is insanely loud, loud enough to be heard in the Scobee parking lot. The TV is still set to Dad volume. I yell over *Wheel of Fortune*, and Mom yells back. Finally, I give up and go upstairs, where I can still hear people buying vowels.

I can't sleep, like Frank Sinatra couldn't sleep. Frank was a notorious night owl, a night fighter—that's the handle he used on his CB radio back when CBs were a thing. He'd talk the night away with truckers on the I-10, because the famous loner could not stand to be alone. Many nights, he worked the phones in the wee small hours, calling friends and sometimes strangers just to hear another voice. Nobody ever said, "Frank, do you know what time it is?" Only Ava Gardner ever hung up on Frank Sinatra.

I would need a damn good reason to call someone at this hour. So I stare at the ceiling while the events of the day play over in my head like that Dinah Washington tape stuck in my car: the trip from Somerville, the detour to the morgue, Jane's body soon to be ashes, Kevin's horrible hate-filled rant, Dad's boxes. All those canceled checks.

Why not?

I pull on my pants and go barefoot to the driveway, taking the first box I touch. Back in my room, I dump it on the bed and fan out the folders and manila envelopes, some with a string that wraps around two little cardboard discs. I grab a folder at random. Nothing of interest. A couple of receipts for washing-machine repairs from McDermott Appliances and the owner's manual for a toaster oven that got tossed twenty years ago. Just random ephemera, including a copy of *The Watchtower* that somehow found its way into Dad's boxes.

Folder by folder, envelope after envelope, I begin the tedious task of exhuming my parents' lives at the molecular level. The first box is a disappointment, but there are eleven more in the car. Ten more. I can't resist. I can't sleep.

I open the box of checks and start rifling through them. Groceries, $19.56; electric bill, $38.00; union dues, $16.50; Cub Scout uniform (Al's), $8.44. Nothing earthshaking, although I did find the receipt from the obstetrician who delivered me: $155. I hope Dad got his money's worth. I'll save the rest of the boxes until I get home.

Maybe one more. Nine left.

This box is promising. Mixed among the old tax returns (in 1971 my father grossed $9,900), I find loose photographs, mostly black-and-white, many dating to the prewar years. Some of the pictures feature my Aunts Margaret, Bridget, Mary, and Geraldine. They are young girls, and it's not easy to tell them apart except for pudgy Aunt Mary. Bridget and Geraldine wear poodle skirts and bobby socks and would have been right at home at the Paramount screaming "Frankie!" I find a couple of snaps of Mom and even two pictures of a smiling Frank McKenna. I will treasure these pictures because I can think of no others that show him unquestionably happy, not even his formal wedding portrait that hangs in the hallway, a copy of which slides out of a stiff, yellowed eight-by-fourteen envelope that has likely never been opened.

I've seen this picture ten thousand times, but I never really looked at it until now. It's just a rectangle on the wall we pass going in and out of the bathroom. But now, on my knees with the bright gooseneck lamp shining directly on it, it's spellbinding. The center of attention is, of course, the bride. She's beautiful, and I'm not just saying that because she is my mother. Catherine Boyle was a head turner. An Eleanor Powell type.

Standing ramrod straight, looking directly into the lens, is Francis McKenna. My father is wearing his dress uniform with his single private's stripe on the sleeve. Dad is not smiling. Marriage is a serious business for him, a lesson I had to learn the hard way. Aunts Margaret, Geraldine, Bridget, and Mary are beaming in their matching gowns. So, too, is Eamon McKenna, my uncle, Dad's brother, and best man.

Eamon McKenna has been little more than a name to me. He died before I was born, and what little I know I learned mostly from Mom. Eamon has bright eyes in this photo and looks a lot like Sean; rather, Sean looks like Uncle Eamon. He's a McKenna for sure, but not obviously Dad's brother, the way Kevin, Al, and I are obviously brothers. All the male members of the wedding party are in uniform, although I have no idea who they are. Until . . . the little man on the end . . . wait, that's not a smile, that's a smirk.

"I have seen this face. Who is he?" I ask myself. "Is he. . . ?"

And I run to the hallway and grab my parents' wedding photo off the wall, uncovering a stain on the wallpaper where the photo has hung untouched for decades. I look closely again at the skinny little smirking soldier on the end and compare him to the skinny little smirking soldier in the picture I just removed from the envelope.

"Yes!"

I fly down the stairs the way I did when I was thirteen and excited about everything.

"Mom!" I shout. "Mom!"

"What?" she says with alarm. "What's wrong?"

"Nothing," I reassure her. "Sorry, nothing's wrong." I turn the TV down with the remote. "This man," I say, pointing to the wedding picture. "Who is the guy on the end?"

"That's Ray," Mom says.

"Ray?"

"Ray Stankowski. He lived next to us in Bayside."

"Is he still in Bayside?"

"I have no idea. Why do you want to know?"

I can't tell her what I suspect.

"I was just wondering who that guy is."

"Oh, Ray had a thing for me. When we were kids. A crush. It was all silly, silly."

"What's his name again?" I ask.

"Ray Stan-*kow*-ski," she says slowly. "Everybody called him 'Stanky' or 'Stinky.' He just hated that!" And she laughs.

She wouldn't laugh if she knew this man had spat in her dead husband's face.

15

Don't Worry 'Bout Me

The Gods on Mount Olympus clustered around long tables with low-hanging lights as uniformed men with sticks shoved miniature armies and fleets and air wings from country to country. Messengers dashed in and out with urgent telegrams and freshly deciphered intercepts. After dinner, the President, the Führer, the Prime Minister, the Emperor, and the Supreme Commissar sat on their verandas, porticos, and at their dachas and strategized away the lives of millions. Which countries should they invade? What cities would burn tomorrow? Who should be liberated? Who exterminated? The rarified air of the Wolf's Lair, the Chrysanthemum Throne, the Kremlin, 10 Downing Street, and the Oval Office was unimaginable to men like Francis McKenna as they grabbed a few winks in a freezing hole surrounded by arbitrary death. His world was measured in meters, not miles. Yet the private's life hung in the balance of every decision made in those late-night ruminations a world away.

Then, one night, Adolf Hitler had a dream.

Having survived an assassination attempt orchestrated by his own generals, Hitler turned to the only man he knew he could trust, because he had been dead for nearly 160 years. During one of his increasingly frequent drug-induced stupors, Hitler claimed Fredrick the

Great told him to plunge back through the Ardennes Forest and retake Antwerp from the Allies, a hundred miles or so from where Francis McKenna was literally holed up. Every bullet, every tank, every boy and creaky old man would be dragooned into this last gasp. By taking Antwerp, the main port for Allied supplies, the Führer hoped to starve his enemies and tear apart the Anglo-American alliance, allowing him to make a separate peace with England and Canada, far short of Roosevelt's "unconditional surrender." The plan was insane. What wasn't in 1944?

Rain and mud. Mud and cold. Snow, sleet, ice, and more snow. Northern Europe was enveloped by a low-pressure ridge plunging down from the Arctic. Fog and frost merged with drifting snow to obscure the horizon. A man could not see ten feet in front of his nose. The Ardennes became the coldest winter post for any American Army since Valley Forge. Walking twenty yards to the latrine was exhausting. Men froze to death on guard duty, their bluish blackened fingers had to be hacked off their M1s. Francis took his turn on watch. Watching but not seeing.

At 5:30 a.m. on the morning of Saturday, December 16, four days after Private Frank McKenna and private citizen Frank Sinatra celebrated their twenty-ninth birthdays, the Battle of the Bulge began. Eighteen German infantry divisions, accompanied by twenty-five hundred tanks and self-propelled guns, attacked across the Ardennes, rolling directly over the hopelessly overwhelmed 99th Division, scattered loosely along a wide front of the Rocherath Forest.

The men of the 99th were as green as the fatigues they wore, sent to the Ardennes to put their toes in the waters of war. The Big Brains thought this the perfect place to deploy new, untested, unbloodied men, because nothing much was likely to happen there. Suddenly Germans poured across the Siegfried Line by the thousands, as robot bombs and big guns boomed for fifty miles. The word *panic* would never be written into the official histories, but panic they did, with men fleeing to the rear as fast as their half-frozen feet could carry them.

The 23rd was hustled north to cover the withdrawal of what remained of the 99th Division. Private McKenna piled into a deuce and a half with the rest of his platoon for the bumpy ride to hell. An hour later he stood in the cold, waiting and wondering with the others. Nobody knew anything except code signs: "Index" to the rear, "Ivanhoe" going forward.

"Where's the front?" someone asked. "This is the front," came the answer out of the blackness. "It just hasn't gotten here yet." But Private McKenna could hear it approaching, shell by shell.

Captain Warton finally arrived to explain their situation.

A battalion from the 99th Division was defending a ridge to the east. They had been routed by overwhelming force. The survivors continued to fight somewhere between where Baker Company stood and the approaching enemy. They had no reserve force, so B Company was temporarily attached to the 99th to provide cover as the stragglers retreated. Every minute B Company held this position meant fewer telegrams sent home to break hearts. Behind the stragglers would be Germans, lots of Germans, led by a conga line of tanks—Panzers, Panthers, and Königstigers, the dreaded King Tigers that were practically indestructible. Francis looked at his rifle in disgust. The men of B Company now worried about the telegrams that would break hearts in their own homes.

Orders, like shit, flow downstream. A Captain Michaels roared out of the morning mist in a jeep. "Colonel Tuttle wants you to take your company down the road to the left," he instructed Warton. "Beyond that is a draw running perpendicular to the highway. Place one platoon to block the road; swing your other two platoons to the right rear to defend parallel with the road." Warton followed Michaels's finger as he pointed to a map illuminated with a Zippo. "You'll tie in with K Company's left flank at a firebreak." And then Michaels vanished as quickly as he'd appeared. Sergeant Brady brought up a heavy machine gun and ammo, while Francis, Insalaco, and Lugo did their best with shovels and pickaxes to dig a gun pit to help cover the bend in the road.

Around the bend raced two jeeps and a deuce and a half crammed with GIs, the wounded strapped across the hoods to keep them warm. Close behind, a dozen exhausted men ran for their lives. "Tanks! Tanks! Tanks!" they shouted as they raced to the rear.

A gigantic Königstiger rolled into view with its lethal 88mm gun leveled. A bazooka man fired a round. It pinged off the tank, barely chipping the paint. The GI had only three rounds left. As the big tank completed its turn, machine-gun fire erupted from the behemoth's turret, sending B Company diving into the snow. Behind the King were more tanks—Tigers and Panzers—and a column of Wehrmacht soldiers carrying burp guns and rifles, with potato-masher grenades stuck to their tunics like burrs. With a demonic war whoop appropriated from the Apaches, the Germans raced toward B Company fueled by Pervitin, a government-issued methamphetamine that numbed empathy and the normal limits of human endurance. They died as fast as they could be killed, the Germans in the rear jumping over the bodies of their comrades piling up in front, creating a gruesome fleshy berm. This was fanatical behavior, suicidal. Six times the Germans came; six times B Company held the line until the bazooka man bounced his last two rounds off the King, which then established its field of fire.

"Fall back!" shouted Captain Warton redundantly, as every man from every platoon zigzagged to the relative safety of the forest. Only Sergeant Brady stayed at his post, emptying belt after belt from his heavy machine gun, until the favor was returned by the King Tiger's gunner, literally slicing Brady in half. Still, he had covered the scramble to the woods, and the men who made it home would forever be in his debt.

"Momma!" yelled someone.

The cry was ignored. The Germans were notorious for shouting Maydays in English to lure Americans into the open. But the crying was relentless, and Insalaco recognized the voice of Travis Lugo, who was stuck in no-man's-land, halfway between the approaching tanks and his own retreating platoon. Lugo was balled up in a snowbank, paralyzed by fear, not the cold.

"It's Travis," said Insalaco.

"Cover me," said Lieutenant Suits.

The two of them serpentined their way to Lugo and dragged him to the tree line. They deserved a medal. Lugo said nothing. He could not speak.

B Company drifted deeper into the woods and even lower to the ground. There was no defensive position, just a single rifle company scattered in a forest with nothing to suggest their survival. They couldn't go forward, and they couldn't go back, but they sure as hell couldn't stay where they were.

"Fall back!" Warton shouted again. "Get back!" And in twos and threes, B Company took turns shooting into clumps of Germans while their buddies scurried farther to the rear. They had bought time for the retreating 99th. Maybe twenty minutes. Not much more. More could not be asked.

The Battle of the Bulge was the largest engagement in all of World War II. At its peak, one million men fought on land and in the air, often hand to hand. The Wehrmacht pushed forward for eight full days before the Allies finally recovered their equilibrium and stopped the advance. The fighting then settled into a stalemate, a costly harvesting of men and machines producing no tactical or strategic advantage other than the culling of human life. The weather remained Germany's ally, with snow and sleet grounding the Army Air Corps and RAF, just as Hitler had foreseen. The shelling and shooting continued unabated, until the Reich's fuel supplies ran low, and the weather finally cleared.

On January 1, 1945, wave after wave of P-47s rained death on the Nazis, turning tanks, even the King Tigers, into smudge pots and supply trains into flaming steel snakes. "Happy New Year, Adolf!" was scrawled on the five-hundred-pounders, but the recipients didn't live to read the salutations. The tide had turned. By February the battered Wehrmacht had been forced back until the Bulge in the Allies line was gone. So, too, were nineteen thousand American lives, along with countless Germans and civilians.

Francis McKenna survived with only a small gash in the fleshy part of his calf, halfway between his ankle and his knee. During a particularly intense barrage, he had stood with his back flat against a tree trunk to expose as little of himself as possible to the shells. But the Germans knew the woods were crowded with Americans and aimed accordingly, calibrating their artillery for the treetops, showering the Americans with a downpour of spear-like splinters. A shell drove a six-inch shard deep into McKenna's leg. He didn't know he had been hit until he felt the warmth of his own blood filling his boot. This qualified him for a Purple Heart he did not get because, true to form, he never told anyone he had been hit.

Francis X. McKenna had now killed other men, of that there is no doubt. How many? Who knows? In the pandemonium of that first desperate day in the Ardennes, he fired his weapon madly at men and machine alike. Did he see men drop? Unknown. Did it trouble him? Unknown.

The kitchen trucks brought up hot meals and then, platoon by platoon, B Company enjoyed their first showers in forever. Francis had been bathing out of his helmet for a month and enjoyed every near-scalding second he spent in the shower tents with endless hot water, thanks to the engineers who rigged pipes to an improvised boiler. The men joked and wrestled and took turns scrubbing each other's naked bodies with uninhibited joy. Fresh from the showers, they grabbed new fatigues, their old uniforms so caked with filth they practically stood by themselves. Private McKenna stuffed his pockets with extra socks, as did every man, until the footwear ran out. It was easier to get the clap than clean socks.

Replacements arrived to fill the ranks. As the newbies climbed out of the transports, McKenna gave them the same stink eye he had received. Dugan was now a battle-tested veteran. He had not broken under fire. As one of the oldest men in his unit, Private McKenna was treated with deference by the fresh meat who were nearly as afraid of the veterans as they were of the enemy. Occasionally, the Jerrys would send over a barrage of shells to remind everyone they were still there, but after the mayhem of the Bulge, only the greenest men took shelter.

A short while later he wrote a letter—Number 68—to Catherine:

Bunny,

Well, your ol' Jack R. is quite the hero now. I got a scratch on my leg. A splinter. By the time I get home, I'll make a mountain of it. And I'll tell everyone how I rassled Himmler to the ground all by meself. Sleeping late now. Eating like Mary.

(Don't let her see this!) Mail truck is leaving. More to-morrow.
Don't worry. I'm as healthy as a horse.

Your husband,
XX

During this lull, the rumor mill picked up steam. While the specifics were always wrong, they were universally correct in spirit. The 23rd Regiment was moving out, heading east, deep into Germany. Having earned points with the brass for the delaying action fought at the bend in the road, Captain Warton and B Company were given the honor of leading the tip of the spear in what was to come next.

"Some honor," said somebody on behalf of everybody. "The fuck-ups stay in the rear, while we get our balls shot off."

The order came to move out, and Francis McKenna stowed his gear, secured his bedroll, and climbed aboard yet another truck without a grumble. They had come this far. They would finish the job so they could go home and live their lives.

16

Bang Bang
(My Baby Shot Me Down)

Ray Stankowski. Stanky. Stinky. Where is he? Does he still carry a torch for my mother? Does he hate my father for winning her hand? Did he come to Dad's wake to spit in his face over an unrequited love from half a century ago? Why come to his funeral? Why the salute? Why sign the registry "Compliments of Willie and Joe"?

I sit at my old desk with pen and paper to organize my thoughts. He has to live nearby. He knew about Dad's death. How? From the *Daily News*, of course. He has to be close enough for a man his age to make two trips to Little Neck, first to the wake, then the funeral. Would he be in the phone book? Which phone book? Queens County? There are two million people in Queens County. All five boroughs? Some four hundred thousand live on Staten Island alone. There's another two million in Nassau County. A million more in Suffolk. Then there's New Jersey, Connecticut, upstate New York.

There are probably a million Poles in the tristate area. Every year, the Pulaski Day Parade brings out a sea of red-and-white flags along Fifth Avenue, with throngs of Kowalskis, Jankowskis, Wojicks, Wojciechowskis, and Wozniaks enveloped in the dueling aromas of kielbasa, pierogi, and kopytka hawked from pushcarts on every corner. There's likely a thousand Stankowskis alone, but I am now confident Rajmund "Ray" Stankowski, formerly of Bayside, Queens, New York, is the man who defiled my father's corpse and undoubtedly planned further mayhem at his funeral if I hadn't beat him to the punch. I must find him.

Phone books will take forever. If I knew how to use a computer, there might be a way. Then, it dawns on me—he's a veteran. That means the V.A. and a pension. That means a paper trail that didn't burn up in St. Louis. A man who can still snap a salute after fifty years is likely a member at the Veterans of Foreign Wars or American Legion even if my father was not.

But where?

The next day I draw a couple of suspicious looks from behind curtained windows as I stare at the house in Bayside Stinky Stankowski once shared with his brother, Connie, his five sisters, and his Polish immigrant parents while dreaming of fucking my mother.

I stop a dog walker and ask if he remembers the Stankowskis. He docs not. Nobody here knows anything. I drive to the local senior center and ask around. Half can't hear my questions, the rest jumble the Stankowskis with Stankowitzes, Stankiewiczes, and Stankofskis, raising and dashing my hopes. Then I go home to regroup, and my mother remembers:

"You know who might know? Your Aunt Mary," she says while ironing a dish towel. "She stayed in touch with some of the Stankowski girls. Mary will love hearing from you."

This would be an awkward call under perfect circumstances. I haven't telephoned my Aunt Mary since high school, when I thanked her for a graduation card. I have not seen her since the disaster on the altar. She sounds nervous on the phone.

"I hope I'm not bothering you, Aunt Mary," I say, pouring oil on troubled waters.

"What bother?" she says, returning my serve.

I give her an abbreviated version of what I want, leaving out my belief that Ray Stankowski spat in my father's face and trolled his funeral.

"Oh, it's been years," she tells me. "His sister Lucky moved to South Carolina. I lost touch with the rest." Then she hollers to her husband. "Eddie!" she bellows. "Do you remember where Ray Stankowski moved?"

"Ray who?" yells Uncle Ed from another room.

"Stanky Stankowski!" she screams. I hold the phone away from my ear. This is how they live, shouting at each other from room to room and sometimes when in the same room.

"Who wants to know?" hollers Uncle Ed.

"Danny!"

"Kate's Danny?"

"Yes!"

"Christ! Why's he asking us?"

"How do I know?"

"New Jersey, I think! He moved to Jersey! That was twenty years ago. Thirty. He could be dead."

But he's not dead. And now I have a lead. I thank Aunt Mary profusely and ask her to thank Uncle Ed as well.

"Danny says thank you," she screams, as I hang up.

At the Little Neck library, I throw myself on the head librarian who pawns me off on a reed-thin woman of indeterminant age. Miriam something, I don't catch her last name, but I assume she's Jewish, because every Miriam I've ever met is Jewish. I wonder why this even pops into my head. Miriam runs technology services; Little Neck has entered the computer age. Maybe there's hope for me? My eyes glaze over as the names and addresses of VFW halls and American Legion posts scroll up and down the screen. I ask Miriam to print a list of every post and lodge in New Jersey. It will cost ten cents a page, so I narrow the list by eliminating northern Passaic and most of southern Monmouth County, saving three dollars.

Back at Mom's, I start dialing.

"Hello? I'm trying to reach Ray Stankowski."

"Who?"

"Ray Stankowski."

"Never heard of him."

"Stankowski. World War II vet." I repeat post after post, lodge after lodge.

I feel like I'm twelve again, prank calling the pizza place Kevin worked at in high school. "This is Jack N. Hoff," I'd say with my pitchy, pubescent voice that never fooled him.

I call each VFW hall and American Legion post on my list, asking for Ray and immediately hanging up if they don't know him. When nobody picks up, I circle the number, so I'll remember to call again. Occasionally, the voice on the other end asks, "Who wants him?" which raises my hopes and forces me to identify myself. That I mustn't do. Ray Stankowski can't know I'm on to him. "Bob Apodaca," I say, coopting the name of a former Mets pitcher who mysteriously pops into my head. I haven't thought of Bob Apodaca in years. Why now?

"My name is Bob Apodaca, and I'm trying to find a member named Ray Stankowski."

"Nobody here by that name." *Click.*

"My name is Bob Apodaca, and I'm trying to find a legionnaire named Ray Stankowski."

"Nobody here by that name." *Click.*

When I hit fifty dead ends, I realize I've begun to sound like those people who call selling storm windows reading their pitch from a script. I dial so many places so quickly, I haven't even considered what to say if the voice on the other end says, "Hold on, he's sitting right here."

Then it happens. The phone rings at American Legion Post 113 on Cleveland Street, in Fairview, New Jersey.

"Is Ray Stankowski there?"

"Not tonight, but he'll be here tomorrow for sure," says a deep, baritone voice. "You want to leave a message?"

"Um, no." *Click.* "I found you, you motherfucker!" I yell directly at the telephone.

I've never heard of Fairview, New Jersey, so I go to Dad's car and pull out the big road atlas from the side pocket. Back in my bedroom, now CENTCOM for Operation Find Stanky, my finger slithers around the Garden State, finally landing on Fairview, almost directly across the river from Grant's Tomb, only twenty miles as the crow flies from Little Neck. A doable drive.

I call Information and push buttons until I get a person. I ask the operator for Ray Stankowski in Fairview, New Jersey. The operator finds an "R. Stankowski" at 24-22 Reddick Road, in Little Ferry. Excitedly, I scribble down the address and phone number, then read it back to make sure I have it right. According to the map, Little Ferry is only a few miles from Fairview. It all fits.

My heart pounds so quickly that I go to the window and open it wide, sucking in the warm summer air. This isn't a panic attack, rather an adrenaline rush. I draw in a deep breath, and my pulse slows enough so I can think.

After dinner and yelling over the TV with Mom and Sean for an hour, I take a long shower and try to read myself to sleep. I end up getting out of bed twice to go over my checklist for tomorrow.

———

I take Dad's car into the city because my car is stuffed with his boxes, and that would mean an early Christmas for the smash-and-grabbers who would pick the car clean.

As I crawl through the Midtown Tunnel, the radio fades out as it always does when you go under the river. I have things to decide: Where should I scatter Jane's ashes? If I knew her better, or at all, maybe I'd have some idea. Did she like the water? I could put her in the river or Little Neck Bay or take her to Jones Beach. I could even bring her home to Somerville and scatter her at the Cape next time I go. Then, there's Stanky. What am I going to do when I find him? The radio comes back to life as I emerge onto 37th Street. I forget about Jane and Stanky and everything other than the jerkoff who drove a motor home into Midtown and is now blocking the grid. I lean on the horn.

Lyons & Sons is on 14th Street between Seventh and Eighth Avenues. I consider double-parking out front, but I have no idea how long this will take, and it would be my luck to get towed. I circle three times before I find a spot. As it turns out, I could have double-parked. They have Jane ready to go.

"That's it?"

"Yes. That's Ms. Freeman," says the mortician, as he hands me a paper sack.

"No urn?"

"Would you like an urn, Mr. McKenna? You didn't request one, but I'd be happy to show you what we have."

I give the sack a little bounce in my palm. This isn't a regular paper bag. It's thicker, like the kind cement comes in or a bag of grout. About six pounds. I'm surprised it's so heavy.

"This is fine," I say, pocketing a receipt.

Out on 14th Street, I blend in with all the other people carrying bags. Bags tell a story—Dick's Sporting Goods, Macy's, D'Agostino, Barneys, Kate Spade. Jane's bag says nothing. Her epitaph. I put her on the passenger seat.

The news station says the Lincoln Tunnel is a mess, so I take the Holland across to New Jersey. A couple of working girls selling blow jobs wave at the cars as they enter the tunnel. Freud would have a field day. A truck with Delaware plates stops, and the skinnier of the two fat hookers climbs in. Her butt crack is showing between two large love handles that spill over the top of her black sequined hot pants. The rips in her fishnets are big enough for an entire school to swim through. She'll finish her business before the truck reaches the Jersey side, then she'll flag down a john for the ride back to New York. Shampoo, rinse, repeat. This vignette didn't make *Pretty Woman*.

When you come out of the tunnel into Hoboken, you face a mishmash of highways and crisscrossing surface streets. If I blink, I'll miss my turnoff, and then I'm screwed. I speed past Sinatra's hometown without giving it a look.

I make it to Route 9, north to Secaucus. The Hackensack River is on my left. At Ridgefield/Palisades Park, I merge onto the Jersey Turnpike with the lyrics to Freddy "Boom Boom" Cannon's "Palisades Park" colliding in my head with Steve Clayton's old radio jingle, "Come On Over!"

The amusement park wasn't actually *in* Palisades Park; rather, it was on the Palisades, in Fort Lee, high above the Hudson River. I only went once, but in my mind's eye it was better than Disneyland will ever be. Mothers hawked up loogies and threw hot-dog wrappers on the ground, and told their children it was okay to litter, while men cursed and smoked and blew their noses by pinching their nostrils together. Try that in Anaheim, and you'll get tased by Mickey. Everybody drank canned beer and fists flew, always. Palisades Park was Paleolithic. It's where New Jersey came to play.

I turn onto Route 46, an ugly ribbon of gas stations, shoe stores, discount mattress warehouses, and billboards for urban radio stations, gentleman's lounges, and soon-to-be-indicted politicians. Sinatra once said, "You know what we thought growing up? We thought everybody was on the take. We knew the cops were taking. They were right in front of us. But we thought the priests were on the take, the schoolteachers, the guy in the marriage-license bureau, everybody. We thought if God came to New Jersey, he'd get in line to pick up his envelope." I'm not on 46 long before I enter Little Ferry. Two lefts and a right put me onto Reddick Road. And there's 24-22.

Not bad. Better than my place in Somerville. The smallest on the block, from what I can see. Two stories with a couple of bedrooms facing the street, maybe two more in the back. The first floor has been redone with faux brick; the upper level is vinyl-sided with freshly painted brown shutters around the windows. The lawn is perfect, not a dandelion or leaf or twig to be seen. He's one of those guys—obsessive-compulsive. He must diaper the birds so they don't crap on his lawn. He lives better than I do.

I drive around the block, so I can park across the street rather than directly in front. I'm willing to wait all night until I see him, until I'm absolutely sure I have the right guy. I don't want to author my own "Wrong Door Raid," like Sinatra and Joltin' Joe DiMaggio barging into Marilyn Monroe's pied-à-terre, only to find Florence Kotz, a secretary, sleeping in her own bed. She screamed in terror, believing she was about to be murdered by strangers, one of whom looked exactly like Frank Sinatra. I will sit and wait until I'm positive I've found *the* Ray Stankowski. I take the yellowed wedding-party photo out of its envelope and lean it against the sack of Jane's ashes. My reference point.

"Christ almighty, doesn't he ever leave the house?" I say after only ten minutes have passed. I'm bored out of my skull. How do cops do this? I should have brought a book. I turn on the radio but quickly shut it off, afraid to run down the battery. I'm sweating like salted pork. I want air-conditioning, but an idling car sends up even more red flags than a parked car.

I wait. A Gulfstream comes in low with a whoosh on final descent to Teterboro, which is only a few blocks away. Cessnas and Pipers buzz into the air or float down for a landing every few minutes. They go right over the house, lower and louder even than the jets leaving LaGuardia that pass over our place in Little Neck.

A mailman comes and drops a few letters in the box by the front door. No dog barks. Nobody comes to collect the mail. I take a huge gamble. I run to the mailbox and grab today's haul, mostly junk addressed to "Resident" but also an exterminator bill and bank state-ment for "Rachel Stankowski."

"Shit!" I put the letters back and dash to the car.

"Rachel Stankowski!" The R. Stankowski I got from information is not Ray; it's Rachel!

What do I do? Maybe that's his wife? The phone could be in his wife's name.

A car turns onto Reddick Road. I slump down a little. The car doesn't stop. It keeps going and turns into a driveway fifteen houses down. I slump again when two more cars pass. I start the car and drive around the block, mostly to cool off but also to think. Nobody has noticed me. If they had, the cops would've been here by now. I'm highly suspicious. I *feel* suspicious. I start to rehearse stories I can tell a neighbor if challenged. I settle on car trouble. I consider popping the hood but that will draw instant attention. Jersey is filled with gear-heads. Someone will try to help me.

I continue to sit, numbed by the near total absence of life in this neighborhood. No children play. Not a squirrel on the wires or a cat slinking across a lawn. Then the door opens. Out comes a woman.

She's about my age, too young to be his wife. A daughter? She's a little chubby, wearing a gray pantsuit. A professional type. A realtor? This is Rachel. She turns and shouts back into the house.

"Hurry up, please." She looks at her watch. "I can't be late!"

And that brings him to the door. Shriveled, stooped, skeletal, giant ears, cane, and if I needed another reason to hate him, a Yankees hat covering his bald, veined, liver-spot-brindled head. I glance at the photograph. It's him. Ray Stankowski. The spitter. Definitely.

Stanky fumbles with the zipper on his windbreaker. It's ninety degrees. He doesn't need a jacket. But he's old, and I suppose he's cold, because old people are always cold. He's colder than most. Finally, the coat is zipped, and he steps out. The daughter offers him her hand as he navigates the one step he has to descend. He waves her off.

"Wait here. I'll get the car," she says.

A big DHL cargo jet takes off, making a huge racket. He stands there looking at nothing. There's no way this feeble old man drove all the way to Little Neck twice. He can't even zip his coat. He had to take the train. Or a bus to the city and then the LIRR to Little Neck. What an effort! What madness made him do this?

A minute later Rachel backs a green Subaru out of the garage. She stops the car at the walkway and gets out.

"Come on," she says, holding the car door for him.

"You're always in a goddamn hurry!" he barks back.

There's another delay while he fumbles with his seatbelt. She tries to help him, but he swats her away. I can't hear what they say, but like a silent movie, the action tells the story. Finally, the backup lights come on, and she pulls into the street. She makes a right on Robby Road. I start Dad's car and follow slowly, gladly letting two cars get between us.

She makes a left on Niehaus; I make a left on Niehaus. We drive past a VFW hall. Why doesn't he go here? It's half a mile from his house!

I see a sign ahead: "Entering Borough of Fairview. Established

1894." She turns left on Fairview Avenue. They slow down a bit. I can see her eyes in the rearview mirror. Does she know she's being followed?

No, instead she fixes her lipstick and picks up speed again. She makes a right on Cleveland. I do the same. Then suddenly, she pulls to the right and stops. American Legion Post 113. I drive past so I can circle back and come in behind them. When I do, she's out of the car holding the door. She gives him a kiss on the cheek. She loves this prick. He walks stiffly toward the entrance as Rachel drives off to wherever she's in a hurry to get to.

American Legion Post 113 is a one-story brick building with two smooth white columns supporting an unadorned entablature. A big flagpole ringed by benches and circular flower beds share the front lawn with a M101 howitzer of Korean War vintage. If it weren't for the big gun, this could easily be mistaken for a nursing home, even more so once inside.

It smells old in here. Stale, like everybody's grandmother's house. Bleachy. Fifty years of pancake breakfasts, Monte Carlo nights, clambakes, Italian festivals, St. Patrick's Days, Pulaski Days, and every other day that can conceivably be celebrated has been celebrated in this building. Half a century of ethnic cooking permeates the curtains, carpets, linoleum, and even the ceiling tiles. The place stinks of sauerkraut, corned beef and cabbage, kielbasa, marinara, tobacco, draft beer, and urine.

The décor, if you can call it that, is midcentury bulletin board. Legion halls love signage. There are flags, of course, and bald eagles, and Washington and Lincoln, but mostly there are flyers and posters warning not to X this or Y that. A row of portable coatracks line one wall, with three or four orphaned jackets still waiting to be claimed. Post 113 is what the world would look like if there were no women.

Down a hallway, by the restrooms, big, round tables with collapsed legs lean against the wall like giant poker chips waiting to be rolled out for the next event. Rentals keep the doors open: weddings, baby showers, baptisms, post-funeral collations, retirement parties, fundraising dances, food by the ton, an ocean of alcohol, gallons of sweat from blubbery White people dancing to Sly and the Family Stone. Life has been lived in this building.

Now it's dying. All the founding members are gone. Even the youngest guys, the Vietnam vets, are in their fifties, and the Gulf War–age guys aren't joiners. Stankowski is one of the last of the Greatest Generation who still answers the bell.

And there he is, at the bar, elbows down on either side of a gin and tonic, guarding his drink as if someone is trying to steal it.

I sit on the stool next to him.

"Remember me, Stanky?"

"Should I?" he says, as he looks at me, puzzled. Then his eyes widen. "You?"

"Yes, me."

"What are you doing here?"

He's rattled. I love it.

"We have to talk," I say.

"About what?"

"You know this guy?" the bartender asks Ray.

"He's the McKenna kid. The one I told you about. The fuckup."

"Are you in the Legion?" asks the baritone-voiced bartender.

"No," I say.

"You can't be here unless you're in the Legion."

"I have business with Stanky here." And I punch the Stanky, but nobody reacts. They call him Stanky, too.

"I don't have any business with you," says Ray.

"Okay, buddy, out," says the bartender.

"This prick spat in my father's face. At his wake! Right into the casket!"

"Out!" repeats the barkeep.

"Your father was a yellow coward. A fucking deserter!" screams Stankowski, the veins in his neck pulsing with half a century of rage. His blood pressure has to be 190. He's close to a stroke.

"What are you talking about?" I shout back.

"You know."

"I don't know."

"Leave or I throw you out!" threatens the bartender.

"He ran from his unit," says Ray, spraying me with spittle. "He was court-martialed." More spittle. "Did a stretch, the lucky bastard! They should have shot his ass like Slovik!"

"What shit is this?" Now I'm rattled.

"You're *that* McKenna's kid?" asks the bartender. "The kid that busted up the funeral?"

"Fucking coward! Someday I'll piss on his grave, too."

"Hey, this is the McKenna kid!" shouts the bartender to four other drinkers. Then he turns back to me. "We all thought that was just more of Stanky's bullshit."

"A goddamn coward he was, and you can drop dead, too, as far as I'm concerned."

"Fuck you, Stanky!" I scream right into his face. "My father fought his way across Germany. Where did you fight? Fort Dix?"

"I fought, punk!"

"Where?"

He says nothing. His lips quiver.

"France? Italy? North Africa?"

"I don't got to tell you!"

"The Solomons? Iwo? Okinawa?"

"I got nothing to say to you."

"You got nothing, because you never went anywhere. If you did, you'd be at the VFW, not the American Legion, wouldn't you, Stinky?" And I hit the Stinky hard.

Ray takes a big swig of his drink. Then, "At least I didn't run. I gotta piss."

And he shuffles to the men's room.

"Don't let that old goat get you going. He's a nut," says the bartender sympathetically. "I don't know how his niece puts up with him."

"Rachel?"

"You know her?"

"She's not his daughter?"

"His niece," he says. "A saint, that one is."

"He spat in my father's face."

"I'm telling you, he's a nut."

"And this shit about Dad being a deserter . . ."

"Stanky's got a bug up his ass. When Sinatra croaked, Christ, he wouldn't shut up. We had to take 'My Way' off the jukebox."

"My father fought in the Battle of the Bulge!" I shout to the ceiling.

"And don't get him going on Slick Willie or Hanoi Jane," says the barkeep.

Stanky has not returned. I look over my shoulder toward the hallway.

"What's taking him so long?"

"The head's that way," says the bartender pointing.

I go into the hallway, make a left down another hallway, and find the men's room. He's not at the urinals. I check the stalls. Not here. "Fuck me!" I check the ladies' room. Empty.

I rush back to the lobby, past the folded-up tables and the racks with the unclaimed coats, past Washington and Lincoln, the bald eagles, and a big poster announcing next week's Octoberfest, even though it's only July. And then I see him through the window, he's waving at a car in the parking lot. He gestures in my direction. The driver leans over and throws whatever's on the passenger seat into the back. I rush out to stop him.

"Wait!"

Stankowski drops into the seat and motions for the driver to go. The car lurches before he even pulls the door shut. I'm running now, chasing him like a dog chasing a tennis ball, only joylessly. I turn toward Dad's car. I fumble with the keys. The car starts.

I drive like mad back to Rachel's, arriving just as Stanky shuts the front door. I ring the bell a million times, then I pound on his door with two clenched fists, playing a tattoo.

"Open up, you fucker! Who's the coward now, Stinky?"

He yells back from the other side. I keep pounding and yelling, and he keeps cursing me, but mostly my father. This brings a few neighbors out on their lawns and then a police car arrives, and I am spoken to.

"Whatever he may or may not have done, sir, you are trespassing and disturbing the peace," says the cop.

Stanky wins.

———

I drive from Reddick Road in a daze. Instead of a left, I make a right, then I make a right, when I should go straight. I am lost. My head spins. I'm like a drunk driver. I open all four windows and let the hot night air slap me around. It's Arizona hot. I stop at an Arby's to splash water on my face. I get back on the road. The road to where? Where do I go with my head filled with thunder?

Friday traffic. Getaway day. Every road is jammed with Jerseyites heading to the shore. I go home. To Little Neck. I see a sliver of light leaking from under my mother's bedroom door. I tap lightly.

"Mom?" I ask as I walk in.

"Danny?"

She puts down her prayer book, a pamphlet really, something the Society for the Propagation of the Faith sent her for mailing them ten dollars. My mother is an easy mark for anything church-related. She gets dozens of these pamphlets every week, along with calendars, laminated saint cards—like baseball cards for Catholics, only without the stick of gum—rosary beads, vials of holy water allegedly blessed by Pope John Paul II, and a cornucopia of Jesus tchotchkes. Her bed is littered with envelopes and collateral materials from various groups asking for a handout. Her checkbook is open. She's in a giving mood. I'm hoping she can give me some answers.

"It's late. Have you eaten?"

"I've eaten," I say, sitting on the edge of her bed in a nonthreatening manner.

"I don't think your brothers are home."

"Mom, I have to talk to you." Her antenna goes up. She knows whatever I am about to say is bad.

"I saw an old friend of yours today."

"Of mine?"

"Ray Stankowski."

"Stanky?" she says with real surprise. "Where in the world?"

"Mom, he told me something about Dad that shocked me. Really shocked me."

"What did he tell you?" she asks with alarm.

"He said . . . during the war . . . Dad . . ."

"It's a lie!" she says ferociously, cutting me off.

" . . . deserted."

"A lie!"

"He told me Dad was court-martialed. Sent to prison!" Emotion takes prison up an octave.

"Ray Stankowski doesn't know shit," she says, throwing the covers off and jumping out of bed, sending her saints and checkbook flying.

"Ray said everyone knew . . . when Dad came home from the war. Yellow, he called him. YELLOW!" And I lose it.

"Frank a coward? Where are your children?" she asks with contempt in her voice.

"My what?"

"Your children!" she shouts, even angrier this time. "Where are they?"

"I don't have children," I say, confused.

"Why not? At your age your father had four children!"

"Mom, I'm just asking because Ray said . . ."

"Your father fought in the war," she cuts me off again. "He came home different. Terrible things. But he was a good man. A good husband. A good father. Did you ever go to bed hungry, even once? You had a roof over your head, didn't you? You went to all those schools you went to, didn't you? Don't talk to me about cowards and yellow until you raise your own children!" And she starts to sob.

I stand speechless. I am physically unable to form words. A verbal hay-maker has struck me dumb. Am I a coward because I don't have kids?

Children do frighten me. They're all feelings, and I feel too much. Children never stop breaking your heart, like I'm breaking my mother's right now. I've made her say "shit," maybe for the first time in her life. I go to hug her. She pushes me away with both hands.

"Get away!"

She crosses to her closet and reaches on her toes to the top shelf, pulling down a big round hatbox from the '50s. She shoves the box violently into my gut like a quarterback tucking the ball into the hands of a fumble-prone halfback.

"Here!" she barks.

The Greatest Generation had women, too.

As I close her door behind me, my mother howls like a wounded beast.

I empty the hatbox on my bed. Five bundles of yellowed letters tumble out. Each packet is tied with twine. I start to untie a stack; the brittle twine snaps in my fingers from age. Dad's wartime letters. The postmarks go back to his stay at Camp Upton, his earliest days in the army. My mother numbered them in pencil, carefully collating them in chronological order. Incredible!

This is the first letter with his spelling and punctuation intact:

Dear Bunny,

I'm here. You won't believe who my Sgt. is. Larry Kirby. I sold his people bread and cakes. He now has everyone calling me, "Dugan" like it's my name.

Hair all cut off short. It feels funny when I rub my hand on my head. Prickly like when I rub you. (Wink, wink)

This is going to be just so you know I'm here. The train took forever. Thanks for The jar of jam. There was nothing on the train.

All my love from you're,
Jack Rabbit

"Bunny" and "Jack Rabbit," sometimes just "Rabbit," appear throughout their correspondence. It doesn't take the cryptanalysts at Bletchley Park to crack the code of their pet names. I am shocked, then amused, then moved, and even amazed. My prudish, virginal, repressed mother had a pulse after all. These were names rarely said later in life. In moments of tenderness, a Bunny might slip out from his lips, but I can only recall her calling him Jack Rabbit once, at his eightieth birthday at Patrick's Pub, the last time all of us were together. Occasionally, she'd snap at him, "Watch yourself, Jack!" when he got on her nerves, but even that was rare. Letter Number 1 is like finding the Rosetta Stone to my mother and father's marriage. There are a hundred more.

I can't read them tonight. It's too much. All of it. Jane, Stinky, this whole day. This life. Each of these letters will need to be digested. I turn off the light and nearly pass out from cognitive dissonance.

17

Let Me Try Again

Today Sinsig is a picturesque village on the banks of the Rhine River, a little less than fifty miles southeast of Cologne. It was equally picturesque in March 1945, occupied as it was by a Panzer-Grenadier battalion and treated as if it were the soldiers' own hometown. For several dozen, it was. As the American war machine approached, Sinsig was hastily abandoned without a fight and therefore spared the fate of so many idyllic European villages that were plastered by shot and shell.

The men of B Company were not greeted as liberators. The locals eyed them with suspicion, fear, and hatred, or—worse—fawning, sycophantic obsequiousness.

"*Nicht Nazi! Nicht Nazi!*" they shouted, protesting too much.

There were no cheering, flower-strewing mademoiselles as in France, or even the neutral Belgian *jonge dames*, who had been whipsawed back and forth between the various occupying forces and were unsure whom it was safe to kiss. The fräuleins of Sinsig, and every town going forward, would stare with angry eyes, wondering if the men marching into their town had killed their husbands, their beaus, their brothers, and, of late, even their grandfathers. Sinsig was a village of women, children, and geriatrics, a town stripped of its vital manhood like every city, town, and hamlet that had embraced Hitler's degeneracy.

The local *Burgermeister* was pressured to say something. He approached Colonel Tuttle and, in halting English, demanded to know how long the Americans would stay. "Until your Führer burns in hell," said the colonel. The Burgermeister did not translate this for the others.

The men of B Company called Sinsig "Zig-Zag," like every Yank who passed through. They would remember it fondly. Their principal activity was counting enemy planes on their way to attack the bridgehead at Remagen, a last doomed attempt by the Germans to keep Patton and his tanks west of the Rhine. Bets were placed. Eight bandits fly over Zig-Zag; only two fly back. The winners cheered while the losers handed over cigarettes or scrip.

Private McKenna's billet was a school building where all the GIs slept. Captain Warton, Lieutenants Suits, Chase, and the other officers bunked in the command post, a storybook medieval castle with crenellated towers missing only a captive damsel with long golden hair. Warton did not often coopt luxury, choosing instead to share the same hardships as the men he led. But after the shock of December 16, no one begrudged the captain his warm bath and electric lights, because the castle offered a panoramic view in every direction. The Germans would not take them by surprise a second time.

The hours turned to days and days into weeks, as the final push to Berlin awaited resupply. Zig-Zag became an accidental rest stop with little to do but write letters and smoke. A week in, Francis volunteered with two others, Privates Anthony Insalaco and Steven Herndon, for a covert mission, Operation Beefsteak, an unauthorized sortie whose sole objective was a lone cow lazily grazing in a pasture just beyond their schoolhouse barracks. The cow was taken without incident, her carcass dragged to the cooks via a weasel, a small-tracked vehicle used to evacuate the wounded.

"Where'd you get that?" asked Captain Warton sternly after wandering into the kitchen.

"Stepped on a mine, sir," said Private Insalaco.

"I like mine medium," said Warton. The men laughed. Then Warton asked, "Anybody know where Dugan is?"

"I saw him by the latrines," offered Herndon.

Captain Warton found McKenna shaving, his bayonet doubling as his razor.

"Dugan?"

"Yeah, Cap'n?"

"You got a minute?"

"Yeah, Cap'n."

"Sit down."

Francis sat on a case of 60mm mortar shells, his soapy bayonet dripping onto his pant leg. Warton handed him an envelope. The private looked at the envelope, then at Captain Warton. He opened it and read:

> The Secretary of War desires me to express
> his deepest regret that your brother,
> Sergeant McKenna, Eamon Aloysius, was
> killed in S.F., California, on the 27th of
> February. Letter follows.
>
> Ulio, the Adjutant General

Eamon was more than Francis's brother; he was his best friend and maybe his only friend. He would keep the telegram for the rest of his life.

"I'm sorry, Dugan," said Warton.

"When did he make sergeant?" asked Francis rhetorically.

"You're on light duty, Dugan. My condolences."

Eamon had been the lucky one, Francis thought. He had landed cushy duty in Oakland, part of a secret program known as SIGSALY, the first draft of modern-day digital voice, data, and video transmission. Churchill, FDR, then Truman, needed real-time encryption to speed up communication across the oceans. All SIGSALY personnel were handpicked for their special talents, and that's how Eamon McKenna came to be part of the group. The man whose math prowess impressed the nuns at St. Barnabas and who once crunched numbers for Dugan's bakery was tapped to crunch numbers for Uncle Sam. Unable to reach Fiona McKenna in Ireland, the War Department sent its telegram to Francis as next of kin.

A follow-up letter said Eamon McKenna died from injuries received in a fight outside a bar in San Francisco. His assailants, two sailors from the heavy cruiser U.S.S. *Louisville*, had been arrested and were awaiting court-martial for murder.

———

In the latrines, at chow time and before the GIs hit the sack, the latest news from *Stars and Stripes* was debated; the pessimists read the worst into every story, while the optimists saw rainbows in every sentence. It was hard to say who was more irritating. By all appearances, the Germans were licked. Just that morning thousands of POWs marched through the center of Zig-Zag on their way to prison camps in the West, some sent all the way to Nebraska and Oklahoma.

As if by secret signal, the streets of Sinsig emptied. The prisoners passed by their American captors stoically, arrogantly, eyes straight ahead toward the middle distance. A few had the gall to bring their fingers to their lips, hoping some soft-touch GI would toss them a Pall Mall or Chesterfield. Still, even the most fanatical Nazis among them knew they had hit the jackpot by falling into American hands rather than Russian. When the order to move out finally came, the reverie in Zig-Zag was over.

It was time to kill again.

At 4:45 the next morning, Baker Company advanced south along the west bank of the Rhine with the rest of the 23rd Regiment. In trucks, half-tracks, jeeps, and atop tanks, the soldiers traveled sixty miles through Bad Breisig, Brohl-Lützing, and Andernach—one nothing town in the way of the next. Still, each town was a potential ambush and therefore approached with caution. It was not until the regiment crossed the Rhine near Neuwied that the advance scouts ran into the rear guard of the German Army. The Nazis had chosen the hillside town of Stromberg as the place where they would make their stand. Before B Company could get to Stromberg, they would first have to punch through a string of tiny villages, one more deadly than the next, a gauntlet designed to sap their strength before the big battle. The villages of Heimbach, Weis, and Schloss-Sayn are bunched so closely together, it was hard to tell when you left one and entered the next.

In Heimbach, the resistance was light, misleadingly so, a false indication of the Germans' willingness to die for the Fatherland. Two men from the 2nd Platoon were killed outright by snipers: a corporal from Murfreesboro, Tennessee, and a private from Long Island who had ridden with McKenna on the same train to Camp Upton. In the next village, Weis, the 23rd slowed to a crawl; every window was a potential sniper's perch, every culvert a possible machine gun nest.

Two Panzers churned up the cobblestone road from Schloss. "Tanks!" echoed through the ranks, as the men took what cover they could. Lieutenant Suits grabbed the walkie-talkie and called for the 155s to open up. "Concentration, queen, one, six, three! That's queen, one, six, three!" Sixty seconds later three salvos of shells exploded atop the Panzers. The concussion was tremendous, toppling the shop walls on both side of the Stadtplatz. One Panzer literally flipped ass over teakettle and spun on its turret like a giant steel turtle. The other tank smoldered for a few seconds and then burst into flames. Both hatches opened, and burning men screamed as they popped out and rolled on the ground. A rifleman shot them dead as an act of compassion.

As the war moved into the next village, Schloss-Sayn, two more GIs were hit by snipers.

"Take three men and clear out those houses," barked Captain Warton to Lieutenants Suits and Chase. "Check the attics and basements."

Suits grabbed the first three guys from his platoon. Lieutenant Chase was more selective, deliberately tapping Corporal Joseph Cosgriff, Private Anthony Insalaco, and Private Francis McKenna. Lieutenant Suits's squad went left, while Chase took his men to the right.

The first house was a two-hundred-year-old stone-and-timber chateau with leaded-glass windows and multiple chimneys and dormers jutting out from a slate roof. Today it's a pricey bed-and-breakfast favored by Dutch and Austrian honeymooners. In March 1945, it was prime real estate for a sniper. McKenna and Insalaco took positions on either side of the door. "*Achtung*, fuckers!" yelled Lieutenant Chase, as he and Corporal Cosgriff kicked in the door.

It appeared empty. These places always did. Silently, the men fanned out, searching each room on the first floor. Corporal Cosgriff went up the steep staircase toward the attic, while Lieutenant Chase covered him from behind. Privates McKenna and Insalaco cleared the kitchen. A warm loaf of bread cooled in a basket next to the stove. Whoever had been there was likely still there. Insalaco tore the loaf in two. He pocketed half and offered the rest to Francis, who stuffed it into his pocket. He silently mouthed "The cellar" to Insalaco. They cautiously looked down a dark stairwell.

"*Hände hoch!*" shouted Insalaco, employing two of the six German words he had picked up since arriving in-country. Silence followed. Nothing is more frightening in war than silence. Insalaco shouted again, "*Hände hoch!*"

Francis McKenna pointed to a pull chain. Was the electricity still working in Schloss-Sayn? It was out in Weis and Heimbach. He gave the chain a yank, and there they were—a terrified family. Grandparents, daughters or daughters-in-law, and five grandchildren, two boys and three girls, all huddled together. The grandfather spoke rapidly, incomprehensibly, including the obligatory, "*Nicht Nazi!*" The women wept, while the children hid behind the adults, all but a steely eleven-year-old girl with droopy curls and middle-aged eyes who looked directly at the two Americans pointing rifles in her direction.

"Hands up!" shouted McKenna in English.

"*Hände hoch!*" shouted Insalaco.

Slowly they raised their hands, and Insalaco motioned with his rifle for them to go up the stairs. The mothers shooed the children forward. Then, from the shadows, a greenish-gray blur, and *BANG!* A shot ripped straight through Insalaco's head, taking out his right eye and splattering a stunned Francis McKenna with blood and brains. The others screamed and ran for the stairs; their thundering footsteps caused the basement ceiling to undulate, sending a shower of dust down from above. The sniper worked the bolt on his rifle for a second shot. Before he could chamber a round, *BANG!* Private McKenna's shot sent him tumbling backward into a rack of homemade glühwein, which shattered on the stone floor. The blast from the two gunshots filled the low-ceilinged cellar with grouts of smoke. Lieutenant Chase and Corporal Cosgriff rushed to the kitchen.

"Dugan? Insalaco!" shouted Chase from the top of the stairs.

"Are you guys okay?" yelled Cosgriff.

Both men cautiously crept down the stairs, rifles at the ready. They saw Insalaco dead on the floor, his blood merging with the blood of the sniper and a pool of crimson from the broken bottles of wine.

"What happened?" asked Lieutenant Chase.

"That bastard," Francis said, pointing to the dead German.

"I hate this goddamned country," said Cosgriff.

There were nine more houses to clear.

Lieutenant Chase dragooned Travis Lugo to take Insalaco's place.

Across the street more shots were fired as Lieutenant Suits's squad took out a pair of snipers, fortunately without suffering any losses themselves. The search continued. McKenna and Lugo went upstairs in the next house, while Chase and Cosgriff took the basement. Another family cowered, this time in a coat closet, but no sniper was found.

House by house they went, kicking down doors and terrifying occupants as they hunted the hunters. Finally, they came to the last house. Once this place was cleared, B Company could advance up the road to Stromberg, the 23rd's final objective of the day.

McKenna took the lead, with Lugo ducking behind him, his hand on Francis's shoulder for cover.

"Goddamn, Dugan!" said Lugo. His fingers were smeared with brain tissue from Insalaco's skull, which still clung to McKenna's shoulder like a macabre epaulet. Francis did not have time to be horrified as they approached another dark cellar staircase.

"Shit on this," said Travis Lugo, before tossing a grenade and diving for cover.

KA-BOOM! A cylinder of flame and debris rocketed up the stairwell like a tongue of lava, blowing Private McKenna backward into a cabinet filled with stacks of Meissen china. Dinner plates, saucers, cups, cruets, and carafes tumbled to the floor, exploding into porcelain shrapnel. And so began a new life of near total deafness for Francis McKenna, an imposed silence that isolated him from music, laughter, whispered confidences, and the affection of his children.

"You okay, Dugan?" asked Lugo as he dusted himself off.

Francis did not answer. He was stunned, likely concussed; blood trickled from his ears. Slowly, he gathered his bearings.

"What happened?" he asked, but Lugo had already gone into the basement.

"All clear!" shouted Lugo. Francis did not hear that either. He slowly got to his feet and steadied himself before cautiously going down the cellar steps.

It took a bit for his eyes to dilate in the swirling smoke and murky light. Then he saw them—nine children, or pieces of nine children. Maybe it was only eight; it might even have been ten, all blown to bits by Lugo's reckless grenade. Some of the kids were still alive; they made a high-pitched, extraterrestrial screech, a wounded-animal sound so intense even McKenna's ruptured ears could make it out. Lugo looked to his platoonmate like the child he was.

"Well, shit, Dugan," said Lugo. "Little Germans become big Germans."

And Francis McKenna shot him dead.

Private Travis Lugo fell where he stood, facedown onto of the pile of children he had murdered. Francis made no attempt to run or tamper with the crime scene, neither Lugo's or his own. Instead, he waited for Lieutenant Chase and Corporal Cosgriff, who he knew would be the first to arrive.

"Dugan! Lugo!" shouted Cosgriff from the top step. But either from deafness or trauma, Francis McKenna did not answer. Cautiously, the corporal and the lieutenant came down the stairs. They froze until they could process the horror before them.

"Holy Hannah," whispered Cosgriff.

"What happened here?" asked Chase with bewilderment.

Francis did not answer. He counted the children's heads. There were nine kids, ranging from three to fourteen years old, but he was no judge of children and never would be. Some were clearly siblings, others cousins or the neighbor's kids. Lieutenant Chase grabbed Private McKenna by the shoulders and shook him.

"Dugan, how'd this happen?" Again Francis did not speak.

"Dugan!" shouted Chase, slapping his face. Francis McKenna dropped his rifle and then his sidearm, still hot from the shot that killed Lugo. He never touched a gun again for the rest of his life.

The explosion in the basement drew others: guys from Lieutenant Suits's platoon and then Suits himself and a sergeant from across the street. They took turns peeking down the stairs. Three of the GIs puked, sickened by the sight of the dismembered children. Lieutenant Suits demanded answers.

"How did Lugo get it?" asked Suits. "Did one of the kids kill him?" he asked sarcastically. Francis said nothing.

"I think he's out of it, Lieutenant," said Cosgriff, dabbing at the blood running from McKenna's hemorrhaged eardrums.

"Have Walsh look him over," said Lieutenant Chase, but Francis would never see the corpsman.

In a last-ditch effort to keep the 23rd from reaching Stromberg, the Germans launched a rare late-war tactical raid by the Luftwaffe. The Shermans were juicy targets, wedged between the stone houses in the narrow streets of Schloss-Sayn. As the Stukas dipped their wings, every GI opened up, but the small-arms fire did nothing against the planes. Two five-hundred-kilogram bombs landed in the center of town, ripping up the lead Sherman and toppling the church steeple and the parish hall, killing the local Burgermeister, who died with his family when their home collapsed on top of them.

Lieutenant Suits and his men abandoned Francis and joined the others firing at the Stukas. Chase and Cosgriff fled the house as well, eager to get off a few shots of their own. Meanwhile, McKenna—ignoring or oblivious to the mayhem surrounding him—walked west on Weiser Strasse. He did not run, but away he went. Away from the madness, from the dead American private—Travis Lugo of Albany, Georgia—who had murdered nine children only to be murdered himself. The term is *fragging*, and it's as old as warfare.

As half-tracks, jeeps, deuce and a halfs, weasels, and Shermans headed east toward Stromberg, rifleless, grenadeless, ammoless, deafened Francis McKenna walked west, away from World War II.

A lone Stuka, a straggler, appeared out of nowhere, carrying a single thousand-pounder. Swooping low over the village, the pilot leveled his wings and released his payload, scoring a direct hit on the trailing tank. The explosion tore the tank to shreds and instantly killed Lieutenant Suits and the private with him. Lieutenant Chase and Corporal Cosgriff died from their injuries the following day. The houses on both sides of the street caved in, including the north-facing walls of the house where the children had been murdered and McKenna killed their killer. A ruptured gas line would keep the fire burning for three days. Francis kept walking.

He continued north and west, passing through all the towns Baker Company had traversed, walking unmolested by the occupying forces left to hold the towns he had helped take. Outside of Gladbach, McKenna caught a ride to Neiderbieber in an empty deuce and a half driven by a private like himself.

"Need a lift?" asked the driver.

Francis could see his lips move but could not make out the question. He pointed to his ears. The driver tapped the seat next to him. "Hop in," he shouted.

The driver prattled on, but about what Francis did not know. They bounced and swayed with each hump and hole in the road. At Neiderbieber, McKenna parted company with his chauffeur, who turned north, while Francis continued west to the Wied River, a tributary of the Rhine. It was dark and cold, and he was hungry and lost, not geographically, but psychically, maybe spiritually. He could not fathom how the Book of Fate had seen fit to send him into one house too many. He slept that night in a barn, covering himself with hay.

He awoke the next morning, trembling with a chill, soaked from night sweat. It had come to him. A decision. Right or wrong, he would continue west until he was stopped, neither seeking capture nor eluding it. When confronted by MPs or whomever, he would answer every question truthfully and accept whatever followed. He would not make excuses. He would not justify his actions. With this decision made, a burden was lifted. He was famished and remembered the half-loaf of bread Insalaco had given him. He gobbled it greedily, which only made his hunger more acute. Just after sunrise he made his way to the banks of the Wied, where he paid an elderly German two cigarettes to ferry him to the other side.

On foot, he passed through Rodenbach, then by horse cart he arrived in Feldkirchen, facing the Rhine. He was surprised when he walked without resistance against the flow of traffic over a Bailey bridge thrown up by the engineers to speed along the endless stream of trucks and tanks and every kind of vehicle hauling God-only-knows-what to the front. As McKenna crossed the mighty river, a dead German bobbed in the water, spinning clockwise as the current eddied around the bridge supports. *Where will he wash ashore?* wondered Francis. Then again, where would Francis wash ashore?

Having crossed the Rhine unmolested, he made his way through Pellenz and used the last of his scrip to purchase a lump of cheese from a hausfrau. He nibbled a few bites, saving the rest for later. There had been plenty of opportunities to pilfer cheese or wine or whatever he wanted to grab from homes or bomb-damaged shops along the way, but he was determined to do no more harm. If it had been possible to levitate and leave the soil itself undisturbed by his footprints, he would have done so. How different Frank McKenna was from Frank Sinatra and even from his youngest son, who would dream of leaving huge footprints.

For two more days and nights, he walked west. An African American corporal driving a jeep saw him and pulled over.

"Where to?"

Francis tapped his ears.

"Get in," said the driver, pointing to the empty seat next to him.

They traveled south toward Koblenz, but Francis never made it that far. Ahead, he saw a roadblock manned by MPs. He shouted at the driver to pull over, unaware how loud he was speaking.

"You sure?" asked the corporal.

"THANKS FOR THE LIFT!" shouted Francis.

He walked the half mile to the check point where he was stopped by two MPs—one tall and thin, one short and stocky, like Abbott and Costello in *Buck Privates*.

"Where do you think you're going, Mac?" asked Abbott.

Francis shook his head. He pointed again to his ears.

"What are you, deaf?" asked Costello.

Dad pantomimed writing. The tall MP fetched a pencil and notebook from a Jeep.

"Who are you with, Private?" asked Costello.

Again, Francis pantomimed. The MP wrote out the question and handed him the notebook. Francis shouted his answer.

"PRIVATE MCKENNA, FRANCIS XAVIER. THREE, TWO, SIX, NINE, FOUR, ZERO, SEVEN."

"Who are you with, Private?" The MP pointed to the notebook again.

"NO ONE."

"No one, sergeant!" barked the MP.

And they continue to shout and write and pass the notebook and pencil back and forth, until McKenna made himself understood.

Q: "What are you doing here, soldier?"

A: "GOING HOME, SERGEANT."

Q: "Don't be a jackoff, McKenna. Go back to your unit."

A: "I CANNOT DO THAT, SERGEANT."

Q: "Why not?"

A: "I KILLED A MAN," Francis shouted. "ONE OF OURS."

"It happens. Go back."

"ON PURPOSE."

"Shit," said Abbott and Costello in unison.

And with that, the MPs put him in cuffs and took him away.

That same day Earl the mailman delivered a telegram to Mrs. Francis McKenna of Bayside, Queens, New York:

> The Secretary of War desires me to express his deep
> regret that your husband, Private Francis X. McKenna has
> been reported missing in action since the 28th of March in

Germany. If further details or further information is received, you will be promptly notified.

Major General James Alexander Ulio,
Army Adjutant General

Catherine's shrieks could be heard three houses over and brought the neighbors running, including Mrs. Stankowski.

Pappy Boyle did his best to be positive. "He's missing. It doesn't mean he's . . ." But he couldn't bring himself to finish the sentence, because he didn't fully believe it himself. The man who had four daughters feared he had lost a son.

Mrs. Stankowski bawled the loudest of all. She had received her own telegram three years earlier, when Connie was killed, and seized every opportunity to wail, even when her grief upstaged her neighbor's.

The Boyle family circled around Catherine, offering what solace and hope they could. A week passed. Catherine returned to work, her suffering laminated to her face. Her coworkers and regular customers at Gertz gave her space. Then a second telegram arrived:

It is my duty to inform you that your HUSBAND, PVT. FRANCIS X. MCKENNA, was placed under arrest by Military Police near Pellenz, Germany, on the 31st of March. He is charged under Article 85 of the Articles of War with desertion in the face of the enemy. PVT. MCKENNA will stand for court-martial when a panel can be convened.

Major Blackshear M. Bryan, Provost Marshal,
United States Army

"He's alive!"

"Desertion?"

"Cowardice?"

"Yellow?"

"Not Francis!"

"I don't believe it."

"It has to be a mistake!"

"At least he's alive."

"At least the German's don't have him."

"That would have been better!"

"Shut your mouth!"

"Why? Why? Why?!"

And with that, Catherine ran up the stairs and slammed the door of her bedroom and did not come out for two days. Nobody went to console her. They needed consoling themselves. They needed time to figure out what they would tell their friends and neighbors.

It would be no comfort to Catherine or the Boyle family to know that desertion was anything but uncommon. In every army, in every war, in every epoch of history, soldiers have taken a hike. In World War II more than twenty thousand Americans and fifty thousand Brits deserted, the overwhelming majority in the European Theater. It's not that men were braver in the Pacific; there simply wasn't any place to desert to. Military justice was surprisingly lenient for those who agreed to return to their units. So were the frontline combat troops who welcomed them back.

Not everyone was forgiven. Some deserters left the battlefield to commit freelance murders of passion or profit, including contract killings, armed robberies, and rapes leading to murder. These men hid, sometimes in plain sight, finding refuge in the vast wartime black-market economies of Brussels, Paris, Naples, Liège, and even London. They turned to crime or ran away specifically to commit crimes, seeing vast opportunities for riches on a continent unmoored from morality.

White-helmeted MPs, "Ike's Snowballs," were deployed by the thousands to patrol the cafés, nightclubs, railroad terminals, dance halls, and bordellos of occupied cities, where men on the run found employment as dishwashers, waiters, or muscle. Paris became so riven with roaming gangs of violent GIs that the City of Light became known as *Chicago sur la Seine*.

Then there were the men broken by battle who would rather face life in prison, or even a firing squad, than one more night in a rifle pit.

The Unified Code of Military Justice ranks desertion in the face of the enemy as the most serious offence short of treason. Yet, of the twenty thousand American deserters in World War II, only one, Private Edward Slovik of Detroit, Michigan, would pay the ultimate price.

Slovik was caught in an artillery barrage and refused to advance. He spent six weeks hanging with a rear-guard Canadian unit, until he was finally discovered and sent back to his company. That night Eddie Slovik wrote a note saying he was "not army material," then hit the bricks, surrendering to a cook. Three days later he was court-martialed, convicted, and sentenced to death.

On December 23, 1944, as Private McKenna was fighting for his life in the Battle of the Bulge, Eddie Slovik wrote a letter to General Eisenhower begging for mercy. With thousands of men being slaughtered in the Ardennes and thousands more AWOL, Ike was not in a magnanimous mood. On the last day of January 1945, Eddie Slovik, stripped of all symbols of rank and regiment, was strapped to a post in a courtyard in Sainte-Marie-aux-Mines, France, and shot to death by firing squad. His death went unreported at home, but every rifleman in Europe knew of his execution, because Ike wanted them to know. Fifteen years later, Frank Sinatra hired blacklisted Hollywood Ten writer Albert Maltz to write a screenplay about Private Slovik's execution, but the Kennedy campaign put the kibosh on the project.

The morning after turning himself in, Francis McKenna was escorted to a truck and shackled to a canopy post. They drove for hours, Francis nodding off, smoking, and nodding off again. The transit of the sun told him he was heading west, away from Germany, away from the war, so he had no complaints.

He spent the night lying flat on the cold bed of the deuce and a half, guards rotating every two hours, even though he had no thought of escape. After cold coffee and colder rations, he was under way early the next morning. When the truck pulled into Bruyères, headquarters of Brigadier General Dahlquists's 36th Division, McKenna was ordered out.

Bruyères had been hit hard, but the town jail survived without a scratch. Go figure. McKenna was caged with a thief, a drunken half-track driver who ran over a field kitchen, and a psychopath whose erratic behavior included driving a pickax through the skulls of dead Americans while moving corpses.

In the early evening, Francis McKenna was taken to a cluster of hospital tents, where the medics treated his damaged ears, saving some function on his right side. After a few days, he recovered enough hearing to converse and was sent for an interview with the divisional psychiatrist who certified Dad competent to stand trial. The next morning, he was introduced to the man who would defend him.

Major Kelly Kellenbach was a lawyer in civilian life, which was not always the case in military tribunals. Kellenbach was an experienced defense attorney but grossly overworked with twenty-two cases currently on his docket. After a few general questions, he cut to the chase.

"If given the opportunity, are you willing to return to your unit?"

"I've done all the killin' I'm going to do."

"They're going to ask you."

"I'm done killin'."

"You are aware the penalty for desertion in the face of the enemy is death?"

"Sir, I am done killin'."

"Did you tell the MPs you killed one of our men?"

"I did."

"Do you want to tell me what that's about?"

"I'd rather not, sir."

"Will you tell the court?"

"I'd rather not, sir."

"Very well," said Kellenbach, as he stashed his notes into a file folder. "It's your neck."

And with that, Major Kellenbach led Francis into the improvised courtroom. They had spent less than ten minutes together.

Private McKenna's court-martial convened in a three-hundred-year-old chapel, part of a group of parish buildings commandeered by the 36th Division as its headquarters. With the exception of two stained-glass windows that had miraculously survived a monthlong bombardment, the chapel had been stripped of its icons by MPs readying the church for a different kind of judgment day.

The panel consisted of eleven officers, none of whom McKenna had ever seen before. The presiding officer, Major James B. Jordan, sat dead center at a long table placed in the transept. The trial judge advocate, prosecutor in civilian lingo, was another major, Martin Melchionni, a career army staffer. These were hard men, as hard as all men who fight in wars become.

A corporal, acting as court stenographer, took down as much as he could.

"The accused is alleged to have violated Article 85 of the Articles of War," read Major Jordan from a sheaf of papers. "Specification one: in that Private Francis X. McKenna, Company B, 23rd Infantry Regiment, 2nd Infantry Division, being present with his company while it was engaged with the enemy, did, in the village of Schloss-Sayn, on or about the twenty-third of March 1945, shamefully abandon said company and seek safety in the rear." At that moment, an African-American orderly entered with a tray of coffee for the court. Major Jordan took a sip from a mug. The coffee was molten and burned the major's tongue. He continued reading but with a slight lisp.

"If convicted, the penalty for misbehavior before the enemy is death or such other punishment as a court-martial may direct. Do you understand, Private McKenna?"

Francis did not answer.

"Yes or no, soldier," snapped the Major.

Major Kellenbach jumped in, requesting the tribunal speak up, given his client's damaged ears. Major Jordan ordered it thus.

"How do you plead, soldier?" shouted Jordan.

"Private McKenna pleads not guilty," answered Kellenbach on behalf of his client.

Prosecution Exhibit A, Private McKenna's psychiatric evaluation, was introduced into the record and accepted without comment. Specifics were then read by the prosecutor in a booming voice that made everything seem even more terrible than it was. The defense did not challenge the allegations. The army had only one witness to call, Captain Walter Warton, commander of Baker Company, who had just arrived in Bruyères from the front.

After swearing his oath, Captain Warton confirmed that B Company was actively engaged with the enemy on the twenty-third of March, clearing the town of Schloss-Sayn of snipers, then fighting off an artillery and aerial counterattack in advance of the push toward Stromberg. Major Melchionni asked Captain Warton when he discovered that Private McKenna had deserted. Warton was not entirely clear, citing the fog of war and the large number of dead and wounded after the air attack.

"I checked with my platoon leaders and the corpsmen for casualties," answered Warton. "We had ten killed, fourteen wounded. Three unaccounted for," added the captain. "Two of the three had been evacc'ed. I assumed Dugan . . . Private McKenna . . . was taken to a field hospital. But a day later, after checking with Battalion, we still couldn't find him, and that's when I began to suspect he was AWOL."

Major Kellenbach cross-examined Warton while seated. He was too weary for theatrics.

"You are Private McKenna's C.O., correct?" asked Major Kellenbach.

"Yes, sir," said Captain Warton.

"Do you consider Private McKenna a good soldier?"

"I did, sir," he said, using the damning past tense.

"Has Private McKenna ever exhibited reluctance to fight?"

"No, sir."

"Has Private McKenna ever shirked his duty?"

"No, sir," said Warton. "Sir, if I may . . ."

Kellenbach looked to the presiding officer, who gave a nod.

"Go ahead, Captain."

"I was greatly surprised to learn that Dugan . . . Private McKenna . . . was AWOL."

"The charge is desertion," barked Major Melchionni.

"Yes, sir," said Warton. "I just want it to be on record that Private McKenna fought bravely in the Ardennes and every town and village B Company entered. Even in Schloss-Sayn. I want the court to know that."

"So noted," said Major Jordan.

"No further questions," said Kellenbach.

But the prosecution had more questions on rebuttal.

"Captain, Private McKenna told the MPs in Pellenz, 'I killed a man.' We have their written statements. Prosecution Exhibit B. 'One of ours,' McKenna said. 'Deliberately,' McKenna told the MPs, or words to that effect. What do you make of this, Captain Warton?"

"Objection," said Major Kellenbach. "The judge advocate's question is speculative."

"Sustained," said Major Jordan.

"Captain Warton, do you have any reason to believe Private McKenna may have murdered one of your men?"

"Lieutenant Chase was his squad leader that day."

"Did Lieutenant Chase note anything unusual in Private McKenna's behavior?"

"I wouldn't know, sir. Lieutenant Chase was killed with the others. Schloss-Sayn was hell, sir."

"Has Private Travis Lugo been accounted for?" asked the prosecutor.

"No, sir."

"Is he one of your KIAs, Captain?"

"We have remains that can't be identified. Three in fact. There was a fire in the house, a gas line. Schloss-Sayn was hell, sir."

"No further questions," said Major Melchionni.

Warton snapped a salute to the court and gave a nod to McKenna as he left the chapel. He had done all he could. They would never see each other again.

"The defense rests, gentlemen," said Kellenbach.

The presiding officer spoke next.

"Private McKenna, is there anything you would like to say to this court?" asked Major Jordan.

"No, sir."

"Nothing?"

"No, sir."

"Private, I want you to think about what I'm about to ask you before you answer. Will you return to your unit and fight if given the opportunity?"

"I've done all the killin' I'm gonna do."

"Did you hear me clearly, Private?"

"Yes, sir."

"Will you go back and fight? Yes or no, soldier."

"No," said Francis. And then added a belated "sir" as a show of respect and character.

"So noted," said Major Jordan.

And with that, Francis McKenna's fate was in the hands of the panel. The deliberations did not take long—fifteen minutes, tops.

"Please stand," said Major Jordan. Private McKenna stood ramrod straight as Major Jordan lowered the boom. "After taking a secret ballot, the members present concurred in each of the following findings: of specification one, guilty. Of the charge, guilty."

Francis had no visible reaction. He was ordered to sit and remained seated while the panel withdrew again, this time to discuss his sentence. Major Kellenbach opened the file for his next case and began reading. "You can smoke if you want," said Kellenbach, without taking his eyes off his papers, but Francis was not about to light a cigarette in a church, even if it had been desanctified.

The officers returned, having taken longer to reach agreement on the sentence than they had on guilt or innocence. Of course, the delay could also be explained by the long walk to the latrine, which was on the other side of the parish grounds.

"On your feet, Private McKenna," ordered Major Jordan. He said it without hostility. These cases saddened military men as much as they enraged them.

"Private Francis X. McKenna," read Major Jordan, "Army serial number three-two-six-nine-four-oh-seven. You are to be dishonorably discharged from the service, to forfeit all pay and allowances due or to become due, and to be confined at hard labor, at such place as the reviewing authority may direct, for the term of your natural life."

Thanks to Captain Warton's testimony, Francis had dodged a death sentence. It was unclear if he had done him a favor.

Even before Catherine McKenna opened the telegram informing her that her husband and lover, Private Jack Rabbit, had been convicted of desertion and sentenced to life in prison, Francis had already been shackled and convoyed by MPs to a prison camp, along with a dozen other GIs convicted of capital crimes.

Stripped of his private's stripe, Francis McKenna was now classified as S.U.S., "Soldier Under Sentence," and put on a train under guard. After two days of travel, slowed by traffic on the mostly destroyed French rail system, he arrived at the Gare de l'Est in Paris, where he was met by two fresh MPs who escorted him to an uncovered jeep for the long, cold ride to the Loire Disciplinary Training Center.

They stopped briefly at a canteen for military truck drivers, where they ate a silent, smoky, midnight breakfast before getting back on the road. Their route took them through the medieval city of Le Mans, the place where, in 1908, Wilbur Wright had made his first public flights in a practical flying machine. The town was still digging out from the devastation that had rained down from the progeny of the Wrights' miracle.

After more driving, the MPs finally turned off the road onto a dirt trail leading through the woods, then into an open field. In the pre-dawn darkness, two crisscrossing searchlights revealed the perimeter of the stockade in which Francis would be imprisoned.

At the main gate a guard signed for Francis as if he were a FedEx package. With that, Francis Xavier McKenna began his life as a convicted felon, a deserter, a fallen soldier, an object of scorn and universal contempt.

There was roll call every morning, calisthenics on the parade ground, and then work constructing barracks to replace the cold, damp tents the inmates were housed in. The prisoners threw themselves into the barracks project, working with enthusiasm for obvious, self-serving reasons. When the barracks were finished, boredom overwhelmed them. The endlessly repetitive life of roll call, jumping jacks, and other menial tasks followed by hour after hour of smoking, spitting, and jerking off was broken only by the appearance of the executioner who dispatched the murderers twice a month, a macabre relief from the oppression of tedium and caged testosterone.

Not long after settling into camp life, Francis tackled what must have been the toughest moment of his life, letter Number 90.

Dear Catherine,

I want you should hear it from me. They have convicted me of
desertion. I am guilty of desertion. I am guilty of worse even. I
want you to know. You must know who you are married two.
If you want to be married to this man.

I killed a boy. One of our men. He murdered a cellar-full
of children so I shot him. He was not more than a child hiself
and I should not have done so.

When he fell dead I can kill no more. Not even the Krauts
so I left.

Don't feel sorry for me. I am sorry enough for both of us.
Tell you Mom and Pop I say thanks for making me like a son.
They are good people.

I will love you forever. Now I must pay for my crimes.
Forget we met and live happy.

Francis
PS: Eamon is dead.

What Catherine wrote in reply was not in the hatbox and therefore
lost to history.

In April, as the noose around Hitler's neck tightened, Franklin
Roosevelt complained of a terrific headache, then pitched forward.
As the Free World mourned the loss of its leader, the Allies continued the race toward Berlin. The Red Army got there first, storming in
from the east, bringing a pandemic of rape and retribution with them.
Then, a few days after celebrating his fifty-sixth birthday, with bombs
exploding above him, the Führer, Adolf Hitler, married his longtime
mistress, Eva Braun, and poisoned his beloved shepherd, Blondi, a
test of the cyanide Mrs. Hitler would use to end her life the next day.
Once the groom was sure his bride was dead, he put a pistol to his
temple and did what he should have done as a young man, sparing
humanity its greatest stain.

On May 7, 1945, the Nazi government surrendered uncondition-
ally. The war in Europe was over. Francis McKenna's war was not.

On September 2, 1945, the Empire of Japan signed surrender terms aboard the battleship *Missouri* in Tokyo Bay. The war in the Pacific was over. Francis McKenna's war continued.

On April 19, 1946, my father was given a second chance at life. A general amnesty signed by President Truman enabled Dad to walk out of the stockade that had been his home for a year, one of the thousands of deserters and other wartime miscreants paroled by the president. It was time to heal, time to move on to the Cold War. But Francis's war would go on for another fifty-three years, until his heart finally gave out in our driveway while he listened to the New York Mets.

Dad hitchhiked his way to Cherbourg, astonished to see how much rebuilding was under way and how much still needed to be done. The mood in France had changed. Gratitude has an expiration date. Champagne now came with a tab, and French women returned to the arms of French men. The ripped stitching on Dad's sleeves added to the cold shoulders he received everywhere, the ghost outline of his former rank a military scarlet D, for deserter.

He made the rounds of the steamship offices, hunting for the lowest possible fare. Passage was hard to find at any price. Many of the surviving ships were in dry dock, being readied for their return to civilian service. Francis was trapped in a dry dock of his own, but nobody had readied him for a return to civilian life. With the last of his army pay, he purchased a secondhand suit and a third-class ticket aboard a Dutch steamer, the S.S. *Nieuw Amsterdam*. Then he sent the only telegram he would ever send.

Arriving 5/8 Nieuw Amsterdam. Pier 46.

Francis

She saw him before he saw her. She shouted his name and waved, but Catherine's voice was swallowed by the cranes and crowds and river sounds of the West Side of Manhattan. As Francis disembarked, his head swiveled, searching the faces for the only face that mattered. Then he saw her, literally elbowing cigar chompers and Negro porters out of her way, as she ran to her husband. Francis did the same, rushing to his wife pell-mell, bumping past stevedores and cab drivers, stepping on toes, his eyes dewy with love and relief, until finally they enveloped each other in a hug they swore would never end. Yes, like in a movie.

He was not welcomed home with ticker tape, but he was welcomed home. The Boyles accepted him under their roof and withstood the shunning they received from the neighbors, especially the Stankowskis, who did not speak to them for nearly a year. Pappy took Ma Boyle and the girls to the mountains for a week, leaving the house to Francis and Catherine. The husband and wife reintroduced themselves. This Francis McKenna was different from the one Catherine had married; he was deafened and shamed and burdened with a guilt that would never be absolved. Could she love him as she loved the other Francis? She said she could and spent the next fifty years proving it.

When the Boyles returned home, Francis sat with Pappy and answered his every question. He told him all the gruesome details. He held back nothing. Then, after that one long night of talking, the war was never spoken of again.

Nine months later, Al was born. Four years after that, Kevin arrived, then Sean. Finally, in 1957, I completed the family.

The world moved on. Another war was fought in Korea, then Vietnam, the Gulf—then all the wars after 9/11. Today nobody remembers what my father did or didn't do. No one except one unforgiving man in New Jersey, *Pan Kichot*, a Polish Don Quixote, forever titling at cowards and deserters because they lived, and his brother Connie had not. He is gone now as well.

Many of the questions I had about my father have been answered over the past seventeen years; his wartime letters, stashed in a hatbox in my mother's bedroom closet, opened doors previously slammed shut. Since his passing, blanks have been filled in by my deep dive into after-action reports typed and filed from handwritten notes by those who were there, from diaries, and with good old-fashioned shoe leather. I haunted archives and libraries and searched the web until I nailed down the truth, or what we call truth. But it was only in the last years of my mother's life that Frank McKenna and Private Dugan became one. My mother told me things she had told no one, things her husband told her and only her when he came home from war. It was she who put the flesh and blood of Jack Rabbit McKenna on the historian's dry facts. Today I have only one unanswered question: What if Dad *had* been yellow? Would I have loved him any less?

I often wonder how I would have behaved after Pearl Harbor. Would I have enlisted Like Ray and Connie Stankowski, or waited for the draft like Dad and Uncle Eamon? Or would I have angled like Sinatra to have myself declared unfit, if that's what he really did? I like to believe I would have stepped up and served in World War II, because we always see ourselves on the right side of history.

Had I been of age, I surely would have marched with Dr. King. I would have stood with John Lewis on the Edmund Pettus Bridge. In my mind, I would have sat on the bus with Rosa Parks. I would have condemned the internment of Japanese Americans and voted for Truman over Dewey. I would have defended the Suffragettes, fought for Honest Abe and the Union against those traitorous Rebs, who valued their slaves more than their country. I would have opposed the Trail of Tears, wintered at Valley Forge, and shouted "Give us Jesus!" not "Give us Barabbas!"

Still, if I am to be truly candid, I would have cheered on Joe McCarthy as he sniffed out godless communism because the Rosenbergs got what they had coming. Cross out Stalin and insert Hitler and tell me anyone would blubber over Julius and Ethel? I'm trying to be honest here. And if I am to be really truthful, I cannot guarantee, had I been born in Berlin in 1927 rather than New York in 1957, that I would not have goose-stepped in line with millions of my fellow countrymen who allowed themselves to be seduced by the promise of glory restored, vengeance, and blind hatred. This thought gives me chills. History, like real estate, is often location, location, location.

"In times of peace, sons bury their fathers," wrote Herodotus in his *History*. "But in war it is the fathers who send their sons to the grave."

So what if Dad *had* been yellow? Would I have loved him any less? Let me answer that now. He was my father, and I love him. The end.

"Hey! You shouldn't be up there!" shouts a voice from the back of the church.

I take a big swig from a plastic Poland Spring bottle. My throat is raw from all this talking.

A janitor under the St. Anastasia choir loft wheels his big plastic trash can in from the vestibule.

"I'm almost done," I tell him.

"You shouldn't be on the altar!" insists the janitor, his voice thundering like the voice of God in the empty church.

"Okay, I'm done," I say as I close my folder and look up at the rows of empty pews.

My wife, Abigail, sits about halfway back, accompanied by my stepdaughters, Melissa and Maddie. My children.

The girls are relieved; the pews are uncomfortable, and Abbie wouldn't let them look at their phones, which is practically child abuse. I knew the girls would be bored listening to a long eulogy for a man they never met, a man who died seventeen years ago, before they were even born. Abigail insisted they be here. "They should know who your father was," she said. "He should be more than a face in a picture frame."

Is there any doubt why I married her?

Abigail meets me in the center aisle. We hug, then the girls join us. We stay in each other's arms.

"Can we go now?" asks Melissa.

"Yes, we can go," I say, while wiping a single tear from the corner of my eye.

Family.

18

A Hundred Years from Today

Today is the twelfth of December 2015. Exactly one hundred years ago, Francis Albert Sinatra entered this world. This will be Sinatra's last hurrah. Nobody commemorates the 101st anniversary of anything.

Francis McKenna would also have been one hundred today. My do-over eulogy at St. Anastasia was my way of marking this milestone. Abigail was game, as she always is when something is important to me.

After leaving St. Anastasia, we drive east on Northern Boulevard, and I point out the locations of long-departed shops that once made up the landscape of my life. The girls are not interested or even listening; their faces are buried in their phones. I don't blame them. My travelogue is really for my benefit. Even Abbie can only muster an occasional, "That's nice," or "Cool," as a courtesy rather than curiosity.

Little Neck is now almost entirely Korean. All the signs are in Korean, and I don't know what anything is. I remember what used to be, so I narrate what is missing rather than what is. The movie theater is now a chain pharmacy. The little upstairs office where Jean Nidetch founded Weight Watchers a million pounds ago is some kind of immigration office. Korvettes is gone. Patrick's Pub is gone. The brick facade of the Little Neck Inn stills stands, but the Inn itself is no more.

The Little Neck Inn had weathered World War I, the Spanish Flu, Prohibition, the Great Depression, the Cold War, Vietnam, and everything else history could throw its way. For more than a century, we told our stories there, toasted our victories, and drank away our dreams. Now the big front window is papered over, the door chained shut. A sign in several languages promises the April opening of a dim sum shop. I've counted six dim sum shops already.

Diagonally across the street is the Doyle S. O'Connell Funeral Home, one of the few survivors. It's been sold twice, and I don't know who runs the place now. The green neon sign flickers; the "S" is out completely. The awning has been patched, and the patches have been patched. A funeral home is always the last to go. The Irish have left feetfirst for eternity. Now it's the Koreans' turn. Fat Tommy Boyle himself was zipped into one of his own black bags and delivered to his resting place. He had been ill off and on for most of his last years, dropping so much weight that people who had called him Fat Tommy their whole lives took to calling him simply Tommy.

Here and there, a few weathered "Let's Go Mets!" posters still cling to phone poles or yellow in store windows. Five weeks ago, the Mets played in the World Series. They lost. Oh, well. Wait till next year. Or the year after. Or never.

The Scobee Grill is also gone, plowed under and replaced by a franchise coffee house. Madness. The Scobee served coffee, also Reubens, pancakes, waffles, lox and eggs, and a seven-layer cake people fought over. How is this progress? Abbie tells me I sound like the "get-off-my-lawn guy," and I laugh because it's true.

I make the left at the light and park behind a heavy equipment hauler in front of our house, the McKenna house, my house. On Monday, the big steel bucket on a front-end loader will smash holes in the roof and scrape away Sean's attic retreat. Workmen will pull apart Mom and Dad's bedroom, Al's and Kevin's old room, my bedroom in the back, the bathroom we all shared, and the upstairs hallway where my parents' wedding picture hung forever with smirking Ray Stankowski waiting to settle scores.

Ed Henning's house will go, too, as will all the houses on Little Neck Parkway and 44th Avenue. A big sign on the corner advertises townhouses starting in the mid-six hundreds. The little hill our house sits upon will be leveled to the street, then excavated to accommodate below-ground parking. The small garden where my father grew tomatoes will be cemented over. The line on which my mother hung our laundry, the pole that once supported a basketball hoop, the spot where Dad buried Snoopy and her stuffed penguin, the tall hedges that were our Green Monster during heated games of Wiffle ball—all of it will disappear. My childhood is being erased to make way for other people's childhoods. They will have their own landmarks, their own hopes and dreams, and their share of disappointments, too. This isn't sad; it's life.

I invite everyone out of the car for a look, but only Abigail comes with me.

I press my nose against the cold glass of the living-room window. It's empty, and I didn't expect to see anything other than the bare walls and fireplace. Yet, in my mind's eye I see everything exactly where it was, where it will always be in memory.

"Would you like to go in?" I ask.

"How?" asks Abigail.

"I know a way."

We go around back to the kitchen door. I lift the knob with both hands while pressing my shoulder against the door. The latch pops, as it has always popped.

"After you," I say, with a theatrical sweep of my hand.

"You go. I'm cold," she says with a wife's intuitive understanding. "I'll get a coffee across the street and wait with the girls." This is my goodbye, not hers.

The kitchen is as empty as the rest of the house—no Formica table, no refrigerator, no pot holders or teakettle or Brillo pads. No Catherine Boyle McKenna. Mom is with Dad now. She passed ten years ago.

Kevin lived with Mom until the very end, proving to be more

hindrance than help. He kept her busy cooking, cleaning, even doing his laundry. He came and went as he pleased, weaving his way up the stairs, dropping like deadweight on his bed. He had started to soil himself at night. Sean told Kevin he had to go. I told Kevin he had to go. You can imagine how that went over. But my mother couldn't do it. She loved him despite everything. That's what mothers do.

She did not have a quick exit like Dad. Her health followed the usual trajectory, with the normal stiffness, aches, and problems of age. Then suddenly, she lost her appetite and her balance and then incontinence put her in adult diapers, a humiliation she could not bear. Mom tried to hide everything, but Sean noticed and raised the alarm. Tests confirmed what we feared: stomach cancer. The doctor told us she had more time, that she was stable. She died alone with nobody squeezing her hand or kissing her cheek or dropping a tear on her gown.

My mother's funeral was sparsely attended; her surviving sister, Aunt Mary, a widow herself after Uncle Ed's passing, sat in the front pew with Abigail, Melissa, Maddie, and me. Beth, Jay, and Gail sat with Sean, who gave the eulogy and did a wonderful job recapping Mom's life of devotion to family, friends, community, her husband, and the Lord, Jesus Christ, her Savior, in whom she had an unshakable faith. He even squeezed in a few laughs by describing some of Mom's eccentricities in an endearing way.

Kevin McKenna attended his mother's funeral. He was sober and bereft and wept loudly several times during the service. He lives still.

As the groundskeepers lowered her casket, a light rain began to fall, because it always seems to rain at cemeteries. The rain sent everyone dashing to their cars. I lingered, happy to have a moment alone with my mother and father, my first-ever visit to Dad's grave.

I ran my fingers over his name on the stone. The edges of the letters were still sharp. I waited until the last car door closed, then motioned for Abigail to bring her big purse. She held it open, and I carefully removed the brown sack containing Jane's ashes. I ripped open the bag and scattered her remains behind Mom's and Dad's headstone. I shook the bag to make sure it was empty, then joined the others in the limo.

"What were you doing out there?" asked Sean.

"Nothing."

"Took long enough," said Kevin.

"Here," said Abigail, passing me a handkerchief. "Dry yourself. You'll get a cold."

I find a dime on the floor of my old bedroom. I pocket it. My sway-back desk is gone. I open the window and it stays up by itself. The last owners finally fixed it. I leave it open because, why not? I look in the closet expecting to see a row of school uniforms from St. Anastasia or neckties I wore to Bishop Malloy; instead I find a single wire coat hanger and another dime. I'm up twenty cents.

After Mom's funeral, we had Uncle Eamon's remains moved from the military cemetery in Oakland to the family plot at Calvary, bury-ing him next to Mom and Dad. This was Sean's doing. Sean had an interest in Eamon McKenna, the bachelor uncle he believed was mur-dered because he was gay.

"Let's see what we can find out," I said.

Sean did all the work. The internet had become a thing since my hunt for Stanky, and what would have taken weeks took only minutes. I steered him to databases and archives, and he struck gold when he found the MP report from 1944.

Eamon McKenna was found on a sidewalk at 900 Market Street, San Francisco. The address was significant. A few storefronts away was The Old Crow, a notorious gay bar that opened in 1935 and stayed open until 1980. Google has pictures. The sailors who killed Eamon were acquitted at trial, only to die at Okinawa when a kami-kaze hit their ship.

Working with Sean brought about a long-overdue rapprochement, although I'm not sure that's the right word, because we never had a falling out; we simply failed to bond and drifted past each other like blood strangers. Then, in the aftermath of my epic meltdown, my epiphany, and sobriety, there was no longer a pretext for secrets. All my cards had been dealt faceup, and I decided Sean's should be, too.

"What's it like being gay?" I asked, out of an ignorance so pure he could not possibly be offended.

"What's it like having teeth?" he said. My brother is witty! Who knew?

We talked past our differences, learning to forgive each other and Mom and Dad, finally concluding neither had ever, in word or deed, expressed bigotry toward gays or lesbians, unless obtuseness counts as bigotry. I reminded Sean our mother was equally uptight about regular sex. To which Sean said, "Sex is never regular." Funny guy, my brother.

I take the steep stairs to the attic two at a time, a perk of not smoking, the one thing Abigail insisted on. Sean's old box spring is still here, the only McKenna relic left in the house. The horn honks. It's time to go.

Thirteen years ago, in 2002, Marshall College hired a brand-new director of development, Abigail Bruce-Hefley. We sat next to each other at her introductory luncheon. I introduced myself as Daniel McKenna. She called me Daniel and, by the end of the lunch, Dan but has never called me Danny, not ever.

We didn't rush it. Nice 'n easy does it. Finger snaps. Abbie was still licking her wounds after divorcing Paul Hefley, who left her and his daughters for the au pair girl. I was still shell-shocked from September 11.

At precisely 8:46 a.m., American Airlines Flight 11 impaled the North Tower of the World Trade Center between the ninety-third and ninety-ninth floors. Of course, I knew Al worked there, but I couldn't conceive that his life was in jeopardy. Then Flight 175 slammed into the South Tower.

At 10:28 the North Tower collapsed. I sprinted from my classroom to my office to collect my cell phone. I had voice mail messages from Kevin, Sean, Mom, Beth, and Al. Yes, Al! I fumbled with the buttons, my hands trembling so badly I misdialed three times.

"Danny, I'm fucked," he said with great urgency. "There's a fire." I could hear people coughing. There were no screams. "You have to promise to take care of Beth . . . and the kids . . ." And that's where he broke down, as I did on my end while listening. "I love you like a brother," he said. That was his joke to me, always.

> *Who knows when some slight shock,*
> *disturbing the delicate balance between social*
> *order and thirsty aspiration*
> *shall send the skyscrapers in our cities toppling?*
> *Does that sound fantastic?*

—Richard Wright, *Native Son*, 1940.

The car horn honks again, more insistently. The girls want to go. I close the door behind me and give it a good shake to make sure it latches.

"Did you see what you wanted to see?" Abbie asks.

"Every day," I say looking directly into her eyes. I put the car in gear and aim it for home.

———

I've spent my life telling other people's stories professionally, in a doctoral dissertation and books and essays and papers about men and women from another time and place, an America that no longer exists, just as our world will yield to the next. Now you also know a bit about my brothers, Kevin, Sean, and Aloysius McKenna; my mother, Catherine; and my father, Francis Xavier. I've told you about Kimberly Anne Clark and my wife, Abigail, and our children. And I've told you what I know of Jane Freeman. While telling their stories, I have shared mine. It's here now, on paper and in pixels, where it will stay forever, my tiny slice of secular eternity. I appreciate the arc of my story, my journey through unhappy decades lusting for fame only to discover happiness through anonymity. I'm finally walking through my own confetti, even if I'm the only one throwing it.

Ultimately, we have just one story to tell, our story, intersecting as it does with other lives, bits and pieces and fragmentary snippets of the people whose paths cross ours. I have also said quite a bit here about a man I never met, Francis Albert Sinatra, but he's been part of my life, too. I wrestled with the coincidence of his birth and death coinciding with my father's birth and death and what possible connection there could be. Now I know.

Me. I'm the connection. It's only though me their lives intersect. We have that power, all of us.

I am cured of the past and live in the present, free to spend the balance of my days living, just living, not looking back, but rather in the moment, with no ambitions other than the love of family to sustain me until respiration ends. We don't leave footprints; we leave shadows, fleeting shadows.

That is enough.

Acknowledgments

With sincere thanks for the early encouragement and intelligent notes of trusted friends and fellow writers Jim McGrath, Jay Abramowitz, Kevin Kelton, and Vince Passaro. Additional thanks to Joseph Cosgriff and Mark Teitelbaum who went above and beyond.

Many thanks to Dean Kay not only for writing "That's Life," but generously allowing its use in these pages.

I am indebted to my personal hive: Buck Jordan, Devon Brady, Kimberly Ng, Buzz and Bowie Jordan, and Marc Germain—who has never read a book in his life and won't read this one either. Without Mike O'Connell, I couldn't live in Los Angeles. Michael Considine, Jim Giattino, Doug McAward, Patrick Hayes, and, as always, Paul McDermott are foundational friends. Lucky me.

A shout-out to Patti Tenaglia and the Moles of Stonehill College and my former radio and TV colleagues who taught me so much about storytelling. Special thanks to the late, great Jean Shepherd whose voice coming out of a transistor radio tucked under my pillow opened up a new way of seeing the world.

I am indebted to Rick Atkinson's *The Liberation Trilogy* for Dugan's darkest secret, and the late Charles B. MacDonald's *Company Commander* for allowing this Baby Boomer to come as close to life in a rifle company as he ever hopes to get. Lt. Brian Suits (ret.) explained wartime fragging, and former military attorney Michael Imprevento the reality of wartime court-martials.

Special thanks to the Sinatra sidemen I pestered for stories: Bill Richmond, Al Viola, Ron Anthony, Bill Miller, and Frank Sinatra Jr.

The Greenleaf Book Group has been a joy to work with. If you have a manuscript, by all means send it to them. Special thanks to Lindsay Bohls and Morgan Robinson, who calmly and diligently steered a neurotic and obsessive-compulsive author through his first manuscript. Thanks as well to Cameron Stein, Jordan Smith, Claudia Volkman (who stayed at her post through Hurricane Ian), Leah Pierre (who managed the paperback production), and the wonderful Joan Tapper. Don't edit without her.

Finally, Peter McGovern lost his father on May 14th, 1998. This book resulted from that sad event. Not a fair trade for Pete.

About the Author

Doug McIntyre has worked on stage, radio, television, and film—having written for the hit series *Married . . . with Children*, *Full House*, *WKRP in Cincinnati*, *Mike Hammer*, and the PBS animated series *Liberty's Kids*. For twenty-five years he hosted *Red Eye Radio* and *McIntyre in the Morning* on KABC in Los Angeles and WABC in New York. Onstage, McIntyre has appeared with Trevor Noah, Steve Martin, Robert Redford, Lily Tomlin, Betty White, Goldie Hawn, Jane Fonda, John Cleese, and many others, including prominent historians David McCullough, Douglas Brinkley, and Ken Burns. His newspaper column appears in the *Los Angeles Daily News*, *Orange County Register*, and *Long Beach Press-Telegram*, among others.

Born and raised in New York, Doug still suffers through every inning of every New York Mets game, which he understands is a cry for help. Together with his wife, actress/writer/producer Penny Peyser, he cowrote, produced, and directed the award-winning feature documentary *Trying to Get Good: The Jazz Odyssey of Jack Sheldon*. He lives in a decidedly unhip corner of Los Angeles, where it's too hot and expensive. www.DougMcIntyre.com